A Garden
IN THE Rain

Lynn Kurland

BERKLEY BOOKS, NEW YORK

This is a work of fiction. Names, characters, places, and incidents either are the product of the author's imagination or are used fictitiously, and any resemblance to actual persons, living or dead, business establishments, events, or locales is entirely coincidental.

A GARDEN IN THE RAIN

A Berkley Book / published by arrangement with the author

PRINTING HISTORY
Berkley edition / September 2003

Copyright © 2003 by Lynn Curland.
Cover design by George Long.
Cover illustration by Griesbach/Martucci.

For information address:
The Berkley Publishing Group,
a division of Penguin Group (USA) Inc.,
375 Hudson Street, New York, New York 10014.

ISBN: 0-425-19202-4

BERKLEY®
Berkley Books are published by The Berkley Publishing Group,
a division of Penguin Group (USA) Inc.,
375 Hudson Street, New York, New York 10014.
BERKLEY and the "B" design
are trademarks belonging to Penguin Group (USA) Inc.

PRINTED IN THE UNITED STATES OF AMERICA

10 9 8 7 6 5 4 3 2 1

> To my aunt Kay, godmother and friend

Acknowledgments

M*y* heartfelt thanks to . . .

My editor, Gail Fortune, who comes up with perfect titles, for unparalleled support and freedom to write the books of my heart.

Ashley Blakely, who spells much better that I do, for invaluable help in keeping up with business, for the love she has for my girls, and for her tender care of them while I grabbed a couple of hours each week to write. We love you!

Molly Wiscombe, who kept me organized last fall so I could think and who kept my house unburied so I could work without things falling on me.

My cousin-in-law, David Lyddall, for his continuing insights on all things Scottish—especially things to do with fast, expensive cars, speeding tickets, and travel times between UK cities that only he could make a reality. (His accomplishments in this field are legendary . . .)

Melissa R., who worked miracles in getting me a computer that worked. You are a saint!

My mom, for Friday Gaga days.

Matt (who types really fast for a guy), for sacrificing sleep and vacations to help me get this finished by typing out my very illegible handwritten chapters.

My little girly girls, who make my life a wondrous garden of sweet delights.

And lastly but not least, to my Auntie Kay, who once said, "You get to the point in your life where you have the urge to go dig in the dirt." She was right, of course.

Chapter 1

S *cotland in the Fall.*
    Were there any other words in the Mother Tongue that could possibly conjure up more romantic thoughts and feelings than those? Madelyn Phillips let her luggage slip to the ground, closed her eyes, and breathed deeply. No, those were the words, this was the country, and she had two weeks stretching out in front of her with nothing to do but enjoy. That she was poised to visit the Highlands when the air was full of the briskness of fall was simply the stuff of dreams.

"Get a move on, ducky."

Madelyn moved, thanks to a friendly shove on her backside by the man standing behind her. Thank heavens he had used his suitcase. At least she *hoped* he had used his suitcase.

She looked around her and realized belatedly that she was blocking the exit from the train station. In her defense it *had* been a very long day. Or maybe it had been two days. At this point she just wasn't really sure anymore. It felt like weeks since she'd slept in a horizontal position.

She moved out of Mr. Ducky's way, pulling her suitcase along behind her and trying to ignore the fact that one of the wheels had somehow become fused to something else during a too-lengthy stay near her radiator on the night before she'd left the States. She paused at the station's entrance, looked, then smiled at the sight of people driving on the wrong side of the street. She listened to the conversations wafting past her and sighed in pleasure at the lilting sounds that cascaded over her.

It was better than she'd dared hope, and she'd dared hope a lot.

She yawned suddenly, then rubbed her eyes and gave herself a shake. She didn't have time to sleep. She had much to see, much to do. Sleep could wait. She pushed away from the wall, hauled her carry-on and violin case farther up over her shoulder, took a firm grip on the handle of her no-longer-rolling roll-along suitcase, and made tracks for the local rental agency.

Half an hour and several dubious looks later—it was possible she'd yawned one too many times—she was the possessor of keys and a very unsatisfactory map of the Highlands. She put it into her notebook with great reluctance, though she supposed she didn't have to look at it. After all, she had directions to the inn where she was staying from the proprietor himself. He could no doubt tell her where to find a map that had more roads drawn on it than this.

Unless these were all the roads there were.

Then again, fewer roads, fewer people. Less things to run over on her first day. Maybe that was a good thing.

She hauled her gear to the car, put it in the trunk, and managed to get herself behind the steering wheel on the correct side of the car without any undue stress or confusion.

"Drive on the left," she reminded herself as she negotiated her way through the parking lot. That was a little unsettling in and of itself, but it was nothing compared to trying to blend in with the local traffic. She wondered why rental agencies didn't grill potential renters about their level of jet-lag before handing over any keys.

She took a deep breath and put her foot on the gas. She had a few hair-raising near misses with pedestrians, cars, and other bits of unyielding curb material, then she was quite suddenly on the road out of town. The road narrowed and the accompanying traffic eased up as well. She relaxed her death grip on the steering wheel and let herself smile.

She was in Scotland. It was almost too good to be true.

She could pinpoint the precise moment when her fascination with the country had begun. Her father had come home from a conference in Edinburgh and brought her a little statue of a Highlander playing the bagpipes. And for some reason, that had set fire to her ten-year-old's imagination. Her father had never traveled to the UK without bringing her back something Scottish, even if he'd purchased it at Heathrow. Child-sized bagpipes, kilts, books: All had served to deepen her fascination with a land that boasted so many lochs, such a rich history, and such a fiercely independent people.

Of course, an elaborate teenage fantasy about an ultra-buff Highland lord who would fall madly in love with her the moment he saw her hadn't done anything to blunt her enthusiasm, either.

She'd wanted to come to the Highlands for years. She'd wanted to touch the stones with her own hands, to roam the land on her own two feet and imagine who might have walked there before her, see the lochs and mountains with her own eyes and envy those who called them home. Even when school and career had taken the lion's share of her time and money, she'd always kept Scotland in the back of her mind.

And, she had to admit with a good bit of chagrin, she'd always kept that daydream of that handsome Highland lad in the back of her mind as well.

It was a good thing she'd just recently sworn off men, or she might have been distracted on her trip. After her last relationship, she'd decided to give them up for at least a decade or so. She just couldn't imagine anyone changing her mind. Besides, she was in Scotland to see the country, not find a man. That Highland lord could just look elsewhere.

She put all thoughts of impossible fantasies behind her and concentrated on the fields and forests that were full of autumn color. She rolled down the window and savored the chill in the air. Fall was by far her favorite season. It was full of promise for mornings spent lingering over a hearty breakfast before going outside to shovel leaves, afternoons spent watching the leaves wearing their autumn colors, evenings spent reading next to a roaring fire. Sweaters, boots, scarves: even the clothing worked for her.

Of course, she didn't have any of that really great fall-type clothing. What she had was a suitcase full of business attire, very *expensive* business attire, but that was a different story entirely. At least the obscenely expensive black shoes she was wearing were comfortable. It almost made up for the nylons that had slouched their way down her thighs and seemed determined to slide even farther. She didn't dare tug. They were her last pair, and she didn't have any money for others.

So to take her mind off her migrating legwear, she forced herself to admire charming stone houses separated by equally charming stone fences and pay attention to the delightfully winding road leading past them.

After a while, though, the road began to feel like one endless ribbon that wove its way in a rather haphazard fashion through the countryside, and she began to feel a little disconnected. Soon she wondered if she'd slipped into a trance. Things were becoming very peaceful.

Or at least they were until she glanced in her rearview mirror and found a black car of indeterminate origin suddenly crawling up her tail as if it had every intention of taking up residence in her trunk. She was invited to pull over with a series of friendly toots on the horn.

All right, so the guy was actually leaning on the horn as if he'd collapsed there. Not even being passed, seeing a ferocious scowl tossed her way as the man slowed in his passing to make sure she knew he was irritated, followed immediately by an acceleration so rapid she had to roll up the window to avoid road dust blinding her, was enough to sour her determinedly cheerful mood. She happily flipped the rapidly disappearing sportscar the bird and continued on her way.

The road continued northward and soon it began to wind with more enthusiasm. Her driving skills were definitely improving because she found herself growing used to driving on the wrong side of the road. She even managed to avoid various and sundry bits of animal husbandry that seemed to find warm, fallish tarmac to be to their liking. She'd never thought of sheep as a road hazard, but there you had it. When in Scotland, look out for white, fuzzy impediments to your journey.

If only the natives would take that advice, they would probably get a lot farther in their travels.

This was something she decided as she rounded yet another corner and found herself facing a traffic tableau that brought her foot into forceful and sudden contact with her brakes.

Mr. Black Sportscar was standing by the side of the road, looking at his beautiful car, which was now facing the wrong direction and sporting an enormous scrape down one side. Madelyn pulled over. No sense in adding to the tragedy by becoming a road hazard herself. She rolled down her window and poked her head out to look at the man who was speaking quite enthusiastically in a language she supposed had to be Gaelic. He was coming close to tearing his hair out.

Then he stopped and turned to look at her.

And she felt her mouth go dry.

All right, so she was sleep-deprived. She was also probably overloaded with too many expectations and too much airline food. And it was also possible that her social life was so far in the toilet that anything that looked passable in jeans and a black sweater seemed like a dream come true.

It was possible.

Or not.

Nope, there was just no denying that the man before her was simply, undeniably stunning. Tall, dark, unbelievably handsome. She tried valiantly to remember why it was she'd sworn off men. Not that it would have mattered. This guy was reason enough to deep-six that resolution.

And surely he had a fabulous personality to match that incredible face and impressive physique. Charming, strong-willed but chivalrous. She could only imagine what sort of gallant reply he would give to the offer of aid she couldn't not give. Really. It was the right thing to do.

"Need help?" she asked in her most helpful tone of voice.

He stopped his swearing and turned to look at her.

So it was more of a glare than a look. Maybe he'd had a bad day.

"*Help* me?" he snarled. "*Help* me? Nay, you can*not* help me, unless you'd care to go along before me and sweep the sheep from the bloody road where they don't belong!"

She blinked. Okay, maybe his chivalry had been buried under all the paint he'd scraped off the side of his car. She couldn't blame him. But as far as sweeping sheep went, she doubted it would do all that much good. His car didn't look as if it was going to go far enough for sweeping to become an issue. She turned her mind to more practical matters.

"Need a ride?"

He swore at her—she was quite certain he had—then stomped over to his exceedingly scratched door, opened it, threw himself inside. He managed to get the door shut with only a minor struggle. He whipped a U-turn, then flung his damaged car down the road with rather unwise abandon, to her mind.

Well, looks were deceiving, it seemed. His car was fully functional, but his manners were definitely not. She sighed. So her first contact with indigenous culture had been a bust— her father would have been appalled at her inability to ascertain the man's linguistic origins in ten words or less—but in spite of all that, maybe things would look up soon. After all, no sheep were lying dead on the road, she still had her car intact, and she'd been witness to a helping of just desserts.

Not bad, considering the alternatives.

She put her car back in gear and continued on her way, happily humming a tune and looking forward with eagerness to a decent dinner and a good night's rest. The sooner she was acclimated to her new time zone, the better use of her time she would be able to make.

It was rather late in the day when she finally reached the village of Benmore. She didn't bother consulting her map of the village because she'd already memorized it. She wound her way up to Roddy MacLeod's small inn.

She parked next to a very expensive-looking Jaguar, then turned her car off and sighed deeply. Safe and sound with a bed in her immediate future. Miraculous.

She dragged herself from the car, grabbed her purse from the front seat and her violin from the trunk, then made tracks for the front door. The entryway was neat and clean, but humble. She loved it on sight. But she hadn't taken but a handful of steps inside before she came to a screeching halt.

She sniffed.

A feeling of horror washed over her.

Not Eternal Riches cologne.

She rubbed her nose vigorously on the off chance that she was imagining things. But no, she wasn't. After all, who could mistake that for anything but what it was, especially given the permeation ratio she was currently experiencing?

Before she could decide between swearing and screaming, a middle-aged, ruddy-haired, ruddy-complected man came out, wiping his hands on a towel. He looked at her with a smile.

"May I help you?" he asked.

"I'm Madelyn Phillips. I have a reservation."

The man stared at her in surprise. "Miss Phillips," he said, blinking in surprise. "Aye, you did have a reservation, but . . ."

Did? Did he say *did*? Madelyn ignored the sinking feeling in her stomach—and the fierce itching in her nose.

"I called before I left the States," she said. "To confirm. You are Roddy MacLeod, aren't you?"

"Aye, I am," he said, beginning to look very unsettled. "But Mr. Taylor said you'd made other arrangements at the last moment."

Madelyn gritted her teeth. "He didn't. He couldn't have."

"Ah, but I could and I did."

Madelyn looked to her right to see a man emerging from the darkness of the hallway like a damned vampire come to look over the evening's offerings and offer his opinion on how they were lacking.

Bentley Douglas Taylor III. Her former fiancé. The man who had left her with no money, no job, and no apartment.

Was it bad to loathe another human being?

She glared at him. "You stole my reservation," she said, putting her hand over her nose so she wasn't quite so assaulted by his cologne.

"It was the honeymoon suite—such as it is, and it isn't much. I didn't think you would want it."

"What I wouldn't want is to share it with *you*."

Bentley removed a toothpick from between his teeth—he carried them in a silver case in his shirt pocket—and sucked those teeth, probably to retrieve whatever expensive lunch he had stowed there for later inspection. "Madelyn, you aren't being a very good sport about this."

What in the world had ever possessed her to agree once upon a time to marry the man standing in front of her? Obviously some sort of momentary loss of all rational thought. Bentley Douglas Taylor III was suave; he was handsome; he was powerful. He had also dumped her six weeks before their wedding only to turn around and become engaged to someone else approximately six minutes later. Just what in the hell was he doing here, fouling up her vacation?

"Food's not bad," he said, continuing to dig around in his teeth. "Not the civilization I'm used to, of course, but it'll do."

Yes, she'd been blinded by perfect teeth, lovely hazel eyes, and unassuming freckles across his nose. The fact that he was the über-lawyer at her firm with the accompanying stench of power that clung to him like perfume had likely had something to do with her fascination.

"Hey, Roddy, got a McDonald's around here?" Bentley asked, giving their host a friendly punch in the arm.

Too late, Madelyn decided, too late had she realized that the stench that clung to Bentley wasn't just power and Eternal Riches cologne, it was Eau de Fast Food. Over the six months she'd dated the man, she'd learned to differentiate between McDonald's, Burger King, and Jack-in-the-Box in three whiffs or less.

"McDonald's?" Roddy asked, looking appropriately horrified. "Nay, I'm afraid not."

"Why don't you try real food, Bentley?" Madelyn asked. "You know, fruits and vegetables."

"I prefer fries and burgers," he said archly.

"How do you survive on that junk?" she asked, but her incredulity was gone. She'd seen him throw back a triple-patty, slathered-in-sauce death sentence followed by fat-saturated fries and lard-soaked dessert and have not so much as a discreet burp to hide in his monogrammed hankie afterward.

"Superior physique," he said. "Teflon arteries. I eat whatever I want, in whatever quantities I want, and never do anything but flourish." He looked at her critically. "You've packed on several pounds, I see. I thought you would bear up under my rejection much better than this."

"I am bearing up very well," she shot back. And she was. Getting dumped by him was the best thing that had ever happened to her. But to have him potentially turning Scotland in the Fall into Vacation in the Toilet?

Not a chance in hell.

She'd figure out just why he was standing in Roddy MacLeod's unassuming foyer later. For now, she had more pressing matters to attend to. She looked at Roddy MacLeod.

"I need a place to stay since my room has been illegally and immorally purloined by the scumbag here."

Roddy clasped his hands together and began to wring them. "Ach, but all I have is a very small room—"

"I'll take it," she said quickly. "If it has a bed and I can become horizontal very soon, I'll be happy."

"Of course," Roddy said. "And I'll not charge you—"

"I'll pay a fair price," Madelyn said. "I won't stay for free."

"Take him up on the free thing," Bentley advised. "You don't have a job."

"Thanks to you," she reminded him.

"I did you a favor by taking you out of the partner's race. You never would have made a good one anyway. Look at you. A little stress and you eat your way out of your business suits and into matronly muumuus."

"I am still wearing my business suits, thank you very much, and you did more than just take me out of the partner's race. If memory serves, you had me fired as well."

"Did not."

"Did, too."

"Did not."

"You did, too!" Good grief, how could he stand there and deny it? He'd signed her termination notice! And the events leading up to it had come so quickly and so efficiently, she'd known it had to have been him, ruthlessly following a hastily jotted down list.

First had come the termination of their engagement. Then, in the order of appearance, had come the cessation of invitations to the partners' dining room, losing her best clients, being ignored by paralegals who had once quivered in fear before her, losing her crappy clients, losing her secretary, and finally, and by far the most humiliating, having her parking pass shredded by the lot attendant. She'd been forced to shell out ten bucks in advance to get into the garage.

Her pink slip had been taped to her door.

Of course, Bentley had been behind it all. With one stroke of his foul pen he had crushed any and all dreams she might have had of continuing her meteoric rise at DiLoretto, Delaney, and Pugh. Too bad it couldn't have ended there. Unfortunately, with all the people he knew in Seattle—and all the names she'd called him as she'd taken his pink slip to his office and thrown it into the ketchup on his china plate—she'd be lucky to get a job slinging burgers.

Would Roddy MacLeod call the police, she wondered, if she were to just reach out and plant her fist in Bentley's nose?

"Barbie Patterson was a better choice all the way around," Bentley said, chewing on his toothpick. "Less likely to cave under pressure. Less argumentative."

"I'm a lawyer. I'm supposed to be argumentative. And in case you didn't notice, Barbie is a lawyer, too."

"But she's a lousy one," he said pleasantly. "Couldn't argue her way out of a preschool dispute. But she'll look damn good in the annual report. Now, let's get down to business. Are you planning to stick to our itinerary?"

"Go to hell."

"Hell is where we are," he said, removing his toothpick and examining it. "I cannot believe I let you talk me into Scotland for a honeymoon. Scotland, a country where perfectly reasonable men dress in skirts."

"Kilts," Madelyn corrected.

"Plaids," Roddy MacLeod said, his nose beginning to quiver.

Bentley, unsurprisingly, was oblivious to the undercurrents of irritation flowing around him. "I suppose if I stay next to you, I will avoid any unwanted advances from light-steps in skirts."

"You're not going to be near me," she said firmly. "I don't want to see you. I don't want to sightsee with you. Sniff your way on your own to fries and unidentifiable burger material."

"You'll be much happier with me at your side."

What was he, nuts? The man was engaged! She might have suspected jetlag to be the cause of his lunacy, but he'd no doubt flown first class and she was sure they didn't have jetlag in first class. She could see she had only one choice.

She'd have to ditch him at first light.

Madelyn looked at Roddy. "May I have my key?"

Roddy retrieved one from his reception desk. "Here it is, lass. Fresh sheets, bathroom down the hallway. You don't think twice about asking for whatever else you need from me. Happy to provide it, happy indeed."

Madelyn hoisted her gear, then made her way down the hall and decided, as Bentley began to engage their host in a conversation regarding pubs and what kinds of unhealthy substances might be found therein, that the rest of her luggage would keep. She could wash her face tomorrow. Her teeth would survive a night without being brushed or flossed. She suspected that even her bladder might leave her alone if she asked, but there was no sense in overdoing things.

After a quick trip to the bathroom, she eased her way into her minuscule room and cast herself gratefully upon Roddy MacLeod's second finest mattress. She could deal with the wreckage that was her life tomorrow. For now she had a comfortable bed beneath her, and she was no longer trapped by any kind of moving mode of transportation.

Scotland in the Fall.

Despite everything, it was almost as fabulous as she'd dared hope.

With her last few thoughts, she wondered how the man who'd done serious damage to his black sportscar was sleeping. Not well, probably. Who would be, when contemplating that kind of repair bill?

At least she'd managed to avoid his fate. Her car was sitting undamaged in front of Roddy MacLeod's safe, pleasant inn.

She fell asleep with a smile on her face.

Chapter 2

Metal whistled as it traveled through the air, set up a fiercesome clang as it encountered an opposing metal force, then shrieked as it traveled along that bit of opposition, coming to rest quite forcefully against yet more metal that halted it in its forward progress.

Patrick MacLeod grimaced. If he hadn't known better, he would have thought himself inside his astronomically expensive Aston Martin Vanquish, listening to its pristine black side screech as it traveled the length of a stone fence. He felt himself again helplessly coming to rest with sickening finality—facing oncoming traffic, no less—on a stone-banked portion of the A785 that several sheep seemed to find a handy place for a nap.

Not that he cared overmuch for sheep foolish enough to use tarmac for a bed. In another lifetime he would have skewered the creatures on the end of his sword and been happy for a nice meaty supper. But that was then and this was now. Now he lived in a very civilized world where one did not flatten other people's mutton for the sheer sport of it.

Then again, given his mood the day before, he supposed the only reason he hadn't ignored modern conventions and done the little blighters in was because of the potential damage to his car.

Damage he'd done just the same by trying to avoid them, damn it anyway.

"Can you not at least *pretend* a bit of interest in this goodly exercise?"

Patrick looked at his brother's face a hand's breadth in front of his own, separated by their two swords, and gave him a casual smile. "When the swordplay demands my attention, I'll give it its due."

Jamie, his brother and his laird, reacted predictably with a great deal of cursing, a hefty shove that left Patrick no choice but to stumble backward a pace or two where he might again find himself within the range of Jamie's quite lethal blade, and a ferocious attack that did indeed require quite a bit of Patrick's attention.

As he endeavored to keep his brother at bay, he couldn't help but admit that it was indeed the perfect morning for that sort of thing. The sun was still below the horizon so there was enough chill in the air that a vigorous workout was not unpleasant in the least. He also couldn't deny that he enjoyed the association with his elder brother. He'd gone a very long time without Jamie's companionship after he'd left home and found himself living quite a different life than he'd ever expected—

Jamie ceased suddenly with his swinging, jammed his sword into the dirt, and placed his hands quite forcefully atop the hilt.

"Had that been a real battle, you wee fool, you would have been dead."

How was it his brother could still speak to him as if he'd been no older than ten-and-two and do it with a straight face?

"Fortunately for me," Patrick said pleasantly, "we do not find ourselves in a fight for our lives and I can afford a distraction or two."

"My sword is as sharp as it would have been then."

"But you love me and it would distress you greatly to lose me."

"I shouldn't be forced to worry about protecting you," Jamie continued with irritation. "That is your task. I rely on you for a satisfactory morning's sport, which you are certainly not providing me with of late."

"Sorry to disappoint," Patrick said with a low bow.

Jamie resheathed his sword in disgust. "I do not understand these foul moods of yours."

Patrick didn't, either, but there was no point in telling his brother that. The saints only knew what Jamie would do with that glimpse into Patrick's psyche. Not only had Jamie acquired a host of new relationship skills during the course of his marriage to Elizabeth Smith, he'd also come to believe that the handful of pop psychology books he'd read over the past year were actually useful and he was the only one who knew how to use them to their best advantage. And Jamie was, as it happened, laird of their little clan and had always felt responsible for the well-being of his clan members.

Well, that and he still looked at Patrick as if he were that laughing, carefree twelve-year-old who had loved nothing more than to get into trouble as often as possible and watch his older, more responsible brother come clean up the mess after him.

"You drive too fast," Jamie announced. "If you drank, you would drink too much. In regards to wenching, who knows? You never bring anyone to supper, so I can only assume you find them, bed them, then send them on their way before the sun sets."

Patrick knew giving his brother the truth of the matter would just send him off for another foray into his library, so he shrugged casually. "Just because you're the responsible one with a wife, two lads, and another babe on the way doesn't mean you have to begrudge me my indulgences. I have time, money, and freedom. What else am I to do with my largesse?"

His brother ground his teeth. Patrick coughed to cover up a laugh. If Jamie hadn't been so easy to bait, he probably wouldn't have done it so often. But how could he help himself? It was one of his little pleasures, and, as he had just told his brother, he wasn't about to deny himself what little pleasure came his way.

Jamie might have been relieved to know that he didn't drink, but he surely would have been unsettled to know that Patrick hadn't done anything with the women he'd dated, either. Casual intimacy had never set well with him, and no one he'd met in recent memory had interested him enough to make the relationship more than casual.

Maybe Jamie would have been pleased to know that he wasn't the only one Patrick was frustrating lately.

"You're five-and-thirty years old," Jamie said, reaching out to jab Patrick in the chest with his index finger. "Old enough to have done something with your life."

"I did something with my life and look where it got me."

Jamie hesitated, then scowled. "So you were once wed and you lost her—"

"And the child she carried," Patrick said easily. He only said it easily now. He couldn't have done the same six years earlier.

Had it been six years?

He shook his head in disbelief. It felt like yesterday. He'd almost been a father, almost held a bright-eyed, squirming babe in his hands and felt his life shudder because of it.

Almost.

"Perhaps 'tis time you ceased grieving and moved on with your life. On to something constructive."

If it was only grief he felt, he might have been able to move on. Unfortunately there was a great deal more to the tale than a simple loss and Jamie knew it. Jamie opened his mouth to speak, and Patrick could see in his brother's eyes that such was precisely the matter he intended to discuss.

But Patrick had no desire to discuss the matter at all, so he agreed quickly with his brother. "I should move on. Definitely."

Jamie pursed his lips, but let the moment pass. "You should do something more useful than that foolishness you do to earn your gold. You have more than enough with what I've given you. You should cease with that other work."

Patrick had no answer. They'd been having this conversation for years. Jamie didn't like Patrick's choice of occupations, and Patrick didn't like his brother telling him what he could and couldn't do. It was his life; he could risk it if he wanted. Besides, there was far less risk involved than Jamie suspected. He'd spent the whole of his youth preparing in one way or another for his current line of work.

"You should also," Jamie said, "go write your feelings down."

Patrick blinked. "What?"

"Write them down. We'll study them later."

Patrick could scarce believe his ears. "You're daft."

"I am not. Write down what you're feeling, and I'll put my considerable intellect to the challenge of determining where you've gone wrong."

"When hell freezes over," Patrick said crisply, "and not a moment before. You've no idea what you're doing."

Jamie stiffened. "I've spent my life studying the men about me and divining their innards. These books have only strengthened my gift for it."

"Divine elsewhere," Patrick said.

"I'll look for richer pastures when I've finished with you," Jamie said stubbornly. "And at least I'm interested in doing something with your sorry self. Far better that than wasting my life doing nothing, which is what *you're* doing."

Patrick was not sitting about doing nothing and his brother bloody well knew it. He earned a living honestly. He spent time with his family. He was a fabulous uncle. And he might marry again someday. Aye, an older widow with children safely tucked away at university where he wouldn't have to see them too often, wouldn't have to grow close enough to them to love them.

But even if he never looked another priest in the eye to repeat marriage vows didn't mean he wasn't living a goodly life. Who the hell was Jamie to discount that?

Patrick found himself with a sudden urge to cut off his brother's head. And given that he had a reputation for indulging his whims at any given moment—a reputation he seemed to have acquired thanks to his brother's wagging tongue—there was no sense in not living up to it.

Jamie's eyebrows went up as he ducked down to miss Patrick's first mighty swing. He came back up with a mocking smile on his face, and Patrick knew that he'd started something he would be finishing whether he wanted to or not.

Fair enough. He needed the distraction.

An hour later Jamie took a step back and held up his hand. "Peace," he said.

Patrick dropped his sword and leaned on it, breathing heavily. Nothing else he did in life to keep his body fit equaled swordplay before the sun was truly up and about.

Too bad he couldn't discipline his thoughts so easily. He sighed, then turned toward the stables.

"Stay," Jamie said, catching him by the arm and stopping him. "Stay for a meal at least."

Patrick looked at the sun peeping over the horizon. "Tempting, but perhaps another day."

"Damnation, Patrick, I didn't buy you that bloody wreck so you'd spend all your time there."

"I never asked you to buy me anything, and I protested quite loudly when you did. But since you felt compelled to purchase me a house of my own, you've given me no choice but to go live in it."

"I never intended—"

"And as if it wasn't enough to buy me a house, you had to buy me a title to go with that house," Patrick continued. "So much responsibility, being lord of my own hall. I'd best go see to restacking the rocks atop one another so I'll have a respectable place to entertain guests."

Jamie grunted. "Wouldn't worry about stocking my larder any time soon, if that's the case. 'Twill be years before you're entertaining aught but ghosts and rats."

Patrick paused and looked at his brother. Jamie stood before him, well over six feet of muscle, tolerable looks, and gruff affection. But damn him if he wasn't just as close-mouthed about his motives for doing anything as he always had been. Patrick looked at his brother searchingly. "Why did you buy me that hall anyway?" he asked.

Jamie only shrugged.

"I could have bought it myself," Patrick announced unnecessarily. Jamie knew just exactly what Patrick could and could not afford, given that he had been the one to divide up the family inheritance. And Patrick *did* have money of his own. It wasn't a fortune, what he earned, but it kept his belly full of sustenance and his cars full of petrol. In spite of that, Jamie had one day up and presented him with a deed and a fancy bit of paperwork that granted him some bit of lordly title. A year ago, as a matter of fact. Patrick had begun to suspect that his descent into perpetual grouchiness had begun at the same time.

And why not? Jamie's castle, their own ancestral hall, loomed up behind them; a gray, unforgiving place that was filled with love.

Patrick's house was filled with rotting tapestries.

"Were you weary of having me underfoot?" he prodded mercilessly.

"Of course I wasn't weary of you," Jamie said gruffly. "Thought you might want some responsibilities of your own."

At that moment Patrick almost regretted having baited his brother. There the poor man stood, supremely uncomfortable, borne down by the weight of love and too many self-help texts. Patrick sighed as he reached out and clapped a hand on his brother's shoulder.

"I thank you, brother. I'm grateful for a hall of my own and I know why you did it."

"I daresay you don't—"

"Perhaps I'll come for dinner tonight. But now I'll go home and actually do something responsible, such as take a broom to the place."

"Shovel, more like," Jamie muttered.

Patrick laughed. "Aye, you got quite a bargain."

"Ha," Jamie said. "Fair beggared myself to do it. You've no idea—"

"Actually, I do. You've told me repeatedly." He re-sheathed his sword and headed toward Jamie's stables.

"Patrick, wait!"

Now, that was a voice he would stop for without fear of having his innards examined for fatal flaws. He turned and waited as his sister-in-law waddled over to him. She leaned up and kissed him on the cheek.

"You're staying for breakfast," she said, not making it a question.

"Elizabeth, my love," he said with a smile, "the last thing you need with a baby due any day is me eating through your larder."

"We have enough to feed you."

He cast about for a decent excuse, but by the time he'd

formulated a very inadequate one, she had put her hand on his arm and smiled, an understanding one.

"All right," she said gently. "Go. I'll call you when the baby's here."

"It's not the—"

"Of course it is."

He sighed. "Very well. Ring me."

"Go charge your cell phone. It's dead."

"I know."

She pursed her lips. "You're impossible."

"But charming."

She turned him around and pushed him toward the stables. "Good-bye."

He smiled over his shoulder at her, then made for the stables. It was safer that way, not to be at the hall. He didn't begrudge Jamie and Elizabeth their bairns; he just didn't want to be there when those bairns made their entrance into the world. It was damned idiotic, he knew, but when did sense have anything to do with wounds of the heart?

He retrieved his horse and headed across Jamie's land to his own humble hut, northeast of Jamie's hall. It took him less than fifteen minutes, not because his house was close, but because his horse was fast and Patrick gave him his head. He often wondered if he enjoyed speed simply for the pleasure of it or if it had some kind of deeper meaning, like trying to outrun his ghosts.

He decided that today was not the day to determine the answer to that.

He slowed his mount down and walked the gelding into his courtyard. *Courtyard* was giving it a lofty title. It was more of a front area boxed in by a crumbling wall. It would keep no enemy at bay, but it did give some sort of structure to the front of his house, and for that he was grateful.

His house had once been the hunting lodge of a seventeenth century English nobleman with delusions of being a medieval lord. The entire place was constructed of stone and bore some resemblance to a small castle. It sat on a very beautiful bit of land. Patrick had admired the place from time to time, given that it was so close to the borders of Jamie's land and he'd had ample opportunity to see it, but he'd never considered buying it. It was, put quite simply, a complete wreck.

It did boast its share of chambers, true. There was a great hall, a kitchen, a pair of bathrooms, and several bedchambers. Indeed, one of them contained the same sort of massive fireplace the gathering room did. And it was also true that the owners over the years had modernized both the kitchen and the bathrooms—after a fashion. Not that he cared overmuch. He'd made do in the past with less and been quite happy. But to make the place comfortable?

It was almost more work than he could comfortably contemplate.

He looked over the outside of the house. It was in slightly better shape than the inside. The courtyard was surrounded by a low stone fence, and contained the house, stables, and a garage that in its day had likely housed four or five carriages. The stables and garage were in remarkably good shape. Unfortunately for the house, the descendants of the first Lord of Benmore hadn't had either his means or his enthusiasm. The last resident, a distant nephew several generations removed, had let the entire thing go almost entirely to ruin before he'd sold both the house and his very small, very insignificant title to none other than James MacLeod, who had bought it to give his feeble younger brother something to do.

Patrick sighed and went to stable his horse. What he could say for himself as the new owner was that he'd filled the stables with very fine horseflesh and he'd certainly done justice to the garage. The house, however, was still a disaster. He supposed it might have been less expensive to tear the whole thing down and start over, but he hadn't been able to bring himself to do it. Maybe there was more of a romantic inside him than he cared to admit. He couldn't help but wonder who had lived within those walls, how had they loved, what had they lost. . . .

Well, the last he could readily imagine because what they had lost was his gain. Patrick sighed. He really should do something about fixing the place up. Buy some furniture. Fix the walls. Install something in the kitchen besides an ancient Aga stove and a periodically functioning icebox.

But not this morning. He didn't have the heart to build anything today. This morning he would take another of his very expensive, very fast cars and drive very fast until he'd left his demons behind.

He walked inside the house, then came to an abrupt halt in his great hall. He sniffed. Pipesmoke?

He considered. It wasn't the first time he'd smelled the like. Maybe it was something locked in the decrepit tapestry hanging on the wall. But he didn't dare clean the thing. It would disintegrate.

He shrugged, resigning himself to smells he couldn't rid himself of, then headed for his shower, stripping on the way. At least he had indoor plumbing. It could have been worse. He'd lived in worse; he knew how bad it could be.

He stood in his shower, rested his hands against chipped tile with his head bowed, and willed the water to wash away more than just dirt and sweat. It didn't, of course, but he quite happily ran out the hot water in the attempt.

He dried off, grabbed fresh clothes from his armoire, dressed quickly, then headed out to the garage. He'd only made it midway across the courtyard before he froze.

Were those bagpipes?

He shook his head. There was no one at Jamie's who played the pipes. Well, perhaps that wasn't exactly true. There were pipers who came and went, but Patrick never exerted himself to make their acquaintance. He had better things to do than converse with those of their particular ilk.

Maybe this lad was a stranger using the mournful Scottish hill behind his house for a little practice. Might as well go tell the fool he was trespassing. Patrick hopped over the wall and walked slowly up the hill. He stopped well below the summit.

There was no one in sight.

And yet the pipes played on.

Patrick closed his eyes. He could imagine quite well a man standing there, his plaid and his music carried about by the breeze. He allowed himself the pleasure of enjoying music he was certainly only imagining. Apparently he had a damned good imagination, because the sound of the pipes stirred something in his soul he hadn't felt in a very long time. It was music from another time, music that belonged on a deserted, windswept hill, mournful music that was almost enough to make a man give in to his grief and weep it all out without shame.

He opened his eyes. There, at the top of the hill, was the piper. His plaid flowed in a breeze that Patrick most certainly could not feel; his music was carried by that same breeze, coming to Patrick's ears in snatches that were all too real. The man finished his song, turned, and made Patrick a low bow.

And then he disappeared.

Literally.

Patrick stared at the summit of the hill and cursed fluently. Damnation, wasn't it enough that the walls were falling down around him? He had to have ghosts, too?

He turned away and walked swiftly back to his house before he could give any more thought to that. He was losing it. It was the only logical explanation. He was not hearing a piper on his hill, he was not *seeing* a piper on his hill, and he was not going to indulge in any more of this Jamie-inspired speculation about his own mental state.

There was, he had to admit, far too much magic in Scotland for his own good.

He went to the garage, no firm destination in mind. The only direction he could come up with was *away*, and he'd had enough experience pursuing that one to know it was a good one. He opened the garage doors and stared gloomily inside. His Vanquish that sat there, a perfect wreck. Damned sheep. He should have flattened them.

He decided on his black Range Rover. Not as fast, but more sensible should he choose to pursue paths unknown.

He got in, slammed the door, then realized something was amiss. He climbed back out, saw the flat tyre, then swore with great enthusiasm. He was not having a good week.

Half an hour later, he was on the road and heading away for parts unknown. Civilization was what he needed. Maybe

Inverness. It was a goodly bit more culture than he'd grown up with. It would do for the moment. Besides, it would be a good thing to drop in on his mechanic and set up the fetching and repairing of his car.

He set his face forward and left the past, and that bloody ghostly piper, behind.

Chapter 3

Madelyn dreamed she was being attacked by giant mosquitoes. They buzzed fiercely around her head, settling with disturbing finality near her left ear. She pulled a diaphanous white mosquito net over her head, hoping to ward off any substantial bites, and wondered why in the hell she was in the Tropics. Big bugs, big spiders, big bright sun endlessly shining down.

Not her kind of place at all.

She woke with a start, realizing she was suffocating herself with her pillow. The alarm clock on her nightstand was buzzing incessantly. She groped for it, turned it off, and sat up before she was tempted to succumb to more blissful sleep.

Then again, maybe sleep wouldn't be so blissful. Heaven only knew what kind of insect she'd find herself bitten by in her dreams this time. She should probably cut her losses and limit the conjurings of her subconscious to something she could easily swat.

Besides, the day was a-wastin' and she had a very long list of sights to enjoy. The sooner she was out of bed, the sooner she would be out living her dream. And the sooner she could ditch Bentley to do it.

She could hardly believe the events of the day before. Had Bentley actually come to Scotland to ruin her vacation, or had she merely hallucinated the entire episode? Did hallucinations have smells? She could still smell his cologne, but perhaps that was due to residue left behind in her sinus passages from six months in his company.

Fresh air was obviously the thing for her.

She swung her legs over the side of the bed, then leaned over to find her slippers. It was then that she realized two things.

One, she'd fallen asleep in her clothes.

Two, there wasn't room to lean over while sitting on the bed.

She gingerly put her hand to her head—fully expecting to find blood gushing from a wound the size of the Grand Canyon. She fumbled for the lamp switch, hoping the blood hadn't ruined her suit.

She looked at her hand. No blood. She felt her head. Not much of a lump. She looked around her. Not much room for her suitcase either unless she let it share the bed with her.

She cursed Bentley Douglas Taylor III as she rose and carefully stretched so she wouldn't crack her elbows against the wall.

Well, the upside was she wouldn't be tempted to hang out in her room instead of getting out and seeing the sights. But since that had never been anything she'd anticipated having to fight, she went back to cursing Bentley for sticking her with a room that barely contained a bed, no matter that the bed was actually comfortable.

She sighed, then turned—carefully—and eased her way between bed and wall to the door. She put her ear to the wood and listened for the huffings and puffings of an ego-tistical trial lawyer who might or might not be lingering outside her door. She heard nothing. That, at least, was something to be grateful for.

She made tracks for the bathroom, made use of the facil-ities, then splashed cold water on her face. She peered blear-ily at herself in the mirror. Her hair hung down past her shoulders in big, fat Shirley Temple curls she usually spared no effort to straighten. She knew people paid huge amounts of money to have hair like hers, but all she wanted was to have hair that looked as straight as if she'd ironed it. Obvi-ously the lovely Scottish clime was going to do nothing to help her in her cause. The humidity had sent her hair into never-before-reached spasms of curliness.

With a sigh, she put her hair up in a ponytail, then turned to face her day—or at least her trip to the car to get her suitcase. She poked her head out of the bathroom, saw no one in the hallway, and dashed to her room. She grabbed the keys sitting on the bed, carefully exited the room without bumping anything, and headed quickly for the front door.

"Breakfast?" asked Roddy as she sped by.

"Sure," she threw over her shoulder on the way out the front door. If she could just get her stuff, grab a bite, and get going before Bentley woke up, she'd be in business.

She saw his car still parked outside. He was no doubt sleeping the sleep of the dead, without remorse, in the room that was to have been hers. He had paid for it initially, true and under unsettlingly loud protests, but when they'd been negotiating the dumping conditions, she'd traded him out their accommodations in Scotland for the horrendously expensive bridesmaid's dresses—violent pink bridesmaid's dresses insisted upon by his three vile sisters—and the deposits for caterers and sundry she'd been out.

At least she didn't have to worry about paying for her hotels. What she did have to worry about, she supposed, was fighting Bentley for each and every room. She could just see him racing her to each B and B just so he could get there and make her life hell. And considering he had the Jag and she had a little touristmobile, he would probably win every time. Well, she would deal with that when she had to. Maybe she would take off a day early and get a jump on their next destination.

She put her key into the lock to grab her suit jacket from the front seat only to pause and realize that her car was open. Had she forgotten to lock it? She honestly couldn't remember. The past several days were nothing but a blur. She peered inside. The radio was still there. Her suit jacket was still there as well, so she picked it up. She went to open the trunk.

She found that she didn't need the key there either.

She lifted the lid gingerly, hoping she wouldn't find a dead body placed inside.

No, no dead body.

No luggage either.

It was tempting to panic, but she took a deep breath and forced herself to relax. Roddy had probably gotten her suitcase and overnight bag for her. After all, her keys had been sitting right there on the bed. But hadn't she put them in her purse the night before? She shrugged to herself. Impossible to remember.

She walked back to the inn. Roddy was waiting for her inside with a welcoming smile.

"Ready for breakfast?" he asked.

"I've got a problem to fix first," she said. "Have you seen my luggage?"

He blinked. "Your luggage? Didn't you bring your things in yesterday?"

She shook her head. "Not my suitcase."

Silence descended as they both considered the ramifications of that.

Roddy spoke first. "Stolen?" he ventured.

She grimaced. "I hope not, but I don't know what else to think."

At that moment who should have come oozing out into the foyer but Bentley Douglas Taylor III himself, in tweed. Apparently he was dressing for success. At least he had foregone the kilt. She was certain the local population wasn't ready for his knees, knees she had fortunately only seen once at a company luau. One time too many, actually.

As she stared at his immaculate self, a nasty thought occurred to her. Had Bentley stolen her suitcase to hold it hostage?

She went on the attack. It was Bentley's favorite ploy and it tended to confuse him when females used it against him. "Why did you steal my suitcase?" she demanded.

"What?" he asked innocently. Far too innocently.

She looked at him narrowly. "You stole my reservation. Why would you stop there?"

"I don't steal," he said, puffing like a steam engine. "I am the epitome of honor, forthrightness, and virtue. I would never inconvenience you—"

She snorted in disbelief.

"—by stealing your suitcase," he finished.

Madelyn scowled. He was probably telling the truth—in his own twisted way. Bentley was completely committed to his version of the facts. That his version of the facts might be altogether incompatible with reality didn't trouble him. She often wondered how he managed to sleep at night.

"I don't believe you," she said, folding her arms across her chest. "I want to search your room."

"As much as you'd like to see the inside of the local jail?" he asked with one raised eyebrow.

"At least I'd get a few free meals there," she shot back. "And considering the state of financial ruin you've left me in, that sounds pretty good at the moment."

He shrugged. "Go look. You won't find anything."

"Only because you've hidden it so well," she muttered as she stomped back down the hallway.

She searched thoroughly, rumpling his shirts and mismatching all his socks as she went. It left her vaguely unsatisfied. What the man needed was a few days on the rack, stretched until his pinkie ring wouldn't stay on any longer. Unfortunately, she didn't know anyone with any kind of torture devices, and it was beneath her to mess with his very expensive mousse, so she trudged back to the foyer.

"Find anything?" Bentley asked politely.

She didn't think that deserved an answer. She set her luggageless sights on the dining room. Maybe breakfast would cheer her up and provide her with energy for the necessary sleuthing activities.

Before she could avoid it, she found herself with Bentley's arm around her. "Come on, Madelyn. Not that you really need breakfast with all that excess weight you've gained recently, but you can have something small. Then I'll take you shopping before we head out for our day of sightseeing."

She dug in her heels. "I am *not* going sightseeing with you. I have no plans to spend my vacation with you. You dumped me six weeks before our wedding, you jerk. Why would I want to spend any time with you?"

"Because you have a forgiving heart."

"I don't. I'm very vindictive. Besides, in case it has slipped your mind, you are engaged to someone else. Go home and sightsee with her."

"That's complicated," Bentley said dismissively.

She snorted. "I'll just bet it is."

He looked down at her with what for him was a look of sincerity. "Madelyn, I fear I may have acted precipita . . . precipita—"

She suppressed the urge to roll her eyes. Big words were not Bentley's strong suit. "Precipitously," she supplied. "In stealing my room? Yes, you did. Now, let go of me so I can get some breakfast."

His chin quivered. It was his Your-Honor-this-story-is-almost-too-painful-for-me-to-tell look. Heaven only knew what he was up to now, but it would no doubt entail her doing something she wouldn't like.

"I wasn't speaking about the accommodations," Bentley said, his eyes glowing with sincerity. "I was talking about my *precipitous* decision regarding us—"

"Ha," she said. "If you think I'm interested in any of your heartfelt confessions, think again."

She managed to escape his octopuslike embrace and sit herself down at the table. Unfortunately, Bentley sat right next to her. Suddenly she had the unsettling vision of an entire two weeks passed with Bentley sitting right next to her. "Need to pee," she blurted out, leaping to her feet.

She thought fast as she sprinted down the hallway. If her car wasn't safe, maybe her room wasn't either, because no matter his protestations, she knew Bentley had swiped her stuff. Not only was he truly in touch with his own reality and ready to lie to convince others of its validity, he taught off-site classes to the junior partners of DiLoretto, Delaney, and Pugh on how to lie and enjoy it. Her clothes were probably stashed in the back of his trunk for easy transportation to an unsuspecting Dumpster.

She paused at her room, gathered her notebook and everything else of value in her utilitarian black tote, shoved her violin under the bed, then made for the bathroom. She quickly put her hair up in her best business chignon to give herself courage, then continued with her plan.

The bathroom, as luck would have it, sported a much bigger window than her bedroom.

She made full use of it, sneaked around the side of the house, and eased her way into her car. It made loud crunching sounds as she peeled out of Roddy's parking lot, but that couldn't be helped. By the time Bentley realized what she was up to, took the time to douse himself in more Eternal Riches, then secure his hair in place with handfuls of mousse, she would be long gone in a direction he wouldn't anticipate. While he relied on the itinerary she had so lovingly and painstakingly crafted, she would venture off to parts unknown.

Once she felt she could safely pull over and give her direction thought, she stopped and reached for her notebook. Since she'd planned to use Roddy's as a base for her first week's travel, most of her scheduled destinations were in the general area of the inn, or easily reached with a minor bit of travel. She looked at her carefully laid plans and swore. Damn Bentley anyway. She'd plotted her sights to be seen with meticulous care, taking into consideration what to see in what order to best take advantage of the time allotted her. That she should have to abandon such carefully laid plans because of counselor Taylor was almost more than she could take.

It almost killed her to do it, but she knew she had no choice. She closed her eyes and jabbed her map with her finger. Inverness? Well, she'd planned to see the sights thereabouts on her way back to Edinburgh, but it was certainly a place Bentley wouldn't look for her today. She forced herself to peel her fingers away from her itinerary and turn to her maps. She determined her route, reminded herself to drive on the left, and headed out for the first day of her dream come true.

It wasn't much later that she found herself with a shiny black Range Rover trying to insert itself into her trunk. She glared at the sight of it in her rearview mirror. What was it with these guys up in the Highlands anyway? Fast black cars and no road manners—and she'd always heard what polite drivers the Brits were. Then again, maybe all the Highlanders left after all their years of troubles didn't truly consider themselves Brits, and the road rules, therefore, didn't apply.

The guy flashed his lights, then gunned his SUV around her. She would have flipped him off if she hadn't needed both hands to clutch the steering wheel to avoid being swept off the road by his jetwash.

His taillights disappeared into the distance.

Madelyn dismissed him, then settled down to serious driving, keeping the occasional lookout for Bentley in her rearview mirror. Surely he wouldn't be equal to the task of determining where she was going. He was, after all, the very stuff that bad lawyer jokes were made from. He was cunning, he was ruthless, but sometimes he just wasn't all that bright, especially when it came to ascertaining the intelligence of the fairer sex.

Nope, she was safe.

Unfortunately, not having to keep her eyes peeled for one annoying lawyer left her far too much time for idle thoughts and irritating observations. The first thing that leaped—or crept, as it were—to her attention was her hose. They eased upward every time she shifted as if they, being her final pair, couldn't resist giving her a final pantyhose wedgie. It wasn't as if she could take them off. How would she look in her Cole Haan flats and obscenely expensive black silk business suit without nylons?

She'd look like an out-of-work lawyer, that's how she'd look.

She gritted her teeth and said a foul word. Better that than crying. And with the mess she'd left behind in the States, crying was looking pretty darn appealing. She let the countryside roll by as she reexamined the mess, on the off chance that she might have missed something positive in the rubble.

Employment? No, she had no job, even after having invested countless hours and thousands of dollars in a Juris Doctor—at Harvard, no less—then sacrificing more untold hours studying for and passing the bar.

No money, thanks to the wardrobe she'd been convinced she needed to have to make the perfect partner, clothes that required all manner of uncomfortable undergarments to pull off properly. She'd blown all her savings on them, flush with the rosy glow of a new engagement and the promise of partnerdom within a couple of paychecks.

No money also thanks to all the times Bentley hadn't

seemed to have had his wallet on him—most often after they had enjoyed a very expensive meal. Amazing that the man could drive so often *sans* his credit cards and identification. Maybe he just kept his driver's license in a vestigial skin pouch.

And as if all that weren't bad enough, the bum had tried to bum a fast twenty off her on his way out the door for the last time.

There was no ray of sunshine so far.

Her parents had been prevailed upon to cover her student loans for a couple of months—but that had come with the hefty price tag of having to listen to lectures on the perils of pursuing a career outside academia. The tortures wouldn't end when she returned to the States because she would have no choice but to continue to crash with her parents while she looked for work.

Unfortunately, she knew that while she was looking for a job, she would also be listening to her parents argue any number of linguistic arguments in a dozen different languages and suffer more indignities as they required her to answer in those languages so they could point out where she was misconjugating the verb *to work*. That would no doubt be followed by more lectures on the necessity of her going back to school so she could follow in their footsteps and find herself a full professor of some obscure linguistic specialty so she could in turn find herself arguing their ridiculous arguments from morning until night.

It was no wonder she'd left home as soon as possible to pursue filthy lucre—their term, not hers—by defending low-lifes and high-lifes living a low life.

Her other alternative was to cast herself upon the mercy of her sister, but Sunshine Phillips was far too granola for her taste. Herbs, massage, holistic mumbo jumbo, and food that hadn't seen the north side of a frying pan. A stay with her would no doubt include some sort of herb for restoring Madelyn's good sense where men were involved.

On second thought, maybe that wouldn't be such a bad idea.

She shook her head. She could endure her parents' couch

for a few more days until she got her life together. At least her mother believed in ice cream and hot-fudge sauce. Madelyn suspected she would be partaking of both quite often as she tried to sort out the mess of her life.

But for now she would leave her job prospects, astronomical loan debt, and lack of housing and decent wardrobe behind her—

Wardrobe? Damn. Most of her wardrobe had been in that suitcase. She'd had to consign everything else just to get enough money to pay for food on her trip.

Which meant she had, basically, nothing but what she had on.

Could her life worsen?

She suspected it could and there was no use in dwelling on that. Such pondering invariably led to all cosmic retributional forces honing in on the hapless ponderer and rendering him quite unfit for anything but crawling into bed and pulling the covers over his head. Sunny said so. Sunny, being Sunny, would know.

Madelyn smoothed her hand over her black suit with renewed appreciation and continued on her way.

She made it to Inverness without mishap. First on her new list was a stop at Culloden. Between good signage and a big fat red line on her map, she managed to find it. The sight, what she could see of it from the parking lot, seemed quite unremarkable. Nothing gave away the carnage that she knew had happened there.

She checked her visitor's map, then hurried through the visitor's center. She had planned several sights for the same day she'd intended to visit Culloden's field. No sense in not efficiently checking them off her list while she was out. After all, she didn't have much time and she really wasn't one to waste time—

She came to a sudden, uncomfortably abrupt halt.

It was as if her feet had suddenly become glued to the ground.

She turned to her left, looked down, and saw a gray, rather unremarkable rock on the ground, a round, headstonish kind of rock. And on it was written the name *MacLeod*.

She looked around her. The path she was on was flanked by the same kind of stone markers she stood in front of. Simple stones with a clan name inscribed on them. She looked back at the MacLeod's marker. A chill went down her spine.

She backed away. These kinds of otherworldly sensations lay in her sister's domain, not hers.

She turned to look at something else, rubbing her silk suit-covered arms. But wherever she looked, she saw markers of death. This hadn't been on her list. What she wanted was nice, safe, comfortable examinations of historical sights. She *didn't* want to be blindsided by the first thing she saw.

She turned and walked resolutely away. It had been a fluke. Maybe jetlag was catching up with her. She might have been better off to take the day and remain ensconced in Roddy MacLeod's broom closet.

She came to another unwelcome halt. Had one of Roddy MacLeod's ancestors fought on the field she had yet to see?

She walked on before she could think about it. It was one thing to speculate on those lives lost from a safe emotional distance. It was another thing entirely to have it personalized. Maybe that was why she enjoyed being a lawyer. She got to savor the justice that would be brought to bear without having it be brought against any of her relations. At least no justice had as of yet been levied against any of her relations.

She paused. Maybe she should check to make sure those were really herbs Sunny was growing in her basement, not pot.

She continued on her way, neither looking to the right nor to the left so as to avoid any more encounters with head-stones, and didn't stop until she'd marched right out onto Culloden's field—

And into the final stages of the battle.

She dropped to the ground, squeezed her eyes closed, and covered her head with her arms. As she felt her legs be liberated from their sheer-as-silk coverings, she realized that she was losing her mind. Either that or the fact that she'd had no breakfast was getting to her. She would really have to eat something tomorrow morning. No more hallucinations like this, no sir.

She didn't move until the gunfire ceased. She opened her eyes, lifted her head, and saw through the smoke a field littered with the fallen bodies of men wearing plaids. All except for the man standing at the front line. Madelyn could hardly believe there was anyone still standing, yet there he was, one lone man standing in front of his fallen comrades, his plaid flowing about his knees, his sword flashing silver in his hand. His long black hair was a tangled mess swept back from his face. His eyes were closed, his face set in lines of grief, his posture rigid as if all that kept him on his feet was pride and the sound of the pipes behind him.

A sound she could readily hear even with her eyes open and her imagination shut safely up where it should be.

She knelt there in the heather for what seemed like hours, listening to a battle dirge played by some unseen bagpiper and watching a man standing in the midst of carnage, swaying a little himself with the breeze and the music. The complete hopelessness of the scene before her was too much to take. Tears streamed down her face.

Then a handful of birds took startled flight from a bush nearby and the spell was broken. She blinked and saw that the field before her was once again a flat, barren plain that stretched out to an unassuming motorway. It was not filled with the wounded and the dead.

It was, however, filled with one man still standing, though this one was dressed in jeans and a sweater, not a kilt. Keys dangled from one of his hands, flashing silver in the sunlight. His black hair was cut short around his ears.

But his face was the same one.

His face, she realized, was a familiar face. He was the one who'd wrecked his car to save sheep. What was he doing in the middle of a battlefield, taking part in her hallucinations?

She would have given that more thought, but he turned suddenly and looked at her.

And time again ceased to be. It was the same sensation she'd had at the headstone, only this time it was stronger.

And it seemed to have everything to do with the man before her. Half a dozen potential explanations for that raced through her mind, but she ignored them. What she knew, and she couldn't have said how she knew—obviously some unsettling legacy from her kooky sister—was that the man in front of her was connected to her in some way.

And she knew, beyond reason, that she had to make contact with him before he walked out of her life forever.

She hadn't come to Scotland expecting this.

But she had the feeling this was why she had come.

She lurched to her feet, then stumbled a pace or two toward him.

"Um," she began, fumbling in a most unaccustomed way for the right words.

He turned to look at her.

The wind kicked up suddenly, so suddenly she found herself having to shout to be heard.

"I think we're connected!" she yelled.

He frowned.

"I think that we're meant to be!" she bellowed.

The man looked at her as if she'd lost her mind.

Which, upon further reflection, she suspected she just might have.

Good grief, what was she doing? Begging a stranger to stay and be her soul mate? Spooky feelings or no spooky feelings, she wasn't going to stick around and make a bigger fool out of herself. She was going to just turn around and march right off the field.

Soon.

The minute she got her feet unstuck from the sticky bit of destiny she seemed to have stumbled into.

She stared at the man in front of her.

She could do nothing else.

Chapter 4

Patrick stared at the woman standing in the heather with her stockings in shreds and flinched at the way the past and present seemed to be layering themselves over her. One moment she was dressed in long skirts and a shawl, with her hair whipping around her face from a breeze only he seemed to feel, the next she stood in a black suit fit for any number of corporate endeavors.

What was she doing here, planting herself in the incredible delusion he seemed to be laboring under? And why was she staring at him as if she'd never clapped eyes on a man before?

By the saints, he hadn't come here for this.

He'd come to Culloden's field to brood. He came here when he felt troubled, for it reminded him of how fortunate he was to live in the hills with forests and beautiful places to wander.

But this time when he'd stepped onto the flat, unbelievably ridiculous place for a Scot to fight, he'd found himself thrust back into that fight. Gunfire had exploded from the British ranks before him, his countrymen screamed as they fell all around him. He alone had stood there, unharmed, in the midst of a battle that had been doomed from the beginning, in a locale no Highlander would have chosen if he'd had the choice.

The smoke had cleared, but his grief had not. And it had been in the midst of that grief that he'd noticed something move out of the corner of his eye, then turned to see a woman standing there, that woman, dressed in the eighteenth-century garb of a Highland lass. The wind had blown her skirts about, carried her voice off in a direction he couldn't follow.

Then he'd blinked and in the place of that Highland

woman had been a modern-day business type who looked as if she'd just stepped out from the office for a brief romp in the heather.

So now he stood, staring at her, wondering what in the hell he was doing standing there gaping at a stranger.

And wincing at the feelings of timelessness that washed over him at the very sight of her. He took a step or two closer to her, which was against his better judgment given that entirely unsuitable flash of feeling she engendered. He shrugged it aside with great effort and concentrated on something else.

"Did you say something?" he asked loudly.

"I . . . um . . ."

He made the grave mistake of looking her in the eyes again. The jolt that went through him startled him so badly, he stumbled backward. With skill and grace even Baryshnikov would have admired, he avoided landing fully upon his arse, but it was a near thing. As it was, he left his dignity behind as he hopped about in the heather trying to regain his balance.

"Out with it, woman," he demanded, his pride quite stung. "I haven't the entire day to wait for you to find your tongue."

The words were out of his mouth before he could call them back, though he wished quite suddenly that he could. It wasn't his habit to be rude to strangers, especially strangers who happened to be women.

The woman went quite red in the face. "Nothing," she said briskly. "It was nothing at all. My mistake."

A Yank. Patrick watched as she turned and practically bolted from the field. Perhaps 'twas just as well. The last thing he wanted to entangle himself with was a foreigner.

Never mind that both his brother and his cousin had married Americans and found themselves quite content with their situations.

Nay, such bliss was not for him. He wanted a Scot, someone who loved his land as much as he did. He had no intentions of hopping across the Pond to live on yonder fruited plain. He had no desire to eat McDonald's three times a day, unravel the ridiculous rules of baseball, or drive on the right.

Besides, he found Americans, when they weren't rudely tramping over his land wearing Hawaiian-print shirts, generally quite too solicitous for his taste. He was surprised that wench in her black suit hadn't asked if he'd needed help getting off the field. She'd had that look about her. Did he truly appear so feeble? Was it his fault that everyone seemed to find him desperately in need of aid of late? Take the woman the day before who had stopped her car and offered—

He froze.

It had been her. The same one who'd extended an offer of aid after he'd made that great hash of his Vanquish. She'd probably chuckled all the way to her hotel with visions of his repair bill. He hoped she'd been properly amused.

The breeze picked up again, blowing his hair about and tugging on his coat. He jammed his hands into his pockets and scowled, fully dissatisfied with the course his morning had taken. The only thing he hadn't done was wreck another of his automobiles.

The strains of a battle dirge wafted his way.

"Bloody hell," he bellowed, "will you cease!"

The piper seemed not to take offense, but played on.

First a woman who unsettled him to the core, then a damned ghostly player who seemed to have nothing better to do than to haunt him. If there was a deeper meaning to it all, he didn't want to know. The pipes he could ignore. More difficult was the woman, but her impact he could put down to the fact that he'd seen her yesterday and she'd certainly been eager to help him during a thoroughly humiliating moment—

It is more than familiarity . . . .

Patrick ignored his heart. Fickle, unreliable bit of him that was forever leading him astray. The woman seemed familiar because he'd seen her the day before.

'Tis more than that . . . .

Aye, the ridiculousness of a woman traipsing about a graveyard in a black business suit. What was she then, some traveling executive slaying time between meetings? She'd have to pop into Boots for a new pair of stockings if she had the high and mighty to meet with that afternoon.

Go after her . . . .

To what end? She would find her way back to the visitor's center easily enough, her bruised feelings would heal, and she would manage to get herself a new pair of hose. Let her see to herself. He had his own business to attend to. Not that any came to mind right off, of course, but he would work on that after he'd finished brooding. He stared determinedly out over the field, waiting for dark thoughts.

None came.

In fact, as the breeze blew over him and the pipes behind him began to play something altogether quite undirgelike, he felt a brush of something quite unexpected wash over his soul.

Something sweet.

Some bairn downwind with an iced bun, no doubt. He scowled, hesitated, then scowled some more.

He was not having a good day.

He jammed his hands farther into his jeans and ignored the urging from his heart. He didn't need to apologize to a woman he didn't know. She would have a perfectly lovely afternoon without any more of his input.

He stood there, listening to the pipes, feeling gentleness tug at his soul, and found that he just couldn't brood any more. Maybe he'd been brooding too long. Perhaps it was time to move on with his life, leave the past and its horribly befouled tapestry behind him.

By the saints, had he listened to his brother once too often?

He walked off the field before he could give that any more thought. He was going to find the wench not to apologize but to offer her his aid. Besides, it was in the national interest to leave her with a good impression of Scotland. And he was nothing if not a good citizen.

He turned down the path. She was quite a goodly distance in front of him. It was tempting to let that be excuse enough not to follow her, but a coward he wasn't, nor was he lazy. Speak to her he would.

He was a dozen paces behind her when she suddenly ducked behind a bush. She'd obviously not realized that she was completely visible from behind. He stared in astonishment as she hiked up her skirt, pulled off her stockings, then shoved her feet back in her shoes and her stockings in her purse. She adjusted her skirt before she sailed serenely forth from her small hiding place like the HMS *Victory*.

He wasn't sure if he should laugh or be appalled. His faint smile faded as he watched her stop in front of his clan's marker. She was very still for quite some time, then bent to touch the rock. She shivered so forcefully that it was plain even to his eye.

It felt as if she'd touched his soul.

His heart began to beat uncomfortably hard in his chest, and the tremor that ran through him had nothing to do with the fall chill in the air.

He didn't want this.

He didn't want any kind of connection with a woman he didn't know and was certain he wouldn't like if he did. She wasn't his type. He preferred casual clothes, casual women, casual entanglements that went no further than his heart could bear—not that he'd had any of those in quite some time, but his standards hadn't changed.

Where was his Scottish widow too old to have any more children who could break his heart?

The woman straightened suddenly, then looked around her, as if she wondered who might have seen her do something foolish.

He dived into the bushes at his right.

He waited several minutes until he was certain she was gone, then crawled out of the underbrush only to face a very suspicious-looking National Trust employee.

"Sir, what are you doing?" she asked sternly.

"Looking for my keys," he lied. That was all he needed—to run afoul of some governmental do-gooder. He brushed off his jeans, rubbed his hands together purposefully, and walked away before he could be questioned further.

The woman was gone. Patrick touched his clan's headstone in respect as he passed, then continued on to the visitor's center.

No Yank without stockings loitering there.

He walked swiftly out the entrance and stopped at the edge of the car park. She was getting into her car. He waited until she had pulled out, then ran for his car and jumped in so he could follow her.

She had, after all, paid her respects to his fallen clansmen.

His heart whispered its approval.

Patrick cursed it to silence.

The woman drove slowly. It was no wonder he'd almost run her over before he'd seen her. Then again, what else could he expect of her? It wasn't as if she'd had the benefit of several years of driving on the proper side of the road like he had.

She stopped in Inverness. Patrick remembered the first time he'd seen the place. It had seemed, to him who had grown up with only his family about him, like an enormous metropolis. The sights, sounds, and smells had overwhelmed him at first, but he'd soon grown used to them.

His Yank found herself a car park and simply sat with her head resting against the steering wheel. Patrick felt an unaccustomed sense of remorse wash over him, and he honestly hoped it was weariness and not his own callous treatment of her to cause her distress.

He rubbed a hand over his face. Maybe he was coming down with something. He'd felt more emotions in the past hour than he'd felt in the past year.

Frightening.

He made his own parking place where he probably shouldn't have, then caught up with her in the crowd. Inverness wasn't Edinburgh, to be sure, but it did have some shopping and the accompanying crowd to hide in. Patrick watched her look in windows, but she didn't buy. Given that the suit she was wearing was obviously very expensive, perhaps she couldn't find anything fine enough here to suit her.

She stopped at a small grocery. Patrick followed her in. It was an easy thing to spy on her without being noticed. It was, after all, one of the things he did best. He made himself scarce in the crisps aisle whilst she chose fruit. He loitered near the vegetable bins whilst she rummaged through day-old breads. He pretended a great interest in feminine hygiene products as she chose something to drink, then he managed a long-distance look in her basket. Bread, fruit, and water.

Not exactly a gourmet lunch.

He followed her from the store, then leaned uselessly against a wall as she ate her lunch on a bench. Watching her eat made him realize that he hadn't eaten himself, and after his morning with Jamie he surely deserved something. He popped back inside the grocery, grabbed the first things he laid his hands on, paid, and then exited quickly. He looked at the bench.

She was gone.

He was halfway down the block in a panic before he realized what he was doing. Stalking a stranger, for starters. Caring about someone whose name he didn't even know, for a finisher.

Obviously, he hadn't been sleeping enough.

"Murderer."

The sound of that voice caused the hair on the back of his neck to stand up. How long had it been, he wondered absently, since he'd heard that voice speak to him with anything but vicious accusations? Never, actually, even when the man had had reason to speak to him kindly. He certainly had no reason to now. Patrick turned and gave his former father-in-law a casual smile.

"Father," he said.

The older man's face tightened. He looked as if he would have given anything to have gotten his hands around Patrick's throat and squeezed, but they were in the middle of the street, and Gilbert McGhee was nothing if not civilized.

"I told you," Gilbert said, "never to call me that."

Patrick tossed his apple up into the air and caught it with a shrug. "It slipped. As I'm sure your kind title for me did."

"It was no mistake—"

The man standing next to Lisa's father, her uncle as fate would have it, put his hand on his brother-in-law's arm. "Leave it, Gil. Go get us a table. I'll be along shortly."

Patrick met Gilbert's hate-filled glance with a mild stare of his own.

"I'll see you hanged for killing her," Gilbert snarled. "See if I don't."

Patrick had nothing to say to that. He'd never had anything to say to that. He watched Lisa's father walk away and wondered what else he might have said at the inquest that he hadn't already said. He'd never been formally accused of killing his wife, but he'd been accused of it more than once by her father.

Only there was so much more to it than what the inquest had revealed, so many things that would never come to light if he had his way. Out of respect for the baby he'd lost and the fragile mental stability of Lisa's mother. Someday, perhaps, he would give Gilbert McGhee the full truth.

But not today. Today he was more than willing to put his dark past behind him and move on to things he could do something about. He turned to Gilbert's brother-in-law and smiled. "Slumming today, are we?"

Conal Grant put his hand on Patrick's shoulder and shook him gently. "I've been calling you for days. Where have you been?"

Patrick shrugged. "I'm having trouble recharging my mobile phone batteries. Bloody things."

"Buy a generator, Pat. I even left messages with Jamie."

"You know he won't give them to me. He doesn't approve."

"I know," Conal said with a sigh. "He told me the like very clearly. Thus you see how desperate I was to even subject myself to one of your brother's tirades."

"What did you need that was so dire?"

"I have work for you."

Patrick looked at his employer, the man who had first given him something he had been supremely suited for. He'd been pruning Helen Grant McGhee's roses when Conal had come along, looked him over, and somehow decided that there was more to him than skill with plants.

When was it that they had become less employer/employee than partners and friends? Sometime after Lisa's death, no doubt, when Patrick had worked around the clock practically every day of the year. It had been then, when he'd been trying to bury himself in something besides earth, that he'd made a friend out of his former uncle-in-law.

"Work?" Patrick echoed with a yawn. "Why would I want to work?"

"So you can pay for the restoration—and I use the term lightly—of that wreck you're camping in. You'd be happier in a caravan."

"You'd be happier with me in a caravan," Patrick countered, "for when I failed to show up when you deemed I should, you could simply attach a lorry to my front and drag me, house and all, to my next assignment. What is my next assignment, by the way?"

"Rich lad on holiday."

"I'm still on holiday myself."

"Not as of today, you aren't. The lad likes you. Asked for you specifically."

Wonderful. He was immediately assailed by visions of hours of attentive listening to youthful woes. "And where am I to keep track of this giddy lad? London?"

"Where else?"

Where else indeed, Patrick thought with a sigh. It was all available in London. He'd seen it all in London. Now, sampling was another story entirely. He would be a personal bodyguard to visiting monetary aristocracy, scout out the security of their locations before they arrived, then baby-sit them after they'd come, but indulging himself was out of the question. He'd seen too much of London's seedier side to have it hold any appeal for him. Given the choice, he would have preferred being at Jamie's, sitting at the long table and visiting with family and friends. But he needed to work— more for himself than his bank account—and Conal counted on him.

"When?" Patrick asked.

"Reconnoiter tomorrow, nanny in three. Which, I might add, is why I've been trying to ring you. I was almost to the point of driving up to see you."

"Horrors," Patrick said with a shiver.

"I certainly think so. Now, are you equal to it?"

"I'm always equal to it," Patrick said. "You'll have the papers ready for me on the plane?"

Conal nodded. "As usual."

"There are times I feel very secret-agentlike."

Conal smiled. "Aye, and there are many such agents who would be very envious of your skills, especially all that karate business you're so fond of."

"It's so much less messy than going about hacking at people with a sword." And learning it all had given him something to do besides sleep during that first year when the grief had been heaviest.

A slight, almost imperceptible shiver went through Conal. "I've seen you go at your brother with a sword. And there are almost times I believe you both about where you learned to use it." He rubbed his hands together. "Now, on to more interesting business. Though I can guarantee you no Bond girl as a prize for your labors, I would like to see you find something suitable on your own."

Patrick nodded, but his head had begun to pound. Conal had told him not to marry Lisa, but he hadn't listened. He wished, not for the first time, that he had. For his sake. For the baby's sake.

And, six years later, he could honestly say he wished it for Lisa's sake as well.

"Anyone promising lately?" Conal asked.

Patrick shook his head. The vision of a woman leaning over his clan's marker came immediately to mind, but he pushed it away. "Nay," he said firmly, "no one."

"There's time, my lad. So, Thursday, then," Conal said. "Get back to me when you land."

"I always do."

Conal grasped his shoulder again briefly, then walked away. Patrick didn't envy the man the trouble of soothing Gilbert.

But that wasn't his problem anymore, appeasing that man, and for that he was grateful. He retraced his steps and sat down on the Yank's bench. He plowed through his lunch with single-mindedness, then rose, tossing his garbage, and made for his car. He was walking down the sidewalk when whom should he see but his prey herself.

He dashed for his car.

And as he did so, he cursed himself. By the saints, he had do-it-yourself projects galore at home. Stones to restack. Plumbing to see to. Broken windows to fix. He didn't have time to play cat and mouse.

But he caught up with her just the same just outside town. She took out a curb and left a hubcap behind.

He got out, threw the hubcap in the back, then jumped back into his SUV and took up the chase again. And he decided, as he tracked her like a hapless rabbit, that he was tailing her because it was good practice. It wasn't because he was losing it. It sure as hell wasn't because he was intrigued by the woman.

She went to Cawdor Castle.

He skulked about in the car park.

She stopped at half a dozen other places, even simple vistas that he passed on a regular basis and had no more awe for. What in the hell was she doing? Going down a bloody list?

Somewhere during that long afternoon he parked. And then he snoozed. And when he woke, she was nowhere to be found.

Damn.

He was so numb from his touristy travails it was all he could do to point his Range Rover in the direction of home and hope it got him there. What he wanted was another nap. He couldn't remember the last time he'd had a nap. He was quite certain it had been decades.

That this woman should inspire the like in him was no doubt a sign.

As he drove, he realized he'd neglected to contact his mechanic. It appeared that he would have to charge up his mobile phone after all. Either that or go use Jamie's phone, but he knew where that would lead: to another of his brother's forays into his library or a lecture on the evils of playing bodyguard to the rich and irresponsible. At least Jamie wouldn't berate him for owning several hideously expensive cars, given that Jamie had his own share of luxuries.

The mechanic would have to wait. There would be time enough on Thursday before the plane took off to make those arrangements.

He drove home in leisurely fashion, with his windows rolled down and stereo blaring to keep himself awake. He almost ran into the ubiquitous Ford rental before he realized what he was doing. He couldn't decide if he should be relieved or indulge in a curse or two. His Yank, still doing twenty clicks below the speed limit.

He backed off and followed her until it was time for him to turn off to home. He considered quickly. There wasn't much up ahead save the village. Perhaps she was staying there.

His car seemed incapable of turning right. He followed along behind the dark blue car until it turned off, slowly and cautiously, into the village. He flipped himself around and headed back the way he had come.

The village wasn't big enough to boast more than two lodging facilities and he wondered which she had chosen and why she had chosen a place so remote. Then again, if merely roaming the Highlands had been her goal, she had chosen a likely enough place.

Comfortably close to his home, actually.

Though that didn't really concern him, of course. He had much to do and needed to be about doing it. Let the Yank see all the sights she wanted. He was far better off not dozing in any more National Trust car parks. He was quite certain he'd seen all the sights he cared to in this lifetime.

He considered taking her hubcap to her, but the thought was just too exhausting. He would do it in the morning.

For now, it was all he could do to limp home to his empty house.

Chapter 5

Madelyn thought her slide into ignominity had stopped. She thought the list of indignities visited upon her innocent—all right, so she had crushed a few paralegals under her spiked heels, so she wasn't all that lily white—her *mostly* innocent person had ceased.

Apparently not.

And that had everything to do with the pile of clothing on her bed.

As she stared at it, her mind drifted back to the evening before. She'd returned to Roddy's inn after a successful completion of her day's list. There had been that horrible business with Mr. Rude at Culloden's field, but she'd shucked off that slight with the same alacrity she had her trashed nylons. She had proceeded with her sightseeing *sans* hose and *sans* any unwholesome and unwelcome entanglements with men who obviously were better left in her delusions.

She put her hand to her cheek, sure she'd find some sort of residual burning from the embarrassment she'd felt the day before. Had she actually babbled words to the effect that she was his soul mate and he'd better get with the program?

She honestly hoped that he'd been telling the truth when he'd said he hadn't heard her.

She'd quickly gotten over that humiliating moment and moved on. Eventually she'd moved on back to the inn to face an irate Bentley, who'd demanded to know where she'd been and why she hadn't followed their itinerary. It had been almost enough to convince her to give up list-making for good.

She had left him frothing at the mouth in the foyer and retreated to her room to contemplate her next move, when she'd stumbled upon the gifts left for her. She'd shared the bed with the pile the night before, simply because she'd been too tired to do anything but lie down next to it and succumb to slumber.

In the daylight, though, she had the coherence and leisure to look at the clothing. She wasn't quite sure just how she should go about being grateful. She'd pulled enough money out of her stash the day before to buy several pairs of panties and a toothbrush, but she hadn't dared do more than that. She still had thirteen days in Scotland, and she would have to eat at some point during them. She'd been prepared to make do with fresh underwear, no nylons, and her black suit.

But now she wouldn't have to. She searched through the things Roddy's wife had apparently pulled out of the attic. They were fifties vintage—Miriam MacLeod's mother's gear apparently—and sported the colors associated with that era: lime, bright yellow, orange, hot pink. It was Gidget, only she wasn't going to look nearly so cute. She was sure the shirts would barely reach her navel and the pants would look like capris—and that was assuming she could get them past her thighs and bum.

Sightseeing in floods and expensive black shoes.

She would look like a dork, but she had honestly never been more grateful for anything in her life.

Forty-five minutes later she was ready for the day. She emerged from her room dressed in short, tight, plaid orange pants and a matching orange shirt. She'd also found a white sweater (also too small) in the pile. That and her black shoes certainly completed the outfit. She'd pinned her hair up in her power chignon just to give herself courage.

"Good heavens, what *are* you wearing?"

Madelyn's hair stood on end, even through her clip. Had she ever found that voice pleasing? Unfortunately, she could remember all too well when. She'd found it appealing up until the moment he'd called her on the phone to dump her. She scowled. One floor away in their building and he couldn't be bothered to take the elevator down to deliver his happy news in person.

Typical.

Madelyn turned and glared at him. "I'm wearing gifts from

my gracious host. Gifts, I might add, that are meant to replace my wardrobe that you, one, made me buy; and, two, stole from me and disposed of in some Scottish landfill."

That he didn't immediately fall to the floor and begin to writhe as he screamed his favorite pep squad cheer "libel, slander, sue, sue, sue" told her all she needed to know about his illegal activities two nights prior. She gave him her most formidable look of disgust and continued on her way to the dining room. She hadn't had money for dinner the night before. It was in her best interest to tank up while she could. She quickly put her bag on the seat next to her. No sense in giving Bentley anywhere to sit.

"Good morning to you, Miss Phillips," said Roddy MacLeod, coming in with a smile. "Ready for a bit of something strengthening?"

"Just a bit, though," Bentley said, sliding into the seat across from her. "She's busting out of her seams already."

Madelyn didn't bother to reply. Instead she smiled at a very uncomfortable-looking Roddy. "He gets like that when he hasn't had enough partially hydrogenated oil. And yes, I'd love something strengthening."

"A small portion—"

"Shut up, Bentley."

He looked perplexed. It was the look he customarily wore when anyone of the fairer sex put up any kind of show of spine. He didn't wear it very often because usually any and all women in his general vicinity were too busy being mesmerized by his stench of power and the few, perfectly proportioned freckles dusted across his nose to notice they were being patronized. She shook her head in amazement that she'd ever been one of them. Dazzled by dermatological phenomena. Pathetic.

"So," Bentley began slowly, lifting his fork and looking for all the world as if he was merely admiring its construction, "what are our plans for the day?"

She wasn't fooled. She'd seen him pull the same thing in court a million times with whatever prosecution exhibit was handy. *Distract, then broadside* was his motto. "They aren't our plans, Bentley, they're *my* plans, and I don't want you mucking them up."

"Unkind, Madelyn," he said, shaking his head sadly.

"And canceling our wedding six weeks before the fact wasn't?"

"We've been over this before. We weren't right for each other. At least," he said, pausing dramatically and waiting for her to look up and make sure he was still breathing, "at least that was what I once thought."

She could hardly believe her ears. "Bentley, you jackass, you're engaged!"

"That's true, technically—"

"Technically?" she echoed. It was no wonder he'd been able to jilt her so easily between his 10:30 and his 10:45. She gratefully accepted a hearty bowl of porridge from Roddy. "Thank you."

"More to come," he assured her. He disappeared back the way he had come.

"Your travels would be more comfortable with me," Bentley said. "And then we could talk."

"Don't want your money," she said around her spoon. "Don't want to talk."

"You were certainly willing to talk about taking my money to get here."

"It was a fully negotiated trade for unrefundable wedding expenses and you know it."

"But you never would have gotten here without me."

"Untrue. I've wanted to see Scotland for years."

"So you used me as your ticket here—"

And he called her argumentative? There was no point in trying to discuss anything with him. Besides, he had a point about the fact that she probably wouldn't have gotten to Scotland on her own, but it wouldn't have been for a lack of funds. Cheap, though, would have been the order of the day given the balance on her school loans. She was good at cheap. Her parents had taken their summers each year in a different country, to polish their language skills of course, and they'd taught her well how to get along with little money.

No, it wasn't about money. She liked to think it had been because she'd romanticized Scotland so much that seeing it alone would have been unthinkable. Or perhaps it was just that she hadn't been willing to take the time away from her career. She had been pretty obsessed with clawing her way to the top. Maybe she should be thanking Bentley for relieving her of that opportunity.

But grateful or not, she wasn't about to let him tag along with her. He was still Bentley after all. And if she hadn't known better, she would have suspected he wanted to either get back together with her or fling with her while in Scotland. With both alternatives leaving her wanting to go shower, she put her head down and plowed through breakfast, ignoring all Bentley's attempts at further conversation.

When she'd finished, she rose. Bentley didn't try to stop her. Counting that as an auspicious sign, she gathered up her gear for the day, made certain her violin was still resting safely under her bed, then walked outside to the car park. Still Bentley didn't follow her.

She rounded the corner of the house.

And came face-to-face with the reason why.

He'd blocked her car with his. Not blocked, pinned. Trapped. Boxed in so there was no hope of escape.

Damn him anyway. She marched back into the house. Bentley was leaning negligently against Roddy's little reception desk.

"Shall we go?" he asked smoothly.

"Go to hell," she said angrily. "But let me out first."

"I would be remiss in my duties as your almost husband if I didn't see you properly escorted on this trip—"

"Move your car."

He merely stared at her blandly. "No."

She was so furious she could hardly speak. So instead of reaching for the handiest sharp instrument she could find and plunging it into his brain, she turned and stomped off toward the bathroom. She locked the door behind her, sat on the edge of the tub, and fumed. She fumed until the bathroom started to feel a bit steamy. She was just certain the mirror was going to fog up soon, but heard a light tap on the window before it could. It wasn't a Bentley tap, so she pulled the curtains back and opened the window.

Roddy stood there, looking around furtively. "Can ye ride?" he whispered.

"A bike?"

"Nay, lass, a horse."

She gulped. Did one terrifying ride on the back of a semi-comatose nag at Girl Scout camp twenty years ago count? It did, if the day spent with Bentley was the alternative.

She put her shoulders back. "Sure."

Roddy nodded his head to the left. Madelyn climbed out the window and followed him to what appeared to be a modest stable.

"Mr. Taylor is in the lounge," he said.

"Tied to a chair?" she asked hopefully.

"I convinced him there were no sights within walking distance. He thinks you'll come to your senses soon enough and return."

"Are there sights within riding distance?" she asked.

"Oh, aye, lass. A nice castle up the way. Manor houses. All sorts of ruins and other interesting things."

Well, this was most definitely not on her list, but it seemed as though none of her vacation was going to be on her list. Besides, who knew where a bit of serendipity might take her?

To the local hospital for the setting of numerous broken bones, no doubt.

Roddy's horse appeared far too soon, saddled and apparently ready for action. He looked enormous, but she wasn't exactly one to judge, given her dismal lack of experience with those of the equine persuasion.

The horse looked at her doubtfully.

She understood completely. "Um, Mr. MacLeod," she began hesitantly, "do you have something less . . . shifty?"

"Shifty, lass?"

"Well, he's moving around a lot. I thought horses were more stable than this."

Roddy looked at her pityingly. "You haven't ridden all that much, have ye, lass?"

Why bother to lie? He'd know the truth the moment she put her foot in the stirrup. And just how in the hell was she supposed to get her foot all the way up there? That didn't even begin to address getting any of the rest of her into the stratosphere.

"No, I haven't ridden all that much," she admitted.

Roddy, that obviously quite gallant soul, didn't blink. "Well, lass, he's your ticket to freedom today, so you'd best learn fast. Even my wee grandchildren can ride Whoa Bullet."

" 'Whoa Bullet'?" she echoed.

"He's a gentle lad, despite his name. Here, let me have your gear, lass. You won't need it."

"But—"

"No need for money up the hill. The sights are free."

Well, he would know. Madelyn surrendered her small suitcase of a bag, then examined her next task.

She suspected it would be easier to deadlift a Yugo than to get her own sorry backside up in that saddle, but she managed it with a great deal of undignified grunting. At least the seams of her orange plaid pants had held up under the strain.

"Steering wheel?" she asked from her perch atop the bucking bronco.

"Reins. Go left, go right, go straight," Roddy said, with the appropriate demonstration.

"I hope I won't break him. Do you have insurance?"

Roddy laughed. "If you fall off, he'll come fetch me. And to be sure, he's endured worse than you atop his back."

Madelyn opened her mouth to thank him, then saw his wife come trotting out with a hefty sack.

"Lunch," she announced, deftly packing it in a saddlebag and attaching it to Madelyn's saddle. "Have a lovely day, lass."

Madelyn almost didn't manage to get words past the lump in her throat. Food, transportation, and vintage clothing as well. "I can't thank you enough. I'll sue someone for you later if you want."

Roddy only shook his head with a smile. "We're happy to help."

"Sorry to leave you with Bentley."

"Aye, well, we'll speak of repayment for that later. Now, be off with ye and enjoy your day." Roddy turned her horse around and led it out of his back gate. "Up past the keep, laddie, and show the gel the land."

Madelyn started to wave, then realized that waving could be very dangerous. She limited herself to a slight nod of thanks, then clutched her reins, the saddle, and a handful of the horse's mane just to be safe as the horse walked on.

The trip through the upper part of the village passed without incident, most likely because she let the horse go where it wanted to. It stopped at the main highway behind the village. Madelyn looked both ways, then urged the horse forward by what she was sure was an age-old horsey command.

"Go," she said.

He went, stepping lazily.

Until they were safely on the other side of the road, that is. Then the horse took off as if someone had shot him in the butt.

"Whoa, Bullet!" she shouted.

Apparently, that didn't translate. Then she remembered that was the damned horse's name.

"Stop!" she bellowed. "Damn it, I don't speak Gaelic!"

Luckily for her, her hands were so tangled in reins and mane that falling off was an impossibility. So she held on for dear life.

Scenery passed. Actually, she passed by scenery. Trees, flora, fauna; she saw it all. From a distance, of course.

She burst through a forested area into a meadow. And the sight of the forbidding gray castle sitting in the middle of it was almost enough to surprise her into releasing her death grip. She continued to clutch, however, as her horse flew up the meadow toward the castle—

Past the castle.

"Hey," she said crossly, "we're supposed to stop there!"

Obviously, her horse had different ideas.

She looked over her shoulder for one last glimpse of the keep. The horse plunged into more forest. She fended off branches with one hand, praying it wouldn't cost her her precarious perch. Her mount left the trees with the same enthusiasm he'd entered it. Indeed, his happiness seemed to increase with every yard he put behind him. His speed increased exponentially.

She realized immediately that she was in deep doo-doo.

"Help!" she squeaked.

The horse didn't answer. Maybe he wasn't listening. Maybe he couldn't hear for the wind rushing by his ears. Maybe he thought if he just ran a titch faster he might break the sound barrier.

She supposed the scenery would have been breathtaking— she was in some sort of plateau-like bit of country with sharp mountains rising around her—but she was quite frankly too terrified to enjoy it.

"Stop or I'll sue!" she squawked.

The horse remained unimpressed.

She panicked, she prayed, she might have screamed. And just at the moment she was certain she would just have to cast herself into a vat of total despair, she caught sight of something flying toward her. Plane? Alien spacecraft? Whatever it was, it was headed straight for her.

She knew death was unavoidably near—or it would be if she didn't do something drastic. So she dredged up superhuman strength and hauled back on the reins.

Miracle of all miracles, the horse tossed his head a time or two in frustration, then stopped.

Didn't matter. She was so flat-out terrified, she did the only sensible thing she could: She slid off the horse so she could faint more closely to the ground.

Much as she'd done twenty years earlier at Girl Scout camp.

Only there, the horse had been shorter.

Yes, definitely shorter because the slide down had ended much sooner. Maybe that horse had actually been a pony. She tried to factor in that new information with the differences in her height, weight, and flexibility, but found she didn't have the time. The ground came up to meet her backside with a great deal of inflexibility. The pain in her tailbone might have been enough to send her into oblivion if she hadn't slid off what she vaguely realized was a rock, tipped over, and cracked her head on another.

She was trying to judge how much that hurt when the sunlight was blocked by a large shadow. She squeaked in fright, then realized the face looming over her was none other than Mr. Black-Sports-Car himself.

"How'd you get here?" she asked. Her words were slurred, she noticed with alarm.

He pointed back over his shoulder to where his black horse stood. "I rode."

"Hmmm," she said, "so did I."

"For a bit, at least."

"I," she said archly—no small feat given her current condition, "am just learning to do it."

"You're off to a glorious start."

"I think so, too."

"Anything damaged, do you think?"

His voice was very far away and growing farther by the minute. Madelyn closed her eyes. It was a shame to block out such splendid scenery—and the countryside was pretty good looking as well—but she found darkness closing in relentlessly.

"I'm tired," she breathed.

"Then take your rest, lass," a deep voice said. "I'll keep you safe."

But who would keep her safe from him and his bad-mannered self?

Chapter 6

Patrick watched the woman before him slip peacefully into oblivion and gave himself over to the contemplation of life's ironies. He'd been tracking this wench for the better part of the day yesterday, yet here she was, having deposited herself quite handily on his land without any effort on his part. He should have repaired homeward after Culloden and left her to her own devices. It would have saved him a mighty kink in his neck from his nap in the car.

He looked up at Roddy MacLeod's Whoa Bullet, who was currently and quite contentedly nibbling a few dainties. So that's where she was staying. He could only assume 'twas Roddy himself who had lent her the horse. That man needed to more thoroughly ascertain the riding skills of his guests before loaning them any horseflesh. Someone was going to wind up in hospital one of these days.

He paused, then swore. He was beginning to sound like his brother. With that terrifying thought to keep him company, he turned his mind to the more practical matter of seeing how seriously the woman was injured.

And then he froze, his hands outstretched.

What, by all the saints, was he thinking?

He sat back on his heels and dragged his hands through his hair. He closed his eyes and concentrated on stilling his appallingly rapid breathing. It was a bloody lucky thing Jamie wasn't nearby; he would have been overjoyed to have seen his younger brother undone—and over something as innocent as thinking to use his hands for something approximating healing.

He stretched out his hand again.

It trembled.

"Bloody hell," he muttered, making his hand into a fist.

"Utter rubbish." He dug deeper for a few fouler things to say, which made him feel slightly more himself, then blew out his breath and set to work. He ignored his raging thoughts and thoroughly and methodically checked his Yank for any fractures.

Fortunately for the condition of her orange trousers, no bones had broken free of the skin. Patrick gingerly felt her head. There was a nice-sized bump, but he suspected she would survive it. He'd seen, and endured himself, far worse.

He patted her cheeks, but all he got in response was a brief opening of her eyes. She groaned, rolled toward him, then closed her eyes again and began to snore.

Jetlag?

A man could hope 'twas but that and not a reaction to his own sweet self.

He looked at her curled up in front of him, then reached out and smoothed the hair back from her face. She was not beautiful in the exotic way that the women he was used to dating were beautiful, but he couldn't deny that there was something about her that was very appealing. Fresh-faced American wench, he thought with a small grumble. Either she bathed in milk or she passed far too many of her hours hiding in an office.

Aye, that had to be it. She likely didn't have much to do with weather and such, what with going from meeting to expensive clothier and back again. He stared down at her current garb. It gave him pause, but perhaps it was high fashion. So high it was beyond him, but there you had it.

Well, whatever the case, she was still sleeping and he had to get her somewhere to either continue her nap or bring her back to her senses.

He looked over his shoulder. His house was a good half hour's walk, perhaps longer with dead weight to carry. It looked as though he would have no choice but to impose on one of his brother's tenants. He looked at the woman lying before him once again. No broken bones. No spinal injury or else she wouldn't have been able to roll. Anything else that ailed her could be taken care of at home. Probably just as well. He himself had no use for doctors—

He stopped his mutterings before they turned into a rant. Aye, he still had no use for doctors, but after Lisa's death, he suspected he didn't have much use for herbs, either.

He turned away from those troubling thoughts and looked at the horses. They weren't going anywhere any time soon. He slipped his arms under the woman and, with only a minor amount of grunting, heaved her up into his arms. He shifted her so her head rested against his shoulder, then set off for his destination. Moraig's house wasn't easily found, but once found, a body never seemed to have trouble finding it again.

Jamie said she was a witch, but Patrick knew better. Jamie's healthy distrust of anything and everything she had cooking on her fire at any given time never stopped him from inviting her to dinner now and then. *Better a witch makin' stew to sustain you than one brewin' potions to kill you* was what he inevitably said after having gone north to deliver his invitation, which delivery also inevitably included having had a polite bite at her fire.

Patrick had had his own experiences with the woman, and his opinion of her was far different from his brother's.

He paused at the edge of the forest and looked down at the path he was poised to put his foot to. He shivered in spite of himself as he remembered vividly the first time he'd done the like.

He'd been a score and six at the time and as reckless as Jamie was responsible. He'd decided to test the rumors about the forest near his home, rumors of magic lurking deep inside where the sun rarely reached. He'd anticipated returning victorious, full of bold words to tease the old ones with and show them how wrong they were.

Ach, such arrogance.

He'd spent the night in the forest, to fully test his own courage and stamina. He'd woken, just as he'd known he would, still under the trees, still wrapped in his plaid. The rain hadn't troubled him so deep in the forest, but he'd anticipated a good soaking whilst hurrying back to the keep to boast.

He'd left the forest and come to a complete and teetering halt. Aye, his ancestral home had been there, but certainly not in the condition it had been the day before.

It had been in ruins.

His bluster had left him abruptly.

Cold, soaked to the skin, and frankly quite terrified, he'd wandered the high meadow until he'd come to the forest before him. He'd never been more grateful for anything than he had been for the path before him that promised aid up ahead. Never mind that it led to a place that even in his day had been rumored to be a haven for all manner of supernatural creatures. He'd seen smoke from a fire. It had been enough.

Moraig had opened her door, taken one look at him, and welcomed him in with words in his native tongue. Gladly he'd set his gear aside and sat in front of her fire as his clothing steamed. He'd accepted food, drink, and an offer of shelter for as long as he'd needed it. He'd remained with her for a pair of fortnights until he'd been ready to venture further afield.

Of course, he'd worked for his keep. Moraig had gotten a new roof, a winter's supply of chopped firewood, and enough herbs gathered to make potions far into her old age. She'd cheerfully invited him to come back often, which he had, even after he'd made his own way in the world and had had no more need of aid.

He supposed she wouldn't mind yet another refugee in need of her skill with brews. He shifted his burden and set off down the path. It took only a few minutes of good walking to come within sight of his destination. Moraig's house looked as if it had grown out of the forest itself. The walls were wood, covered with moss; the roof was thatched, also covered with moss. Maybe calling it a cottage was conferring upon it too grand a title. In truth the place looked like a bird's nest, but it was a comfortable, welcoming nest.

He was five paces from the front door when his Yank apparently decided she'd had enough of a nap. Her eyes flew open, and she flung herself out of his arms. He tried to catch her but was unsuccessful. She landed quite forcefully on her backside.

She blinked furiously and gasped in much the same manner. Patrick knelt down in front of her.

"I think perhaps you should cease with your jumping off things for a bit."

"Me, too," she gulped. "I think I broke something this time."

"Hmmm," he said. "Well, 'tisn't as though we can slap a stiff plaster on it, is it? I'm sure Moraig has something lying about at least to ease you until I can get you home."

He stopped when he realized she wasn't saying anything. In fact, even her gasping had subsided into the kind of careful breathing a body used when trying to not cause itself any more pain. He took that opportunity to look at her.

Her eyes were dark, but translucent somehow. Like a deep green pool in a glade with stray bits of sunshine filtering down into it, touching the bottom and revealing the earth beneath. They suited her excessive fairness perfectly. Without thinking, he reached behind her head and pulled off the clip that held her hair. It fell down around her shoulders in a riot of unrestrained curls completely at odds with the otherwise quite constrained air she projected.

Then he made the grave mistake of looking into those eyes of hers.

The jolt that went through him almost made him lose his balance—again. At least here he wasn't going to make a fool of himself hopping about in the heather. He managed to catch himself with his hand before he fell backward upon his arse. He looked at her. She was apparently just as affected, if the look of surprise that crossed her features was any indication.

"Who *are* you?" she asked.

He searched his vast repertoire of cheeky replies for something suitable, but came up with nothing. It would certainly have been useful to draw attention away from the highly unsettling feeling of timelessness he felt by just looking at her, but it was apparently not to be.

The longer he knelt in front of her, the more intensely he found himself wishing they could remain there forever. It was all he could do not to reach out and pull her into his arms. He didn't dare, and for more reasons than just her

damaged tailbone. So, instead of doing what he wanted—
which he was quite sure would be the height of idiocy—he
merely reached out and touched her hair.

She closed her eyes and shivered.

He understood.

The saints pity him, he did not want this. He prayed for a
distraction of monumental proportions. A rain shower, an
earthquake, a tempest of any kind. Anything to break the
spell.

Bagpipes started up in the distance.

Her eyes flew open. "Did you hear that?" she asked.

"Oh, aye," he said, in relief.

"It's just like at Culloden. Playing that same song." She
looked at him. "A friend of yours?"

He managed to shake his head. "Never met the bloke, but
he seems to haunt me quite regularly."

"Haunt? Haunt as in 'it's such a haunting melody,' or
haunt as in 'it's being played by a ghost'?"

"The latter."

She shook her head. "I don't believe in ghosts."

"Neither do I," Patrick said. He didn't, and technically that
was true. Belief ceased to exist in the presence of sure knowledge, didn't it? "Can't deny the lad has some skill, though,
whoever he is." *And in whatever century he learned his
trade,* he added silently. For himself, Patrick thought the
piper's battle dirges sounded quite a bit like fourteenth century, but that was just his opinion. He held out her clip, then
kept his hand outstretched after she took it. "Now we have
our exit music, shall we go?"

She put her hand in his. She shivered.

He was hard-pressed not to.

"I don't know you," she said, sounding as if she were
trying to convince herself.

"I'm Patrick MacLeod."

"That's not what I mea—oh, never mind." She shook his
hand. "I'm Madelyn Phillips."

"A pleasure."

She looked at him for another moment or two, then took

a deep breath and looked away from him. "This is some place you have here."

"Hmmm," he agreed.

"It's like we've gone back in time."

"By the saints, I hope not," he muttered. He stood up and reached down for her other hand. "Carefully, now. Up you go."

She stood, swayed, gasped, then got her feet under her like a newborn colt—namely very unsteadily and with not a great deal of grace. But she didn't complain.

"I don't think I can walk quite yet," she said.

"Could you bear to be carried?"

"I don't think I can handle that, either. I can get there myself. Just give me a minute."

He waited patiently, then put his arm around her and helped her the last five feet to Moraig's house.

He raised his hand to knock on Moraig's door but found that was unnecessary. The door opened.

"Ah, Patty," she said with a smile, revealing several teeth already gone the way of all men. "Ye've brought your lady."

He made a noncommittal noise. His lady? The saints preserve him if that was the case. But he said nothing to contradict Moraig. He brought Madelyn in and set her down in a comfortable chair near the hearth. He let the soothing sounds of Moraig's muttering in Gaelic wash over him. It made him feel at home—Moraig's pointed looks notwithstanding.

"So," Moraig said, looking at Madelyn closely, "what ails her?"

He answered in Gaelic. "Fell off her horse and landed upon her fetching backside. I couldn't see carrying her to my house."

"Especially since you've nothing there to aid her." Moraig looked at him with disapproval. "A few herbs might serve ye, laddie."

"Might," Patrick agreed. He didn't even own an aspirin. He wasn't about to stock his cupboards with anything else.

Moraig was seemingly unimpressed. She began barking orders at him, and he obeyed before he thought better of it.

He was halfway through making Moraig's healing tea before he realized what he was doing. He shot Moraig a quick look only to find her staring at him with a smile. He scowled.

"I'll finish this for you, old woman, only because I have great respect for old women, you in particular."

"You have healing hands, Patrick. You shouldn't deny your gift."

"My hands have no gift left, as the past amply demonstrates," he said shortly. He handed his Yank her tea. "Here," he said in English, "drink this. It will cure what ails you."

"Thank you," she said. She turned to Moraig. "Thank you," she said in Gaelic.

He wondered if he should be embarrassed to have spoken so freely in front of her, or if she deserved it for not having told him what she knew. "Where did you learn Gaelic?" he asked.

"I don't know it. You've heard the extent of my repertoire," she said. "My parents are linguists."

"What else do you speak? Just so I'm prepared."

"A romance language or two—Italian, French, a little Portuguese. Some German. Enough Russian to get to the bathroom. You?"

"Bathroom phrases in a language or two," he admitted. No sense in giving her more details than she needed. His travels hadn't been in vain. "Are you a linguist, too?" he asked.

"Nope. A lawyer."

"Interesting choice."

"I have an interesting family."

Patrick had to stop himself from asking any more questions about her. He didn't want to know more. He didn't want to like her. He didn't want to like the way she smiled, nor the way her eyes twinkled, nor the way she squeaked when she hurt. By the saints, what he needed was a woman with some endurance, not a lawyer in orange plaid pants who couldn't keep her seat on a useless nag. He stood back in the shadows and let his list expand.

She was a less than perfect patient. After her first swallow of tea, she demanded all sorts of information about what was in it, what would come next, and why Moraig lived in the woods.

Argumentative. Irritatingly so.

"I don't believe in the woo-woo herb business," she announced as Moraig felt her head for lumps.

Impolite as well.

"I think I regret setting foot on that horse," she said as Moraig felt down her spine.

Weak-minded, he decided. She should very seriously regret getting on Whoa Bullet's back.

"Do you have any Advil?"

Well, there was little sense in even commenting on that.

"You need to sleep," Moraig announced. She looked at Patrick. "See her home, my lad."

He looked at Madelyn. "I'll be right back, then we'll get you back to the inn."

"Oh." She rubbed her tailbone uneasily, but didn't put up a fight. "If you think so . . ."

He didn't like the way she gave in. Why wasn't she demanding to know his plans?

And why did she have to have that bloody mass of riotous curls, curls that Moraig's firelight seemed to have been created to dance in?

He left Moraig's humble home before he had to look at her anymore. He strode back up to where he'd left his horse. The Black was there keeping company with that silly Whoa Bullet who'd already gotten his reins tangled in a particularly troublesome bit of brush.

Patrick took off Bullet's bridle and stored it in the saddlebag almost on top of what on further inspection looked to be Miriam MacLeod's best veggie pasties. He reconsidered. Maybe he would be doing Miss Madelyn a favor by keeping her lunch safe in his icebox. Then again, with his icebox's notorious reputation for powering off without provocation, perhaps it would just be best to eat them at his earliest opportunity.

He liberated the saddlebag, fixed Bullet's bridle to his saddle, then sent him home with a slap on the rump. Bullet, now that he had no passenger, seemed to find the journey worth no more than an amble.

Patrick swung up on Black and turned him toward home. He enjoyed the ride, especially since he was sitting comfortably. He didn't envy Madelyn her next pair of days.

He quickly made his way home, but pulled up short outside his walled courtyard. He slid off his horse and landed softly. What was this? Trespassers were rare, but he did get them occasionally. But generally not ones as nosy as this one.

He was waiting in the shadows of a tree as the intruder rounded the corner. Not a professional thief, if his lack of stealth was any indication. Just a snoop, probably.

The man bent to peer into Patrick's kitchen window. Patrick stepped up behind him and poked a stick in his back.

"Who are ye?" he snarled. "And what do ye want?"

"Assault!" the man squeaked, throwing up his hands. "I'll sue!"

"Be a bit hard to sue if ye're dead," Patrick said.

The man went still. "I am Bentley Douglas Taylor III, Esquire, and if you hurt me, I'll see you in jail for the rest of your life."

Patrick snorted. "Again, that'd be a bit hard to do if you're dead. Fortunately, you're not worth the effort." He tossed his stick aside, put a hand on Bentley Douglas Taylor III, Esquire, and spun him around. "Now, my friend, what are you looking for?"

"My fiancée."

"Your fiancée," Patrick repeated. Would some daft wench actually agree to wed with this buffoon?

"Madelyn Phillips. Perhaps you've seen her."

All the more reason not to like that dark-haired wench. She obviously had no taste in men. Patrick looked at Bentley Douglas Taylor III coolly.

"What does she look like?"

"Tall, dark hair, overweight. Dressed in horrendous orange plaid pants. I'm surprised she hasn't busted out of them already."

Patrick took an immediate and thorough dislike to the man. "May have spotted her somewhere," he said.

"Where?" Taylor demanded.

Nowhere you'll be able to follow. He looked at Taylor sternly. "Best get yourself off my land before you find yourself in more trouble than you'll fancy."

Taylor looked primed to argue, then seemed to reconsider. He pursed his lips, then walked slowly back across the courtyard. Patrick watched him until he'd put himself quite slowly and apparently unwillingly in his Jaguar.

Patrick watched him for a moment or two to make certain he was turning his car on and leaving, then he saw to his own business. He put up Black, had a pasty or two, then walked across his courtyard. Taylor was sitting in his running car, a frown on his face. Patrick got into his Range Rover and headed for Moraig's. Taylor could stay and snoop if he wanted. Nothing to steal that he could put into his car and carry away. The house was safe.

Taylor seemed less determined to stay than to follow. Patrick wondered, as he watched the man in his rearview mirror, what had ever possessed Madelyn to find herself attached to the wretch. Insufferable prig.

The Jag slowed.

The Jag stopped.

The Jag slid around a bit, then eased backward into a very well-formed bog.

Taylor got out, stepped up to his knees in muck, then began waving and hollering.

Patrick smiled grimly. Served the fool right. He supposed he'd have to fetch him soon enough, if only to get him back on the road.

But later. For now, he'd best rescue Madelyn from Moraig. The saints only knew what kind of tales that feisty old woman had been telling. Not that he cared what Madelyn thought, no indeed. He didn't like her. She would be easy to get out of his mind.

Very easy indeed.

And he would start putting her far from his thoughts immediately after he'd dropped her off at Roddy's, where he wouldn't have to look at her, listen to her, or, the saints pity him, touch her again.

If he felt that electricity one more time, he just might never rid himself of the feeling.

Chapter 7

M adelyn sat—very uncomfortably—and listened to Moraig MacLeod chat easily in perfectly passable English. Of course, her *r*'s still trilled like a flock of songbirds and her other vowels and consonants danced about to music Madelyn doubted she could ever play, but she was on the whole quite intelligible.

Not that being able to understand the woman was of paramount importance at the moment, as this stop was most definitely not on the agenda. Neither was falling off her horse, but that was another story. She needed to get back on that horse and get going so she could decide if the surrounding flora and fauna—or any of the buildings she'd so briefly had a glimpse of—was indeed on her list.

Take the castle down the way. She was pretty sure it had been magnificent. Gloomy, gray, and very well preserved had been the brief impressions she'd had. She was eager to get back there and see if a brief glance had been accurate. And she could hardly wait to get her hands on the rock, smell it, put her cheek against it, see if it was as cold as it looked. How would it have been to have grown up in such a place? Or to live there now?

Almost too marvelous to contemplate.

But the sooner she was off contemplating it at close range, the sooner she would be doing a bit more roaming and hopefully checking a few more things off her list. Then she could get back to the hotel and see if Roddy had an ice block to sit on. She suspected that might be the only thing to help her.

Though she had to admit that Moraig's tea was starting to make inroads into something. She was still in pain, but she was starting not to care. She opened her mouth to ask Moraig what she'd put in her brew, took one look at the woman sitting on a stool near the fire, stirring something in a black kettle with a long wooden spoon and cackling wildly, and thought better of it.

Moraig seemed to be content to stir and chuckle, so Madelyn took the opportunity—or, rather, seized the distraction in a desperate attempt to forget she was trapped with a woman who in any reasonable fairy tale would have been classified as a witch—to look around and see how Moraig had chosen to decorate her house.

It was, just like the woman herself, straight from a fairy tale. The room was crooked, as if some illustrator had been slightly inebriated when he'd drawn it. Herbs hung in bunches from the ceiling, from the hooks on the walls, from twine that was wrapped around a worktable. The smell alone was enough to make her light-headed. Sunny would have been in seventh heaven. She could have identified each and every one of those weeds, enumerated their virtues, expounded at length upon their uses.

The fairy tale feeling didn't end with the fauna hanging everywhere. The pot over Moraig's cooking fire was ancient, as were the other pots stacked on a rickety shelf. The pots kept company with a few wooden dishes and bowls, all stacked haphazardly, all looking as if they'd been made several centuries ago and weathered the storm somewhat badly. Madelyn wasn't sure that the outside of the cottage hadn't come through the walls and was growing on the inside. It was difficult to tell where the herbs ended and other kinds of underbrush began.

She would not have been at all surprised to hear the strains of dwarf-song coming through the ancient leaded-glass windows, celebrating the fact that they were finished with their work for the day, or to have had faeries and sprites pop out of the corners and dance a jig upon the weathered table.

But the longer she sat, the more normal things seemed to become. Good grief, what was in that tea? Madelyn sipped, but found herself completely incapable of identifying the taste. Was Moraig hiding a bottle of Valium there behind that dried bunch of flowers? Hard to say.

Madelyn shifted slightly and her backside set up a horrendous protest. All right, no Valium in the tea after all. Just herbs.

But despite the pain, she began to unwind. There was something hypnotic about the way Moraig stirred her brew. Even the smell was soothing. Madelyn couldn't decide if her head was clearing or she'd sniffed a bit too much of nature's bounty.

Maybe it was just the peace inside the small house. She could see Moraig's bed over in the corner, made up with a surprisingly comfortable-looking duvet. The kitchen was small, but serviceable. The living room boasted a pair of old but comfortably overstuffed chairs and the kind of sofa that took a person prisoner and didn't let him go until a serious nap had been accomplished.

And it was more than the simplicity of the furnishings. There was simplicity in the lifestyle. Madelyn suspected Moraig gathered herbs, cooked, walked in the woods, and not much else. No television, no radio, no defending spoiled executives from stacks of parking tickets. It had to be a very unfettered, very free kind of life.

Sort of like Sunny's, actually. Madelyn loved her sister, though she'd never understood Sunny's method of rebelling against their parents' very organized, very clinical existence. Sunny's place was a lot like Moraig's except Sunny believed quite firmly in electricity and hot showers. But her sister had the same kind of relationship with simple things. Birth, death, the cycles of the earth. She was a midwife, an herbalist, a brewer of potions and maker of healing sachets.

Sunny wore lots of linen.

Madelyn didn't mind linen. It beat the hell out of polyester.

She took another sip of tea, then another. As she neared the bottom of the cup, she began to wonder if perhaps she had dismissed Sunny's way of life too quickly. She could get into natural foods, natural fibers, natural cosmetics. She could recognize a few important herbs, like basil and oregano. Really, was there much more to it than that? It might be good for her to get out of the sterile environment of a law office.

She reached for a bunched bit of dried herb and brought it to her nose. She sniffed deeply.

She sneezed heartily.

Well, maybe giving up her allergy-free environment wasn't quite for her at the moment.

Then she looked at Moraig and realized the woman had been speaking—and that she'd said something important. Madelyn blinked.

"What?"

"A fine lordling," Moraig said, looking up from her stirring.

"Who?"

"Patrick, the young Himself."

Madelyn frowned. "What does that mean? The young Himself?"

"Himself proper lives at the keep down in the meadow," Moraig said, as if she hadn't heard. "Patty's older brother is he. Both lords of their own halls."

"Interesting," Madelyn said, wincing as she shifted. At least she was only wincing. Half an hour ago she'd been on the verge of tears. Whatever Moraig had put in her tea was potent stuff. But Patrick a lord? He didn't look like one, but she supposed she wasn't much of a judge. Maybe he had scores of servants at his command to polish his black cars. He would need a whole troop of them to bang out the dings he'd acquired on the highway.

"Interesting is the tale of those two brothers," Moraig said. " 'Tis a tale that would interest *you*, to be sure."

"Would it?" Madelyn honestly couldn't imagine why. Patrick was very handsome, he had rescued her quite nicely that morning, but he was most certainly not her type—her unsettling experience at Culloden's field, and the subsequent flashes of it, aside. He was rude. He drove too fast. He probably knew a dozen really lousy lawyer jokes he liked to trot out at the slightest provocation.

And he was most certainly *not* her soul mate. She was

pathetically grateful he hadn't heard her bleating that out like a lovesick sheep the day before.

"Oh, aye," Moraig said, tasting, then putting her spoon aside. She turned to look at Madelyn. "What a fine, strong, braw pair of lads they are."

Madelyn smiled politely. "How nice."

"Both of a height, both with hair the color of night, and both with eyes the piercing green of the rightful King's finest emerald."

Madelyn looked at her skeptically. Maybe Moraig was hiding a few romance novels under those herbs. She would give her this much: Patrick MacLeod was drop-dead gorgeous. But she wasn't all that sure about his manners. He hadn't been overly friendly at Culloden. And he'd tried to plow her over not once but twice. Never mind that he'd certainly gotten his just desserts the first time. He could have caused her to have a serious accident.

But he carried you here.

"Hrumph." She ignored her conscience. She had a harder time ignoring whatever it was about him that pulled at her soul, that haunted her just like the otherworldy music that seemed to follow her from place to place.

Briefly, her long-cherished fantasy of being swept off her feet by a handsome Scottish Highlander swept over her with such force, she had to catch her breath.

Good grief, she really had to get out more.

"And ever willing to extend themselves to aid another," Moraig continued. " 'Tis that sort of nobility that a body doesn't see these days."

"Nobility?" Madelyn echoed, dragging herself back to the present. She looked at Moraig in shock. "Nobility? Why, he almost ran over me!"

Moraig waved her hand dismissively. "An excess of energy and lack of purpose. 'Tis a hard thing in these times to find cattle to raid and enemies to slay."

"Yes, society frowns on both those things as diversions."

"Today, aye."

Madelyn frowned, then shrugged. It was becoming increasingly difficult to try to unravel what Moraig was saying. Either her accent was growing thicker, the air in the cottage was growing thicker, or the mysterious ingredient in the tea was kicking in in a big way. Madelyn rubbed her eyes. Then again, maybe jetlag was just finally and thoroughly catching up with her. It was all she could do to keep her eyes open.

"Today?" she repeated sleepily. "What does that mean?"

"It wasn't so in ages past."

"What wasn't so?" Madelyn asked, hardly caring about the answer. Would Moraig be offended if she crawled over and made herself at home in that comfortable-looking bed? How about the couch? It would certainly do.

"Different sorts of ways to pass the time," Moraig said with a meaningful wiggle of her eyebrows.

Madelyn yawned. "What does that have to do with Patrick?"

"And his brother, Jamie."

"And his brother, Jamie," she repeated dutifully.

Moraig leaned forward and smiled a conspiratorial smile quite devoid of several critical teeth. Madelyn leaned forward as well, suspecting that it was the polite thing to do. Then realized she was leaning too far. She caught herself with her hand on the floor before she fell flat on her face. She pushed herself back into a sitting position and peered blearily at Moraig. "Yes?"

Moraig paused dramatically. "It has," she said, pausing again for maximum effect, "everything to do with them."

"Hrumph," Madelyn said wisely. It was hard to make herself sound wise when all she wanted to do was take a nap, but Moraig seemed to expect it. "Everything?"

"Aye, everything."

Madelyn frowned. "I'm confused."

"Their upbringing, girl. 'Tis what made them the men they are."

Madelyn looked at her hostess and began to have serious doubts about her grip on reality. Too many fumes from all the herbs cluttering up her cottage. "That's the case usually, isn't it?"

"Nay, lass," Moraig said impatiently. "Not with them."

"They're special then, is that it?"

"Nay," Moraig said, waving away Madelyn's words. " 'Tis

their upbringing in a time far distant from ours that makes them the men they are."

"Patrick doesn't look that old," Madelyn said.

"He doesn't look half his age," Moraig said with another meaningful nod.

"And how old would that half be?" Madelyn asked, wondering if Moraig had any Novocain in amongst her pots and sundries and if she could be prevailed upon to cough some of it up for a girl in need.

"Several centuries."

"Yes, well, men never age," Madelyn said, looking around for a likely repository for the serious stuff. Her tailbone was really starting to hurt. Then she looked at Moraig. "What did you say?"

"Several—"

"Things that are really beyond belief," a deep voice from behind her said.

Madelyn jumped up in surprise, staggered, and would have landed in Moraig's cooking fire if Patrick hadn't stopped her fall.

She clutched his arms and stared up at him. Moraig had a point. His eyes were magnificently green. And his arms were spectacularly muscular. She was definitely on the verge of a serious swoon. So she clutched and reminded herself to breathe. Then again, if she swooned, maybe he would pick her up again—

"How do you fare?" he asked.

"I've had better mornings," she wheezed.

"No doubt you have," he said. He looked over Madelyn's head. "Thank you, Mother. I'll see her to Roddy's."

"Come back, lass, when you've a ready ear for a fine tale," Moraig said meaningfully.

"I think she's heard quite enough for a day," Patrick said dryly.

"She's hardly heard enough," Moraig countered, "but 'tis your tale to tell. I'd be about telling it, if I were you."

Patrick grunted at her. "I'll give it no thought at all, if it's all the same to you. Now, can I return briefly this afternoon and offer some kind of aid?"

"If you like," Moraig said. "I can think of several things—"

Madelyn listened to them then talk over and around her and came to a conclusion or two.

First, Moraig didn't actually sound as if she was delusional. She chatted quite freely and happily with Patrick. And while she might have been fanciful, she wasn't a liar. Madelyn had worked with enough liars to spot one a New York city block away. Whatever nonsense she was spouting, it was nonsense she fully believed.

But men from a different century?

Preposterous.

Maybe it was just a euphemism for growing up in the Highlands. It was, after all, a rather rural place. Beautiful, but not exactly bustling.

Second, Patrick MacLeod, his driving flaws aside, was a complete stud muffin. He was tall, he was gorgeous, and he smelled good. Not a doused-in-cologne good. A woodsy, sunshiny kind of good.

Or he could have just had a brush with Moraig's herbs. Who could tell for sure?

Third, if she didn't get herself somewhere flat soon, she was going to cry.

"Put your arms around my neck."

She looked up and felt a little light-headed. "Huh?"

"Hold on to me. I'll carry you to the car."

"Oh," she said weakly. Then her ears perked up. "Car?"

"You didn't think I was going to make you ride back to Roddy's, did you?"

"I wasn't sure what you were going to make me do."

"Put your arms around my neck," he said easily.

"Well, I suppose if I have to."

He made a sound that might have been a half laugh, then very carefully lifted her into his arms—and that without so much of a grunt of exertion.

"You're rather strong," she managed as he ducked out of Moraig's doorway.

"Swordplay," Moraig offered from behind her.

"Bench-pressing each day several old women who talk too

much," Patrick threw over his shoulder. But he said it affectionately.

Moraig only laughed happily.

Madelyn found herself wishing quite suddenly that he would speak that way to her.

Obviously she'd been breathing too many uncontrolled substances. Not good for her common sense. She had places to go, sights to see, items to be able to place in the *accomplished* column. She didn't have the time or the energy to be sidetracked by some muscle-bound, devastatingly handsome Scottish lord who didn't huff and puff when he carried her in his arms.

She blinked.

What was she, nuts?

Contemplating the condition of her sanity was something she'd have to put on hold, because at the moment it was all she could do to bite her lip and hold on so she didn't make a fool of herself by whimpering. Patrick was careful, but still every step jarred. She sighed in relief once she was sitting in the front seat of the SUV that had almost plowed her over the day before. Patrick started to buckle her up. His very nearness was almost enough to do her in. She looked at his face so close to hers and felt distinctly weak in the knees.

"You don't have to do that," she managed.

He looked her in the eye. "Aye, I do."

"I can—"

"So can I. Stubborn wench," he added, but he said it with the same tone of voice he'd used on Moraig.

Madelyn almost passed out.

This was *definitely* not on her list.

He buckled the seat belt, then straightened partway. "The ride back won't be comfortable."

"It beats walking," she managed.

"We'll see."

"But Whoa Bullet," she said with a sudden feeling of guilt. "Oh, no. I left that stupid horse wandering around in the meadow."

"He'll find his way home. He always does."

"Has he lost many riders?"

Patrick actually smiled.

She wondered if he would notice if she began to hyperventilate.

"He loses at least half a dozen tourists a season."

She blinked in surprise. "But Roddy said he was pokey!"

"He says that to everyone. He lies." He straightened and shut her door.

She wondered briefly if Patrick knew Roddy well enough to know that, then shrugged it aside. If Patrick thought Whoa Bullet would get home, who was she to argue? Especially when all her energies were being concentrated on keeping herself from swearing as Patrick eased his car out of the forest. She closed her eyes and held on.

"Well," Patrick said suddenly, "he's still there."

Madelyn opened her eyes. She could hardly believe what she was seeing. "Don't stop," she begged.

"We should."

"We shouldn't."

"He's your fiancé."

"Ex-fiancé."

"Not to hear it from him."

"Keep driving."

"It wouldn't be polite."

"Polite be damned."

Apparently it wasn't to be damned enough because Patrick stopped a safe distance away from none other than Bentley Douglas Taylor III with his car bogged down in a ditch. Madelyn closed her eyes and pretended to be unconscious. That grew increasingly difficult after Bentley opened her door and began to chide her for being foolish and precipitous. It grew almost impossible to keep her eyes closed as he instructed Patrick to hurry up and get going.

Madelyn looked at her erstwhile fiancé. "He's doing you a favor. Use your fawning defense attorney voice on him."

Bentley frowned. "He's an uneducated backwoods Scotsman. He'll respond best to an authoritative tone."

"Geez, Bentley," she said, "can you possibly be that dumb?"

"Ask him what his degree is in." He turned toward Patrick. "What's your degree in?" he bellowed.

Patrick looked up from where he knelt in the mud. "I was . . . homeschooled," he volunteered.

"Did they teach you to hurry?"

Patrick stood. Madelyn hoped he planned to punch Bentley in his aristocratic nose.

No such luck. He merely got back in the Range Rover, reached over Madelyn with an "excuse me," and pulled her door shut. With not even a flicker of concern, he backed up and pulled the Jag out of the ditch. Then he took his Range Rover out of gear, turned, and looked at her seriously.

"Do you want me to put you in his car?"

"Are you out of your mind?"

"I take it he was an aberration?"

"You can take that wherever you want it; just take me out of here."

He got out of the car and unhooked his rope from Bentley's Jag. Bentley spun his tires, causing a great deal of mud to coat Patrick's front.

Madelyn held her breath for the eruption.

Patrick merely turned and walked back to his car. He stowed his gear, then wiped his hands on his jeans and got back inside, mud and all. He smiled at her briefly.

"Ready?"

She could hardly believe her eyes or ears. "You have amazing control over your temper."

Patrick shrugged. "Didn't want him littering up my land. Best not to leave him in pieces on it then, aye?"

"He's a jackass."

"So I noticed."

She would have said more, but they were moving and all her attention became focused on retaining her dignity by not howling.

"This is your land?" she asked as he slowed and eased them over a particularly nasty rut. Maybe there was something to the lord thing. He certainly drove in what she assumed was a lordly manner—as if the road belonged to him and only him.

"Aye," he said. "Part mine, part my cousin's, the rest my brother's."

"Has it been in the family long?"

"You could say that." He looked in his rearview mirror. "Your friend is following us, but he doesn't look particularly pleased. We'll reach a proper road soon. He'll find that more to his taste, no doubt."

"You should have left him in the ditch."

He shrugged. "I'm helpful."

"That's dangerous."

He turned vibrant green eyes on her. "I offered *you* aid."

"I imagine it was spurred on by feelings of guilt. You've almost run over me twice."

He laughed, only briefly, but the sound was breathtaking. Madelyn wondered if he would do it again if she asked.

"Aye, I suppose that's true. Or perhaps 'twas merely the sight of you screaming your way across my meadow that prodded me to action."

"You would have screamed, too. That stupid horse was about to take flight."

"When you can sit again, I'll show you how to stop him."

She looked at him in surprise. "You will?"

The hesitancy was brief, but she was a good lawyer and quite adept at reading body language.

"Unfortunately, I've got a long list of sights," she said lightly. After all, he wasn't obligated to her. Besides, she *did* have plans. "I'll be busy seeing those sights."

He nodded briefly. "Of course."

Madelyn was momentarily tempted to try to unravel the mystery of his reactions, then thought better of it. She only had twelve days left. Not really enough time to plumb the depths of Patrick MacLeod's black soul. Maybe she was the only one who felt anything crackling like lightning between them. Maybe she was romanticizing him in a way he had no desire to be romanticized.

Maybe she should take that block of ice she wanted at Roddy's and put it on her head instead of her butt.

They soon reached the inn. She was unbuckled and halfway out the door before she realized she still couldn't move.

She clutched the door frame and let the tears roll down her cheeks unimpeded.

Large, open hands soon appeared in front of her, hands that were calloused and work-roughened. Not the hands of a man who fondled expensive pens for a living.

Madelyn was about to be briefly grateful for those hands when their owner was hip-checked aside.

"I'll see to her."

Madelyn opened her mouth to protest. And damn Patrick MacLeod if he didn't acquiesce with a little bow. She watched as he retrieved a hubcap from the back of his car and headed toward hers. She continued to watch as he knelt and attached it quickly to one of her wheels.

She would have said thank you, but she was soon wheezing courtesy of a cloud of Eternal Riches. She was manhandled—accompanied by much grunting and complaining—to her room.

"None of this would have happened," Bentley panted as he dumped her on her bed and leaned over her, "if you had just been reasonable—"

"Go to hell," she said. "But close the door behind you first."

He straightened, looking supremely dissatisfied. "You'll see things my way," he stated as he left her room.

Madelyn rolled her eyes. Where was her knight in shining armor when she needed him? Probably awaiting a court date because Bentley had filed a lawsuit against him.

One place she knew he wasn't was up in those mountains behind Roddy's inn, roaming around in his Range Rover and rescuing maidens in distress.

Without so much as a grunt of exertion.

"Don't eat while you're laid up," Bentley said, poking his head back inside the door. "It won't do your thighs any good."

The door closed with a bang.

Madelyn closed her eyes and sighed.

Chapter 8

P *atrick* leaned back into the exquisite comfort of Conal Grant's leather chair. It had been a very long night, and the Learjet's seat was a welcome respite from hours spent investigating the nooks and crannies of London for potential problems with his next charge's proposed itinerary. Given that he'd watched over the boy before, he was fairly certain there would be no surprises.

Unfortunately, closing his eyes brought no relief. It was a wonder he hadn't gone completely gray with the lack of sleep he'd had over the past six years. Somehow, though, his body seemed to function quite happily on very little. He suspected that couldn't last.

All the more reason to consider doing something else with his life.

What, he surely didn't know. Teaching? Aye, possibly. Writing? Nay, he hadn't the patience for it. There was the business of plants and such, he supposed, and he certainly was in the proper country for catering to gardeners. But it was a long fall from high-priced, highly skilled bodyguard to a lowly tender of shrubberies.

Not a fall he fancied he could make any time in the near future.

He opened his eyes and stared out the window, watching the land beneath him from a vantage point that men centuries ago could hardly have imagined. It still stunned him at times, that view, and he'd spent countless hours traveling in planes over the past several years.

They were passing over the Lake District at present. Patrick looked at the shimmer of blue below and decided that he really should take a proper holiday soon. A few weeks spent in a little cottage near the water—or perhaps in a very expensive hotel where his every need would be catered to. Aye, that was what he needed. A vacation, something more serious than just the escape from work he'd taken the previous fortnight. That didn't qualify as rest. It had been more of a mental health break, given the annoyance of his last charge.

She'd been a very rich, very spoiled college girl determined to spend as much of her da's money on as many illicit pleasures as possible. And when she hadn't been squandering her sire's gold, she'd amused herself by taunting him about his apparent lack of education and his obvious lack of funds if this was what he resorted to for employment. She'd been old money from a sleepy New England town he hadn't bothered to remember.

He shook his head at the memory of her taunts. They hadn't been all that original, but they'd been constant. He'd been tempted to tell her that he had money her father could only dream of and that he had taken a degree in classic literature with highest honors at Edinburgh University.

Of course, she wouldn't have been impressed to know he'd gone to school during the day and continued to work for Conal during the evenings and on weekends.

And all in an effort to impress Lisa's father.

What a useless exercise that had been.

That young American wench wouldn't have been impressed, either.

So he'd kept his mouth shut, his expression inscrutable, and his thoughts to himself. He'd tossed his report at Conal as he'd gotten off the plane, then headed directly for home. Perhaps he'd cared more than he wanted to admit about the opinion of one silly, immature wench, given how long he'd avoided contact with the general public thereafter.

Then again, perhaps that girl had merely been the last in a long line of people who were perfectly content to look down on him—often quite vocally—except for those fleeting and all-too-easy-to-forget moments when he was saving either their lives or their reputations. Becoming a recluse for a bit had seemed a fairly mild reaction.

He wondered, not for the first time, if he'd been doing this too long.

At least his current client would be far less a pain in the arse than his previous one. This lad came from a large family of merchants whose name Patrick would immediately forget after the job was over. Patrick could do the drill in his sleep. Indulge but protect. If the lad wanted to ruin his nose with drugs and his body with prohibited pleasures, Patrick wasn't one to pass judgment. He was merely there to make sure the boy was coherent enough to get back on the plane home— and be coherent enough himself to hoist the lad on the plane himself if the boy wasn't.

Which was, given his own practice of abstaining from controlled substances, never a problem.

Conal was waiting as the Lear pulled up to an inconspicuous hangar.

"Any trouble?" he asked, as he had asked regularly for the past six years.

Patrick hoisted his bag over his shoulder and handed Conal a sheaf of papers. "He has a drug problem, but we knew that. I can keep him alive long enough to get him back on the plane."

"Lads these days."

"Too much money; no common sense."

Conal looked at him sideways. "And it wasn't the same for you when you were younger? If you ever were," he added under his breath.

"I heard that," Patrick said easily. "And your assessment of my character is sorely mistaken. I'm the happy-go-lucky one of the family, remember?"

"Or so your brother says."

"He would know." Patrick smiled briefly. "Winter in the Highlands is very long, my friend. We had no money, ample ale, and willing women."

"I'll bet you did."

"Idle hands are the devil's workshop, you know."

Conal snorted, but clapped Patrick on the shoulder. "Some day I want the entire story of your youth, nothing held back."

"I gave you a great deal of it."

"Aye, but I didn't believe it. I want the entire tale. Someday when I have at my disposal something strengthening."

"You find your strong stomach," Patrick said, "then let me know. Until then, I'll concentrate on my nannying."

Conal nodded. "The plane will be waiting at 1700 Friday. Let me know when you get home."

Patrick nodded, then made his way to his car. A few more times, he decided suddenly. He would do this a few more times, then be done. He wasn't afraid of the danger. He'd left more than a few would-be thugs crumpled up behind rubbish bins with his bare hands alone.

It also wasn't the travel. He'd had the chance to become passably fluent in a handful of languages, see many famous sights, and eat things that would have upset all but the staunchest of stomachs. It wasn't even the time away from home. Time away made homecoming even sweeter.

It was just the people he risked his life for. Spoiled, ungrateful children with no appreciation for the virtues of self-denial and self-control.

Maybe he was just getting old.

He stopped in to see his mechanic. It was going to be very expensive, but he had no choice. He arranged the details to suit himself, them headed home. There were no Yanks or sheep to run over, and for some reason that was almost depressing.

He rolled down the window in an effort to douse himself in cold air.

It didn't help much.

He wondered if she could sit yet. Madelyn. Madelyn Phillips, the former fiancée of that insufferable clod Bentley Douglas Taylor III, Esquire. How she had ever gotten herself entangled with that great buffoon was beyond him.

He continued to ponder the improbabilities of that relationship—could Taylor possibly appreciate the tumbling cascade of curls that framed her face, or had he never bothered to pull her hair from its prison at the back of her head?—but it very quickly gave him a headache, so he stopped.

After two hours spent behind an enormous line of cars he didn't have the wherewithal to pass, he signaled right, then suddenly slammed on his brakes and came to a screeching halt in the middle of the road. The road to his house lay to the right, winding up northward. The road before him led straight on to the village. He'd been ready to go home, but he'd been caught suddenly off guard by the unbearable emptiness that awaited him.

He had to take a very deep breath.

Of course, he could go to Jamie's, but he wasn't sure he could bear that, either. The hall would be full of family, all preparing for the blessed event. Nay, he could not go there. The happiness and anticipation that would be filling the hall was simply more than he could stand at the moment.

He put his car back in gear and continued straight on, trying not to think about his destination. The pub, aye, that was a decent choice.

Pity he didn't drink.

But he could get a decent meal there. Of course, 'twas early enough in the morning that he'd have to sit outside and wait three hours for MacLeod's Brews and Tasties to open, but it was a fine day and he had nothing better to do with his time.

Oddly enough, his car seemed to have a mind of its own. The Vanquish never did things like this, he thought with a scowl. He allowed himself to be led into the humble car park of Roddy MacLeod's equally humble inn. He parked, then looked about him.

Taylor's Jaguar was there, but Madelyn's car was not. He stroked his chin thoughtfully. Had she gone out already to pursue her Highland itinerary? Perhaps Moraig's brew had done a goodly work on her after all. Either that or she'd driven herself to hospital on her own with a mouthful of complaints about Highland healing techniques.

And if that was the case, she was more than welcome to her sore backside.

He rested his hands on the steering wheel. There was no sense in not going in since he'd come this far. Miriam MacLeod set an uncommonly fine table for breakfast, and he would be more than happy to see to a few chores in return for a plate of sustenance. Whoa Bullet could perhaps use a morning spent learning some manners.

He got out, then paused. There was music in the air.

It wasn't, the saints be praised, bagpipes.

It sounded quite like a violin.

He walked into Roddy's inn. The music was coming from down the hall.

"Patty, my lad," Roddy said, coming into the hallway, "what brings you down from yon mountain? Or should I guess?"

Roddy was his nephew—by way of a *very* convoluted family tree. It fascinated Roddy to no end, the twistings and turnings of that formidable conifer. Patrick shared his fascination, but it wasn't for a genealogical discussion that he sought Roddy out at present. He nodded his head down the hallway. "Who's the fiddler?"

"Miss Madelyn. A right proper one, isn't she?"

"She's here?" Patrick frowned. "Then where is her car?"

Roddy winced. "A bit of trouble with finances, or so the car company said when they came to collect it early this morning."

"Well, she certainly doesn't dress the part of the idle rich."

"Those were Miriam's," Roddy said with a twinkle in his eye. "Her mother's leftovers. She fished them out of the attic when Miss Madelyn's suitcase was stolen."

"Stolen?" Patrick echoed. "Here?"

"If you can believe it."

"No word of it?"

"None."

Patrick stroked his chin again. Granted, the village had its share of trouble, but it was very difficult to steal a tourist's suitcase and not have someone catch wind of the deed and immediately tell anyone who would listen. There was more to it than a simple theft. "Has she paid you for her lodging?"

"Mr. Taylor paid for hers originally, or so I understood. But of course he then took the reservation himself. I wasn't going to charge her, seeing as how she lost her lodging through subterfuge."

Patrick considered. Madelyn certainly didn't look like she was down on her luck. She was an attorney, for pity's sake. Surely she made enough and squandered little enough that she could afford a few days in Scotland. It wasn't as if Roddy's was some high-priced five-star hotel in London's theater district.

But having her car repossessed? There was something foul afoot there. He looked at Roddy.

"Does she know her car is gone?"

"I didn't have the heart to tell her yet."

"Where's Taylor?"

"Still asleep."

"Convenient."

"Aye, I thought so, too."

Patrick wasn't one to jump to conclusions, but it was hard to avoid here.

"Roddy, mate, let me use your phone," Patrick said. He obtained the rental car company's name from Roddy and the number from the operator.

In less than ten minutes, he had the entire story. He hadn't been able to get her a new car, but he had been able to get her a refund to be sent to the States. It wasn't ideal, but it had been the best he could do without driving down and personally putting pressure on the players involved.

Patrick looked at Roddy. "Apparently, Taylor called and told them her credit card was no good."

"Bloody wretch," Roddy said. "Can he do that?"

"Apparently he did. Perhaps he has friends."

"Difficult to believe."

"Hmmm," Patrick agreed. "So, what of Madelyn? Is she walking yet?"

"Not today. But tomorrow, aye. She vows to sightsee if it kills her."

"Don't tell her of the car. I'll see what I can arrange."

"You could loan her one of yours."

Patrick shuddered. "My altruism stops at the door to my garage. Besides, all I have left is the Range Rover and the Bentley. I've seen how she drives."

"How?" Roddy asked with a smile. "Slowly, or just poorly?"

"Slowly. I'm just certain it would be bad for the engines."

"Hrumph," Roddy said.

"Think about how the Bullet fared," Patrick said. "That should tell you something."

Roddy smiled. "He found his way home all right. My thanks for putting his tack up. I did notice what Miriam sent along as lunch had mysteriously disappeared from the saddlebags."

"No sense in letting a good meal go to waste."

Roddy laughed. "Aye, well, she'll be very flattered you felt the need to poach her goods." He rubbed his hands together. "I'd best go help with breakfast. Do you care to stay?"

"Of course, especially since my other choice is to either go home, or go to Moraig's and endure yet another lecture on the beauties of entangling myself with a certain Yank."

"You could do worse."

"I've no intention to 'do' at all."

Roddy clapped him on the shoulder. "She seems a fine lass, Patty. Miriam likes her. Best be saying good things about the girl if you've a care for your tummy."

Patrick bowed. "If that's the case, then nary a slight will pass my lips. Can I help?"

"Go sit. Enjoy the music. She'll quit once Mr. Taylor comes out."

"Has he no stomach for it?"

"None. The great idiot," Roddy muttered as he walked away.

Patrick retreated to the lounge, sat in Roddy's most comfortable chair, closed his eyes, and promptly fell asleep.

He dreamed of clan wars, of bloodshed and strife. He tramped over blood-soaked fields, fought until he could scarce lift his sword, hid in trees as an overpowering enemy passed by underneath. And through it all, music washed over him, bathed his soul in a feeling he couldn't quite identify.

Not terror.

Not despair.

He listened more closely. The melody was mournful, full of longing and unfulfilled dreams. Yet underneath, like a swiftly running brook, there bubbled up something that made him want to press on.

It was—

"Oh, no. You again. Don't you have some kind of menial labor to perform?"

Patrick decided he really should tell Madelyn how fortunate she'd been not to have to wake up to that voice every morning. He didn't bother to open his eyes.

"Did it all already," he said.

"Perhaps you should get your filthy jeans off the proprietor's good furniture."

Patrick opened his eyes slowly. "Perhaps you should find out whom you're speaking to before you overstep your bounds."

Taylor snorted. "Don't need the name of a common laborer."

"I am Patrick MacLeod, Lord of Benmore. You may call me Lord Patrick."

Taylor opened his mouth to speak, but was saved by Roddy coming in to deliver the call to breakfast. Taylor looked down at Patrick.

"Lord or not, you'll never have her."

Patrick lifted one eyebrow. "I imagine that really isn't your determination to make. The lady may have something to say about it."

"Not while I'm around, she won't." He bent close to Patrick. "Back off, Scotty. You'll regret it if you don't."

"Ach, no bloodshed," Roddy said nervously. "Mr. Taylor, your food grows cold."

Taylor straightened, straightened his clothes with a pair of sharp tugs, then marched into the dining room. Roddy looked at Patrick.

"He's a complete arse," he said in Gaelic.

"I could not have put it more truthfully myself." Patrick clapped his hands on his thighs. "Lead on, nephew. Not even sourness of that magnitude can ruin your lady wife's cooking."

"She'll be pleased to hear it."

Patrick followed Roddy out of the lounge and indulged in a brief regret that he didn't live in another time when he could have tossed Taylor in his brother's dungeon and left him there to rot for a few months. If nothing else, it would have spared the souls around Taylor the misery of his company. Patrick wondered how Madelyn had borne him even for a short time.

He paused outside the dining room to listen to Madelyn's final notes. He tried to find the feeling he'd almost identified.

But it was gone.

Perhaps he would ask her to play for him, sometime when she had peace and quiet and no one to judge her harshly. Perhaps then he would be able to identify what it was she stirred in him.

It was, he decided slowly, something quite sweet.

Something worth investigating further.

Something, he feared, that might involve entangling himself with a certain Yank, just as Moraig had suggested that he do for almost the whole of the previous afternoon. It was amazing how many suggestions an old woman could bludgeon a man with whilst he was about chopping wood for her fire.

It wasn't something he was sure he could do with any success.

Involve himself with Madelyn, that is, not chop wood.

He clapped his hand to his head before he drove himself mad with his own ridiculous thoughts, took a deep breath, and went in to breakfast.

Chapter 9

Madelyn eased her way off the bed, clutched the sides of the window, and pulled herself carefully to her feet. She gasped only once—a great improvement over the day before. Once she was certain she could stand, she leaned her head against the window to rest a bit. It was conceivable that she perhaps should have seen a doctor wearing a lab coat instead of a witch wearing bits of forest in her hair. Then again, Moraig's tea had at least relaxed her. What could a doctor have done? Put her butt in a sling?

She wasn't sure it wasn't there already.

She sidestepped her way around the bed, then paused before she gathered up her clothes to gather her strength. While she was leaning against the wall, she noticed her notebook lying unused and unappreciated on her bed. Thursday already and so few sights seen.

Except, of course, for that exquisite vista of Patrick MacLeod's rugged face, but that was another story entirely. That had been but a brief sight, soured by the haste with which he'd dumped her in Bentley's arms and disappeared. She supposed she couldn't blame him. Bentley had been vociferously staking his claim to her person, and she'd been in too much pain to protest.

She thought about reaching down for her notebook, but didn't bother. She didn't need to look to know what was on her list. Castles, gardens, ruins. How in the world was she ever going to get to any of them when she could barely sit, much less walk?

It was tempting to blame Bentley—in fact, that was a damn good idea—but it wasn't all his fault. Well, all right, it *was* all his fault—except for falling off the horse, but reminding herself of that didn't make her feel any better. She was injured and time was slipping away. She needed to move past the havoc Bentley had caused and get on with life.

But first things first. She couldn't hobble from place to place until she was dressed. She dragged the sleeve of Miriam's mother's frilly peignoir across her eyes and turned to open the door. It would have been too great an effort to step over the shopping bag, so she stepped around it. The sack contained clothes Bentley had bought for her, clothes which were woolier versions of what she'd been robbed of. She knew this because she'd peeked in the sack briefly the day before, hoping that perhaps Miriam had found her something of her own era, perhaps in tie-dye. Unfortunately the glimpse had revealed nothing but things appropriate for court, and that alone had immediately told her who the purchaser had been.

No chance in hell she'd be wearing anything from that bag any time soon.

She shuffled to the bathroom. A gentle shower, a comb through her hair, and the foregoing of makeup later, she inched her way back to her room.

She dressed very gingerly in lime capris and the accompanying too-small lime green sweater. Her hair had all the charm of a tangled mop, so she gathered it all up at the back of her head with a ponytail holder. She didn't care what she looked like. She was just concerned about how she was going to sit in the car.

She looked at her violin. Take or leave? Roddy's was probably safer than her car. She left her room, locked it securely, then hauled her bag up over her shoulder and limped slowly down the hallway toward the foyer. Damn Bentley. It *was* his fault she'd ever had to take a perilous ride on a stupid horse. It *was* his fault that he'd bewitched her with his freckles. It was also his fault she was wearing clothes made for a woman five inches shorter and twenty-five pounds lighter than she. Yes, it was all his fault and he deserved whatever Fate had in store for those who took the perfectly good vacations of others and put them in the toilet.

And he'd better not have blocked her car. If he had, he'd best be prepared to fork out money for a hefty towing fee.

She hobbled out into the foyer, cursing Bentley thoroughly with the most grumbly mutter she could manage, then pulled up short. Her hair stood on end.

She was not alone.

There were deep shadows in the foyer near the door, shadows that the faint morning light coming in from the front door's high window door didn't illuminate. And in that dark space, looking just as dark and forbidding as a shadow, sat none other than Patrick MacLeod himself.

Despite her not-quite-formalized plan to thoroughly ignore him the next time she saw him as punishment for abandoning her to Bentley's foul clutches, she felt her knees grow weak. What was it about the man that rendered her unfit for anything useful?

Side effect of a bruised backside, she reassured herself quickly.

Patrick didn't move. She couldn't make out his expression. The rest of him was equally as hard to discern. What in the world could he possibly want? To mock her riding skills? To torture her with potential rescues from Bentley when he fully intended to ditch her with the jerk later?

Well, whatever he wanted, she wasn't interested. She frowned in his direction.

"Do you always wear black?" she asked, trying to sound cool and aloof. Aloof was good. Aloof didn't leave any room for any softer, romantic feelings. And if there was anyone who had neither the time nor the inclination for romance, it was she.

A boot came down from its perch atop his other knee and made no sound as it met the floor. "Black?" he echoed. "Aye, I suppose I do."

"Why do you do it?" she demanded. "So you can more easily intimidate your serfs?" She'd given a lot of thought to his status during her hiatus in bed. The man had to have some variety of servants, didn't he? If his brother owned the castle up the way, that brother most certainly had servants. It was a sure bet that Patrick had grown up in the lap of luxury himself. Moving away from home couldn't have blunted his need to be waited on.

"Intimidate my serfs?" he asked, sounding almost appalled. "I don't have any serfs."

"Paid servants, then."

What could have been mistaken for a mild snort of humor came from the dark. "I fear I have none of those, either." He rose and stepped forward. "Would such a lack prevent you from allowing me to act as your tour guide for the day?"

Damn her knees. Where were they when she needed them to be rock-steady beneath her? Madelyn reached out to hold herself up against the wall. "Tour guide?" she asked, trying to sound doubtful. "I already have plans, actually. You would be bored with them."

"The Highlands never bore me."

She scrutinized his expression, looking for any indication that he was lying. Well, he wasn't lying, but he didn't look overly eager, either. He would probably drop her like a scalding spud the next time Bentley reared his ugly head.

Though she was incredibly tempted. Tour guide? And she was saying no? What was she, insane?

Well, better insane than heartbroken. She put on her most independent smile.

"Thanks anyway," she said brightly, "but I think I'll be fine."

Patrick didn't reply. He merely clasped his hands behind his back and stared at her. Madelyn wanted to look away, but she just couldn't. The man was nothing short of stunning, in a majestic, breathtaking kind of way, yet he somehow projected an accessibility that made it very hard for her to remember why she shouldn't just slip her arm through his and go in to breakfast with him.

"Good heavens, Madelyn, what *are* you wearing? I bought you a handful of perfectly lovely things. Go back and put something suitable on immediately."

And thus the spell was broken. Madelyn sighed deeply. She looked at Patrick. He looked almost disappointed. Either that or he was about to sneeze due to the tsunami of Eternal Riches that had arrived seconds before Bentley had.

"Breakfast anyone?" Roddy asked cheerfully, popping in from the dining room.

"Yes," she said.

"Lovely," Patrick said at the same time.

"Will it be fried?" Bentley asked.

Madelyn rolled her eyes and pushed off the wall. A black-leather-covered arm came into view. She spared it a brief look of surprise before reaching out to take hold—

Of a tweed-covered arm. She jumped back, yelped in pain, then threw Bentley a glare.

"Haven't you done enough?" She hitched past him and watched out of the corner of her eye as he muscled his way into Patrick. Patrick merely stepped back and let Bentley rumble past. Madelyn scowled. There he went again, letting Bentley push him around, letting Bentley push *her* around. Patrick looked like he should be tough. Obviously, looks were deceiving.

Roddy saw her seated. Bentley pushed Patrick out of the way to plop himself down next to her. Patrick looked at him mildly and went to sit down across from Madelyn.

"What are your plans for the day?" Patrick asked with only a vague-sounding interest.

"I'm not sure yet. I'm working on a list."

Bentley snorted. "Of course you are. I wish I had a dime for every list I watched you make."

"I'll give you a dollar," Madelyn said tartly, "if you'll watch me make one about all the reasons you'd make a lousy husband."

Bentley clucked his tongue. "Slanderous words, my dear."

"Sue me."

"You have no assets."

"Thanks to you."

He patted her hand. "I could remedy all that—"

She jerked her hand away. "I'd rather starve, thanks just the same." She took several deep, cleansing breaths. She had to get away from this man. The irritation of his mere presence was beginning to get to her.

Roddy entered with platters and bowls piled high and saved her from evil thoughts concerning her fork and several tender, meaty places on Bentley's physique. Madelyn turned her attention to the food. It was impossible not to notice the man sitting on the other side of it. His expression was positively inscrutable. Then he looked up at Roddy and smiled.

And that sight was enough to force her to draw several more cleansing breaths.

"My thanks, nephew," Patrick said.

"A pleasure, uncle," Roddy said.

"Madelyn, stop hyperventilating," Bentley said, sounding annoyed.

Madelyn ignored him and concentrated on Patrick. "He's your nephew?"

Patrick set to breakfast with gusto. "Aye."

"But—" Madelyn began.

"Inbreeding," Bentley said with a sneer. "He's probably married to his sister."

Madelyn didn't expect Patrick to jump up and defend his honor, and he didn't.

"Don't have a sister," was all he said through a mouthful of oatmeal.

Madelyn laughed in spite of herself. Bentley seemed to find that less than amusing. He began a rant that included everything from complaints about the food to comments on the quality of the local women. Madelyn could hardly eat. The only reason she managed it was that she didn't have money for anything else later in the day. Her breakfast, though, didn't sit very well, and she suspected with the way it was quickly becoming a rock in her stomach, she wouldn't be *able* to eat later.

She rose. "Thank you, Roddy," she called toward the kitchen. "It was great."

He came out, wiping his hands on a towel. "Where are you off to today?"

"It's a secret." Actually she didn't have a clue. *Out of here* seemed to be a good start. She would work out the particulars later. She looked at Bentley. "Your car better not be in my way."

Bentley only smirked at her. She looked at Patrick, but he was staring at Bentley without a trace of expression on his face. Roddy was wringing his towel as if he intended to expunge any and all traces of moisture from it.

Well, it looked as if everyone was anxious for her to leave. She turned and walked away with as much spring to her step as she could manage.

That lasted until she got to the foyer, then she had to clutch the front door frame and recover. What she needed was a week flat on her back. Unfortunately, she didn't have the luxury of a week to recuperate. She'd have plenty of time to recline on her parents' couch when she got home.

That thought was enough to propel her out the door. She practically trotted around the corner of Roddy's inn.

Once again, she pulled up short.

Bentley's jag was there.

Another low-slung black sports car—Patrick's no doubt—was there.

Her little rental was not.

Her heart leaped in her chest. Good heavens, had her car been stolen? Horrifying visions came to her of having to work the rest of her life to pay the upped insurance premiums for a car that was no doubt being stripped of all usable parts at that very moment in some hidden locale used for such nefarious purposes.

"Ow, ow, ow," she said as she ran back into the house. She came to a skidding, quite painful halt in the foyer. Facing her was a little tableau she suspected she wouldn't soon forget.

Patrick was leaning back against a wall, in the shadows, as usual. Roddy was further torturing his dish towel. Bentley Douglas Taylor III, that pompous ass, was dangling his keys from his pinkie, not bothering to hide his look of triumph.

"Shall we go?" he asked pleasantly.

She could hardly believe the events she'd been plunged into. "You took my car?" she asked in disbelief.

"Your credit, it seems, is not very good," he said.

Her bag landed with a thud at her feet. "I can't believe you took my car."

"I didn't take your car."

"You *liar*," she breathed.

"Careful, Madelyn," he said calmly. "You're walking on thin ice."

"Take it, had it taken. You jerk, it's all semantics."

He drew himself up, looking highly offended. "Semantics are my lifeblood."

"I can't believe it's legal," she said, stunned. In fact, she wondered if she could ever stop shaking her head. When was the nightmare with this guy going to end? "What'd you do," she asked, "call up one of your cronies at American Express and have them cancel my card?"

He smiled. "I have a wide circle of friends."

"How, I don't know," she said.

Then it hit her.

She looked at him in horror. "You didn't have my card canceled."

He only continued to smile.

She looked at Roddy. "Where's the phone?"

He pointed miserably to the desk. Madelyn went, made a quick phone call to one of the myriad phone numbers she had memorized, then slowly hung up the phone.

Her credit card was frozen. And no, they were very sorry, but they could do nothing about that. Her credit, it appeared, had suddenly taken an irreversible nosedive and American Express could no longer extend to her any of their privileges or benefits.

She could hardly believe it, but believe it she had to. She quickly made a short list of what that meant.

No rental cars.

No cash advances.

She had £200 in her purse. Enough to eat. Not enough to eat, rent a car, put gas in a car, or even have a car to make it to the next B and B she had reserved. She looked at Bentley.

"I don't suppose I still have any paid lodging anywhere else."

"I don't suppose you do," he said without even a flicker of remorse. "Since you had no mode of transportation, I thought it best to cancel the rest of your reservations. Unless, of course, you care to travel with me—"

"Never." She looked at Roddy. "Is my stay here still covered or did Bentley cancel that as well?"

"You're all paid up for at least another week," he said, nodding his head vigorously.

He was an awful liar. She doubted that even the full series of workshops at Bentley's private prevarication seminar could fix that. It was all she could do to nod in an equally perjurious manner, and she *had* learned how to at Bentley's knee.

Bentley snorted. "She most certainly—"

"She's covered," Roddy said, shooting him a glance that Madelyn was proud of.

Bentley pursed his lips, but said no more.

She wanted to sit, but that would have hurt. She couldn't look at Patrick—she was too humiliated. She couldn't look at Roddy—she was too damned grateful. She couldn't even look at Bentley—if she'd had to look him in the eye, she would have wrapped her hands around his neck and cheerfully throttled him.

"Well," Bentley said pleasantly, "let's go, shall we? But first, toddle on off and change clothes so you don't embarrass me."

Was he out of his mind? He'd just made her life a living hell and now he wanted to make it worse? Was it possible it could get worse? She suspected it could.

She wondered what she was supposed to do now. A quick list of options came immediately to mind, things she dismissed one by one.

Bum money off Sunny was the first, but she couldn't ask her sister to raid her savings when Sunny rarely took vacations herself, and if she did, they were usually taken within walking distance.

Bum money off the folks was the second, and it went the way of the first without hesitation. If she called her parents, she would be subjected to a lengthy lecture on the virtues of traveling on the cheap and probing questions as to why she wasn't doing so. That would be followed by the inevitable discourse on the evils of her profession, the failings of her taste in men, and the possible justified retribution due one who had left the sacred path of academia to pursue the almighty dollar.

No, the price there was just too high.

She would have to think of something, but she wasn't going to be doing any thinking standing in Roddy MacLeod's entryway, facing three men who were staring at her for completely different reasons.

She stuck her chin out to keep herself from crying, turned, and marched over to the front door.

She made a mental note not to do any more marching. It was excruciating.

Maybe she would head to the pub and pick up some Gaelic. Her father would be proud. Maybe someone had a free tourist book she could look at. It would sure as hell be as close as she was going to get to anything she'd planned on seeing.

She was tempted to speculate on how much farther she was going to have to slide before she reached the bottom of the abyss, but that kind of speculation was never a good idea. Besides, she had the feeling that the slide wasn't over.

"Where are you going?" Bentley bellowed. "You haven't changed your clo—"

She shut the front door behind her. She could be happy in the village. There were lots of sights to see there. Local color. Interesting architecture. Cheap entertainment.

She heard the front door open and close behind her. "Go away, you jerk," she said over her shoulder. "Haven't you done enough? Or do you have to follow me to make sure I'm completely miserable?"

Footsteps crunched in the gravel behind her. "You forgot your purse. I thought it might serve you later."

Madelyn closed her eyes briefly, then she turned and looked at Patrick. "Thank you," she said, taking her bag.

"No need." He reached for her hand. "Come on."

She shook her head. "You don't want to get involved in my life. It sucks. And I think it's still heading south."

"Directions change."

"Huh-uh," she said, shaking her head. "Not this time. This is the real thing. Vacation in the Toilet. I'd be scared if I were you."

"I don't frighten easily."

"Maybe you should."

"Why?"

She would have come up with a witty reply, but she found herself a little unsettled by the feeling of his hand around hers. His hand was sending some sort of electricity up her arm. Sunny would have been able to explain the karmic ramifications of that, but she didn't bother to try. She was just afraid all that zinging would soon fry her brain.

She dug in her heels for a last-ditch effort to save Patrick from her and her disaster of a life.

"Really," she said. "You should rethink this."

He stopped and looked down at her with a grave smile. "I'll survive."

That smile was going to be her undoing. "That's what I used to think," she managed.

"Perhaps you think overmuch."

"I have been accused of that on occasion," she conceded.

He tugged on her hand. "Think later. Walk now."

"But—"

"Taylor's behind us."

She didn't have to hear that twice. She limped right along with him as fast as she could and didn't protest as he helped her lower herself into his car.

"How many of these do you have?" she asked as he squatted down beside her.

"This is the last one."

"Any other colors?"

He looked at her and lifted one eyebrow. "Black suits me," he said.

"I like black myself," she offered.

"And I like your lime."

She smoothed her hand over her pants. "Thank you," she managed.

He leaned over her with the seat belt. She thought she might faint.

"Breathe," he said, not looking up as he fastened it.

"Tailbone pain."

He looked at her and smiled, a wry curling of his mouth. "Sure."

"You don't affect me," she lied.

"Don't I? You disturb the hell out of me—"

A strident voice interrupted him. "Now, wait just one minute—"

Patrick sighed lightly, then rose. Madelyn craned her neck to see what was going on—after she'd locked her door, of course. She wasn't a fool.

Bentley was blathering on. Patrick only shrugged, moved past Bentley, and walked away. He got in the car, turned it on, and backed up. Madelyn looked at Bentley to find that he had hopped in his car.

"Oh, no," Madelyn said.

"He's not going anywhere," Patrick said as he pulled away.

"How do you know?"

"I just know."

"Did you destroy the Jag?"

He looked, unsurprisingly, horrified. "Woman, are you daft? I should sooner do damage to my brother. Nay, I merely made a few adjustments to his spark-plug cables."

"Bentley will never figure that out."

"I didn't imagine he would. And he'll surely offend any mechanic in the area before he can get them out to offer aid. I daresay we're safe for the day."

She blinked, hard, then looked out the window when that failed to halt the tears welling up in her eyes. "I hardly know how to thank you. This is just all so awful. I had such big plans." She looked down at her purse and realized she'd left her list on the bed. If that wasn't the last straw, it was close. She ignored the tears running down her cheeks. "I don't even remember what I had on my list for the morning."

"Leave your plans be and let me see to the day."

"But I can't let you—"

"I am accustomed," he said, glancing briefly her way, "to seeing to the necessities and comforts of the women in my company."

A man who would pay for dinner instead of forgetting his

wallet? Was this possible, or had she stumbled into a fairy tale? She stared at him in surprise. "Do you have any faults?"

He laughed and the sound of it was as breathtaking as sun breaking through storm clouds. Chills went down her spine and she almost wept. Hormones. It had to be hormones, and intense tailbone pain combined.

"Flaws? Aye, and you would be acquainted with several."

She honestly couldn't have said she knew what he meant. He flashed her a brief smile, one full of conspiratorial good humor. It was so sweeping a change that she felt as if her feet had been pulled from beneath her by a riptide.

Flaws?

Nah.

Too good to be true?

She wasn't sure she wanted to know.

And then he reached over and took her hand. He squeezed gently and continued to hold on until they reached the main road and he had to shift gears.

"Be at peace," he said with a smile. "I'll see that the day stays out of the loo."

She actually laughed.

It felt marvelous. And if the rest of the day was that wonderful, she would be thrilled.

He took her hand again.

Things were definitely off to a good start.

Chapter 10

Patrick pulled the car off the road, turned the engine off, and leaned his head back against the seat with a sigh. Rare fall sunlight glinted off the ocean in front of him, pristine sand stretched out to meet that water. This was, without question, his favorite place to come, regardless of the season. He went to Culloden to brood; he came to the strand to be at peace. There was something about the vastness of the sea, the hypnotic movements of the waves that whispered to him of things much larger than himself. It helped him put himself, in a particularly humbling way, into perspective.

Or perhaps it was just that he liked to stick his toes into the water now and then.

That had certainly been his intention the first time he'd come to the shore. He could remember the day with perfect clarity.

He'd come as a lad of ten-and-six with a pair of his more adventurous cousins. They'd escaped the keep in the middle of the night and fled like outlaws across MacLeod lands. They'd reached the shore at dawn. Patrick had stood on the very strand before him and gaped at the huge expanse of water, something he'd never seen before and had scarce imagined could exist. Its beauty had smote him straight to the heart, touching him so deeply that a part of him had never been the same.

Peace, the sea had whispered as it had ceaselessly caressed the shore. *Peace*.

Of course, that quiet had been broken when his cousins had stripped themselves naked and bolted for the water. He'd done the same, of course, for the sheer sport of it. They'd passed the better part of the morning swimming in the surf. The outing had seemed at that point like a smashing success.

They'd retreated from the water eventually to find the gear they'd left on the beach had been surrounded by less-than-friendly souls.

It had been a bit dodgy there for a moment or two, fighting lads with swords when they'd had naught but their bare arses to flash in defense, but they'd prevailed in the end thanks to their wits and a bit of sand flung in the others' eyes. They were, after all, MacLeods, and a MacLeod did not cower.

Jamie had been furious when they'd returned to the hall with the tale. Jamie had held the clan chieftainship for a handful of years by then and had already been sobered beyond his usual soberness by it. The foibles of youth had been incomprehensible to him. Patrick had told his brother in not so many words to lighten up. 'Twas nothing short of a miracle that he hadn't become intimately acquainted with the nooks and crannies of the castle's pit. Fortunately for him, Jamie loved him too well to punish him overmuch, and he'd ruthlessly taken advantage of it on more than one occasion. He felt bad about it now, but at the time he'd been more interested in his sport than familial loyalty.

It was a bit shocking to think he might have grown up in the ensuing years.

But such growing up hadn't lessened his love for the sea in front of him or the sweet peace that seemed to sink deep into him and still whatever turmoil might be lurking there. He sighed deeply. He should come more often. It was the one place that was his alone, a paradise where he could come and be still.

Which begged the question: Why in the world had he brought company?

He'd certainly never brought Lisa here.

He looked to his left. Perhaps he'd brought company because said company would likely snooze through the entire experience. Madelyn was sleeping quite peacefully, as she had been for the past hour. She'd woken only once to mumble something about him driving too fast. It was the second time she'd snored at him in less than a week.

Was there a deeper meaning to that?

Best not to know.

And best not to know why out of all the places in Scotland he could have taken her for the day, he'd chosen his own private sanctuary.

He reached out carefully and touched her hand. That same fission of electricity he'd felt the first time he'd touched her coursed through him. There was something there; he couldn't deny it. An immense feeling of déjà vu swept through him. He didn't know her, he knew nothing of her, yet he felt as if he'd known her forever.

He pulled his hand back and clenched it. He didn't want this. The timing was wrong.

And when would be right? his heart asked.

Any time but now. He closed his eyes briefly. He was still young enough to be vulnerable, young enough to have a family, young enough to love so desperately that the thought of facing another loss was simply too much to bear. The loss of the woman beside him . . .

Madelyn opened her eyes and looked at him.

She caught her breath.

He couldn't look away.

Before he could give it any more thought, he leaned over, slipped his hand behind her neck, and pressed his lips against hers. He didn't want to close his eyes, but the soul-searing sense of destiny that swept over him left him no choice but to do so. He felt her hand reach up and touch his face as he kissed her, first gently, then quite a bit more thoroughly.

By the saints, he didn't want this.

He hadn't asked for it.

What in the hell was he supposed to do now?

He lifted his head and sat back, breathing raggedly. He looked at Madelyn. She looked as stunned as he felt. He cast about for something to say, but found that all he could do was stare at her, mute.

Had he ever thought her looks pedestrian? Had he never considered the flawless, porcelain beauty of her skin? How could he have missed her sparkling eyes, the little crook to her nose, the beautiful curve to her mouth?

By the saints, Bentley was a fool.

But, by those same saints, so was he. This was not what he wanted. He'd brought her only to be kind, not for any

other reason. He looked forward abruptly at the sea before
him. What he needed was a hefty dose of its bracing wind
to blow a goodly bit of sense back into his feeble brain. He
opened his door and got out before he did anything else
foolish.

He slammed the door shut, closed his eyes, and took several deep breaths. When he thought he might have some sem-
blance of control over his rampaging desires, he rounded the
car and opened Madelyn's door. She didn't immediately get
out. It occurred to him that she might not be able to. He
leaned over to look at her.

"Do you need aid?" he asked.

She stared at him thoughtfully. "You know," she said
slowly, "you didn't have to do it."

"Do what?" he asked, stalling. Kiss her? Desire her? Never
want to let her go?

"Bring me here," she said quietly.

He took a deep breath. "I wanted to."

She looked at him for a moment or two, then smiled.
"Sure. Hey, have you got one of those A to Z maps?"

The saints be praised for a goodly distraction. "Of course,"
he said quickly. He fetched one from the boot of his car with
alacrity, then returned and handed it to her. "Here," he said.
"All yours."

"Thanks," she said, taking it, then fishing pen and paper
out of her purse. She opened the map.

He looked at her for a moment or two, then surmised she
had no intentions of getting out of the car. "Would you care
to come sit on the sand?" he asked.

"Okay," she said absently. She maneuvered herself out of
the car, still staring at the map. She ignored the hand he held
down to help her.

He nodded to himself. He deserved that.

He fetched a blanket, then the food he'd stopped at a grocery to buy. He set everything out, returned to fetch her, and
found that his assistance wasn't required. He supposed he
deserved that as well. There was a part of him that admired
her independence, but another part of him was disgusted that

his actions had forced her to call that independence up. He never should have kissed her.

Or perhaps he never should have stopped.

He stared at the sea and wished for a gale. The wind that blew was far too weak to clear his head.

Madelyn stepped out of her shoes and sat without aid, but she was quite still for a goodly amount of time after she'd managed to get there. Patrick cursed silently as he sat down next to her. Nay, he shouldn't have kissed her. When was he going to learn not to follow every bloody impulse that took him?

He replayed in his head several of Jamie's lectures to that effect as punishment.

He watched Madelyn examine his map and make her lists, then replayed a few more lectures. They didn't assuage his guilt and they certainly didn't do anything for Madelyn. He continued to watch her and suspected her list-making might go on for some time. He cleared his throat. "Are you going to make lists all day?"

She set her pen, her paper, and his map aside, then looked at him.

And it was then that he wished heartily that he'd kept his bloody mouth shut.

Would he never learn?

"This is the thing," she said evenly. "I have no money, no car, and no lodging. Well, I do have lodging, but I have it only thanks to the charity of a very nice man it will take me quite a while to repay." Her eyes began to swim with tears, but she blinked furiously and continued doggedly on. "I am in a foreign country with no friends, trying to take a vacation I've dreamed about my entire life, a vacation, I might add, which will probably only last another forty-eight hours because it's going to take all the money in my purse to get myself back to Heathrow and get on the plane, but that's okay because at least I won't have to tip a skycap to check my luggage because I have no luggage to check. Are you starting to get the picture yet?"

He opened his mouth to speak, but immediately realized his input was not necessary.

"And you can't seem to decide if you want to keep me or pitch me. I didn't ask for a rescue, you offered. I didn't ask you to kiss me. I didn't ask for any of these weird, other-worldly kind of kooky things I feel every time I look at you or touch you—"

"Otherworldly—"

She glared at him.

He shut his mouth.

"Fish or cut bait, buddy, because I've got a list and you're getting in the way of it."

He felt his jaw slide down. "Fish or cut bait?"

She struggled to her feet, a vision of irritation in lime. "Make up your mind. I'm going to go take a walk along the beach, then I'm going to come back and take control of my life with a few well-written lists. And if you ditch me here, I will sue you for breach of contract."

"Breach of contract?"

"Comfort. Necessities. You, Sir Gallant, have a very short memory."

And with that, she took herself and her lime trousers and hitched her way toward the water.

Patrick watched her go. He continued to watch as she slowly made her way to the water and walked right in. 'Twas a mercy her trousers were so short, for he seriously doubted she could have leaned over to roll them up. He should have been there to do it for her.

He rubbed his hand over his face, took a deep breath, and made a decision. So she disturbed him. That was no reason to chasten her for it. And there was also no use in denying the fact that he'd come to Roddy's that morning because he wanted to see her, wanted to be there to rescue her when she learned Bentley had stranded her. He hadn't been obligated to bring her to the shore. He'd done it willingly. And he hadn't been bloody obligated to kiss her senseless. He'd done it, the saints pity him, because he wanted to.

But that didn't mean he had to propose marriage.

It didn't mean that at all.

He could, he decided with an unwholesome bit of relief,

just enjoy her company for the day and leave that kiss as a delightful memory.

So he left his shoes, his socks, and his pride behind and followed Madelyn down to the water. An apology was in the offing and he wasn't above giving it. He approached as she was standing with her feet in the water, facing the west.

She was weeping.

It wasn't loud, but it was sloppy. He came up behind her and put his hands on her shoulders.

"Oh, no," she said, hiccupping, "not you again."

He turned her around and drew her into his arms. He fully expected her to collapse against him and bawl until she was ill, but she didn't. She took two great gulps of air, patted him a handful of times on the back, then pulled away and dragged her sleeve across her face.

"Thanks," she said. "Very helpful."

He wondered if he was losing his abilities with women in general or if it was only this one who was beyond his skill.

"You needn't stop on my account," he offered. "I'm wearing wool. It dries quickly."

"I'm fine," she said, nodding enthusiastically. "Really. Momentary lapse of . . . well, something. But I'm fine now."

"You don't look fine."

"I'm *fine*," she repeated.

"But—"

"Look," she said, meeting his eyes, "if I don't hold it together right now, I'll *really* lose it. I'm tenuous, but not completely threadbare."

He found himself with his hands on her shoulders. And once they were there, there was no sense in not reaching up with one hand and tucking a bit of hair behind her ear now, was there?

And once he'd done that, there wasn't any use in not leaning over and kissing the tears gently from one eye, then the other.

Was there?

He pulled back and looked down at her. She looked at him briefly before she closed her eyes and bowed her head. He drew her, unresisting into his arms.

"I don't want to lose it," she whispered.

"You won't."

"I'm a woman on the edge."

"I'll keep hold of your shirttails, that you don't fall."

She hiccuped a sort of half-laugh, then pulled back to look up at him. "I just don't know how to take you. Or even if I should."

"I understand, completely."

"Then what are we going to do?"

He brushed away more tears from under her eyes with his thumbs. "We're going to walk along the shore until it tires you. We're going to have a fine lunch. You're going to look over the map. We might have a nap."

"That's not what I'm talking about."

He reached down and took her hand. "I know. What do you think we should do?"

She looked away. "I don't know. Make a list, I suppose."

Just touching her was starting to become a distraction. He'd never felt anything like it in his life. It was Culloden again, a faint echo of that awareness, and very unsettling indeed. "You know," he said lightly, "I have a hidden affinity for lists. Make them all the time." So he'd never made one in his life. Whatever he had to do for the cause, he supposed.

She looked up at him and smiled. "You liar."

The sight almost took his breath away. Well, at least it was taking his mind off touching her. He drew her hand through his arm and started along the shore. "How do you know?"

"It's my business to know when people perjure themselves. It's one thing I'm never wrong about. But it wasn't just that you don't lie very well. I imagine you don't make lists because your priorities are quite straightforward."

He lifted one eyebrow. "And those would be?"

"Fast cars. Good food. No drink."

Frightening. "You might be right," he conceded.

"I don't know about women." She stopped so suddenly, she almost pulled him off his feet. "You aren't married, are you?"

He flinched. He didn't mean to, but he hadn't expected her question. "Not anymore," he said.

"Divorce?"

He wondered why he was having such trouble breathing. "You are relentless, aren't you?"

"Curious. Pain is easier if you get it over with quickly."

He wanted to sit down. "I wonder if you've any idea what you're talking about."

"I do, but just in little doses. I'd say yours was a big dose and one you don't really want to talk about."

"She wanted to divorce me," he said in as matter-a-fact a tone as he could manage, "but she died first."

"I see," she said softly.

"She was pregnant."

"Oh, Patrick," she whispered.

By the saints, was he going to weep now? He put his shoulders back. "It's over. It was several years ago."

"But you still miss her."

He looked at her in surprise. "By the saints, nay. Not her."

"I see."

He suspected she did. "Well, that was diverting."

"It was. Let's talk about something else."

"Bentley?"

She looked up at him with a faint smile. "You fight dirty."

"If you only knew."

"I do know. You keep ditching me with him."

"I pick my battles."

"I'd like to see that."

He hoped she never had to. He continued to walk with her, feeling an unaccustomed sense of peace. He'd talked about Lisa and the baby and he was still standing. Maybe she had things aright. Face the pain and be done was a far better practice than dreading it, ignoring it, trying to circumvent it. His brother faced the unpleasant, just marched straight up to it and ran it through. Patrick had done his share of that in his lifetime, but not in the past several years. He'd done everything but look at the grief.

Perhaps it was far past time he did.

Change, whispered his heart.

Aye, a change. Change of occupation, change of attitude, change of outlook.

His heart whispered its approval.

He grunted. All he needed now was that bloody ghostly piper to chime in with a fling to celebrate the decision. He sighed deeply, then searched about for a smile.

"Let's go work on your list," he said. "My offer of chauffeur still stands."

"I might take it. It would only be for a couple of days anyway. I don't suppose it would get in the way of you lording over your serfs."

"Probably not," he agreed.

"What will it cost me?"

"Cost? For a woman who scares the hell straight from me? Why, my lady, that would be *gratis*."

She looked at him in surprise. "Do I scare you?"

"Unsettle," he amended. Visions of her shivering as she touched a rock at Culloden assaulted him. "Unsettle."

She cocked her head to one side. "Are you still offering necessities and comfort?"

"Freely."

"Done, then," she said.

And so easily.

"Let's go make that list," she said.

He woke, looked at the sun, and realized he was going to have to make extreme haste to meet his plane. He looked at Madelyn to tell her as much, then found himself rendered quite mute.

She was staring at him with the slightest of smiles on her face. It was a smile that smote him straight to the heart.

Patrick leaned up on one elbow. "Nice nap?"

"It seemed to work for you."

"You slept as well."

"I did not. I was industriously studying the map."

"Maybe lists do you a disservice," he said slowly. "You miss the simple days on the shore that way."

"After this," she said, looking out over the water, "I might consider using them less." She looked back at him. "But if I did, how would I number all the great things about today? Great food, great scenery, tolerable company."

He smiled as he leaned over and, without thinking, kissed her. He pulled back quickly, surprised that he'd done it. It hadn't been intentional.

It had been just too damned natural.

"Keep your lists, Madelyn," he said, attempting a tone of ease and lightness. "I'll rip them up periodically for you."

She nodded casually. "Sure."

He got to his knees and began packing up. "We need to go. I've got to go catch a plane."

She sat up. "Are you a pilot?"

"Nothing so glamorous. I'm off to play nanny for a day or two." He packed up, rose, then held down his hands for her.

"You don't look like a nanny."

"I don't feel like one, either, but there you have it."

She packed up with him, but didn't ask any questions. That was just as well. He didn't have any answers.

He drove as carefully as he dared back to the inn, to spare her. He was damned late, though, and would have to chance another speeding ticket just to get to the airport on time.

He parked in front of Roddy's. At least the Jag wasn't there, which at least boded well for Madelyn's evening.

"I'll be back day after tomorrow," he said. "Then we'll do your list."

"All right," she said easily. "Thanks for a wonderful day."

He was torn between shaking her hand and kissing her. She merely stared at him as he stood in front of her and dithered.

Damnation, when was the last time he'd dithered?

"I'll be back," he promised.

"Sure."

He patted her on the shoulder, then bolted for his car.

She just stood and watched him go.

He glued himself to the speed limit through the village and for a good half hour out of town before he put his foot down and flew toward Inverness.

He'd just patted a woman on the shoulder when he should have hauled her into his arms and kissed the socks off her.

By the saints, he was pathetic. At least Jamie hadn't been watching.

Too bad Madelyn had been.

He shook his head and drove on.

Chapter 11

Madelyn lay on her bed and stared up at the ceiling. She wasn't easily depressed. She wasn't easily discouraged. She rarely lacked self-confidence. She never felt like curling up in a ball and pulling the covers over her head.

Ah, what a difference a day made.

Was that a song? She didn't want to know. The rest of the words might push her right over the edge into a complete cerulean funk. Hers was still turquoise. She wanted to keep it that way.

The bright spot in the gloom had been those kisses of Patrick's. Whatever else the man's failings, he certainly knew how to use his mouth. She couldn't even fault him for not using it to tell Bentley to go to hell. Far better that he use it for more constructive things.

Now, the whole good-bye, patting business was something she should probably examine more closely, but she just couldn't bring herself to. Better to think about her toes curling in her Cole Haans and Patrick MacLeod's fingers tangling in her hair.

She fanned herself.

It didn't hurt her tailbone to do that.

It did hurt her tailbone to look under the bed, which was what she'd done the day before after Patrick's hasty deposit of her person on Roddy's porch.

She wondered absently where Bentley had stashed her violin.

And least she was wondering absently. The night before, she'd been wondering frantically. Bentley's blank stare when faced with her flaming accusations had only given her more fuel to put on the fire of her absolute fury.

Better fury than grief over its loss that was so deep she was afraid to even peer into its depths.

Bentley wouldn't care, which was why she was so certain he'd done the dastardly deed. He'd never liked to listen to her play. He'd discouraged any and all her attempts to join any ensembles. She was actually a very good violinist. It had been her release from the more serious part of her life. She'd worked very hard on her art merely for the pleasure of it and been amply rewarded for her efforts by a good deal of skill. She'd known, however, that to marry Bentley was to completely give up that joyous part of herself.

It should have been a red flag.

Yet, somehow, Bentley had managed to get rid of her music just the same. She was *sans* violin, *sans* money, and *sans* any way to get anywhere since her chauffeur had gone off to do his baby-sitting.

That was another thing. Whom did he baby-sit?

Her imagination ran rampant at just the thought. Maybe he was a high-priced escort. Maybe he'd fathered children all over the UK and went to tend them instead of paying child support.

Maybe she should stop thinking and get out of bed before she thought herself into never speaking to him again.

She sighed, then sat up. It was more easily done today. Hallelujah, a ray of sunshine in the gloom. She got out of bed carefully, though. No sense in pushing her luck.

To celebrate, she took a sunshine yellow too-short skirt and a sweater with an enormous mum embroidered on the front of it to the bathroom. She lingered in the shower, lingered over her hair, then ambled to the dining room with all the haste of a woman who was all dressed up with nowhere to go.

"Well," Roddy said as came into the room, "aren't you just the picture of sunshine."

She smiled. "I feel like it, in spite of everything." She rubbed her hands together. "Now, where's the kitchen? I'll get to scrubbing a few pots for my keep."

"Now, Miss Madelyn—"

She held up her hand. "Roddy, I know you didn't charge my card."

"I might have," he said stubbornly.

"You, my friend, are a horrendously bad liar. And I can't stay for free."

"You can owe me," Roddy began.

A snort came from the doorway. "Best get in line, my good man. She owes everyone."

A quick glance proved there were no sharp instruments loitering on Roddy's table. A quicker glance exchanged with him proved that he'd done that on purpose. Madelyn almost smiled, but changed it to a glare to toss Bentley's way.

"I do not owe everyone," she snapped. And she didn't. It had cost her having her condo foreclosed on her, having to sell all her stuff to pay off her credit cards, and losing the lease on her car, but she had no debt.

Well, except for that astronomical student loan balance, but that was different than owing money all over town.

"I'd let her scrub pots, old man," Bentley drawled. "It's the best chance you have of getting your cash out of her."

Roddy pulled himself up. "Then that is where you and I differ, for I'd not see a lady put to such work to repay a debt caused by another."

Bentley pulled the toothpick from his mouth. "Down, boy. Meant no offense. And while we're chatting so nicely here, I need to extend my stay for a few more nights."

"Now, that is a pity," Roddy said. "I fear I cannot accommodate you. I have other lodgers coming in tonight."

"Tell them to go elsewhere," Bentley said. "I need the room."

Roddy's mouth hung down. "I cannot," he said aghast.

"Then move the incoming guests into the broom closet. Madelyn can't afford to stay here anymore anyway."

Madelyn watched Roddy struggle to speak. She wondered if he was weighing the risks of throwing Bentley out bodily versus the annoyance of letting him stay. Maybe Roddy didn't think he could physically manage to heave the idiot out the door. She decided it was in her best interest to help Roddy rid himself of the pestilence.

"I'll carry his bags for you," she offered.

Bentley threw her a glance she couldn't quite decipher. Warning? Malice? Then he turned back to Roddy. "Another week, if you please."

Roddy's chin quivered as he stuck it out. "I canna do that," he said. "Ye'll have to be out by eleven o'clock tomorrow."

"Or?" Bentley asked smoothly.

"Or I'll be forced to summon the authorities."

Bentley snorted, then looked at Madelyn. "Shall we go? You'll want to sightsee quite a bit today since you'll be out on your ear tomorrow."

She wasn't going to dignify that with a response. Of course, the ugly truth of not having anywhere to go or money with which to go there was something of a problem. The other problem was waiting for Patrick to get back. Should she even wait? He was very polite, but the truth of it was he probably had things and she didn't have money to pay for a hotel while he decided whether or not he could ignore those things in favor of her.

Maybe she could just go home early. At this point, she just didn't feel as if she had any other option.

But admit that to Bentley?

Never.

"Breakfast," Roddy said to her. "Something strengthening."

"Why?" Bentley asked. "So she can loiter in a delinquent fashion around your house when she could so easily see this uninteresting country in style if she would just go put on something less tacky?"

Madelyn glared at him. "Shut up, Bentley."

He drew himself up. "I beg your pardon?" he said in his haughtiest tone.

"Silence, counselor."

"I—"

"Overruled. We're not interested in hearing anything else you have to say." She looked at Roddy. "Breakfast would be great." Without looking at Bentley, she sat down at the table.

She ate heartily of everything Roddy put in front of her. And somewhere along the way during her second helping of oatmeal, she accidentally glanced at Bentley.

And the look on his face sent chills down her spine.

For the first time in her life, she felt afraid.

Fear was a gift, someone once told her. It tells you when something is wrong. Listen to it.

Then again, this was Bentley. He was rich, he was cunning. He might be stupidly cruel, but he wasn't maliciously cruel. There was a difference.

"What?" she demanded, taking an offensive position.

He blinked. "What?"

"What are you thinking?"

"That you are foolishly stubborn."

She shook her head. "What could you possibly care what I am? You don't want me, remember?"

"I may have changed my mind."

She leaned forward. "Bentley, you're engaged to someone else. You can't change fiancées like you change shirts."

He looked frankly baffled.

"Besides," she added, "it's too late."

Bafflement disappeared abruptly. "The Scot?"

"Who?"

"MacLeod, damn it. You're going to marry him?"

"Good heavens, no."

"Then what's the problem? I'm available and I want you."

"You can't have me," she said. "You dumped me, remember? You had my credit card canceled. You stole my room and I'm quite sure you stole not only my luggage but my violin. If you think there's a snowball's chance in hell I'd ever take you back, you're dreaming."

"Take *me* back?" he echoed. "As if you had the choice!"

"I do have the choice," she said, "and I choose to tell you to get lost."

He lifted his fork and pushed a very fine breakfast around on his plate as if he were looking for something edible. "Stop playing coy. You're only . . . exasperating the situation."

Madelyn pushed back from the table. "I'm done. Get lost, Bentley. I don't want to see you again. And," she added wearily, "it's *exacerbate*, Bentley, not *exasperate*. Though you certainly do the latter to me."

She got her purse out of her room, then walked into the foyer. Roddy came out of the dining room.

"Have an errand to run," he said loudly. "Care to come?"

If it meant avoiding Bentley, she'd go shovel out a barn with him. She nodded and followed him into his little car. He was silent until the doors were closed.

"Patty rang me this morn with instructions that you take his car," he said with a smile. "At least you'll have a bit of freedom for the day."

Had she ever thought an unkind thought about the man? Foolish, foolish girl. "Does he have insurance?"

"He's not loaning you his Bentley," Roddy said with a laugh. "Just his little runabout. I daresay he doesn't even consider it a proper car. You're also to make yourself at home at his place, though he made no guarantees about the contents of his refrigerator."

"This is awfully nice," Madelyn said, more than a little surprised.

"He's a good lad. He's had a rough few years." He slid her a sideways glance. "He could do with a woman who appreciated him."

She just bet he could. She looked out the window as they made their way along a one-lane road that wound through forests and little meadows. What would it be like to have this as your backyard? She couldn't understand how Bentley could look around him and not be moved by what he saw. Probably because he wasn't seeing the inside of a five-star resort. His loss.

Roddy turned up a gravel road and wound through a bit of forest. It opened up quickly into a fairly large meadow. In the middle of that little meadow was a house that greatly resembled a small castle. A little hill rose up behind it. The scenery was breathtaking.

The house was a wreck.

Madelyn gulped. "This is it?"

"Aye," Roddy said. "It wants for a bit of repair."

"I'll say," Madelyn said, taking a deep breath. "I can see why he lives here, though. I'd put up with crumbling walls for the view alone."

"Stay there," Roddy said, getting out. He hurried around and opened her door. He held it open for her to get out. "Smell," he said with a smile.

She held on to the door and did. It smelled of earth and sky with a hint of greenery and heather. She smiled at Roddy. "Heavenly."

"I thought you'd like it. Now, shall I wait or do you want to poke around on your own?"

"He won't mind?"

"He won't. The car keys are in the car in the garage. The house isn't locked."

"Isn't he afraid someone will steal something?"

"What's to steal? We all know each other, so there is no market for goods in the area. And," he added with a twinkle in his eye, "no one would dare face Patrick's wrath."

Madelyn reserved judgment on that. She had yet to see Patrick's wrath.

"Besides, young Pat isn't much for accumulating things besides horses and cars."

"And those are a little hard to steal."

"Aye." He closed the door. "I'll be off then and leave you to your pleasures. You can wander back up the hill, but I'd stay out of the forest."

"Why?"

He looked as if he wanted to say something, then shook his head. "The tale is too long. You're safe in the little meadow here."

"Sure," she said. "Whatever." Then she stopped dead. "What's in the forest?"

He started to speak, stopped, then started again. He shut his mouth, looked around him furtively, then leaned in close. "The trees are full of Highland magic," he whispered.

"I'll be sure to stay away from that."

Roddy nodded in satisfaction, hopped in his car, and drove away with an encouraging smile. Madelyn waited until the sound of his car disappeared before she turned and looked at Patrick's house. Silence descended except for the whisper of the wind in the trees. A peace like she'd never felt before came over her, softly, like a mist, stilling her thoughts.

Was this what he had each day?

It was no wonder he was able to ignore Bentley. She might have been able to as well if this was what she had to come home to each night.

The breeze lifted her hair away from her face, gently swirling around her in some kind of Highlandish dance. Madelyn closed her eyes. If she hadn't known better, she could have sworn she heard the sound of bagpipes, faint in the distance.

Her eyes flew open. That wasn't her imagination. She set her bag on the crumbling courtyard wall, then walked around to the back of Patrick's house. The sound was coming from up the hill. She stared at the silhouette of trees and rocks, trying to make out the figure of a musician.

She saw nothing.

Or did she? She could hardly decide.

That could have been the silhouette of a man.

She was tempted to go up and have a closer look, but decided against it for a couple of reasons. One, she wasn't up to any hiking, and Patrick's hill required a good hike. Two, whatever she was listening to was magic, and she just didn't want to spoil it.

So she walked to the front of the house. The pipes were still audible, even there. The front door was unlocked, as advertised. She opened it, then peered inside.

It was empty—and not just devoid of people. There was no real furniture in his living room. Just one enormous fireplace and a stool or two.

She walked in and closed the door behind her. Normally prowling through an unlocked empty house would have given her the willies. Here, for some inexplicable reason, she felt safe. Patrick's presence was there somehow. She stood in his front room and felt peace descend.

It was blissful.

And it also smelled quite a bit like pipe smoke. She frowned. Patrick didn't smoke, did he? She sniffed, but the smell was fading even as she did so. She shrugged and continued on through the room to go explore the rest of his house. It took quite a while, as there was certainly no lack of rooms, but they were all just as empty as the first she'd seen.

And then she walked into what had to be Patrick's bedroom. It had a bed, a trunk, a rickety chair, and an armoire that had to be a very expensive antique. The armoire looked so out of place in comparison to everything else that she couldn't stop herself from going over to touch it.

And once she touched, she knew she would have to open. *Curiosity killed the cat*, her common sense warned. Well, she wasn't a cat. She put her hand on the wood.

The sound of bagpipes increased. A shiver went down her spine, the same kind of shiver she'd had at Culloden, and that was almost enough to make her rethink her nosiness.

Almost, but not quite. She took a deep breath and, to the accompaniment of some kind of battle dirge played by a bagpiper she couldn't see, opened the armoire.

The light in the room was faint, but substantial enough for her purposes. The armoire wasn't full. Indeed it only contained a handful of things.

A very rustic linen shirt that looked as if it had been hand sewn.

A plaid blanket, the colors muted, the cloth mended in many places.

And, heaven help her, a sword.

She reached out and touched the cold steel of the hilt. It fell over, out of the armoire, and against her as if it had been a live thing.

She screamed and jumped back. The sword clattered onto the stone floor. Madelyn looked around her, her hand to her throat. The room was still empty. She took several deep breaths, then reached down.

The sword was heavier than she'd expected and *very* rustic. But the blade was lethally sharp. She sucked on the finger she'd used to prove that to herself. She pulled the finger out of her mouth and looked at the slice she'd made. Good grief, she'd barely touched the edge.

Reenactment sword?

If so, she felt sorry for Patrick's opponents.

She put the sword back, patted the hilt with a "good sword, good sword," then shut the door, rested her hands on the wood, and contemplated what she'd just seen.

Antique clothes and a weapon.

Weird.

She'd have to ask Patrick later, if she dared. For now, she had things to do and wheels with which to do them. She paused in his kitchen only to find things covered with mold in his fridge and some stale bread in his bread box. Oh, well, she'd eat tomorrow.

She made her way outside, past his stables, and to the garage. She flicked on the light and shook her head. There was his Range Rover, two empty spaces, and a small but quite useful-looking something in burnt orange.

No wonder he chose black.

She opened the appropriate garage door so she could back out, then let herself into Burnt Orange and flipped the keys down from the visor.

"Halt!"

She almost wet her pants. She stared up into a powerful flashlight beam. "Um—"

"Out of the car. Now."

She got out of the car to face one of Scotland's finest. She smiled. "Officer, how are you?"

The officer, who briskly introduced himself as Fergusson, was not moved by her best smile. "Far better than you will be. Breaking and entering, attempted theft, drunk and disorderly," he said, ticking the offenses on his fingertips.

She gaped at him. "What?"

"Breaking and enter—"

"I heard that part," she interrupted. "Repeat that other part."

He glared at her. "Lucky for me I got the tip. Now, come along peacefully."

"You're *arresting* me?"

"Even the worst crook can have a pretty face."

She could hardly believe her ears. "I know the owner. He *invited* me to come borrow a car."

The cop could not have looked more skeptical. "Not that there aren't strange enough goings on up here with all these MacLeods, but I know Pat and I know his cars. And I don't know you."

And that, it seemed, was that. She put up a fight when she found that her purse wasn't where she left it. Apparently Officer Fergusson didn't take kindly to being accused of stealing. She soon found herself sitting in the back of his car, handcuffed and swearing.

"I will sue," she threatened.

He ignored her and sped off.

Damn.

These sights were most definitely *not* on her list.

Chapter 12

Patrick climbed down the jet's stairs and walked across the tarmac, yawning. He'd finally managed to get his charge onto the plane home about six A.M., twelve hours after he was supposed to be on board. That was one boy who hadn't wanted to go back home.

For himself, he was more than ready to be home. He would catch a couple hours' sleep, then call Roddy's to see what new disaster had befallen Madelyn. He'd been gone two and a half days. It could have been anything.

A part of him wondered—more anxiously than he wanted to acknowledge—if she had decided not to wait for him and left already for the States. He told himself it wouldn't matter. Roddy would have her address. She could be tracked down if he was all that interested.

He refused to examine that interest level. He had a good heart; she was having a lousy vacation. 'Twas his duty as a Scot to see her left with a good impression of his country.

He studiously avoided any memories of kissing.

Or patting, for that matter.

Conal was waiting for him in the hangar. "Well?"

"Here," Pat said as he handed the other man his report. He set his shopping bag down on the tarmac, rubbed his hands over his face, and yawned hugely. "Nothing exciting."

"Went well?"

Patrick shook his head to shake sense back into himself. "No arrests and all body parts still intact. I'd say it was a success."

"Good enough. I have something else for you tomorrow—"

Patrick shook his head. "Can't."

Conal blinked. "Why not?"

Patrick almost squirmed. "Duty to one of Roddy's guests. She, um, well, she—"

"She?" Conal asked with interest.

"Aye, she."

"Is she a model?"

"A lawyer, and 'tis nothing serious."

Conal's look of interest didn't fade. "I'll reserve judgment. And don't let her turn you into a recluse again, though I suppose I should be overjoyed you're seeing someone. I'd fancy a wee chat with her, of course, just to see—"

"The saints preserve her, nay," Patrick said, with feeling. "I daresay I want to see a bit more of the wench without you frightening her off."

"Sounds serious."

"It isn't. But I'm still not available tomorrow."

"I suppose Bobby can handle this next one."

Bobby was perfectly suited to the work. Handsome, patient, and lethal. Patrick was always happy to know Bobby was on his side in a fight.

"He'll do well," Patrick agreed.

Conal looked at him searchingly. "Is this temporary?"

"Madelyn? Of course it's temp—"

"Nay, not her. Your lack of enthusiasm for your work."

Patrick smiled briefly. "Conal, my friend, you think too much."

"I'm generally spot on."

"Even worse," Patrick said with a sigh. "Nay, I am as eager as ever to give my all to the cause."

Conal snorted. "Right. Oh," he said suddenly, "Roddy MacLeod's been trying to reach you. Something about not having seen your Madelyn since he dropped her at your house—"

"Damnation, Conal, why didn't you say so immediately? Why didn't you call me?" By the saints, anything could have happened to her. She could have wandered into the forest and gotten lost.

"Your mobile is, as usual, dead. And I couldn't exactly send a messenger after you now, could I? And I didn't tell you right off—"

Patrick didn't hear the rest. He pulled Conal's mobile phone out of the man's own suitcoat chest pocket and dialed.

"Roddy?" he said.

"Oh, Patty," Roddy said, sounding frantic, "she's nowhere to be found. No purse, nothing left behind. I never should have left her—"

Patrick listened to the rest of the ramble with only half an ear. She had disappeared without a trace. Given that he had firsthand experience with that, the possibilities of where Madelyn had gotten herself lost *to* were simply staggering.

"Is Taylor still there?" Patrick interrupted.

"Left two days ago. Moved his stuff to MacAfee's, who dumped two of *his* lodgers to make room. Now I'm scrambling to find beds for them all."

"Unsurprising. Well, I'll be there as fast as the law allows."

"Faster, even," Roddy said. "I'm worried."

So was he.

He handed Conal back his phone. "My thanks."

"Trouble?" Conal asked.

"Aye. It may take some time to sort out."

Conal waved him away. "Off with you then, and mount up on that white horse."

Patrick flashed him a brief smile of thanks before he ran quickly to the car park. He threw his gear into the boot of his car, tore out of the airport, and flew for home.

Ten minutes from Roddy's, flashing lights went on behind him. He pulled over with a curse, then cursed some more at the man who appeared at his window.

"Well, who have we here?" the officer drawled. "Speeding, as usual."

"Fergusson," Patrick said shortly.

"That's *Officer* Fergusson to you, MacLeod," Hamish Fergusson said.

"And that would be *my lord* to you," Patrick said. Perhaps there was some pleasure in having a title, however small. It threatened to drive Hamish Fergusson quite mad each time Patrick reminded him of it. "Now, what do you want?"

"Let me just look at your license—*my lord*," he said with

a sneer, "and marvel at the points you've acquired."

"Just give me the bloody points and have done. I've things to do."

Hamish looked at Patrick coolly. "You should be thanking me," he said.

"For what?" Patrick snorted. "Continually annoying me?"

"I caught a trespasser on your land."

Patrick blinked. "In truth?" Taylor grew bold, it seemed.

"She was trying to steal one of your cars."

"One of my—she?" Patrick echoed. "Madelyn Phillips?"

He shrugged. "So she claims. Had no identification on her. Claimed that was stolen as well. 'My purse was just on that wall,' says she. 'That's what they all say,' says I. No proof of theft, and there's a truth for you. No proof of who she was, either, which is why she's still where she is."

Patrick suppressed the urge to roll his eyes. "And where would that be?"

"In jail. Has been for two days."

Patrick could hardly believe what he was hearing. "Hamish, you idiot, I *told* her to take a car!"

"And you weren't around to verify that now, were you? Off on one of your damned stupid secret missions," he said with a grumble. "Besides, the tip I got was a good one."

"Who called? Another American? Pompous, overbearing lout?"

"How did you—" Hamish wiped the look of incredulity off his face. "My sources are secret."

Patrick grunted. "Aye, well, there's a comfort." He thrust out his hand. "Give me my license back. Then get out of my way."

Half an hour and at exactly the posted speed limit later, he was walking into a very small police station with a single cell, followed closely by the good Hamish Fergusson. Ten minutes and several shouts later, he had Madelyn out of the cell and shivering in the entryway. He fixed Hamish with a steely glance.

"A poor excuse for a blanket and nothing but survival rations. You ought to be ashamed of yourself."

Hamish thrust out his chin. "Even the vilest sort of thief can have—"

"More sense than you," Patrick growled. "She's a lawyer, you imbecile. When she sues you, I'll be her first witness."

"Get out of here, MacLeod," Hamish growled.

"That is *My Lord Patrick* to you," Patrick said coldly. "You forget your manners."

"What I'll forget is the key to the cell when I get you inside it," Hamish shot back.

Madelyn slipped her hand into his. "Could we just go?"

"Of course." Patrick took off his jacket and put it around her. He gave Hamish one final glare, then led Madelyn from the station. He put her in the car, then went around, got in, and locked the doors. He looked at her.

"You look as though you need a vacation," he said quietly.

Two great, fat tears rolled down her cheeks. "I'm not a crier," she said, then promptly burst into tears.

Patrick looked around for a tissue. Finding none, he cursed, marched back into the station, and appropriated the first box he saw.

"Oy, you can't—" Hamish said.

Patrick looked at him.

Hamish shut his mouth abruptly.

Patrick got back in the car and handed Madelyn a handful of tissues. "I'm sorry," he said.

"Not your fault," she gulped, then continued to sob.

His brother would have been terrified by the prospect of comforting a sobbing female. Fortunately for Madelyn, he was not his brother. He stroked her hair, he made soothing noises, he held her and let her drench his shirt. And when she was finished and had pulled away, he handed her another wad of tissues.

"Sorry," she said with a sniff. "This was just too much."

"Aye, it was. And it sounds like Taylor was behind it."

"Geez, does the guy never give up?" she asked, dragging her sleeve across her eyes. "You'd think *I* was the one who dumped him."

"You would think," he agreed. He didn't say as much, but he knew Taylor's kind—a man who would destroy everything he owned or coveted to keep anyone else from having it. A very, very dangerous kind of man.

Not the kind of man to provoke without being prepared to do whatever was required to finish the battle.

"Do you have anything left at Roddy's?" he asked.

She shook her head. "I have absolutely nothing. No money, no clothes, no passport, no violin, and no plane ticket."

Patrick considered. First, he had to get her out of Taylor's scope of influence. He'd demanded that all charges against her be dropped. Hamish was pushing for an inquest in two weeks, but Patrick was certain another visit to the station would make that go away. But if Taylor knew where she was, he could continue to harass and annoy her.

His house was out. Jamie's was as well. Elizabeth didn't need any upsets this close to her baby's birth.

That left his cousin Ian and his wife Jane. They had plenty of room, even with two bairns. And Ian, being of Patrick's particular background, could certainly keep Madelyn safe should that be required.

Patrick put the car in gear, backed up, then drove through the village.

"Duck," he said suddenly.

"What—"

"Bentley."

Madelyn hit the floor without hesitation, then groaned. "I think I broke something."

Patrick passed by Taylor, giving him a bored look. Predictably, Taylor puffed himself up and started shouting as he ran down the street after them.

"What an arse," Patrick muttered as he left the village and sped up. "All clear."

Madelyn moaned as she sat back up. "Just toss me in the local Dumpster. It would be the kindest thing you could do."

Patrick looked in the mirror. No one following. It boded well. "There's life in you yet, woman. We'll see it preserved."

She leaned back against the seat. "Thanks for the rescue. Your Officer Fergusson was most unreasonable."

"He doesn't care for me." That was understating the animosity, to be sure.

"Long-standing family feud?" she asked.

"Aye, you could say that." What he didn't bother to add was just exactly how long the MacLeods and Fergussons had been going at it. No sense in giving Madelyn details she didn't need and likely wouldn't believe if she had them.

"Then why bother with me?" she asked with a yawn. "You'd think he would have been thrilled I was breaking and entering something of yours."

"Taylor had to have made it worth Hamish's trouble. We'll solve the mystery as time goes on, if it interests you. If not, I'll see that it goes away." He glanced at her. "You're well rid of your good Mr. Taylor."

"I would be, if I could actually *get* rid of him. And speaking of discharging troublemakers, where are you going to put me to rest?"

"My cousin's. You'll be safe there."

She went very still. So still that it affected even him and his mind was still racing. He would have looked at her if he hadn't been going so fast.

"Does that not suit?" he asked.

"The kindness of strangers," she murmured.

"I'm hardly a stranger."

"Aren't you?" she asked with a small crack in her voice. "I hardly know you, yet here you are ready and willing to let me impose on your relatives."

"I'd let you impose on me, but I don't have anything in the fridge."

"I didn't mean that."

"I know," he said, "and you won't be imposing. Ian and Jane love company, and you'll be quite comfortable there for a couple of days. Then we'll head to London and get your papers straightened out."

"I can't begin to thank you. I don't know where I would even start thinking about it."

"I always do this for women who disturb me," he said lightly. "Three rescues per maiden in distress."

"I think I've already used two."

"Make your third count."

She sighed. "And how many women have disturbed you, my lord?"

He slowed down. He let out his breath just as slowly. "Just you."

She was silent for several moments. "I can't decide if I should be flattered or terrified," she said finally.

He pulled to a stop in front of Ian's large manor house, then looked at her. "Believe me, I can't, either." He reached out and tucked her hair behind her ear. "We'll think about it later. For now, come inside and be at peace."

She hesitated. "Do they know I'm coming?"

"Nay, but not to worry."

"Oh, Patrick," she said, dismayed, "I don't think—"

"I daresay you do. Too much." He got out of the car and went around to open her door. She wasn't moving. He squatted down next to her. "Madelyn?"

She reached for his hand. "Could you please give them a chance to say no? I just can't impose . . ."

"It won't be an imposition, but I'll go ask if you wish."

"I do. Please."

"Then I will." He leaned down, kissed the back of her hand, then gently shut the car door.

And he did his damndest to ignore the feeling of pleasure he got from thinking about having her stay at Ian and Jane's for a few days.

Given that he also had a room at their house where he camped on a regular basis.

He rubbed his hand over his face as he walked to the door. Obviously, he hadn't had enough sleep over the past two days.

He was five paces from the door when it flew open and a small body sprinted out.

"Unkie Pat!" the boy shouted.

He was cousin, not uncle, but he never bothered to correct the mistake. He scooped Alexander up, then submitted cheerfully to kisses, tugs on his hair, and investigations of all the pockets Alexander could reach. He carried his young cousin to the door and smiled at Ian, who appeared holding his year-old daughter in his arms.

"Cousin," Patrick said.

"Cousin yourself," Ian said. "What brings you? A need for breakfast?"

"Always, and that isn't all that brings me. I have a wee problem. Actually, I have a friend with a problem—not so wee."

"A *woman* friend?" Ian asked with a waggle of his brows.

"If you can believe it," Patrick said dryly, letting Alexander slip to the ground.

"Miracles never cease," Ian said. "Is that wench yonder the one in question?"

"Aye. She is without funds or place to stay."

"Hotel MacLeod is always open," Ian said without hesitation. He shifted Sarah to his other hip. "We've enough room and to spare."

"You never disappoint."

"Aye, I'm a prince," Ian said with a laugh. "Bring the poor girl in. My Jane will be happy for a bit of company."

Patrick turned back to find that Alexander had already gone to do the deed. He had opened Madelyn's door and was examining her closely. Patrick hesitated, then turned back to Ian.

"She's in a spot of serious trouble."

Ian raised one eyebrow and waited.

"Ex-fiancé. A vindictive blighter who doesn't want her—or maybe he does. He had her tossed into Hamish Fergusson's cell."

Ian stroked his chin thoughtfully. " 'Twould be a pity to be forced to do him in. In self-defense, of course."

"Who, Hamish?"

"Him, too. Nay, I spoke of your lady's former betrothed."

"Don't tempt me," Patrick warned. "I've had far too many encounters with him for my taste. And she's not my lady."

Ian looked at him skeptically. "Isn't she? You're powerfully solicitous about her, for her to mean nothing to you."

"I'm a very gallant soul. Giving till it hurts."

Ian grunted. "Not worth commenting on. So, what's her

name? This poor woman you have chosen to protect and defend but care nothing about?"

"It isn't that I don't care—"

"Saints, Pat, what's the wench's name?" Ian asked with a laugh. "If you can leave off defending your position long enough to spew it at me."

"Madelyn," Patrick said curtly.

"Then bring Madelyn, the one who is not your lady, inside the house," he said with a grin. He kissed his little girl. "Come, Sarah, and let Uncle Patty go fetch his sweet Mistress Madelyn. She's come to stay with us for a bit." He looked at Patrick. "We'll make her welcome," he said seriously. "And we'll keep her safe."

" 'Tis that which I wanted to hear."

"I suspected it might be."

Patrick nodded, then turned and walked back to the car. Madelyn would be safe. He would speculate later upon why that concerned him so. For now, it was enough to have her away from Bentley and have them both where they might rest a bit.

He leaned on the car door and looked in. "I see you've met Alexander," he said with a smile. Alexander, as fate would have it, was a storyteller of epic proportions and liked to ply his trade upon any soul who would listen.

Most of his tales involved Legos.

Madelyn looked as overwhelmed as he himself felt after listening to the long, involved adventures of Alexander's plastic connecting blocks.

"Yes," she said, looking as if she needed a rescue, "I have."

Patrick smiled. "Have you no younger siblings?"

"I'm the youngest of two."

"No tending of children in your past?"

"None," she said, sounding as if that might have been a good thing. "I didn't baby-sit; I hung out at faculty parties with my parents."

"A far cry from Alex's escapades."

"Absolutely."

He gave Alexander affectionate hair ruffles. "Begone, you

wee fiend, and let the gel breathe." He pulled Alexander aside, then held out his hand for Madelyn. "Come with me. You're wanted inside." He took her hand and pulled her to her feet.

And once she was there, there was no sense in not pulling her into his arms. He held her close, closed his eyes, and allowed himself the pleasure of feeling her arms go around him.

"We'll stay here for a bit," he whispered. "You'll be safe."

She pulled back and looked up at him. "This is too much—"

He smiled at her. " 'Tis a small thing, in the grander scheme of things. Come and be at peace. Then again, Alex lives here, too. You may not have much peace while he's awake."

"It seems a small price to pay."

"See how you feel ten minutes before his bedtime." He took her hand. "Let's go in."

She nodded, put her shoulders back gingerly, then hobbled with him into the house. Jane MacLeod, Ian's wife of four years, was waiting in the living room. She immediately took Madelyn in hand.

"You look exhausted," she said gently. "What do you want first, food or sleep?"

Madelyn looked at her in surprise. "You're American."

"Born and bred."

"But you're here."

"Ian was persuasive." She took Madelyn by the arm. "It's a great country, but the taxes are bad. Where are you from? What do you do? What brings you to Scotland? How did you meet our Pat?"

Madelyn laughed a little uneasily as she disappeared up the stairs. "He was running over sheep. . . ."

"I did *not* run over sheep," Patrick said. " 'Tis for precisely that reason that my Vanquish sits in Inverness receiving Douglas's loving ministrations." He realized he was speaking to no one, so he sighed and walked into the kitchen.

Ian was busy with breakfast. Patrick took a seat at the table.

Patrick sighed. " 'Tis a rescue, nothing more," he said. "She needed aid; I was at hand."

"Hmmm," Ian said, noncommittally.

"I am not seeking a bride."

"Didn't say you were."

"You didn't have to say it."

"Saints, Patrick"—Ian laughed—"you're a bit touchy about this."

"She bothers me."

"I can see why. Beautiful women bother the hell out of me. I can scarce bear living with Jane because of it."

Patrick scowled. " 'Tisn't that. This is not what I want right now."

"Then walk away."

"She needs my aid."

Ian turned around, spoon in hand. "What a romantic heart you have, cousin."

Would he get no peace from his damned heart? Bad enough that it plagued him. Now the souls about him were reminding him of it as well.

"I'm a fool."

"Love makes fools of us all."

"Not me," Patrick said. "Not twice."

Ian turned back to his shiny red Aga stove. "Love, if it is to endure, must be reciprocated, Pat."

Patrick pursed his lips and stared at the table. "I talk too much," he muttered.

"I am discreet," Ian said, beginning to put food on plates, "which is why you tell me things you won't tell Jamie— much as we both love him."

Ian had it aright. Besides, if Jamie knew half of what Ian did about Patrick's past, it would send him to his library for a year at least, trying to unravel the horrors of Patrick's twisted heart.

Ian set a plate down in front of Patrick. "I'll look her over if you like. Give you my unbiased opinion."

"Oh, aye," Patrick said, " 'tis that that I've been holding out for."

"You could do worse. I'm happily wed."

"And that through no virtue of your own. Jane has a good heart and a blind eye."

"Heard my name," Jane said, walking in and shepherding children. "If you must speak in the native tongue, do it more slowly so I can follow."

Patrick admired the hell out of her. Not only did she endure his cousin, she loved the Highlands with a passion that rivaled Ian's own, and she spoke Gaelic as well as they did—her deprecating words aside.

"How's Madelyn?"

"Exhausted. What did you do to her?"

"Wearied her with scrutiny," Ian said wisely.

Patrick snorted. "I merely rescued."

"She seems nice," Jane said.

"She is," Patrick said. "She is quite nice."

"I have a thought," Ian said. "Why don't you just spend a few days enjoying her company and let nature take its course. You might find that you don't like her at all."

"Or you might find that you love her very much," Jane said.

Patrick honestly wasn't sure what would be worse.

And he most certainly did not want his heart's opinion on the matter. He knew already what it would tell him.

It was too soon.

Not soon enough, it whispered.

He set to his meal, trying to bury his thoughts and those damned whispers under as much butter and marmalade as possible.

Chapter 13

Madelyn leaned on the sink and stared at herself in the mirror. Almost twenty-four hours of sleep, yet she still felt like a zombie. Her wet hair dripped down onto her shoulders, hung around her face. She tugged, watched it spring back, and wished she had the energy to straighten it. Maybe after she'd gotten rid of the dark craters that were her eye sockets. Who knew how long that would take? Probably not before she'd gone home and lost potential jobs due to her appearance.

Too much stress, too little sleep. It was no wonder she looked so bad. Of course, two days in the local jail cell hadn't done much for her, either. She'd threatened to sue so often she'd started to sound like Bentley.

And where was that foul piece of primordial slime? She didn't know, she didn't care. She just never wanted to see him again.

The other person she could do without encountering was that Hamish Fergusson. If she'd had to listen to him rant about the MacLeods one more time, she would have lost it. What was his problem? So the MacLeod she knew best was good-looking, well-off, and quite charming. Was that any reason to hate him and his kin so ferociously? Now, if he'd imparted any decent tidbits about Patrick or his family, it might have been interesting, but all he'd done was complain about their money, their looks, and their fast cars.

It had been, on the whole, a very forgettable two days.

She'd never been so glad in her life to hear a friendly voice as she had been to hear Patrick coming in like an avenging angel. It had made the previous bit of hell almost worth it.

But what to do now? She rubbed her eyes and sighed.

Things did not look good. She was for all intents and purposes quite destitute, quite devoid of her passport, and no longer in possession of her plane ticket. She might as well be invisible as far as her identification went. Her options were few and quite clear-cut.

She would have to get a new passport and that would require calling some family member to overnight her some kind of identification. And that family member certainly wouldn't be either her mother or her father. Maybe Sunny would be willing to go through the files sitting in her parents' garage and find the necessary items. Sunny would exact a price for it, but it would definitely not involve any verbs, and that was a price Madelyn was willing to pay.

She supposed she would also have to get back to London to get her replacement passport, and who knew how long that would take, or how she would get there. The embassy had to have some kind of emergency procedure for renewing passports immediately, didn't they? And the airline would have some sort of pity procedure for those unlucky enough to have their purses stolen, wouldn't they?

A girl could hope.

She splashed water on her face, then left the bathroom in Jane MacLeod's flannel rainbow jammies. She went and sat on the bed. At least she was sitting more easily. She looked around the cheerful yellow room, grateful beyond measure for the kindness of strangers and mortally embarrassed to have to take advantage of it.

Accepting aid was not her strong suit.

She caught sight of a large shopping bag sitting just inside the door. There was a piece of paper sticking up from it. She closed her eyes briefly and swallowed her pride. More gifts from people she didn't know. She made a vow right then that she would return the favor by helping someone else.

But it didn't make any of Jane's generosity any easier to take.

Well, hand-me-downs from Jane had to fit better than hand-me-downs from Miriam MacLeod. She got up, walked over to the bag, and took the note.

Madelyn,

A thing or two to get you by. I daresay this falls under necessities. . . .

Patrick

Madelyn reread the note, but it still said the same thing. She lugged the large bag back to the bed. Maybe Marks & Spencer really meant Marks & Spencer. She pulled out—in her size, no less—clothes that were definitely inappropriate for court.

The man might not be willing to punch Bentley in the nose, but he knew how to shop.

A couple of bulky, luscious sweaters, three pairs of jeans, several shirts, a handful of warm socks, and a beautiful tartan skirt that flowed to her ankles. There were flannel jammies in lime green and two shoeboxes with "not sure about size" scrawled on the tops. Boots came out of one box, boots suitable for Highland hiking. Out of the other came loafers that were buttery soft and fit like a dream.

And in the very bottom, tucked discreetly under a warm corduroy dress, were underclothes wrapped in tissue paper.

She clutched the underwear to her chest, sat down in the middle of a new wardrobe, and began to cry. If she hadn't been so pathetically grateful, she would have cried with more enthusiasm. As it was, all she could do was sit there and let her eyes leak copious amounts of tears. This was really the last straw. How could she ever repay this? And it wasn't just the money, though she could readily add up in her head what the cut-off portions of the tags likely had said. It wasn't even the kindness of a decent wardrobe.

It was the gift of clothes she loved immediately and the effort, however small, that had gone into choosing something she would have liked.

Not an ounce of polyester in sight.

She dragged her sleeve across her eyes, got up, and blew her nose, then went back to the side of the bed and looked down at Patrick's shopping spree. Well, she might be poor, but she was going to look great while she was at it.

She dressed in jeans and a sweater and didn't bother doing anything but running her fingers through her hair.

It felt wonderful.

She left the haven of Jane's cheery yellow guest room and went downstairs barefoot. She would do the dishes. That would be a good start on repaying MacLeod kindnesses. Jane could probably use some baby-sitting as well. Patrick could use a construction crew, but she'd work on that later. She could at least use a broom and dustpan and make inroads over at his place. She knew how to be useful. But that didn't really solve her cash-flow problem at the moment.

She didn't want to think coming to Scotland had been a bad idea.

She was having a hard time coming to any other conclusion.

She paused on the stairwell. She had no choice. She would have to bum money off her parents. Maybe she could make that phone call right after she'd called to beg her sister to do the dirty work of finding her identification for her.

But later. She wasn't going to ruin her last good day in Scotland with either of those phone calls. They could wait until evening. She continued down the stairs and followed her ears to where the most racket was being made. It sounded like breakfast was in full swing.

"Sarah, love, cereal goes in your mouth, not onto the floor," Jane said patiently.

Madelyn walked in to see a little girl now flinging her breakfast onto her mother's head. Jane looked up from where she was kneeling in front of her daughter's high chair. Oatmeal dripped down onto her nose.

Madelyn couldn't help herself. She laughed.

Jane wiped the food off with the back of her hand. "Oh, yeah, it's hysterical," she agreed darkly. "She's experimenting with gravity."

"So I see," Madelyn said.

Jane wiped up the floor, then stood and looked at her kids. "I think a bath for the both of you is in order."

Alexander did not like the idea at all and began to protest

loudly. Sarah took the opportunity of motherly distraction her brother's complaints afforded her to dump her entire bowl of oatmeal onto the floor. Jane pushed flaming red hair out of her face with an oatmeal-covered hand.

It looked as if they all three should go have a bath.

"I'll deal with this," Madelyn said, taking the sponge from Jane. "You have your hands full."

"Thank you," Jane said, sounding disproportionately grateful. "You don't have to—"

"Are you kidding?" Madelyn said. "Piece of cake compared to what you're up against."

"You have a point." Jane looked at her son. "No bath, no Legos. We don't play with sticky hands."

As Madelyn had already learned, Legos were a big thing in the MacLeod household. Alexander abruptly stopped protesting. He looked at his mother with enormous blue eyes.

"I yike Yegos," he said seriously.

"Of course you do," she said, unstrapping Sarah from her high chair. "And you like them clean, so let's get ourselves equally as clean so you can play with them. Maybe you can show Madelyn how they work after your bath."

Alexander looked at her expectantly.

"I'm there for you," Madelyn said readily, hoping she would be equal to it. How bad could it be? She'd already heard one small story about red blocks pinning blue and green ones in an impenetrable fortress. She could hardly wait to hear what he would come up with later.

"Upstairs," Jane said, turning Alexander around and pointing him in the right direction. "Thanks, Madelyn. Help yourself to breakfast."

Madelyn watched them go and paused briefly to examine the fact that the thought of playing with a three-year-old didn't sound completely horrible. He was darn cute and she suspected he wouldn't throw any oatmeal in her hair. Sarah, though, was an unknown quantity. Maybe Madelyn would do well to put her hair up before bathtime was over.

She cleaned up the floor, the high chair, and the table. Dishes were quickly finished, and she was just helping herself to hot cereal from the community pot when it occurred to her that she hadn't seen Ian or Patrick that morning. Were they sleeping in? Somehow she doubted it, but it wasn't as if she knew them very well. Maybe they'd stayed up half the night playing with Alexander's Legos while he was asleep. Stranger things had happened.

Then she finally looked out the kitchen window she'd been standing in front of for twenty minutes.

Her bowl fell from her hands.

Good thing it had been one of the kids' plastic ones. Her oatmeal was in the sink, but did that really matter when compared to what she was seeing outside?

Jane and Ian had an enormous backyard. They had a garden. They had a swingset. They had a deck that was probably full of furniture during the summer but was now empty in preparation for winter. They also had a very large grassy place that looked perfect for the playing of croquet, horseshoes, or a little touch football with a very large extended family. But there was no football going on today.

There were two fools out there hacking at each other with swords.

Madelyn stared, openmouthed, as Patrick and Ian fought. She'd never seen anything like it, not even in movies. In movies, it looked choreographed. She knew it was choreographed so the actors, when brave enough, or the stuntmen, when skilled enough, didn't get themselves killed. They also used, she assumed, swords that didn't have sharp edges.

She'd felt that sword Patrick was using.

Her finger still ached from the cut.

She set her spoon down, walked over to the back door, and eased it open until she could peer out just the slightest bit.

The ring of steel was startling at first, but she soon grew accustomed to it. There wasn't much conversation going on, but what there was of it was being conducted in the native tongue. Ian said something and Patrick laughed, then they both continued to chop at each other as if they had every intention of inflicting bodily harm.

Were they out of their minds?

No wonder they scared the hell out of Hamish Fergusson. She wouldn't have wanted to tangle with them, either.

They must have been quite an asset to their reenactment society.

Cattle raiding . . . enemies to slay . . .

Moraig's words teased the edge of her memory, but she honestly couldn't remember what else the old woman had said. Something about Patrick not being able to do that these days. She could see how he might be good at it, given the way he used his sword.

He gave Ian a shove backward, stripped off his shirt, and continued fighting.

Madelyn fanned herself surreptitiously.

She hoped, not quite so absently, that they'd just begun their workout.

She continued to stare at them in fascination, though in all honesty, she spent more time looking at Patrick than Ian, and not just because he'd taken off his shirt. It was the fact that she'd sat next to the man in a car, sobbed all over him just the morning before, and she hadn't had a clue what he was capable of.

If Bentley could have seen this, he would have peed his pants.

And then the unthinkable happened.

Patrick tripped backward over some sort of children's outdoor transportation device. She started to yell a warning, but found herself rendered quite speechless by the fact that Ian didn't blink. He didn't offer to help, either. He simply took advantage of the fact that his cousin was flat on his back and tried to stab him where he was.

Patrick rolled and was back on his feet, spewing a mouthful of what had to be curses, almost faster than she could follow. Ian only laughed and continued a very relentless assault.

Things took an ugly turn.

They used the deck, they used the rock wall, they even used bits of the kids' very sturdy swingset—nothing was apparently very sacred when it came to trying to kill each other. Curses flew, sweat dripped (she fanned herself more at that point), and the ring of swords was so loud and so fierce she almost had to close the door so she wouldn't have to hear it anymore.

Good grief, who *were* these guys?

She decided on the spot that a visit to Moraig was most definitely in order.

"Oh, thanks for doing the dishes!"

Madelyn almost fell over in shock. She turned toward Jane, who looked a good deal tidier than she had been earlier that morning, and gestured weakly to the great outdoors.

"Have you seen . . ." she began. Well, of course Jane had seen. Madelyn took a deep breath. "Where did they learn that?"

Jane continued to smile, but it was a very careful smile all of a sudden.

Madelyn's BS radar kicked into high gear. A half-truth was coming; she would have staked her career on it. She pretended not to notice Jane wringing her hands.

"Oh, here and there," Jane said vaguely. "It sort of runs in the family."

"Is that so?" Madelyn asked. "Reenactment society and all that, I suppose."

"Sure," Jane said, nodding enthusiastically. "Highland games, that sort of thing. You know boys and their toys."

"Right," Madelyn said. "Interesting toys."

"Aren't they, though. Would you excuse me?"

Madelyn moved aside so Jane could open the back door fully. She called to Ian and Patrick in Gaelic, and they immediately put up their very unusual toys. Madelyn liked the cadence of the language. She was surprised her mother hadn't learned it. Her father knew it. At the moment Madelyn wished she'd spent less time practicing the songs of Scotland on her violin and more time learning its language.

"They didn't have to stop," Madelyn said.

"Oh, well," Jane said uneasily, "they were done anyway."

"I see," Madelyn said.

"I've got to get back to the kids. Sarah's into everything. Want to come?"

What she wanted was to stand right where she was and unravel the mystery of Patrick's morning exercise, but she was nothing if not polite, so she followed Jane into the living room. She sat on the floor and examined Alexander's Legos until Ian and Patrick came through on their way to the showers. They were all smiles.

And no swords.

Something was definitely afoot here.

And she was definitely not one to let a good mystery go unsolved.

"Be back in a minute," Patrick said as he headed for the stairs.

"Sure," she said, smiling briefly at Ian, who followed hard on Patrick's heels. She looked at Jane to distract herself. "So," Madelyn said easily, "where are you from? If you don't mind my asking."

"Indiana," Jane said. "And you?"

"Seattle."

"Then you should like Scotland. It's your kind of climate."

"I love it. So, how did you meet Ian?"

"New York. I was designing bridal gowns and he . . . um . . . wandered into our salon one day."

"You design bridal gowns?" Madelyn asked, stunned. "Do you still?"

"Nah, I got sick of white," Jane said easily. "I weave now, sell a few things down in the village, other things in London. Just to keep a little finger in the pie. The kids are what I concentrate on."

Madelyn couldn't imagine trading in a career like that for the intellectual stimulation of two small children. She needed to think, to fight, to right wrongs in the courtroom. She was sure of it.

At least she was pretty sure of it.

"Mama," Sarah said, spontaneously throwing arms around her mother. She crawled into Jane's lap, snuggled close, popped her thumb into her mouth, and proceeded to sigh the sigh of a completely content child.

Madelyn suddenly became quite unsure of everything.

She blinked several times to keep her tears where they belonged. Good heavens, what was that? Her biological clock chiming with all the subtlety of Big Ben?

Patrick came tromping down the stairs. He walked into the room, picked up Alexander, and tossed him into the air to the accompaniment of squeals of delight. He set the boy down, then looked down at Madelyn.

"Sleep well?"

"Like the dead."

"Quite the change from the continual mutterings of Hamish Fergusson, no doubt," Patrick said, plopping down on the couch. "He's always full of complaints. Damn those Fergussons. Never have liked them." He flashed Jane a teasing smile. "There might be an exception now and then."

"Big of you," Jane said. She looked at Madelyn. "I'm an American Fergusson, and Pat has never forgiven Ian for dipping into the enemy's gene pool."

"Untrue," Patrick said. "Rather, I'm jealous he managed to find a gem amongst the refuse."

"I *think* that's a compliment," Jane said with a laugh, "but I'm not sure. And you know Hamish and I just can't be related, no matter how distantly."

"You'd like to believe that," Patrick said with a smile.

"I have to believe it, though I use our common ancestors to get out of speeding tickets. Hamish feels sorry for me being married to one of those dastardly MacLeods."

"No doubt," Patrick snorted.

Madelyn watched them tease and wondered at the ease of it. They didn't tease in her family. Well, to be honest, her parents didn't tease. Sunny teased and Madelyn tried to figure out what she meant by it.

A by-product of herbs, probably. Sunny sniffed too many things that made her quite happy and content.

Madelyn was tempted to dose herself up with a few when she got home.

"You look beautiful," Patrick said. "That sweater suits you."

She realized he was talking to her. She smoothed her hand over the sweater a little self-consciously. "Yes, it is lovely. I don't know where to begin to thank you."

"Oh, no," Jane said with a laugh, "don't give him that

kind of free rein. He'll be having you muck out his stables if you're not careful."

"Or, worse yet," Ian said as he walked into the room, "he'll have you being his date to any number of social functions."

"I don't go to social functions," Patrick said.

"That's because you don't have a beautiful woman feeling guilty enough to go with you," Ian said, dropping down onto the floor near Jane. "Take advantage of it."

Patrick looked at Madelyn. "Ian babbles. Now, have you given thought to your list? Perhaps we should see a few sights hereabout before we go get your passport."

Had it suddenly gotten hot or was it humiliation burning through her that had made her begin to perspire?

"I chucked my list," she said. "I probably should be getting home anyway."

"Of course you shouldn't," Jane said. "You're here. You should see the sights. Pat is a great tour guide."

"He knows lots of interesting historical facts," Ian said blandly. "If you can put up with his miserable personality long enough to get at them. And if you can get him to be silent about supposed historical inaccuracies the tour guides spout."

Patrick glared at Ian and said something that had to have been uncomplimentary in Gaelic. Ian only laughed and turned to wink at Madelyn.

"He's foul-humored, just as I said."

Patrick rose. "I'll go fetch the maps and we'll make your list."

"No, really," Madelyn said, holding out her hand, "I couldn't. You've all been so kind, and I just can't impose—"

"It's not an imposition," Jane said.

Madelyn took a deep breath. "If I could just use the phone, I can get my parents to wire me some money—"

Patrick put his hand briefly on her head as he passed. "Jane has pen and paper somewhere. She'll fetch that; I'll fetch the maps."

Madelyn wasn't sure she wasn't going to burst into tears again. As it was, she had to blink furiously for several moments to get herself back under control. Jane got up and went into the kitchen. Madelyn couldn't even look at Ian.

" 'Tis a hard thing," he mused, "isn't it?"

She looked at him. "What? Accepting charity?"

He smiled. She could see why Jane had fallen for him. Poor Hamish Fergusson. It was no wonder he was jealous.

"Aye," he said simply. "I had to once and it fair killed me. But if it eases you any, Patrick can afford it. And I daresay he needs time with you as much as you need aid from him."

"How do you figure?"

"A beautiful woman who doesn't care about his bank account? What lad couldn't use that?"

"I do care about his bank account. I don't want to decimate it."

Ian laughed. "Not to worry. He'll survive whatever small dent you might make in it. Nay," he said, shaking his head with a smile, "you're the dose of sunshine he needs. Let him see to you for a few days. It will do him good to be unselfish for a change."

"I couldn't, really," Madelyn said. "He's done too much already."

"Aye, and see what a fine humor it's put him in," Ian said. "Look how he smiles instead of scowls."

Patrick threw a pillow at his cousin, then dropped down next to Madelyn on the floor. He accepted pen and paper from Jane on her way by, then looked at Madelyn expectantly.

"Well?"

She took a deep breath. "I can't, really."

"Then I'll make your list for you."

"Poor gel," Ian said sympathetically.

"Fish hatchery," Patrick said, tapping his chin thoughtfully. "Oil refinery. Waste treatment plant."

"Oh, Patrick"—Jane laughed as she sat down next to her son—"choose some decent things for her to see. There is so much beauty here."

"Aye, precisely as I've told her," Patrick said. He looked at Madelyn. "Do you want the pen?"

She wasn't sure what would be worse, watching Patrick

make a list, or doing it herself. "I can't," she said seriously. "My flight home is on Sunday. I need to be doing business—"

"We'll do all that," Patrick assured her. "In good time. For now, make your list."

"But—"

He held out a pen.

She looked at it.

He took her hand, put the pen into it, then closed her fingers around it. He didn't release her hand.

"Make your list, Madelyn," he said gently.

And just how was she to make a list when she couldn't see the paper for the tears swimming in her eyes? "I suppose I could make a day's worth," she managed.

"Two weeks," he countered.

She blinked. It helped clear away the tears. "Patrick, there's no way—"

He took the pen back with a sigh. "I do know where all the industrial parks are, of course."

"Pat, stop teasing," Jane said. "Madelyn, think of your dream vacation. You don't have to do everything."

She hesitated. It was killing her to say no, killing her to say yes.

Patrick leaned close. That about killed her, too.

"Old, musty train museums," he began.

"I like trains," Ian protested.

Patrick shot him a look, then leaned closer. "A nine-hundred-year look at farming implements," he whispered. "Very interesting. Very dusty. Very sharp."

"Oh, good grief." Jane laughed. "Madelyn, put him out of our misery."

Maybe just for a day or two. A day or two in Patrick MacLeod's company, seeing Scotland from his eyes.

A day or two looking into Patrick MacLeod's eyes.

Could that be so bad?

He leaned even closer. "Ruins. Moldy old piles of stones coated with history. Crumbling stairs, weedy garden patches, monasteries full of ghosts."

Madelyn shivered.

And it had nothing to do with ghosts.

"Aye, do the ruins," Ian advised. " 'Tis better that way, for you'll have no guides to offend. As I said, historical inaccuracies get under his skin and he's quite vocal about it."

Patrick snorted. "I won't get us tossed out."

"It wouldn't be the first time," Ian noted. He looked at Madelyn. "Be forewarned."

Patrick put his arm around her. "I'll keep my mouth shut. Now, pick out a castle or two for the day and we'll be on our way. I promise to behave." He looked at her and winked. "For the most part."

A handful of days with nothing to do but watch him try to behave? A handful of days alone with him, looking at castles, gardens, and ruins, and trying very hard not to fall helplessly into those emerald pools he had for eyes?

Heaven help her, she was in trouble.

Chapter 14

B entley Douglas Taylor III, Esquire, stood in front of a pitifully inadequate pub in the middle of a painfully primitive village in the wilds of rural Scotland and wondered how in the hell he'd managed to let himself be talked into dealing with these kinds of conditions.

It was, as with a great number of things, all Madelyn's fault.

He walked in the door, strode up to the bar, and banged on the counter. The native took an inordinate amount of time to see to him and was reluctant to take his order, but Bentley was hungry and surely the kitchen could be opened an hour early. He retreated to a comfortable—marginally, of course—seat to wait.

Things were just not proceeding as he had planned. His life just wasn't going as he had intended. Damn that Richard Phillips! He hadn't behaved at all as Bentley had expected him to. Stupid academics. They were perpetually lost in their ivory towers, places so out of touch with reality, Bentley often wondered how they managed to feed and clothe themselves.

Of course, when *he* took his seat in yon ivory tower, he would do things far differently.

He drummed his fingers on the table. It was getting into that tower—and getting himself seated on the lofty throne of Dean of the Law School—that was proving to be more difficult than he had anticipated.

His plan had first included befriending Dean Anderson, everyone's favorite shoo-in for all sorts of high honors, and doing so by befriending *his* friend, the brilliant linguist Richard Phillips. As rumor had it, Phillips and the Dean had been roommates during their undergrad years at Harvard.

Concentrating on how to get to Phillips had been uppermost on his mind one winter afternoon last year as he'd been idly scanning the up-and-comer staff list for potential threats to his own status. Whose name should he have noticed but Madelyn Phillips, DD&P's rising young star. She was pretty, she was brilliant, and he had quickly found out that she was related to her father.

Handy, he'd thought at the time.

His pursual of Madelyn had been pitifully easy, but his attempts to get in good with her father had not. Damn the man for his obsession with words.

Words were, as fate would have it, not Bentley's strong suit.

He didn't like to admit that weakness. He also never showed anyone the word-a-day calendar hidden in the locked drawer of his desk, or the tapes that promised he could use Large Words with Confidence in no time at all that lurked under the front seat of his car.

He wasn't stupid, he just didn't have time for trivialities. Or words longer than three syllables. And all that foreign gibberish? It belonged on the foreign soil it had come from.

Unfortunately, Richard Phillips hadn't been impressed by any of his words—which left Bentley wondering if he hadn't used the really long ones correctly—or by his $2,000 Italian silk suits. Bentley had done everything short of actually falling in love with Madelyn to try to get her father to like him.

It had been a complete waste of time.

And once he found out that Richard and the Dean weren't all that close—some sort of falling out over some obscure bit of Latin grammar—what had been the point of having anything further to do with that obnoxiously organized daughter of his?

No point that he'd been able to see.

And once he'd dumped her, irritation over her father's dismissal of him had really begun to get to him, and he'd made a few phone calls to get back at her dad by destroying his daughter financially.

And then he'd seen the Dean and Phillips having lunch together, laughing like the old friends they were, damn them both. That had left him back at the beginning. And with Madelyn destitute and vulnerable, taking her back had seemed like the easiest way to get what he wanted. He hadn't counted on any resistance.

Yet another reason they were certainly not suitable for each other.

Not to worry, he assured himself quickly. He didn't have to marry her. He could simply drag out an engagement with her for as long as it took for her father to recognize his innate intelligence, befriend him, and hastily introduce him to Dean Anderson.

And then his quick rise up the steps of that ivory tower would begin in earnest and he would be able to shove that in his own academic father's face.

Of course, none of that would happen until he found the woman in question. He'd already discovered she wasn't where he'd left her—in that primitive jail cell. That useless Hamish Fergusson hadn't had any idea where she was, only that she'd left with Patrick MacLeod.

He'd looked at MacLeod's house, but found nothing.

He'd gone to James MacLeod's castle, but peeking over the garden wall had shown him nothing but a large man waving a sword around. Bentley had determined immediately that such a man was not one he wanted to converse with, so he'd retreated and wondered if hiring someone to find Madelyn might be a good next step.

It beat the hell out of doing it himself.

Yes, that's what he would do. And when he found Madelyn, he would inform her of his decision to take her back. Convincing her of her course of action wouldn't be a problem. He'd already shown her what he could to do her financially. Other threats could be used as easily.

"Service!" he bellowed.

His food arrived. Not as quickly as he would have liked, but it came.

Good grief, didn't these people know how to deep fry?

He shook his head and decided that the sooner he was

back on his home turf, the happier he—and his stomach—would be. So, therefore, the sooner Madelyn was found the better.

And this time she would know better than to refuse him.

Chapter 15

Madelyn lifted the guest room's curtain and looked out. The view of the countryside was nothing short of breathtaking and she indulged in a brief bit of envy that Jane Fergusson MacLeod called that view hers. How would it be to look at this view every day, to have it there just waiting for you to walk out and enjoy it each morning when you woke up?

She sighed. Well, that view was hers for at least another day or so, given that she would have to wait for old passports and birth certificate to arrive from her sister.

The phone calls had been made the night before. At least one of them had. When she'd started to call her parents to beg for cash, Patrick had taken the phone away from her.

Necessities and comforts, he'd said.

She'd tried to insist.

He'd distracted her with some lovely coffee-table books on castles.

She sighed. She would have to call her parents eventually. Maybe after she'd determined the proper idiomatic Latin translation of "out of the frying pan and into the fire."

She let the curtain drop, briefly fondled the new sweater she was wearing thanks to Patrick MacLeod's exquisite taste, then headed for the door. Jane could use help; she was sure of it. Madelyn might be mooching off them for another day or two, but she wouldn't do it without at least trying to offer some kind of service in return.

She walked down the stairs, following the sound of two children at play. All right, so Sarah was playing and Alexander was trying to keep her from extending her scope of amusement to his beloved Legos, but who was arguing? Familial bliss was preserved.

Madelyn envied them all.

Jane looked up from her referee position between her two children.

"You're up early."

"I think I'm finally adjusted to the time change." She yawned anyway, just on principle.

"How was yesterday?"

Madelyn smiled. "Wonderful, until Patrick got us thrown out. He doesn't suffer fools—or British tour guides—gladly, does he?"

Jane shook her head. "He thinks anyone born south of Hadrian's wall—no, I can't even say that. He thinks anyone born south of Inverness shouldn't be giving lectures on the Highlands. He probably has a point."

"He makes it forcefully."

"He can't help himself. So, did you get to see anything else?"

Madelyn nodded. "Gardens, forests, a few ruins." *Patrick's face for the whole of the day.* Really, could a vacation get any better than that?

Jane began to pick up toys. "What's your plan for the day? The men have gone to pick up Pat's car at Inverness, so you don't have to hurry."

"That was a fast fix."

"Pat's mechanic likes to keep him happy. He always goes to the head of the line."

Madelyn shuddered. "Please don't tell me he's got his cars in the shop that often. I think I still have some traveling to do with the man."

"Generally it's tune-ups only," Jane said with a smile. "He rarely has any other kinds of issues. He and Ian left early, but you'll still have a couple of hours to kill."

She smiled. The perfect chance to pitch in and repay a small bit of their kindness, in spite of any protest Jane might put up. The woman was up to her elbows in diapers, laundry, and toddler toys. Surely she could use a break, a bit of free time to do her nails, read a book, take a bath.

"All right," Madelyn said, rubbing her hands together,

"I'm on duty for as long as you need me. What kinds of games do the kids like?"

"Not a chance. This is your vacation; you need to be taking it. You know, you could go over to Pat's place, if you don't mind the walk."

"But," she protested, "surely you could use help—"

"I'm fine. Ian's taking a break between sessions, so I have all the help I need."

"Sessions?"

"He teaches swordplay," Jane said, without blinking. "To stuntmen types, or rich guys with time on their hands and egos to match. Oh, and the occasional actor into realism."

"Interesting," Madelyn said, trying to sound casual. In reality, she could hardly believe her ears. Ian teaching swordplay? There were actually people who *paid* him to do that sword business to them? She wondered if he broke them in slowly, or humiliated them right off so they knew what they were getting into. "He must be pretty good to do that," she said.

"He is," Jane said with a grin. "He'll tell you how good if you ask. The men he trains would probably say the same thing."

"Where'd he learn it again?"

"Family business," Jane said. "You should see Jamie. Ian and Pat are good, but Jamie's the master. At least we all tell him he's the master. He goes out of his way to prove that when anyone tells him anything else."

"That must be entertaining."

"*Frightening*'s more the word I'd use, but that's just my opinion. Now, go take your walk. You won't regret it."

"But—"

"Go," Jane said, pointing to the door. "Sarah, don't eat that . . ."

Madelyn hated to leave when Jane seemed to be distracted. Grilling her while she was keeping her baby from ingesting small toys was obviously the way to go. Family business, huh? Well, that was an interesting way to put it. Madelyn filed that away with all the other tidbits she'd been acquiring.

This was some family, she had to concede, with some big backlog of secrets.

It was incredibly tempting to try to find them all out.

Maybe a walk to Patrick's house wasn't such a bad idea. She could snoop under the guise of cleaning. Who knew what she would uncover?

"Maybe I will go, if you're sure you don't need help."

"I'm sure, but hold on a minute," Jane said. "You'll want a map. Why don't you grab breakfast and I'll get you one."

"Is it really that hard to find from here?"

"It's not that it's hard to find," Jane said. "It's just that, well, there are a few pitfalls. . . ."

"All that Highland magic?" Madelyn asked easily.

Jane looked at her in surprise. "What?"

"Roddy MacLeod told me to be careful, that the forests here were full of Highland magic."

Jane laughed uneasily. "Well, he has quite an imagination."

"Does he now."

"Oh, yes. Breakfast is still hot."

Madelyn took the hint. She also took the opportunity to get some breakfast. She put her dishes away, then went back into the living room. Jane handed her a map.

"Just avoid all the places marked in red."

"And if I don't?"

Jane paused. She seemed to be weighing the telling of truth against something Madelyn wasn't sure about, then she shrugged. "I just wouldn't," she finished.

The tone of her voice was sobering. Madelyn decided to reserve judgment on what the red dots might mean. If Jane thought she should avoid them, then avoid them she would.

Until she knew more, of course, then she would tramp over them with enthusiasm and no doubt dislodge something very interesting.

"I'll be careful," Madelyn promised, taking the map and folding it up. "How long do you think I have?"

"At least a couple of hours," Jane said. "Pat's going to lose his license if he doesn't slow down, so he'll probably be careful today. He and Ian left early, but not that early.

Oh, wait a minute." She went in to the kitchen and came back with a cell phone. "Take this. My number's programmed in. Call me if you get stuck and I'll come get you."

"Thanks," Madelyn said, taking the phone. "I'll try not to get lost."

"I wouldn't."

There was that tone of voice again. Madelyn suppressed a shiver. "Okay. I'll be back." She patted the kids good-bye, thanked Jane for the loan of her coat, then left the house before she had a chance to think any more about the map she held in her hands or what it might mean.

She stood on the front stoop, took a deep breath and closed her eyes to savor the chill and the lack of exhaust fumes. Life was pretty good, in spite of the fact that she had basically nothing but the clothes on her back—plus the new wardrobe in her room upstairs, of course—and a borrowed phone in her pocket. Did she really need more than that to survive?

Actually, she did, but she wasn't going to think about that right now. She pulled out the map and made an effort to concentrate on what was in front of her. Lots of red dots, but the path that snaked through them was very clear. It was also very clear before her in real life, as if it had been walked over many times.

Or purposely cleared so a person didn't get lost.

She kept to the path and enjoyed the scenery. And it was breathtaking scenery. What deciduous trees there were had their fall colors still clinging to them, but the bulk of the forest came from evergreens. It reminded her a great deal of her own home, but this was far more primitive, as if time had simply overlooked this bit of land. Time and developers, she supposed.

It was forty-five minutes before she reached Patrick's. The journey hadn't been without its hair-raising moments. Entering the forest that separated Patrick's meadow from Ian's had made her unaccountably nervous. She'd walked the faint path with religious attention to where she was going, just on the off chance that those red dots meant something foul.

But now that she was back out in the light—what there

was of it and that wasn't much because apparently the blue skies were gone for the year—she was able to breathe and relax. She walked down the little hill to Patrick's house.

She looked around her carefully. No Keystone cops, no Bentley with evil designs upon her person, no strange creatures springing up from the red dots to make her life miserable. She was set.

She wandered around his courtyard. She picked up the occasional stone she could actually lift and set it back in its proper place. After hefting one particularly heavy piece of rock, she stood back and surveyed the damage. It would take weeks with muscles much more capable than hers to do this work.

She paused and looked at the front door. It was a rustic bit of wood that looked as if it was centuries old. How many people had knocked on it? she wondered. What had they worn, what had they eaten, what had they sat on when they were welcomed into the front room?

Hopefully more than was there, she decided as she walked into the house. Patrick needed to get some furniture. How long had he been sitting on this pitiful stool in front of the fire? It was something even Cinderella probably would have objected to.

Maybe the kitchen needed cleaning. She flipped on the light and looked inside the room. He had a stove reminiscent of Ian's, but this one was not new. There were worn cabinets, a large farmhouse type of sink, and a small refrigerator. She walked across the stone floor and opened the fridge.

Nothing inside.

Either he was good at finishing his leftovers, or he didn't eat here much. She shut the door. The same loaf of moldy bread sat on the counter, but she left it alone. Maybe he was working on a science experiment.

She stood back and surveyed his culinary domain. It wasn't pretty. It had none of the warmth of Jane's kitchen. Maybe it just lacked a family to give it warmth.

Well, that and food, a table, and some dishes.

For a moment, she had a vision of a family in the room,

children laughing, two parents watching over their brood with tenderness and affection.

She was one of those parents.

Patrick was the other.

"Oh, please," she said, rolling her eyes. She really had to get a grip on her rampaging hormones. She turned around and walked away before she really lost her mind.

She found herself quite without warning standing at the entrance to Patrick's bedroom. She flipped on the bare bulb overhead and stared at the armoire.

Sword or no sword?

Only one way to find out.

She opened the armoire and looked inside.

No sword.

She wasn't surprised. It was probably hiding with Ian's at Ian's house. She reached out to touch the very old-looking plaid blanket.

Bagpipes started up in the distance.

She jumped back, shut the armoire door, and rubbed her arms.

"All right, this is just too creepy," she said to no one in particular. It was no doubt what she deserved for poking around in a place she shouldn't be.

She left Patrick's room and made her way out the back door.

The pipes were coming from the top of the hill. She started across the enormous backyard, climbed gingerly over the low rock wall, and started up the hill before she thought to check on either the condition of her tailbone or her position on the map.

Patrick's hill was reassuringly free of red dots and a careful wiggle showed her tailbone to be in remarkably good working order. She paused and listened. The music was still there. Well, whoever it was had better be prepared to be kicked off the hill. Patrick couldn't be happy about trespassers.

She managed to hike up to the summit with only a minor amount of grunting. The music grew louder. She stopped and stuffed her hands in her jacket pockets. It was cold and there was a breeze. Maybe she was crazy to be outside. After all, who cared if someone wanted to play the bagpipes on Patrick's hill? There'd been a guy who'd done the same in an empty lot near her house while she'd been growing up, and she'd never felt the need to make him stop.

She rubbed her eyes. And when she stopped, she saw him.

He was maybe a hundred feet away, playing with complete calm, apparently unconcerned that she was watching him, or that he might be loitering on private property.

Where had he come from so quickly?

As she looked at him, she noticed something else.

His kilt wasn't moving with the breeze.

She thought about that while she stood there and listened to what sounded like some kind of lament.

The song ended.

The man looked at her, made her a low bow, then smiled.

Right before he disappeared.

Her jaw fell down. She knew this because she'd fallen asleep sitting up many times in law school and there was nothing quite like the feeling of your jaw sliding south and you being too exhausted to retrieve it.

"Spooky, aye?"

She screamed bloody murder—well, not those words, but it was a scream worthy of any B movie horror heroine. She whipped around, wishing she had some kind of weapon, only to find the young Himself standing behind her, looking surprised.

"Sorry," he said. "I didn't mean to startle you."

"You . . . you . . . you . . ."

"I thought you heard me come up the hill," Patrick said. He smiled. "In truth. But that was very impressive."

She couldn't seem to form words, so she stopped trying. She pointed back over her shoulder.

"Aye, he's good, isn't he?" Patrick asked.

"Ba-ba-ba," she managed.

"Bagpipes," he agreed. "Very difficult to play well."

"Ahhh . . ."

"He must like you. I've never seen him play for anyone else. Then again, you heard him at Culloden, didn't you?"

She closed her mouth and nodded.

"He's a ghost, I fear."

"I don't believe—"

"After what you've just seen?"

"I don't," she said, taking a deep breath, "believe in ghosts."

Though at the moment, she wasn't so sure of herself. In fact, she wasn't sure of anything.

Patrick stood there, the only thing solid and real in a world that was full of things she'd never expected. It was all she could do not to reach out and take hold of him so she could steady herself until everything around her stopped swirling.

On second thought, that was a damned good idea. She flung herself at him with enthusiasm.

He caught her without so much as a grunt of protest.

His arms went around her, safe, strong arms that seemed to block out all the things she couldn't explain, all the idiomatic phrases she couldn't translate, all the really lousy things that had happened to her over the past week or so.

He pulled the ponytail holder from her hair and began to comb through her hair with his fingers.

She wondered if his strength and stamina were up to standing where they were and continuing that activity for the rest of the day.

It didn't take her long, however, to realize that while he might have been good for the day, she wasn't. Her tailbone was quite a bit better, but it wasn't perfect. Maybe that scream had done more damage than she'd thought. She sighed as she pulled back to look up at him.

"Highland magic?" she asked.

"Aye, I fear it is."

She looked back to where she'd just seen something she couldn't believe she'd just seen, then looked at Patrick.

"This is not on my list."

He laughed. "No doubt."

Neither are you, she almost said, but restrained herself.

"I was going to suggest we go for a drive," Patrick said, "but the places I intended to go aren't much freer of ghosts than my hill."

"And what spooky places do you have in mind?"

"Loch Ness."

She nodded. "Monsters are good."

"We can continue down the inland coast, if you like. 'Tis a beautiful drive."

"Is it possible that the only music we might hear is from the CD player in your car?"

"We can hope."

"Then it works for me. Let's go." She looked behind her just to make sure there hadn't been any reappearance of that figment of her imagination. The hillside was free of anything scary. She turned back around only to find Patrick holding out his hand.

And for some reason, the sight of it caught her in a most unexpected manner.

In the vicinity of her heart.

"Shall we?" he asked with a smile.

For the first time in her life, she lost her heart.

It didn't hurt nearly as badly as she'd thought it might.

So she put her hand in Patrick's.

Bagpipes started up in the distance.

"Someone approves," Patrick said dryly. "Maybe he won't follow us." He led her carefully down the hill. "You'll like the drive," he promised. "Beautiful. Many interesting sights. Probably something already on your list."

Her list, yes, her list. She'd have to get to making it again right away. It would take her mind off the incredible sense of déjà vu she had just holding Patrick MacLeod's hand.

She closed her eyes briefly.

Scotland was full of so many things she hadn't expected.

Chapter 16

P *atrick* shifted in his seat and smiled in pleasure. It was probably quite deplorable to love a car, but if there had ever been a car to love, it was his Vanquish. Sleek, fast, built for the driver who loved to drive. Could anyone blame him for having such unwholesome affection for the beast?

He let his car unwind along with the road. It never protested any turn, no matter the speed. It was truly a marvel, and he felt, as he generally did when behind the wheel, deeply grateful to be driving and not riding. Especially in the fall when the chill seeped into a man's bones and made him wish for a warm fire and a hot drink.

And a car did provide him with the luxury of having company he didn't have to shout at over his shoulder to converse with. He looked at his company. She was clutching the door frame with one hand and scribbling something on a piece of paper with the other. Her knuckles were, predictably, white.

He slowed down without so much as a sigh. She might as well be able to enjoy the view in a more leisurely manner. Goodness knows, he could stand to.

Madelyn put her pen down and looked out the window. "This is beautiful," she said, nodding toward the loch. "I don't know how people stand to live here."

"Why do you say that?" he asked with a smile.

"I'm certain they don't get anything done. I wouldn't. I would just spend all my time staring out the window."

"You don't think you would become accustomed to the view in time?"

"Never."

She stared out the window for some time. He watched her periodically from out of the corner of his eye.

Tears leaked periodically from the corners of her eyes.

He wondered what ailed her. He reached over and took her hand as shifting permitted. He even ignored the opportunity to pass several cars that he might not need to shift to do so. Traveling thusly gave him time to contemplate what he thought might be going on inside Madelyn's head.

Was she worrying over her lack of job? He'd pried that tale out of her on the way to Inverness that morning. It made him want to find a way to do the same to Bentley Douglas Taylor III. He would have to look into that at some point.

Could it be worry over her papers? He contemplated that for a moment or two, then dismissed it. Her sister was sending her the necessary identification, and there would be no problem getting a new passport.

Money was another matter. He'd told her he would take care of her needs. She was uncomfortable with it, he could tell that quite easily, but he wasn't going to allow her to call her parents when he was perfectly capable of seeing to her for a few days. He could easily see to her for more than a few days if she would allow it.

Was it something else entirely? Was it possible she might be missing him already?

He snorted to himself. By the saints, what an ego he had. She was probably suffering nothing more than an attack of allergies.

Madelyn sighed deeply, surreptitiously brushed at the tears on her face, then clasped her hands in her lap. "So," she said, "did you come here a lot as a kid?"

Ah, a distraction from his ridiculous thoughts. He leaped upon it enthusiastically. "Nay, I didn't," he said. "I didn't travel at all, if you can believe it," he said. "We were poor and our neighbors were . . . unfriendly."

"What were you, landlocked? Were there no roads off your property that you couldn't get past your neighbors?"

To where? More unfriendly clans? He smiled briefly. "The Highlands are an interesting place," he said.

"So I keep hearing, and I'm definitely curious about several things," she said. "And since you're my tour guide, guide the tour. Tell me everything about Scotland and start with yourself and your growing-up years."

He downshifted, blew past a caravan, and swung back into his own lane. "Well, there was much of poverty, hunger, and cold extremities," he said. "Very cold winters. Chilly, rainy summers."

"And what about you?"

"I was cold and rained on, too."

She laughed. "Come on, Patrick. I saw, granted it was a brief view, your brother's castle. You couldn't have been *that* poor."

"It would surprise you," he said.

"Then surprise me. Cough up the details."

What was he to do, tell her everything about his childhood and youth, then watch her look at him as if he were completely daft? Worse yet, delusional—perhaps dangerously so?

"I have a list of questions, if that helps."

He blinked. "Questions?"

"Questions for you, about you." She waved a piece of paper at him. "Don't prevaricate. I'll know it if you do. Shall I start?"

"Can I stop you?"

She rattled her paper purposefully. "Where were you born?" she asked.

That was an easy one. "My father's keep."

"When?"

"Thirty-five years ago." *Plus a bit,* he added silently.

"Hmmm," she said, tapping a pen against her paper. "A little lie. Are you clinging to your youth, or is there another reason?"

He grunted. "Move on, ye feisty wench."

"The worst thing you did as a teenager?"

"By the saints, woman," he said, faintly alarmed, "you don't mess about."

"Don't worry," she said with a laugh, "I won't ask you about regrets, past sins, or huge, colossal mistakes you'd like to hide under large rocks so no one could ever discover them."

He slowed for a village and the accompanying traffic, and took the opportunity to look at her. "Do you have regrets?"

"None."

He smiled, then looked back at the road. "I daresay that was given too easily."

"It isn't my turn to give answers."

"I'll be happy to answer anything you'll ask—after you divulge a regret or a colossal mistake."

She sighed. "Well, I do have one. I regret that I didn't grow up soon enough to realize that what I wanted to do had nothing to do with accepting my parents' plan for me, or rebelling against that plan. I would have practiced more and become a violinist."

"It's not too late, is it?" he asked. "You're not precisely geriatric."

"Thirty," she said. "Too old to start something new."

"Hardly," he said. "It's not too late to change."

Change, his heart whispered suddenly. *Aye, change.*

She was silent for several minutes before she nodded. "It's tempting."

"Dreams are."

"All right, now you," she said, shifting in her seat to look at him.

He rubbed one of his hands on his leg. There was no reason to be nervous, but he found himself so just the same. He much preferred it when he was the one asking the questions. "Regrets," he said slowly. "I wish I hadn't tormented my brother so much when we were younger."

"Were you a rotten kid?"

He shook his head. "Reckless. And Jamie was a very sober soul with much responsibility thrust onto him at an early age. I tormented him when I should have stood behind him and offered him aid. And I regret leaving home without saying anything. When I left, I think it grieved him deeply."

And that, he supposed, was a monumental understatement.

"Didn't you ever go back home?" she asked.

"Once," he said. "Once, before Lisa was to have had the baby."

"And after?"

"It was several years before I saw him again."

"Is there no phone at his castle?"

Patrick smiled. "At that time, nay, there wasn't. And it

seemed as if we were millions of miles apart."

"Hmmm," she said thoughtfully. "Interesting."

"Next regret," he said, moving on quickly. Best not to linger where she might ask questions he certainly couldn't answer. "That I married Lisa."

"You're kidding."

"Nay," he said, with a shake of his head. "Her uncle told me not to, but I didn't listen." He smiled at her. "As I said, I was reckless and full of my own opinions."

"You aren't now?"

"I'm no longer quite as reckless."

She laughed. "I'll just bet. Jane said you're close to losing your license."

"Speeding is for the joy of it. Recklessness is another matter."

"All right, I'll give you that. Third regret now."

"That I was rude to you at Culloden."

She was silent so long that he had to look at her. She was blushing furiously.

"My apology moves you so?" he asked.

"You didn't hear what I said to you there, did you?"

He shook his head. "I didn't."

"Thank goodness. Let's move on."

"Nay," he said with a smile, "this is far more interesting. Were you being rude to me?"

"Terribly, so get over it," she said, crossing several things off on her list. "Now back to my questions. You were born, you grew up shivering, and you wish you hadn't been such a pain in the backside to your brother. Where did you learn to use a sword?"

He'd wondered when that would come up. "From my father."

"Just like that?" she asked. "Like learning to tie your shoes? He just up and said one day, 'Okay, Patrick, today we're going to learn to use a medieval weapon. Pay attention or I'll cut your little head off'?"

"Aye, something like that."

She stared at him for several moments in silence. He could have fidgeted, but he didn't.

"You're leaving out critical details," she said. "There's something about your whole family that just doesn't add up for me."

He lifted one eyebrow. "Maybe we all behave this way in the Highlands."

"Possibly," she conceded. "Possibly. I'll give you that."

The saints be praised. He wasn't up to coming up with a decent excuse as to why his family behaved the way they did. If he gave her the entire truth, she wouldn't believe it anyway.

Then again, she might.

At this point, he wasn't sure what would be worse.

He was, he conceded with complete resignation, more bewildered than he had been in his whole life. And it had everything to do with the woman who'd just been distracted from her list by the sight of a castle sitting on the edge of a loch.

"Will you look at that!" she exclaimed. "Look over there! Can we stop? I bet there are lots of stairs."

"Stairs?"

"Stairs," she repeated reverently. "Millions of feet tramping up and down them. Very interesting. Can we get there? Do you mind?"

He smiled at her. "I don't mind. I'm eager to stomp up and down stairs with you. We'll stop wherever you want."

"Thank you."

"It is truly my pleasure."

"And you won't say anything to the tour guide?"

"Nary a word."

She looked vastly relieved. "I'd like to actually get through a castle without seeing the exit prematurely."

"My apologies," he said humbly. "I couldn't help myself. That man yesterday didn't know his tartans from Ralph Lauren bedsheets."

And given that Lisa had always insisted on Ralph Lauren bedsheets—imported from the U.S. no less—he would certainly know of what he spoke.

"Maybe they don't have any guides here," she said hopefully.

He laughed. "If they do, I promise to keep silent."

"Thank you," she said. She put her hand over his.

Chills ran down his spine. He had his doubts it was because he was cold.

Madelyn rubbed her arms suddenly. "Has this thing got a heater?"

He turned it on. "I told you," he said. "Highlands, cold. Together every time."

"I didn't think we were in the Highlands anymore."

" 'Tis still cold," he said. "Let's see if there's a tea shop. We'll find something hot to drink. The chill won't stand a chance against it."

"Uh-huh," she said with a nod, but she didn't sound convinced.

He wasn't, either.

Whatever there was between them had gone far beyond what could be solved by something hot from a kettle.

Five hours, three castles, an uncountable number of steps, a reservation for separate rooms in a B and B, and several small snacks later, he was standing on the castle walls overlooking a bay on the inner coastline in Argyll. There had been stairs enough to suit Madelyn, an adequate guidebook that suited even him, and a sunset that suited them both. He looked at Madelyn and smiled at the look of pleasure on her face.

"You're happy," he said.

"I got to tramp up and down stairs," she said.

"Are you hungry?"

She laughed. "Don't you ever think about anything else?"

"I'm making up for being hungry in my youth."

"Then sure, I'll go eat with you. Just let me look out over the ocean one more time." She had her look, then sighed. "This is just beautiful."

"Aye, it is."

She smiled up at him. "This was a wonderful idea. Thank you."

He looked down at her, saw her shiver, and put his arm around her. "Nay, thank you, Madelyn," he said. "I've enjoyed the day very much."

She smiled weakly. "Aren't we just a picture of politeness?"

He considered that. Politeness? He supposed so. Though politely asking her if she'd mind if he kissed her again was not exactly foremost in his thoughts. What he wanted to do was haul her against him and kiss her until neither of them could breathe. He'd done it before with marginal success.

He lifted one eyebrow.

She laughed at him.

"Feisty wench," he muttered, then slipped his hand under her hair, pulled her against him, and proceeded to kiss her until he had to reach out with one hand and hold on to the wall so he didn't send them both plunging down into the inner bailey.

Madelyn didn't seem to mind.

He didn't, either, but he was beginning to wonder if he might have to sit down soon. She was intoxicating and he was starting to feel just the slightest bit light-headed.

" 'Tis time to close!" called a merry voice from behind them.

Patrick almost fell off the parapet. He lifted his head and looked at Madelyn. "Did you hear something?"

"It wasn't a ghost," Madelyn said, her breathing a bit ragged. "Nope, there he is. Waving at us."

"Damned do-gooders," he muttered.

"Might be a Scottish tour guide," she offered.

"Ha. A proper Scot wouldn't have interrupted us." He took her hand and pulled her along behind him. "Fair knocked us from the wall with his bellowing. Dangerous."

"Very," she agreed.

He grumbled a bit more as he passed the perky soul with the keys, but had no trouble smiling at Madelyn as he walked with her to the car park. The feel of her hand in his was quite possibly one of the nicest things he'd experienced in a long time. He was almost growing accustomed to that otherworldly sensation that went through him occasionally when he touched her.

His mobile phone was buzzing in the car when they got back in. He almost considered not answering it, but perhaps it was Jamie telling him that Elizabeth had delivered her baby. He listened to the message, then sighed.

"Bad news?"

"A job in London."

She waited. "And?"

"We'd have to fly tomorrow."

"I could get my passport," she offered. "And I could see if I can get a replacement for my plane ticket."

"You could," he agreed slowly. "And that doesn't mean you need use it right away."

"My ticket is for Sunday."

He spit out his next words before he thought better of it. "Change it."

He could feel her looking at him. He met her eyes and wondered if the twilight would show things he didn't want shown, things he wasn't sure he wanted to feel. And even if he wanted to feel those things, he wasn't sure he would be able to endure the feeling of them.

By the saints, he was a wreck.

"I don't know if I can," she said slowly. "Change it."

He waited.

"Not that I wouldn't want to," she added.

He took a deep breath. "Let's worry about it tomorrow. My flight leaves early tomorrow afternoon. We've time for a decent dinner, breakfast, then a quick trip back to Inverness."

"Works for me."

And more time with her worked for him. He started the car and drove to a restaurant, unaccountably at peace.

A few more days with her.

What could that hurt?

Chapter 17

Madelyn ducked into the plane, took the seat Patrick led her to, and wondered how it would be to travel in this kind of luxury on a regular basis. It was nothing she should accustom herself to any time soon. Her astronomical loan debt guaranteed her occupation of a coach seat—when she could afford to fly, that is—far into middle age.

So she sat in an exceedingly comfortable leather chair, accepted a preflight drink of orange juice from a beautiful flight attendant, then watched that flight attendant look at Patrick with the same awe and reverence she might have a Greek god come down from Mount Olympus to slum with the mortals for a few days.

The woman, Madelyn had to concede, had a point.

Patrick sat across the aisle from her, leaving her in the seat facing Conal Grant. The downside of that was the scrutiny she suspected Conal would subject her to. The upside was the view she had of Patrick's exceptionally handsome face. And as she took surreptitious glances at that face the same way a parched woman might have at some mysterious elixir of unknown origin, she wondered why she'd fought so hard against letting him take care of her for a few days.

What was she, nuts?

Change it, he'd said about her ticket.

She would be crazy not to. After all, what did she have waiting for her at home besides reality? Her job search could probably wait a day or two as well.

At least she had something in mind. She'd had an epiphany the night before as she slept in a cozy B and B paid for by a handsome Highlander who had kissed her senseless on the roof of a castle earlier that evening.

Why she was having work-related epiphanies and not ones
of another flavor was something she would have to think
about later.

She had decided that when she got back to Seattle, she
would immediately head over to Wentworth and Co. and
apply for a job. It would gall Bentley no end to watch her
rise effortlessly to the top of that food chain, and it would
give Barry "the Barracuda" Wentworth great pleasure to rub
that in Bentley's face as often as possible. She was a good
lawyer with an impressive track record. Her canning from
DD&P was personal, and there wasn't an attorney at either
firm who didn't know that. She would be okay. She would
be better than okay. She would be shopping at Ann Taylor
again and happily trotting off to court to crush prosecuting
attorneys under her very expensive heels. It sounded good.

At least she thought it sounded good.

Besides, what else was she going to do? Wait for a certain
Scottish lord to fall in love with her and carry her off to his
castle? She'd seen his castle and it was a disaster.

The man himself was another story entirely, but that was
something she would also have to think about later.

The plane pulled away from a discreet, unmarked hangar
and she took a deep breath. Flying wasn't her favorite activity. She looked at Conal Grant and wondered if this flight
might be less than pleasant for other reasons than turbulence.
Conal was an older man, distinguished, gray-haired. He
looked nothing like a secret agent. She would have passed
him on the street and thought him nothing more than a successful businessman.

She smiled weakly at him.

He smiled back, but only politely, and that was where the
rub lay.

He was obviously very protective of Patrick, but that hardly should affect her, should it? She was catching a ride on
his plane and that was that. She didn't have to make a good
impression, didn't have to have him like her, didn't have to
score any brownie points. She was tempted to pull out the
documents Sunny had overnighted to her and study them so
she wouldn't have to look at the good Mr. Grant.

Then again, what did she care? And as she sat there, being scrutinized and not caring, she wondered if putting herself back in the position of being scrutinized by any man in a suit was something she ever wanted to do again. She stared out the window, faintly shocked by the idea. What would it be like, to never wear another pair of nylons again? To never put her hair up in her power chignon again? To never walk into a boardroom again where the minute she did, she had to throw up all kinds of defenses, or worse yet, offenses, just to get through a meeting with men who automatically held her to a different standard just because she was a woman?

It would be heaven, that's what it would be.

No, she realized quite suddenly, it would be hell, because whatever else she did, she would still have the incredible burden of her six-figure loan debt on her shoulders. Weaving baskets—or some other kind of low-stress job—might have been fun, but it wasn't going to get her out of debt. It looked as if it was back to the salt mines for her when she got home.

But she wondered, briefly, if she might ever enter a boardroom quite the same way again.

No sense in not practicing now. She smoothed her hands down her very comfortable jeans, then gave Conal Grant a different kind of smile, a smile that said she didn't give a damn what he thought of her.

He raised one eyebrow in acceptance of the challenge.

And then the grilling began.

"So, Miss Phillips—"

"Madelyn," she corrected.

"Madelyn," he conceded. "I understand your vacation hasn't been without its share of difficulties."

She shrugged. "That's life."

"Convenient that Patrick was there to lend a hand."

Madelyn had to appreciate the fact that Conal went straight for the jugular. "He has been very kind," she agreed. "It hasn't been easy for me to accept his help."

"Hasn't it?"

"I'm not accustomed to being in a position to need aid," she said.

"Aren't you?"

It surprised her somewhat to find herself on this kind of barbecue. After all, it wasn't as if she was the one breaking into a royal flush each time she passed Patrick's chair—no, not like that blonde whose legs stretched all the way to her ears and whose cleavage had probably moved lesser men to tears. The plane had apparently leveled out enough that the lone flight attendant could pass Patrick's chair. Often.

Patrick remained seemingly unimpressed.

She found that she liked him for that.

Quite a bit.

". . . work?"

There went that word again. Madelyn dragged her wandering eyes from Patrick's boots—black of course—and focused on his employer.

"Work?" she echoed.

"I assume you do some," Conal said. "What kind?"

"I'm a lawyer."

"A good one?"

"A very good one."

"Where do you work?"

"I'm in between jobs at the moment," she said. "I won't have a problem getting one when I get back to the States."

"Were you sacked from your last place of employment?"

"Yes."

"Hmmm," he said noncommittally, "how interesting. Poor job performance or another reason?"

"Another reason."

He waited.

So did she.

He should have been a poker player. Or a castle torturer. The man had a seemingly inexhaustible supply of patience because he didn't seem to be in any hurry to move on to another question. She looked at Patrick.

"Is he going to offer me a job soon? Is that why he's asking me all these questions?"

Patrick was sitting with his elbows resting on the arms of his chair, his fingers steepled against his mouth. She could tell he was trying not to laugh. His eyes were twinkling. "I've never seen him like this," he said. "I think he thinks you're distracting me from my work."

"That's hardly my fault, is it?"

Patrick shook his head. "It isn't." He looked at Conal. "Stop tormenting her."

"I'm satisfying my curiosity," Conal said mildly. "Permit me, dear boy, my little indulgences." He looked back at Madelyn. "Well?"

"My ex-fiancé, who happened to be a partner in my firm, had me canned," she said. "He followed me here to Scotland, stole all my possessions including my ID and my plane ticket, and had me thrown in jail. Patrick was kind enough to spring me, clothe me, and take me sightseeing—the latter in spite of my protests. Satisfied?"

The slightest of smiles crossed Conal's face. "Within shooting distance of it."

"All right, let's keep going," Madelyn said, rubbing her hands together in anticipation. "I'm not after his money. I can make enough of my own to survive quite nicely. I'm not after his house—it's a wreck. I'm not after him personally—"

Memories of Culloden assailed her so suddenly and with such an overwhelming sense of déjà vu that tears sprang to her eyes.

"I mean . . . um . . ." she trailed off.

She didn't want him personally? Good grief, what a liar she was!

Conal cleared his throat. "Could we have something to drink, Hailey?" he asked.

Patrick came over and unbuckled Madelyn's seat belt and pulled her to her feet. "My turn to have her," he said as he led her over to the seat facing him. He sat her down, then knelt and buckled her seat belt. He looked up at her. "This seat's cooler."

She realized, to her horror, that tears were running down her face. "Is there a bathroom?" she asked.

"Up front," he said.

She excused herself, avoided broadsiding Hailey, and

managed to get herself inside the head before she burst into tears.

Hormones?

Love?

She wasn't sure and she honestly didn't care. She put her face in her hands and bawled until she was almost sick. The feeling of the plane beginning to descend finally brought her back to her senses. She got a paper towel wet and tried to repair most of the damage she'd done, but there was no way to fix a splotchy red face and puffy eyes.

She was a mess.

Falling for a handsome, Scottish lord probably did that to a girl.

There was a discreet tap on the door. "Miss Phillips? We're starting our descent now."

"Coming," Madelyn said. She took a deep, shaky breath and opened the door.

Hailey was putting things away in the galley. She gave Madelyn a look of understanding, then turned back to her work. Madelyn took another breath, put on her happy face, and went to sit back down across from Patrick. She buckled up, then braved a look at him. He looked concerned.

"All right?"

"Never better."

"Liar," he said with a smile. "Try again."

She sighed. "Overwhelmed. Unsure."

"Unsettled."

"Exactly."

"That makes two of us."

It took her a minute to realize he'd said it in French. She looked at him in surprise. "Where'd you learn that?"

"At university," Conal supplied.

She looked at Patrick narrowly. "You told Bentley you were homeschooled."

"I was. For a while."

"Patrick tends to leave out details," Conal said dryly. "I don't suppose he told you he's a third-degree black—"

"Conal," Patrick warned.

"Belt?" Conal finished without hesitation. "Or that he speaks several languages?"

"Or that I can juggle three eggs at a time, raw ones," Patrick added. "Conal, old man, shut up before I begin to blush."

Madelyn looked at Patrick. "No," she answered, "he hasn't told me any of that. He's infuriatingly reluctant to divulge important details. I can't get anything interesting out of him about his growing-up years. Just that he was poor, reckless, and cold most of the time."

"It's accurate," Patrick said.

"But incomplete."

"The precise details are boring," Patrick said. "Oh, look, there's London. We'll be landing soon." He looked at Conal. "Perhaps we should see to our business. Any details for me about what I'm to be doing or must I guess?"

Conal dug out a briefcase and opened it. He pulled out a folder and handed it to Patrick. Madelyn stared out the window and looked at the view below. She wasn't sniffling anymore, which she considered a good sign. She supposed her eyes would get back to normal as well. But her heart?

Patrick eased his boots around one of her feet and held on. She looked down at her feet, then up at him. He looked at her from under his eyebrows and flashed her a conspiratorial smile before he looked back down at his papers.

She clutched her hands together. She was far too close to getting lost in the lush forest that was Patrick MacLeod's heart. It wasn't a place she was at all sure she wanted to wander in.

Oh, who was she kidding? She was already there.

And the way out was a plane at Heathrow.

A plane she was beginning to wish she would never have to take.

Her life back in the States was beginning to look less and less attractive. Jumping back into the rat race with a million other rats was sounding more miserable by the moment. Trying to claw her way up the Barracuda's corporate ladder was sounding about as exciting as cleaning out rat cages for the rest of her life.

Unfortunately, there was no guaranteeing Patrick had any feelings for her.

He started to rub the back of her calf with the toe of his boot.

Then again, maybe she should reserve judgment for a while.

The plane began to land, Patrick finished his reading, and Hailey strapped herself into her seat. Madelyn looked at Conal to find him watching her. Gone was the look of assessment. In its place was another kind of expression, one she couldn't quite identify, but it was definitely much friendlier.

"Any final questions?" she croaked.

He smiled. "Nary a one. You pass the test."

"Why? Because I went and bawled in your bathroom?"

He laughed. "No, my girl, not because of that. Because you have a tender heart."

"I don't. I'm a cold, calculating career woman whose sole goal in life is to bring the chauvinistic members of my former law firm to their knees."

Or at least she thought that was her goal.

Once the plane landed, Patrick handed Conal back his papers, then took Madelyn's hand and led her out into the rain. He collected their small bit of luggage and looked at her. "We'll dump the old man at the gate. I'm not hauling his gear as well."

Conal pulled her hand through the crook of his arm. "Young Patrick will survive. Let's find ourselves somewhere to eat."

She agreed with resignation. She was obviously doomed to be in the company of men who needed to eat often. Well, at least these two were paying for it. It was a very nice change from Bentley.

She spared a brief thought for him. Was he still in the UK or had he gone back to the States to wreak havoc on some other poor unsuspecting girl with stars in her eyes and no brain cells in her head? At least she'd learned her lesson. She would be so much wiser the next time.

Was she being wise this time?

She hoped so. It was hard to tell when she was in the middle of it.

Patrick paused at the gate long enough to hand Conal his bag, sling both his and Madelyn's over his shoulder, and take her hand.

"Food," he said, "a place to stay, then maybe a tourist attraction or two before it gets too late. I'll need to take a look around later this evening, but I'll see you safely at the hotel first."

She closed her eyes very briefly and savored the feeling of his hand around hers and the pleasure of walking by his side and feeling as if there was something connecting them together. Maybe she should start keeping track of these kinds of moments, so she would have something to look back on when she was home, slogging through cases and wishing she were back in this very spot, holding hands with this very man.

"Are you all right?" he asked.

"Fine." She nodded quickly. "Perfect."

It was a lie, but she supposed there might be times where lying to oneself might be the only way to keep from losing it. The truth in her heart would have to be faced.

But later, when she was alone.

For now, she would hold Patrick MacLeod's hand and enjoy it.

*I*t was quite a bit later that they finally made their way back to the small but apparently quite upscale hotel Patrick had taken for them near Buckingham Palace. They'd had dinner, parted company with Conal, and walked along the front of the Queen's modest home. She had decided, in that short time, that she far preferred the wilds of Scotland to the bustle of London. It was impossible to calculate the number of people who had lived in London since the time of its inception. Just walking over the same places that she was certain hundreds of thousands of people had walked before her was enough to give her a headache.

He squeezed her hand. "What do you think of London?"

She shivered. "Too much. Too scary. I've seen some very frightening people since we've been here, and we've only been here a few hours."

"And we're in a fairly thug-free bit of town," he said with a smile. "Safe. Very few muggings."

Or so he thought, apparently.

They were walking peacefully through the park, hand-in-hand, dodging drips from the leaves above one moment; they were surrounded by four men of indeterminate origin but clear purpose the next.

"Money, keys, coat," said one man. "In that order."

Madelyn watched as Patrick pulled out his keys. They weren't his car keys, she knew that much because she'd watched him stow those on the plane. He tossed those to the leader.

"Closest to the surface," Patrick said easily. "What did you say you wanted next, mate?"

"Money," the same man said. "All of it. The lady's purse as well."

"She has no purse," Patrick said. "Believe it or not, lad, it was stolen last week."

A pair of the men laughed.

It was a rather unfriendly sound, on the whole.

"I don't believe it," said one of the men, moving closer to them. "I believe I'll be seein' for meself."

Madelyn found herself landing rather forcefully on the grass, and by the time she realized it was Patrick to shove her there, two of the men were unconscious on the ground. She watched in complete astonishment as Patrick finished number three in like manner with a pair of moves, a slap and a kick that left him groaning on the pathway as well. Patrick looked at the leader.

"Have a gun?" he asked politely.

The man cursed him thoroughly and reached into his jacket.

Apparently that was enough for Patrick. Before the man could pull out whatever weapon he was carrying, Patrick had sent him sprawling. He knelt down, wrenched the man's arm behind him, and removed from his apparently quite numb fingers a very wicked-looking knife.

"I daresay you don't," Patrick said, tossing the knife onto the ground. He jerked the man's arm up and back. There was a substantial cracking sound, the man yelped, then slumped down quite peacefully onto his face. Patrick dusted off his hands and reached over to pull her to her feet.

"Off we go," he said politely. "Quick, before the bobbies show up and we're forced to spend the night in the police station, answering their endless questions."

Madelyn was, quite simply, quite speechless. She made tracks with a man who had incapacitated four other men without any effort at all. She was silent until they'd trotted out of the park, down the street, and into the door of their hotel. Patrick led her up the stairs and stopped in front of her room.

"Have you anything in mind for tomorrow?"

She gaped at him. "I just saw you take out four men your size, and you're asking me what I want to go see tomorrow?"

"Aye."

"You're . . ." She hardly knew what to say to him. "I can't believe you."

"Is that praise or condemnation?" he asked without any inflection to his voice at all.

She stared at him for a moment or two in silence, weighing his words and trying to decide what he was leaving unsaid. Was he used to being condemned for what he'd just done? Did his brother not care for it? Had his wife not cared for it?

Did it really matter what either of them thought?

She decided it didn't. She had her own opinions and it was probably best he hear them right off. She looked up at him seriously. "If I were an important person, I wouldn't leave home without you to protect me."

He smiled, a wry pursing of his lips that was utterly charming. "You *are* an important person and I am at your disposal, whenever you need me."

"Thank heavens."

He laughed softly. He took her key, opened her door, then made her a little bow. "My lady's chamber awaits," he said.

He squeezed her hand, hesitated, then stood back a little to let her pass. "I'm next door if you need me."

"Thank you."

He didn't move.

She hesitated as well. She wasn't sure what a moment of this kind—the kind when you were saying good night to a man who had just saved you from a mugging or worse—demanded, but she was fairly sure it wasn't a handshake.

She put her arms around him, hugged him tightly, then leaned up to kiss him.

"You are amazing," she whispered. "Thank you."

He cleared his throat. " 'Twas nothing."

"It was something and I'm grateful for it." She stood for a moment in his arms, then pulled back reluctantly. "I imagine we should call it a night."

"There is much to see on the morrow," he agreed.

She nodded, went inside, looked at him again, then smiled and closed the door.

Then she turned and leaned back against it.

The man looked perfectly civilized in his worn jeans, expensive wool sweater, and black leather jacket, but she had seen a side to him that night up close, the side that his swordplay had hinted at. There was a very uncivilized, very dangerous, very uncontrollable side to the man and she wondered how it was that only she saw it. She pitied the men who thought to cross him.

She wondered if she should exercise the same caution, then, even more briefly, she dismissed the thought. There hadn't been a moment that she'd ever felt anything but safe with him.

And safe because of him.   .

Enemies to slay . . .

It sounded like the kind of thing a person would have done hundreds of years ago in the Highlands, something when times were not so civilized.

She shook her head, pushed away from the door, and went to find her toothbrush and Jane's flannel jammies she was still borrowing. She'd been almost mugged, but Patrick had protected her.

She wondered why he hadn't done the same thing to Bentley.

Maybe Bentley hadn't been worth the trouble.

She couldn't help but agree.

Chapter 18

Patrick handed over an exorbitant amount of money to the cashier, collected his tickets and his guide book, and followed Madelyn across the bridge to the Tower of London. He'd been here a time or two before, thankfully never as a prisoner, and always found himself surprised by the press of modern humanity in such an old place. Or maybe it was the contradiction of so many humans wandering about with older, otherworldly beings.

Talk about ghosts.

Madelyn looked at the brochure. "Wow, the Crown Jewels," she said enthusiastically. "Cool. Let's go."

Patrick refrained from comment. He'd seen the Crown Jewels before and found himself quite appalled by the sight. Elizabeth was most certainly *not* his queen and that she should have so many useless rocks loitering even more uselessly in glass cases when his country was drowning in poverty irritated him to no end.

"Aye, brilliant," he agreed darkly.

Madelyn only laughed at him. "Now you'll tell me you wish that Robert the Bruce had not only freed Scotland but taken over England as well."

"I most certainly will not," he said archly. "England can keep itself. I just want my country to be free from the tyranny—"

"Please, Patrick," she beseeched, "don't get us tossed out of here, too. At least not until I've seen a few things. The Crown Jewels. The dungeon. The place where Henry had Anne Boleyn's head chopped off."

He sighed. "I'll do my best."

"You do that," she said. She took his hand and pulled him along. "Come on. The day's a-wastin'."

He wondered if he should balk more often. There was something unwholesomely pleasant about having her drag him along after her. He'd almost grown accustomed to the feeling of her hand in his, which probably should have unnerved him.

That it didn't should have scared the hell out of him.

It didn't and that was even worse.

Maybe it was just another in a long list of actions he'd taken that he just couldn't explain. Take that morning, for instance.

Whilst she'd been dealing with her paperwork at the embassy, he'd been arranging an open return ticket for her. That in itself wasn't noteworthy. That he had in fact plunked out a substantial amount of sterling for that privilege likely was.

Let her think the airline was being altruistic, he didn't care.

He just wasn't ready for her to go home yet.

Too many things still to see, he told himself quickly. And his working for a pair of days would take time away from her vacation. And far be it from him to be anything less than the most gallant of hosts possible. It was right that she go home with a good feeling about her time spent in Scotland.

Aye, that was it.

Besides, she would have enough to think about when she returned and had to see to the remains of her life.

He knew this because his list of questions had been answered during their wait at the embassy. He supposed he'd asked the boring things, where she was born, how old she was, how many siblings she had.

He'd learned all about her parents, her summers spent in a different country each year, her sister with the house that looked a great deal like Moraig's.

But what he hadn't asked her were the things he was most curious about. When had she first been kissed, did she want children, was she the sort of girl to sleep with him, then leave him and break his heart? That she hadn't seemed inclined to save him the expense of a second room gave him pause. He'd rarely brought anyone to London with him, but on the occasion or two he had, he'd certainly foregone that expense.

Odd, but now he wished he hadn't.

"Are you daydreaming?"

He looked down into the lovely face of the woman who had seriously worked her way into his heart and wished that he hadn't done several things in his past.

"What is it?" she asked, a small smile on her face. "Thinking traitorous thoughts?"

"Nay," he said with a half laugh. "Thoughts about abstinence, actually."

She stopped still. "Where in the world did that come from? Henry the Eighth?"

"Something like that." He shook his head. "I'm just wondering if it's even possible."

"Difficult, but possible. Now, come on. The line into the keep is almost nonexistent."

"Wait," he said, trying to stop her, "what are you saying, 'difficult'? How would you know?"

"How do you think I would know? Come on, Patrick. I'm seeing steps."

"You can't be serious."

She looked at him.

She was serious.

Patrick went along with her, because he couldn't seem to do anything else.

Obviously this should have been one of his questions. Then again what purpose would that have served? To stun him into silence?

He trailed along after Madelyn thoughtfully. He remained thoughtful through the Tower itself, through a frightening display of torture implements, and through the obligatory, and quite annoying, look at the Crown Jewels.

"You're muttering," Madelyn said with an elbow in his ribs as they moved along in the queue full of gaping spectators.

"It's the best I can do," he said.

"It's a good thing your Stone of Scone isn't at Westminster anymore," she said dryly. "I hate to think of what you would have done."

"I would have admired it from a distance," he said virtuously.

"Right," she said with a snort. "Wasn't it yours originally?"

"Aye, it was."

"And didn't England swipe it, stick it under a seat, and subsequently crown all their kings and queens on it?"

"So the tale goes."

They were, mercifully, through looking at the Crown Jewels at that point. He stepped out into the humid air of October's beginning and took a deep breath. Ah, freedom.

"You seem awfully calm," she said suspiciously. "Doesn't it bug you that they absconded with an important rock of yours?"

He smiled down at her. "How readily you use *they*. When you begin to use *we* just as easily, I'll think you a proper Scot."

"As a matter of fact, my great-grandmother was a Mackenzie, so I am part Scot, and you're changing the subject. What about that rock of ours?"

"It is back in Scotland where it belongs," he said smugly.

"How easily you say that now."

"Believe me, I didn't say it easily when it was captive in Westminster Abbey," he admitted with a grin. "Come, let us be off to Westminster just the same. I'll make disgruntled noises there just to please you."

She laughed as she took his hand and walked with him to the abbey.

He looked at graves with Madelyn, marveled at the famous souls buried there, then paused before the former resting place of the Stone of Scone.

They kept their thoughts to themselves, but Patrick shared a meaningful look with Madelyn. And for the first time in years—or maybe it had been longer than that—he felt as if he had a friend. Not a brother, not a cousin, not a lover, but a friend.

Of course, the lover bit of it wasn't far from his mind, but she was apparently a virgin and he wasn't sure he wanted to talk her out of that condition, even if he flattered himself that he might be able to.

They left with straight faces. Madelyn laughed as they walked out onto the grass in front of the abbey. "You think too loudly."

"I do not."

She smiled up at him. "You're a purist."

"I'm a Scot. We're fond of our national treasures."

"Then we should count you as one of them. I'm faintly surprised all these tourist attractions are still standing after the national pride you radiate. Are you hungry yet?"

"Famished. Let's go to Harrods and have something to eat. Then I'll leave you to shop whilst I take care of a bit of business."

"Shop?" she echoed. "You've got to be kidding."

"We have theater tickets tonight. Are you going to wear jeans?"

She scowled at him. "Patrick, you just can't up and buy me clothes every time you feel like it. You're racking up an incredible tab it's going to take me months to pay off."

"You're not going to repay me. Think of it as choosing to decorate you instead of my house."

"I need clothes less than you need furniture."

"But 'tis far more rewarding to spend my money on you. I've set up an account for you. Just buy what pleases you."

"Ha," she said with a snort. "You have no idea how much I could spend in an afternoon."

"And you have no idea what I have in the bank. You cannot outspend that."

"Have you been to Harrods lately?"

"Have you?"

She looked at him, then laughed suddenly. "No, but I've heard rumors. Patrick, I can't just go spend your money like this."

"Then I'll spend it for you."

She sighed. "All right, I give in. I'll spend less than you

will. Let's go. I'm imagining you'll have to get something for tonight as well."

" 'Tis already done. I'll pick up my suit when I come back for you."

She shook her head. "You and the phone have a relationship I don't understand."

"Neither does Conal, because London's the only place I ever answer my mobile. He's forever trying to reach me at home." He took her hand. "Let's find a taxi. I think I need something strengthening."

Three hours later he walked into the most touristy shopping in London with a goodly bit accomplished. Of course, none of it had been related to his work, but he would never admit that.

He'd found a violin, a good one if the word of a well-known violin maker could be trusted, purchased it, and had it sent to the hotel. He'd talked to Conal, worked out the details of flying Madelyn back to Scotland, then returning to London for his brief bit of nannying before he himself could go home for a fortnight.

He'd also talked his former uncle-in-law into loaning him the Lear for a few nonwork-related journeys during that upcoming fortnight. Madelyn should see Edinburgh and he certainly preferred a trip by plane versus the long, lorry-clogged motorway. They could hop over to Ireland if she liked, or Amsterdam, or Paris. There were other places to see in England as well. Elizabeth's brother Alexander and his wife Margaret had a recently restored medieval keep in England that Madelyn might care to see. There was much to do and little time in which to do it. Wings gave him the freedom he craved. With Conal's plane at his disposal, all of Europe lay at his fingertips.

Of course, the fact that he could have bought a Lear for himself without feeling the pain of it was something he didn't think on very often. Conal enjoyed interrogating him about his destinations, and he rather enjoyed doing his damndest to avoid giving any details.

Unhealthy, no doubt, but there you had it.

He walked into Harrods, checked his watch, and headed for the predetermined meeting place. Madelyn was there, waiting, looking a bit harried. Her hair was riotous, her sweater on a bit askew, and her face flushed.

Not a good afternoon shopping, perhaps.

But she was, he couldn't help but admit, simply beautiful. He stood in the midst of the continual stream of shoppers and stared at her for a handful of moments without moving. Aye, she was very fair.

Not only fair, but amusing, independent, and determined.

And she was waiting for him.

She turned, saw him, and a smile of relief mingled with happiness crossed her face.

It almost undid him.

He started toward her. She worked her way through the throng of shoppers to meet him halfway.

"Crazy place," she said, dragging her sleeve across her forehead. "I should have worn shorts and a T-shirt. Too many people in here."

He nodded in agreement. "That's why I call ahead." He looked down. "One sack?"

"A dress and shoes. What do you want, a whole wardrobe?"

"I admire your restraint, but I had suitcases sent back to the hotel for us and mine is full."

"Things in black?"

"I bought a pair of blue jeans and a red shirt, just for you. Come on," he said, taking her bag with one hand and her hand with his other. "Take advantage of me."

"Don't want to."

He grunted and pulled her along after him. "Stubborn wench," he muttered under his breath.

Amazing, stubborn, marvelous wench.

An hour and a very cross Madelyn Phillips later, he was sitting in a taxi on his way back to the hotel. She had glared at him so long, she'd finally given up and claimed he'd given her a headache from all the frowning she'd had to do.

"A single dress was enough," she said.

"Say 'Thank you, Patrick.'"

"Thank you, Patrick. You impossible man. Does anyone ever get their way around you?"

"Always. I'm quite tractable."

"Sure," she said dryly. She smiled at him. "Thank you. It was very generous."

"You're very welcome."

"I didn't need more shoes."

"You need everything. Your suitcase was stolen, if you'll remember. Miriam is no doubt anxious to have her antiques back, though I hope she'll allow you to keep the lime outfit. I'm very keen on that one."

"Well, a girl can dream."

He smiled. "Aye, and so can a lad." He reached for her hand. "Let's go change, have supper, then head for the theater. Perhaps we won't be mugged tonight."

"I'm not worried." She looked at him seriously. "You don't know how nice it is to feel safe."

And given that his heart had felt safer in the last day or two than it had in years, he had to agree.

He watched from Conal Grant's luxurious leather chair as the Lake District passed beneath him and marveled at the change in his life over the past few days. A lighter heart, a fuller belly, a more cheerful outlook. He looked across from him at the reason for two of the three. She was asleep and he took the opportunity to simply stare at her.

Odd how he had started this entire passing of time with her with the promise to himself that he would enjoy her company and nothing more. He certainly hadn't planned on his heart getting involved.

He tramped down the faint feeling of panic he had at that thought. So his heart was involved. It didn't mean it had to be permanently involved.

Though to say that spoke volumes about himself, didn't it?

He closed his eyes and shook his head. Perhaps he would do well to take an hour or two and flip through a handful of books in Jamie's library. Perhaps he could find something there to aid him in unraveling his own sorry self.

Nay, he needed no book. What he needed was time. Time to see what his heart was capable of. Time to see what Madelyn felt. Time to see what might come of their hearts intertwining together.

He opened his eyes. She was looking at him. He smiled.

"Sleep well?" he asked.

She covered her yawn with her hand. "I can't seem to stay awake. You'd think I wasn't sleeping at night, but I am." She shivered. "Just catching up, I suppose. You know, the strain of too much shopping. It's just exhausting."

He squeezed her foot with his own. He liked that, sitting with her foot cradled between his, finding some way to touch her even when he wasn't sitting next to her.

By the saints, he was indeed in trouble.

"And I was forced to sit up for quite a while after the show, fondling that violin I found on my bed."

He shrugged with a faint smile. "Amazing what hotels these days leave on pillows. I understand 'twas a mere chocolate or two in times past."

"You are completely impossible."

"I do what I can."

"You do too much." Her smile faded. "Patrick, how can I ever repay you? And it isn't just for the things. It's for your time. You've just done too much."

"You don't need to repay me," he said.

"You could come to Seattle."

He looked at her in silence for a moment or two. The thought, for some odd reason, terrified him. But the more he looked at her, the less that ridiculous emotion seemed to hold sway over him. He smiled. It was a weak one, but there.

"I just might," he said.

"It wouldn't be hard. Just get on a plane."

"Seems easy enough."

"It is. Just buy your ticket, pack your gear, and get on the plane. I can promise you a bit of floor in my parent's living room. We'll get them to speak French. You'll like it."

He found it in him to smile truly. "I daresay I'd like it very much."

"Good. Then I feel less bad about imposing."

It wasn't an imposition. In fact, he wished she would impose a bit more, for a bit longer.

The plane began to descend. He wondered if Jamie would mind guests for supper. He tried not to think about what that would mean, him taking a woman to dinner at his brother's.

Something he'd never done with any woman.

Ever.

He made Madelyn go over another of her lists as the plane descended, then collected their luggage and headed toward his car. He begged her to bear with him and stop in Inverness for a bit of lunch. He supposed she might be growing used to that because she only smiled gamely and warned him that she wouldn't be fitting into all her expensive clothing soon if he didn't take her to fewer restaurants. But given the fact that she perpetually ordered the smallest thing on the menu, he doubted she would be growing out of her clothes any time soon.

After a tolerable lunch, he took her hand and walked with her down the street back to the car park. That he should take her hand so casually and so easily should have unsettled him greatly.

That it didn't was almost as unsettling.

He smiled at her.

She smiled back.

He walked toward his car and suddenly the hair on the back of his neck stood up. He stopped and looked around him, but saw nothing out of the ordinary.

"What's wrong?"

He shook his head. "Nothing. Not enough sleep, probably."

"Too much chocolate for dessert."

He laughed. "Aye, 'tis likely that. Poisonous stuff, that chocolate."

"But so fabulous."

He agreed and continued on his way. But he couldn't shake the feeling that he was being watched.

It was probably Bentley, stalking them. Would that the fool would stalk them somewhere in private where he could see to him appropriately.

He shrugged off his unease. Nothing he could do now. He'd deal with whatever mischief Bentley was combining when it came to a head.

Chapter 19

B*entley* Douglas Taylor III, son of academics and aspiring law deity, stood in a crowd on the streets of Inverness and watched as Patrick MacLeod walked with Madelyn down the street. Holding hands, no less. He had watched them get off that very pricey Learjet, holding hands then as well.

He wondered if she was sleeping with him.

That she should do so when she hadn't been willing to with him was intensely irritating, but he would repay her for that later. He'd have plenty of time to see to that once MacLeod was out of the way.

And he had the perfect way to see that accomplished.

His time hadn't been wasted over the past couple of days. First he'd determined who owned the plane MacLeod was using. And while he'd been about that small bit of investigating, he'd also learned that Conal Grant had a brother-in-law, Gilbert McGhee, who had a daughter who was dead.

Murdered, it was rumored.

By none other than her husband, Patrick MacLeod.

Bentley had listened in rapt fascination to all the gossip he'd heard. Murder, mayhem, foul crimes wrought in the middle of the night.

Three of his favorites.

Fortunately for that poor Gilbert McGhee who had obviously lost someone to Patrick's dastardly hands, he was a fine prosecutor and could pull facts, exhibits, and other pertinent items out of thin air.

MacLeod would pay.

Then Madelyn would pay.

He watched MacLeod and Madelyn walk down the street and smirked to himself.

"Enjoy your peace and quiet," he muttered. "It ain't gonna last long."

Chapter 20

Madelyn dressed in jeans and her warmest sweater, put on socks and her boots, then pulled on Jane's coat. She went downstairs and found a note on the table telling her to make herself at home. It would seem that Jane, Ian, and the kids had gone to town for a couple of hours. Patrick had gone back to London sometime during the night to finish up his baby-sitting job.

And there she was, all alone with no one to talk to.

She was tempted to spend the day at home exploring the possibilities of that exquisite violin Patrick had bought her in London—and what in the world had possessed him to do that, she wondered—but she had questions that were simply burning a hole in her brain. Questions about Patrick that Patrick hadn't seemed too eager to answer.

Questions she knew exactly who *would* answer.

She made sure her map was in her pocket—not because she was afraid of the red dots, but because she wanted to be able to get herself back home—then made herself a quick but substantial meal of oatmeal. She would need her strength. She had the feeling it was going to be a doozy of a day.

She took the key Jane had left her and locked up behind her. Maybe they all left their houses open and relied on ghosts to guard them, but she was a guest and thankfully not acquainted with the specter alarm system. She would have to content herself with a key in the lock.

It took her almost an hour to reach her destination, and by that time she was hot, tired, and wishing she'd learned to ride at Girl Scout camp so she could have made use of something from Ian's ample stables.

She put her hands in her pockets and walked down a familiar path under the eaves of the forest. There, just before

her, still sat that humble little house that tilted to one side
and was covered with all sorts of foresty growth. Light
spilled out from paned windows that had to have been centuries old. She scanned the surroundings for any kind of
spell-casting woodland sprites, but found none. Roddy's
warning about Highland magic came back to her, but she
pointedly ignored it. Moraig's entire existence smacked of
Highland magic, and given that she fully intended to delve
into some of it, there was no point in trying to avoid it.

The door opened as she approached.

Apparently, she was expected.

"Good morning, Mother," she said in Gaelic.

Moraig laughed delightedly.

All right, so it was more of a cackle than a laugh. Madelyn
was determined to remain rational. Moraig was, environment
and wild, flyaway white hair aside, *not* a witch.

"Is that all ye know?" Moraig asked.

"So far."

"Ye should learn more," Moraig said. "It would serve ye
well."

How, by impressing her father? By allowing her to eavesdrop on Patrick and Ian? By garnering her better service in
the local pub? Tempting all three, but probably not worth
the effort in the end.

"All in good time, my gel. All in good time," Moraig said.
"Come in. Sit. There is much to discuss."

Bingo, Madelyn thought. This was why she'd come. She
imagined Moraig might know as much as anyone else, and,
more importantly, be more inclined than others to spill the
beans. Patrick tended to give her a few vague answers, then
attempt to distract her with more shopping. She was accumulating a great wardrobe, but not many reliable facts.

She hopped right into Moraig's house and made herself
comfortable on a stool near the fire. She happily accepted a
cup of tea and didn't ask any questions about its origin, or
the contents of the pot hanging over the fire.

It might be lunch.

Moraig gave her stew a final stir, then turned and sat down
on a stool across from Madelyn.

"So," she said with a sly smile, "ye've come for a wee chat, have ye?"

"Yes," Madelyn replied promptly. "And as little of that wee business as possible."

Moraig rubbed her gnarled hands together. "And what is it ye'd be knowing, lass?"

"More of what you told me last time when I was too distracted to pay attention. You were trying to tell me a few things about Patrick. . . ." She trailed off meaningfully.

"Aye, I was."

"Things I should probably know."

"Aye, that as well."

Madelyn tried to look as casual as possible. "Something about cattle raids and enemies. I think the pain of my tailbone distracted me from several important details divulged in that conversation."

"Gel, ye've a silver tongue worthy of any laird's bard, but it won't serve ye here."

Madelyn waited. When Moraig didn't immediately begin to fill in those missing details for her, she wondered what she was supposed to do to pry answers from the old woman. Tap dance? Offer to chop wood? She waited for several uncomfortable moments, then decided just to get the pain over with.

"Then what *would* serve me here?" she asked.

"Honesty."

Madelyn smiled in appreciation of a worthy opponent. "I'm just curious."

"And what motivates yer curiosity, lass?"

Madelyn took a deep breath. "I'm beginning to care for him."

Oh, who was she kidding. She was already knee-deep in a stream of the most ridiculous of romantic feelings for him without a hip-wader in sight.

She was in trouble.

She took a deep breath. "I'm not sure how he feels, of course, and not that it matters, probably. I have a life to go home and try to resurrect—"

"Yer life there will keep."

But her patience and sanity might not. Madelyn wished, briefly, that she had come bearing gifts, like Godiva or a nice Kate Spade purse. Surely Moraig needed something to collect her herbs in. Did Prada make herb-carrying trugs? Too late to wonder now.

"Moraig," she said, leaning closer, "I really need to know some things."

"And what would ye do with the answers, if ye had them, gel?"

Madelyn opened her mouth to blurt out a meaningless reply, then stopped herself. If she had details about Patrick's life, what would she do with them? She looked at the old woman. "Well, I wouldn't use them for gain."

"Hmmm," Moraig said noncommittally.

"I'm discreet."

"Are ye?"

"Completely."

Moraig seemed to give that some consideration. Then she looked at Madelyn searchingly. "Can ye learn to love him?"

Madelyn took a deep breath. "Yes."

"Do ye love him already?"

Madelyn closed her eyes briefly. "I think so. Maybe. Yes."

Well, that very resolute answer seemed to be enough for Moraig.

"Very well, then," the old witch said, leaning forward conspiratorially, "I can't tell ye all, ye ken. Some of this is Patty's tale to tell, if he trusts ye with it."

"Sure."

"Ask me yer questions, and if I can answer them, I will."

Questions? Why, they were her specialty. "When was he born?" she asked.

Moraig didn't blink. "1285."

Madelyn *did* blink. "Huh?"

"Ye heard me."

Heard, but didn't believe. "But that was centuries ago. Centuries," she repeated. "That isn't possible."

"Isn't it?"

"It isn't," Madelyn said firmly. Best get past that ridiculous answer as quickly as possible. "Where was he born?"

"Down at the keep. His ma died when he was wee. Broke his da's heart and never did a woman cross the threshold of that hall for years afterward."

"Interesting."

"Interesting is those two brothers, young Pat and his brother Jamie."

So she'd said before. "And when was his brother born?"

Moraig shrugged. "Sooner than Pat I'd say, aye? Don't know much about Laird Jamie, save he comes quite regular and brings me aught I need without my asking." She grinned at Madelyn. "He thinks I'm a witch."

Madelyn had the feeling she'd have a lot in common with Laird Jamie.

But perhaps there were grains of reality in Moraig's fanciful answers. She would just play along for a while and see where things went. "So," she said slowly, "if Patrick was born in 1275—"

"1285."

"1285, as you say," and she could scarcely say it without adding a very skeptical *right* immediately after the date, "how did he get here? Or has he just lived that long?"

"He came through the time gate."

"The time gate?"

"Aye."

Madelyn couldn't help herself. A "right" slipped out before she could stop it. "Where is the time gate?"

"There are many here. Don't know which was his."

Madelyn had a brief vision of red dots on Jane's map, but quickly dismissed it.

Then again, what else might those dots be? Poison oak? Nettle patches?

She contemplated it for a moment or two, then dismissed the thought. She had other things to concentrate on. She focused on the problem at hand.

"Where did Patrick learn all about swords and stuff?" she asked.

Moraig looked at her as if she'd sorely overestimated Madelyn's intelligence. "Where do ye think, gel?"

She had to take a deep breath in order to even say the words. "In the past?"

"Aye, of course."

"So," Madelyn said slowly, "you're telling me that Patrick grew up in the Middle Ages, learned all kinds of sword fighting there, then came through a time gate to the present where he now lives among modern men."

"Nay."

Madelyn frowned. "Nay?"

"He didn't come to the present."

"He didn't?"

"Nay, he came, seven, nay, eight years past. Maybe nine." Moraig smiled. "My memory fails me."

Madelyn suspected her memory wasn't all that was failing her. "But the rest of it," she prodded, "the other stuff . . ."

Moraig only smiled again.

"Not important," Madelyn conceded. "And the time gate was where again?"

"Hidden."

All right, so Moraig was sharper than she'd given her credit for being. She frowned. She wasn't sure what she had expected to hear, but it hadn't been this. She'd expected to hear that Patrick belonged to a society of secret sword-wielders, or an ultrafanatical group of rich guys with more muscles than sense, or one of those reenactment societies that had perhaps taken things one step too far and actually set up permanent shop in the wilds of Scotland.

But Patrick as a medieval clansman hanging around in the twenty-first century, wearing jeans and driving a sports car?

It was absurd.

"Look to his brother," Moraig advised. "Mark his cousin, Ian. Watch the friends that enter the doors of the laird's hall." She nodded wisely. "Ye'll see."

Madelyn was sure she'd see something, but it wouldn't be a bunch of guys wearing T-shirts that said, "Kiss me, I'm Medieval."

"I'm sure I will," Madelyn said.

"Lunch?" Moraig offered.

"Certainly, if I can clean up."

That seemed to cement the deal. Moraig served her a quite delicious stew, then Madelyn did the dishes with water from the stream heated over the fire. She tentatively sniffed a few herbs as she put things away and couldn't resist a peek or two into darkened corners.

No sprites.

No elves.

No faeries seconding the truth of Moraig's fanciful story.

"Thank you for lunch," Madelyn said politely. "It was a pleasure."

Moraig cackled, took Madelyn's hands and patted them. "Ye'll see, gel. See if ye don't. Ye'll see in the end."

Madelyn nodded as if she believed, then hightailed it out of there before she had to listen any more to the bizarre ramblings of a woman who had obviously come in contact with one too many bunches of lavender.

She walked briskly down the path, turning to wave once, then continuing on with something that fast turned into a trot.

And that was something, considering she was wearing hiking boots.

She ran until she couldn't breathe anymore, then stopped when she realized she probably looked really stupid. What had she expected from Moraig, really? Ask a crazy question, get a crazy answer.

She walked beneath the eaves of the forest, listened to the beat of her own heart and the crunch of twigs under her feet. It sounded like half a dozen feet stomping along with her.

Literally.

She stopped suddenly.

The footsteps that echoed her stopped as well.

Not quite as suddenly.

She tried it another time or two with much the same results.

She looked around her but saw nothing. That didn't mean there wasn't someone there. A twig cracked to her left. Her heart leaped into her throat. She was alone in the woods with a psycho—

Bagpipes, blessed bagpipes, started up so closely she

screamed. The piper appeared thirty feet in front of her, nodded to her, then turned and marched on.

Okay, she could handle that, especially if the alternative was very corporeal, very frightening footsteps following her. Ghost or not ghost, at least the piper was a known quantity. She ran after him.

And never seemed to catch him, truth be told.

The feeling of being watched was gone by the time she reached Patrick's place. She stood hunched over with her hands on her thighs and sucked in painful gulps of air. She either had to work out more or quit running in crisp autumn air. She needed air with smog in it. All this clean stuff was really hurting her lungs.

She straightened when she could, then watched as her piper went and climbed up on top of Patrick's rock wall. He played peacefully. His kilt didn't swirl around with the breeze that stirred her hair. His music didn't come and go on that same breeze.

She was becoming alarmingly accustomed to being serenading by a ghost.

She stood in the ruins of Patrick's garden and listened for a long time, and then suddenly she began to grow restless. Patrick's house was a disaster, true, but the thought of going inside to clean gave her the willies. She needed to be out in the open.

Where she could see someone coming, if she had to.

She pulled Jane's cell phone out of her pocket, turned it on, then set it on top of a rock wall. She looked around and wondered just where to start in the garden. The whole place needed a date with a heavy-duty tiller, but she couldn't do anything about that. The least she could do was derock a little of the place by hand.

She bent down and started to work.

Soon she became too hot for her coat. She went to toss it over the rock wall. She'd only taken three or four steps before she came to a teetering halt.

There were men in kilts standing along the rock walls with their backs to her.

As if they guarded her.

The piper was sitting on the wall as well, watching her, holding his pipes and swinging his leg casually. She gaped at him as well.

"Are they protecting me?" she asked before she thought better of it.

He nodded.

"Are you a ghost?"

He merely smiled, then hopped back on top of the wall and took up a playing stance. Soon she was enjoying a little recital of what apparently passed as gardening music.

She wanted to pinch herself to make sure she was awake, but she knew she was awake, so there was no need for any self-inflicted torture.

So instead, she pondered the state of affairs in her mess of a life.

She was picking up rocks in a garden that really needed a bulldozer taken to it while wearing clothing bought for her right down to her underwear by a Scottish lord whom a witch thought to be of medieval vintage. And she was talking to a ghost who played the bagpipes while she was surrounded by other ghosts who had apparently taken enough interest in her to protect her.

It there was a deeper meaning to it all, she wasn't sure she wanted to know what it was.

She rolled up her sleeves and went back to work.

She worked until her arms were shaking and she wanted nothing more than to go take a nap. She had grown used to the music and the sight of Highlanders—and they certainly didn't look like modern-day Highlanders—standing on top of Patrick's crumbling walls, their swords drawn and gleaming dully in the gloom of the afternoon.

Weird?

Very.

She looked over Patrick's garden. The results of her work weren't all that great, but there was a patch that was definitely rock free. She wondered what would grow here. Probably the same sorts of things that would grow in Seattle, though it seemed colder here in Scotland. She cursed Bentley. These were things she would have known if she'd been able to stick to her itinerary and visited all those gardens.

Instead, she'd had an all-expense paid vacation with a man who muttered in disgust over historical details. She'd eaten at a witch's hearth and lived to tell. She'd found herself being watched over by ghostly Highlanders and serenaded by a bagpiper of that same ilk.

It wasn't a bad trade.

She turned to go back into Patrick's house to wash her hands, then pulled up short at the sight of the young Himself sitting on the rock wall near the gate, swinging a leg casually, watching her silently.

Her heart gave way.

He was, put simply, beautiful. Beautiful and lethal and wearing an expression that said he was glad to see her. Her Scottish lord in black jeans and boots who had wanted her to change her plane ticket for a later date.

She tried not to read too much into that.

She failed.

So she walked over to him. "You're back early."

"It was a quick job."

"Your charge must have gotten tired."

"He passed out," Patrick said with a grin. "I thought it wise to send him home early."

"Kind of you."

"Aye, I thought so." He looked at the walls. "Friends of yours?"

She followed his glance. "Actually, I was going to ask you if they were friends of yours."

"Never saw them before in my life," he said. "But strapping lads, those." He looked at her. "Did something happen?"

"I went walking in the woods and thought someone was following me. I ran back here."

He reached out and took her hand. "I'm sorry I wasn't here."

She fanned herself with her other hand. It was hot. She was hot from all that rock lifting. It had nothing to do with him. It had nothing to do with his handsome face, his perfect mouth, his amazingly green eyes. It had nothing to do with him stroking the back of her hand with his thumb.

It had nothing to do with the fact that he was looking at her as if he thought kissing her might be a good activity for the afternoon.

"You not here?" she managed, finding herself completely incapable of looking away from his mouth. "No big deal. I had the crew here."

"Now do you believe in ghosts?"

"Nah," she said with a smile. "I'm still a skeptic."

He laughed. Madelyn looked at him and smiled in response. He was, without a doubt, the most stunning man she had ever met.

And he looked at her as if he just might like her.

A lot.

"I'd say there isn't much room for disbelief anymore," he said dryly.

"Maybe not." She looked up, then jumped. "Here they come, trying to scare the hell out of me."

Patrick, as luck would have it, made a rather handy thing to hide behind, especially when she pulled him off the wall and put herself between him and that wall. She wasn't a coward. She was conservative. No sense in getting too involved in the whole paranormal thing.

She watched as the Highlanders one by one came and stood before her and Patrick, bowed to them both, then turned and walked away. They each disappeared behind the other side of the house.

It was so surreal, she just couldn't bring herself to believe what she was seeing. Then again, the fact that her guardsmen were walking *through* the rock wall instead of over was something to think about.

And then there was their dress. Their kilts looked like large blankets draped over their shoulders and belted around their waists. Add to that the enormous broadswords they either wore strapped to their backs or to their sides, and you certainly had a recipe for something quite unbelievable.

Unless you were standing there looking at it, of course.

And speaking of looking at things, there was Patrick to look at as well. She looked at him, bringing to mind Moraig's words.

1285? A medieval clansman? A time traveler?

She snorted. Right.

He handed her Jane's coat. "I was thinking perhaps you might like to go to Jamie's tonight. He always has something on the fire."

She nodded immediately. Yet another way to test Moraig's words.

Yet more time to spend with this man she couldn't seem to get out of either her mind or her heart.

"I'd love to," she said.

"Good." He took her hand. "Let's be off then, shall we? I left the car at Ian's."

"I don't mind the walk."

He stopped suddenly, turned her to him, then slipped his hand under her hair and looked down at her with a smile.

There were, she had to concede, quite a few things she didn't mind.

When he let her up for air—and this was some time after her knees had given way and she was upright only because she was digging holes into his shoulders with her fingers—she decided that kissing him was tops on her list of things she didn't mind at all.

"Shall we go?"

"I think I can still walk."

He laughed, took her hand, and gave it a squeeze. "I'll do what I can to keep you upright."

"Great."

Or was great the feel of his hand around hers? Or was great something she should use in a sentence such as "What a *great* big bunch of malarkey I spent the morning listening to"?

Hard to say.

What she did know was that she was happier than she should have been just walking next to the man. DiLoretto, Delaney, and Pugh seemed like a very long way away. Seattle seemed just as far away.

Comfortably far away.

"I hope you'll like my family," he said. He smiled down at her. "They are an interesting group."

An interesting *medieval* group? she wanted to ask, then pushed the question aside. It was ridiculous. The thought of it was ridiculous. It was his family and he wanted her to meet them.

She tried not to read anything into it. It was dinner, that was all.

The Culloden magic whispered over her soul again, a brief hint of it that was nothing more than a faint bit of fragrance on the air.

All right, so maybe it was more than just dinner. Maybe there was a great deal more to it than just that. Time would tell.

And with her plane ticket on hold and nothing pressing to return home to, time was on her side.

Chapter 21

P*atrick* pulled to a stop in front of the keep, turned off the car, and looked at Madelyn. She was staring at Jamie's hall with wide astonishment.

"Wow," she said, sounding a little breathless.

He smiled. "It's just a castle."

"Yeah, but people live here. *You* lived here."

"Aye, there is that. But it seems quite ordinary to me."

"Right," she said dryly. "And this black rocket we're sitting in is just one step up from a lawnmower."

"You have a point there." He smiled and opened the door. "Wait. I'll come fetch you." He went around and opened her door. He helped her out of the car, then caught her as she stumbled. And once he had his hands on her arms, there was no reason to let her go, was there?

None he could think of.

Was it going to be possible, he wondered as he lifted her face up with his hand and kissed her, to stop kissing the woman any time soon?

Would it be possible to actually put her on a plane home?

He could hardly bear the thought.

He lifted his head and stared down at her, marveling at the changes in her. Gone were the constrained tresses he'd seen her first wearing. Her hair was down, curling madly about her shoulders and down her back. Jeans and sweaters suited her perfectly, as did her visage unenhanced by pots of makeup. She was still that fresh-faced American, but now with a bit of Highland untamedness to her.

He was, he admitted uneasily, quite lost.

His heart murmured its approval.

"Anyone home?" she asked with a smile.

He blinked, then shook his head. "Sorry. I was just looking at you."

"Oh."

"Aye, oh," he said with a smile. "And I have to say that 'tis the finest view I've seen out of all the attractions I've had the pleasure of looking at over the past few days."

She blinked. She might have blushed.

"Well," she said finally.

"By the saints"—he laughed—"am I so stingy with compliments, then?"

"It isn't that—"

He took her face in both his hands and looked down at her seriously. "Then what, Madelyn? What is it, then?"

She closed her eyes. "It's just—"

He waited.

"It's just—"

"Oh, Pat's here!"

She jumped back as if she'd been bitten. For himself, he was so surprised, he almost fell over on top of her. He looked up, glared at Ian, who stood at the door grinning like the fool he was, then met Madelyn's eyes.

"I'll kill him later."

"I'll help."

"Jamie has quite a lovely view from the roof."

"I have a coat."

He laughed. "Then we'll rendezvous there later, after I've disemboweled several of my family members."

"Good plan."

He took her hand and led her into his brother's house Easily.

As if it weren't the monumental occasion it really was.

The hall was full of family. Jamie and his two lads were holding court there, imparting the good tidings of a new little girl resting upstairs to any and all who would listen. Ian and Jane were there with their children. Elizabeth's brother Alex and his wife Margaret were there with their children. The only fools who were unattached were he himself, Elizabeth's younger brother Zachary, and a family friend, Joshua Sedgwick, Jamie's minstrel by trade.

So much family.

For the first time in years, he yearned to join in their numbers with a family of his own.

A family made perhaps with the woman walking next to him.

He smiled down at her.

She was smiling the same kind of smile back up at him.

He wanted to be terrified by it, but all he could think of was how perfect it felt.

His heart whispered encouragingly. He didn't bother to contradict it.

"And who is this?" Jamie boomed.

Patrick was torn between wanting to roll his eyes and wanting to flatten his brother. Jamie knew damn well who she was. Patrick hadn't told him—indeed he'd had the happy fortune of not having clapped eyes on his older brother in days—but he was certain Jamie knew all the same.

"This is Madelyn Phillips," Patrick said. "Madelyn, this is my brother, Jamie. Don't call him *my laird*. It tends to go to his head, all that deference."

Jamie smiled his most lordly smile at Madelyn. "Come and sit, my lady. We are happy to have you here."

"Thank you, my laird," she said.

Patrick rolled his eyes at the way his brother immediately took to Madelyn. Patrick was the recipient of a very pointed look that spoke volumes about what he thought Patrick should be doing with Madelyn.

Patrick grunted. He'd get to it, if his bloody family would give him the peace to do it.

Aye, he would see to it.

And for the first time, the thought didn't terrify him.

"Patrick, Elizabeth bids you go to her when you've the chance," Jamie said. "She wants to show off the bairn."

"I'll go." He looked at Madelyn. "She just had her baby a couple of days ago. Do you mind—"

"Go," she said with a smile. "I'll hang out down here and see if I can't get some answers out of your brother as to what it was like to grow up in a castle."

He nodded, shot Jamie a warning look his brother received

with a bland expression of complete noncompliance, then left Madelyn in Jamie's care and went up the stairs to Elizabeth's bedroom. He could only imagine what his brother would tell her.

Best not to know, probably.

He knocked on Elizabeth's door.

"Come in."

He poked his head inside the bedchamber. "Are you decent?"

She snorted and pushed herself up gingerly in the bed. "Give me a break. Come look at this beautiful girl."

He entered, shut the door, stoked up the bedchamber fire, then went and knelt down by the bed. He looked at the baby.

"She's stunning," he said. "Doesn't look a thing like Jamie, obviously."

Elizabeth laughed. "She does, too, but I agree with you. She's beautiful."

He reached out and stroked the baby's cheek. "Long labor?"

"Unmercifully brief," she said. "It seems to get shorter every time."

"Perhaps 'tis a good thing you stay home, then," Patrick said. "You'd likely birth the poor wee thing in the car with Jamie tearing his hair out if you tried to make for hospital."

She shivered. "Heaven help us." She lifted the baby and put her in Patrick's arms. "Hold your sweet niece and tell me about this girl you've been seeing."

"I haven't been *seeing* her," Patrick protested, but he did accept his niece. He looked down into her face and felt his heart melt. "Ah, Elizabeth, she's a beauty." His eyes burned fiercely. "A beauty."

Elizabeth put her hand on his arm. "It isn't too late, Pat. You're thirty-five, not seventy-five."

He didn't have the heart to disagree. "Aye, I know."

"What of your Madelyn?"

"She's a good woman," he said slowly.

"And . . ."

He looked at her seriously. "She has things to return to in the States."

"Does she?"

He blew out his breath and tried to smile. "Aye. At least I think she does. Whether or not she would be interested in living in the wilds of Scotland hasn't been discussed as of yet."

"Maybe it should be. If you like her."

"You're beginning to sound a great deal like your husband."

"I've been married to him for quite some time," she agreed. "He tends to rub off on a person, as you well know."

"Aye." Patrick looked down at the baby in his arms and let himself give the possibility serious thought. Would Madelyn be interested in giving up her life in the States? Could she possibly be at all tempted by the thought of staying home and nurturing his children?

Could he possibly get that wreck of a house in any condition to shelter a family any time in the next millennium?

He looked at Elizabeth. "What did you name her?"

"Patricia," she said with a smile.

He laughed. "You didn't."

"Well, we couldn't name her Patrick. It was as close as we could reasonably come."

"I'm flattered." He kissed the wee babe gently on the forehead, then handed her back to her mother. "Need anything?"

"Company. Come talk to me when you have a few minutes later this week."

"And supper?"

"Joshua's bringing me something in a minute. Go take care of your lady."

"You would like her."

"Give me a day or two to get back on my feet, then I'd like to meet her." She shook her head with a wry smile. "The woman who stole Patrick MacLeod's heart. She must be something else."

Why deny it? He smiled weakly. "She is."

He leaned over, kissed the baby one more time, and Elizabeth too for good measure, then left the room before he could spew out any more admissions he wasn't sure he was fully ready to make.

He thumped down stairs he'd descended for the major part of his life, then paused at the bottom and looked at the scene before him in the great hall.

The high table was just as it had always been, with Jamie's chair at the head and the rest of the seats pulled up on either side. Friends and family sat there, eating and drinking as they had countless times in the past. But there was something different.

And that difference was the addition of one Madelyn Phillips. She was sitting at Jamie's left hand, in front of the fire, laughing as if she actually enjoyed herself.

And Patrick felt something shift inside him, something that had once been hard. His poor heart, most likely. It was nothing but fluff now. Or maybe it had been soft all along, soft since Culloden, when his heart had first begun to torment him with things he wanted but hadn't been willing to reach for.

Things he might have with this woman.

He strode out into the great hall before he could give that any more thought. His place had been saved next to Madelyn, and he took it without hesitation. He looked at his brother.

"Patricia?"

Jamie sighed. "Aye. 'Tis easier than a wee Patrick, I suppose."

"I'm honored, brother."

"Aye, well, the wee lass will need a godfather. It may as well be you."

Patrick laughed. "You overwhelm me with flattery." He looked at Madelyn. "He does this. Damns with faint praise."

"It's an interesting tactic," Madelyn said. She looked at Jamie. "You have a wonderful castle here, my laird. Has it always been in this kind of shape, or did you have to do much restoration?"

Patrick left that question to his brother and concentrated on his supper. He ate with singlemindedness, listening with half an ear to the grilling Madelyn was subjecting his brother to. He smiled at Jamie's stalls and outright lies, then stole looks at Madelyn to watch her as she tried to take his brother apart.

Did Jamie know much about history? What did he think of swords and swordplay? Was there any truth to the rumors of Highland magic in the forests nearby?

Jamie hedged. Madelyn pressed. Patrick looked first at his cousin Ian, then at Jamie's minstrel Joshua. They were trying not to smile. Patrick then looked at his sister-in-law Margaret and found her watching the interplay with fascination.

He wondered what Madelyn would say if he took her aside on the morrow and gave her the answers Jamie hadn't. Would she believe him, or would she look at him as if he'd lost his mind?

Her reaction might be all the answer he needed.

He hoped it would be a reaction he could live with.

He leaned back in his chair and reached for her hand. She looked at him, smiled, then turned back to his brother.

Aye, he would tell her. And if she could accept it, even be willing to think about accepting it, he would think of other things.

Postponing her plane ticket quite a bit longer, for one.

He finished his meal with a very light heart.

And then a banging commenced on the door.

Jamie looked up in annoyance. "Who dares this late?"

"Who knows?" Zachary said. "Are there any more turnips in that bowl? I'm turning over a new leaf with my eating habits."

Jane handed Zachary the vegetables. "Wise choice."

"Yeah, but I probably should have started with something less healthy, like low-fat Twinkies or something. This vegetable stuff is almost too much for me."

"As is that banging," Jamie said, irritated. "Zach, go get the door."

Zach sighed. "Forever at the door. Some day I'm going to open it and find something interesting."

"Like a maid to clean your room," his brother Alex said.

"No, like a beautiful woman," Zach said, rising and trudging over to the door. "One who's heard of me and wants me for my vast architectural skills."

"Dream on," Alex said with a snort.

Patrick sipped his wine, then looked at Madelyn. She was staring at him thoughtfully. "Aye?" he asked.

"Just thinking."

"Pleasant thoughts?"

She smiled. "Pleasant thoughts. Interesting, pleasant ones." She nodded toward the door. "What does Zachary do?"

"He's an architect," Patrick said. "He designed Ian's house. He's itching to get his paws on mine as well."

"He's good," she said, looking faintly surprised. "He's into restorations, then?"

"He has a fascination with all things medieval," Patrick said dryly. "There's great scope for his work here in Scotland."

"I'll just bet there is." She leaned over toward him. "And what about your brother?" she whispered. "What does he do, or does he just do the laird thing?"

He shrugged. "He tends to the land, sees to his tenants."

"That's all?"

"He invests. He travels. The traveling takes a lot of time." That was an understatement, and one Elizabeth would certainly have something to say about, but it was the truth.

"I'd like to hear about his travels."

"And Jamie would like to blather on about them for hours, flush with your flattery, if you asked him. Perhaps after dinner, if you like. Then," he said, pausing and looking at her, "then perhaps we should talk—"

He was interrupted.

It was, he suspected he would no doubt decide later, an interruption that would change the course of his life.

The door slammed back against the wall. Zachary managed to avoid being crushed, but just barely.

Gilbert McGhee strode inside. "Where is the murderer?"

Patrick didn't move. He was, he had to admit, so surprised at having his father-in-law storming into his brother's hall that all he could do was lean back and wait for events to unfold.

Jamie stood, his expression chiseled straight from granite. "What do you want?" he demanded.

"Justice," Gilbert said.

"Justice was done," Jamie said coldly.

"And what would *you* know of it?" Gilbert demanded. "Have *you* lost a child? Have *you* watched the light of your life be snuffed out by the callous actions of a murderer?"

Patrick winced at the pain in Gilbert's voice. Whatever the truth was, there was truth enough in the man's pain.

"I want him hanged," Gilbert said, his chest heaving. He pointed at Patrick. "I want him to *swing* for what he did!"

Alex got up and casually walked to stand behind Patrick's chair. "Maybe you don't have all the facts."

"My daughter's dead," Gilbert spat. "What other fact do I need?"

"I believe the inquest was quite thorough," Alex said calmly.

"The facts were suppressed," Gilbert insisted. "They didn't say how he stole her from me."

Or that she wed me to escape you, Patrick added silently.

"He bribed her with clothes and trips whilst he was working for my bloody brother-in-law."

My fault, Patrick conceded. *Clothes I bought her to prove I was good enough for her and could compete with your money.* Which he hadn't been able to, of course. Not while she'd been alive. It was only after she'd died that he had come into his inheritance.

"She was miserable," Gilbert said, "more miserable with every day that passed."

Patrick couldn't disagree.

"It was all his fault," Gilbert said—stretching out his hand and jabbing his finger toward Patrick. "I saw her before he took her off on a trip—and that too close to her delivering for any man with sense to take a woman traveling. I saw her. I saw her grief. I know the cause."

Patrick looked at his father-in-law. He knew Lisa's grief as well, far better than her father did. Her lover had broken with her for the last time. Patrick had taken her away to keep her from committing suicide in front of the bastard's flat in Glasgow.

"She should have been in hospital."

Patrick couldn't have agreed more.

"He tried to kill her," Gilbert said hoarsely, "with his own concoction of herbs."

Untrue, Patrick thought. He'd given her herbs, that he couldn't deny. Something to make her retch up all the sleeping pills she'd taken, but it had been too late. He'd given her something else to try to pull her out of shock. He'd called for the paramedics, aye, but used his own methods to try to save her until they arrived.

After finding her half dead on her bed.

"He killed his own child!" Gilbert shouted. "His child! What kind of man does that?"

Untrue as well, Patrick thought with a sigh. Hadn't she taunted him with that often enough? " 'Tis not yours; 'tis Robert's," she would say. "How does that please you?"

But Robert hadn't wanted to be a father. Once he'd found out Lisa was pregnant, he hadn't wanted to be a lover anymore, either. Patrick had watched her spend nine months trying to get Robert back.

Bloody business.

Gilbert leaned over the table so quickly, Jane had to duck out of her chair to avoid being smashed by him.

"I'll get you," he promised. "See if I don't."

"Not if we see to you first," Ian said, rising.

He fixed Madelyn with a contemptuous stare. "How does it feel, my dear, to be sleeping with a murderer?"

Patrick rose as well. "Get out of my brother's house."

"I'll kill you myself," Gilbert promised.

"Not if we kill you first," Ian growled.

"Touch me and I'll sue!" Gilbert said.

Patrick walked around the table, took Gilbert by the arm, and escorted him out the door.

"You'll regret the day you clapped eyes on her," Gilbert said, his chest heaving.

"There isn't a day I don't already," Patrick said wearily.

Gilbert gave him one final look of venomous hatred, then stumbled down the stairs and into the passenger side of a Jag.

Bentley Douglas Taylor III's Jag.

Wonderful.

Patrick turned around to find himself facing the men of
his family: Jamie, Ian, Alex, Zachary, and Joshua, all standing in a row behind him.

He'd never been more grateful for anything in his life.

He looked at the supper table.

Madelyn's face was ashen.

He stared at her for several moments, not hearing Jamie's
words, or Alex's, or Zach's stubborn defending of him. All
he could see was Madelyn. All he could think of was what
grief his past would bring her.

A lifetime with Gilbert McGhee haunting him.

A lifetime with Gilbert McGhee hunting him.

Could he do that to her? Could he do that to the children
he might have with her?

He made a decision.

It was the only one he could make.

He nodded to his kinsmen, walked over to the table, and
smiled grimly at the ladies.

"Hopefully that wasn't dessert. If you'll excuse me?"

He didn't wait for a response. He didn't look at Madelyn.
He merely turned and walked up the stairs to Jamie's office.
He dialed the phone.

"Aye" was the answer.

"That job tomorrow still open?"

"For you, always."

"I'll be there. Book Madelyn a flight home tomorrow evening, would you? First class."

There was a long pause. "Patrick, are you sure?"

Patrick took a deep breath. He wasn't sure of anything.
"Aye," he said. "I'm certain."

He hung up the phone. He stood there for several minutes
in silence. Nay, he wasn't sure of anything. But the decision
was made. There was no point in unmaking it now.

Besides, it never would have been possible between them.
He wanted a Scot to warm his bed, not a refugee from a
Swiss finishing school as Lisa had been, nor a Yank lawyer
in a black suit as Madelyn was.

Madelyn would be fine.

And so would he. He would go home, barricade himself

in, and wait for Gilbert to unleash the fury of hell on him.

Something Madelyn didn't need to see.

He turned to go back downstairs only to find his brother standing at the door of the library, his arms folded over his chest, his expression dark. Patrick swore at him.

"Don't you have anything better to do than eavesdrop?" he snapped.

Jamie shrugged. "Nay," he said simply.

Patrick gestured at the phone. "I need to work."

"You need to flee, more like."

"Can you blame me?"

"Oh, aye," Jamie said placidly. "I can."

"You know nothing of my life."

Jamie straightened. The expression on his face might have made Patrick quail, but he was a grown man now and beyond all that.

Besides, Jamie's dungeon had been filled in a very long time ago.

"And you know nothing of mine," Jamie said. "I've killed, in defense and in anger. Do you think I don't bear the stain of that on my hands?"

"But—"

"You lost Lisa through her *own* foolishness, not yours."

"How do you know?" Patrick demanded. "How do you know I wasn't the one to give her what she took to end her life and my child's?"

"If it *was* your child—"

"Are you finished?" Patrick demanded. "Finished with business you know nothing of?"

Jamie stepped aside. "Go then," he said. "Go and ruin your life."

"I'll hardly do that," Patrick said with a snort. "Madelyn was a diversion. Something to pass the time with. I was never serious about her."

Jamie remained silent. That in itself was something, but Patrick suspected it wouldn't last long. Well, it would last long enough for Jamie to pull out several of his bloody books and pore through them. He could hardly wait to find out what sort of emotional ailment his brother would diagnose him with.

He paused at the head of the stairs. It was the best thing he could do. The kindest thing. The best thing for her.

He couldn't drag her through the morass of his life.

He couldn't.

He put his shoulders back and walked down the stairs, his mind firm, his purpose fixed.

Chapter 22

Madelyn packed her last sweater into the suitcase, zipped the suitcase shut, and carried it over to the door. It was surprisingly heavy. Then again, Patrick had been buying her clothes for the past week and half.

He bribed her with clothes and trips. . . .

Why, so that Lisa would marry him? Madelyn shook her head. There were so many things that just didn't add up. She could imagine a woman doing many things with Patrick as her partner, but having to be bribed to spend time with him—or to fall in love with him—just wasn't one of them.

Maybe Gilbert McGhee had an overinflated opinion of his late daughter's desirability.

Madelyn put the thoughts out of her mind. It wasn't really her business anymore. She was convinced of that. She'd been convinced the moment Patrick had walked back into the great hall the night before. She'd seen the change in him from across the room.

When he'd told her on the way back to Ian's that he was going to fly to London the next day, she hadn't been surprised.

When he said he'd managed to find her a really great seat on a flight back to the States that same evening, she'd been even less surprised.

No less devastated, but no less surprised.

She could only imagine his reasons, especially once she'd discovered that Gilbert had driven off in Bentley's car. That information had come by way of Elizabeth's younger brother Zachary, who had been practically frothing at the mouth to get at Gilbert. Patrick had to be anxious to get rid of Bentley.

And since she was connected to Bentley, he was probably anxious to get rid of her as well.

Though for all she knew, there was much more to it than that. Maybe Patrick had just decided he didn't want another relationship. Maybe he'd just decided he didn't want a relationship with *her*. He'd dropped her like a hot potato before. Maybe he was just running true to form.

That didn't account for the way he'd treated her over the past couple of days, but maybe that was an aberration.

She closed her eyes briefly. What a glorious aberration it had been.

She sighed. She would come to conclusions later. For now, she had to get through the day.

She wondered if it would be possible to get one last walk in before she had to go.

She pulled Jane's jacket on over her long skirt and warm sweater, then went downstairs to see what there was to poach from the cabinets that wouldn't wake the family and spoil her plans. She tiptoed down the stairs only to find that the kitchen light was already on. She took a deep breath, put her shoulders back, and walked into the light.

Ian was standing at the stove, thoughtfully stirring something in a pan. He looked up as she walked in.

" 'Tis early," he said. "Couldn't sleep?"

"I'm leaving today," she managed.

"So soon?" He looked surprised.

"Patrick has a job. He thought it would be easier to get me to the airport when he goes to London today than to wait for her another time."

"I see."

"I'm ready to go," she said brightly. "You can only be a tourist so long before it gets really old. Too much excitement and all. I really need to get home as soon as I can."

He approached, dishtowel in hand. He handed it to her. "Your eyes are leaking."

"Allergies."

"I thought so."

She wiped her eyes, then handed the towel back to him with a brilliant smile. At least she hoped it had been brilliant. It felt sort of sick and forced. "Gotta go. One last hike."

"Be careful."

"What's up here but a lot of heather and the occasional ghost?"

He smiled. "True enough."

"Unless there's something else you'd like to be divulging."

"You've been talking to Moraig."

"Yes."

"She's fanciful."

"I'd say." She looked at him. Thirteenth century? Right. Ian looked perfectly modern. "I love her, but she's completely delusional. You weren't born in the Middle Ages, were you?"

"Do I look like I was born in the Middle Ages?"

"That isn't an answer."

"It felt like one to me," he said with a smile. He shoved a scone into her hands. "Be careful."

"What's the worst that could happen?" she asked lightly. "I find myself in a different century?" She didn't believe it. Not really.

Swords and swordplay aside.

"Hurry back."

She nodded and left the house before she could make a bigger fool of herself. She pulled the door shut behind her and managed to get mostly off Ian's property before she started to sob. She stopped under the eaves of the forest, buried her face in her hands, and cried in earnest.

It was a very messy sob session.

She was still blubbering when she decided that perhaps it would be in her best interest to keep going. The sky was barely lightening. Patrick didn't have plans to leave until noon. She could almost get herself to Moraig's and back in that time. Better that than hanging around Ian's, trying to make polite conversation.

The thought of *that* was enough to hastily propel her forward.

She walked swiftly along the way she'd gone the day before. In fact, the path to Patrick's house was becoming all too familiar. She paused and looked into his backyard.

No piper.

No ghostly guardsmen.

So they were all ditching her. It shouldn't have surprised her, she supposed. Maybe she just wasn't cut out for this kind of life. She needed to work. She needed stores with hot bakery goods and stimulating drinks. She needed chocolate shops within walking distance of her labors. She needed clients.

The client thing, she had to admit, might be something she would have to look at differently. Maybe it was time she started working for people who really needed her services, instead of rich, spoiled executives who were too lazy to obey the law.

She found herself quite suddenly in the forest.

And it was then, beyond all reason, that she found herself believing quite strongly in that Highland magic Roddy had told her about.

She stopped. The forest seemed to stop with her and wait while she made some kind of decision.

Forward or back.

She took a deep breath and walked forward. The silence around her was singularly unnerving. She crunched slowly through the woods, holding up her long skirts to keep them out of the wet. She began to feel a little disconnected. It was like having jetlag, but this was much worse. She found herself becoming increasingly tempted to just sit down and rest. In fact, the temptation was almost overwhelming.

She stopped, put her hands over her eyes, and rubbed. Maybe it really was allergies. There was something, some kind of smell that was really beginning to get to her.

She froze.

Eternal Riches cologne.

She whirled around. Bentley stood there. That wasn't a pleasant look on his face. She gave herself a hard shake and went on the defensive.

"What do you want?" she demanded.

"You," he said curtly.

"Forget it. You had your chance and you blew it."

He took a menacing step toward her. "I do not 'blow' things," he said. "And I have no intentions of blowing this one. Now, come along. We'll go back to the States, we'll get married, and then I'll get to where I'm supposed to be."

She heard something there she hadn't ever heard before. Either that, or she hadn't listened closely enough. "Where you're supposed to be?" she echoed.

"Dean of Northern Pacific's law school."

She shook her head. "What does that have to do with me?"

"Can you be that stupid?" he snapped. "Your father? Dean Anderson? Good friends? Do I have to explain every little seance of every situation to you?"

"That's *nuance*, Bentley, and no you don't. I get your drift. I just don't understand why you want to marry me so you can be friends with Dean Anderson. Make your own friends without me."

"No."

"No?"

He leaned forward. "I don't want to be his friend," he said in a low voice. "I want to replace him."

The way he said it sent chills down her spine. She looked at him in a brand-new light. He wasn't a jerk. He wasn't even a compulsive liar.

He was crazy.

Madelyn took Jane's phone out of her pocket. She flipped it open and tried to look where she was dialing while still keeping her eyes on him.

Bentley slapped the phone out of her hand. "Cooperate," he said, "or you'll regret it."

She backed up. "What're you going to do?" she asked shakily. "Kill me? That'll really endear you to my father."

"He'll be thrilled to know I killed your murderer. The man who chased you in the woods that I caught and killed. Unfortunately, he got to you first."

"You're kidding."

"Am I?" he asked. "I've gotten plenty of murderers off during my long and distinguished career. I know how to avoid getting myself nailed."

"You are nuts!"

"I told you never to talk to me that way!" he shouted.

He leaped toward her.

She turned and bolted.

He was right on her tail for quite some time. She brushed aside branches and flung them back into his face. He cursed. He cursed her, cursed her father, and began to curse Dean Anderson. Good grief, did anyone at the firm have any idea what a psycho they had on their payroll?

She ran as fast as she could, then she began to realize something. The faster she ran, the farther behind her Bentley seemed to be. Maybe his Teflon arteries weren't so goo-resistant after all.

His shouts grew fainter and fainter until all she could hear was the crunching under her feet.

She ran until there was silence behind her. But she couldn't stop. Shouting started up again and she continued to run until she realized something rather distressing. The shouting continued, but it was coming from a different direction.

In *front* of her.

She burst out of the trees into what could only be described as a small-scale war.

A small-scale medieval war.

She stood there and gaped. Had she stumbled into some movie set? Some really authentic reenactment group? Some bunch of yahoos who'd given up the corporate life to get back to nature? Based on the bathing standards she could determine from where she stood, that last theory had the best shot at being true.

She backed up.

Into someone who grabbed her by the hair and yelled in triumph.

The fighting stopped, not because of her appearance, but because apparently all the opponents were dead.

And she, it seemed, was the booby prize.

The men, all but the one holding her by the hair, that is, turned to look at her. Whatever shouting there had been faded away to be replaced by grumbles of irritation and spec-ulation.

One man, who she assumed by his stance and the way the others gave way for him to approach was the leader, looked her over in a very unfriendly, very suspicious manner. He said something to her. She couldn't understand a word.

She tried a word of her own. "MacLeod?" she asked.

The man frowned, as if he couldn't understand her at all.

She tried again, with the same cadence Moraig used when she said her name. "MacLeod?" she tried again.

The man's expression darkened considerably. He barked something at the man holding her that she didn't understand at all.

But she understood the hand motion. She suspected it translated across languages into something resembling *render the demon unconscious so we might bind it and examine it later with an exorcist nearby*.

Or something like that.

Good grief, where *was* she?

She didn't really feel the blow.

But she had the wherewithal to hope her head was still attached to functioning vertebrae before the light of her con-sciousness flickered.

Then went out.

Chapter 23

Patrick walked briskly into the kitchen and made straight for breakfast. He'd overslept and that bothered him. He'd had troubling dreams and that bothered him as well. His mind was made up. Dreams about loss and desperately searching for something he couldn't quite find and the utter despair that had come with it—aye, it was nothing he wanted any more part of. It had nothing to do with Madelyn. It had nothing to do with his feelings for Madelyn. It had been a sour stomach coupled with Gilbert stress. When Madelyn woke, he would help her pack, take her to London, put her on the plane, and the tale would be finished.

He could do nothing else.

He looked around him. The kitchen was empty. No family. Cold breakfast. He opened the door and looked out into the garage. Both cars were there. He went back to the back door and peered out.

"Looking for me?"

He almost cracked his head on the door frame, he whipped around so fast. He rubbed at the spot that he'd almost damaged, then glared at his cousin.

"Actually, I wasn't, but you'll do. Where's Madelyn?"

"She went for a walk." Ian looked at him blandly. "Abrupt end to her vacation, wouldn't you agree?"

"It was time for her to go."

"McGhee is mad, Pat. He'll disappear, in time."

Patrick turned and faced his cousin. "And just how will that come about, Ian? Will he simply drop into a hole in the ground and vanish?"

Ian was silent for several moments. "It could happen," he said with a very small smile.

Patrick snorted.

"It could," Ian insisted. "You would know. We both would know."

"That is far in the past."

"Mayhap it should become more in the present for you," Ian said.

"And how would that sit with our fine Hamish Fergusson? He'd have my head."

"What could he prove? That you'd pushed Gilbert onto a particular piece of ground, and he'd fallen back through time into the seventeenth century? Into the Middle Ages?"

Patrick turned away. "I cannot hear this today," he said, wishing he could stick his fingers in his ears. "Not today. I must find her, take her to London, and let her be about her own business."

"And what if her business is with you?"

Patrick ignored the question and applied himself to investigating the depths of Ian's cupboard. Stale biscuits not even Alexander would tolerate fell out into his hands. He shrugged, opened the package further, and began to eat. He looked at Ian.

"Anything else to ask?"

"The question still stands."

"I don't care to answer it. Any more advice? Any more calls to change my mind about her?"

Ian leaned back against the counter. "I don't think changing your mind about her is really what's at issue here, is it?"

"By the saints," Patrick said in disgust, "you've been loitering in Jamie's study."

Ian smiled. "And become potential fodder for his experiments? Surely you jest." He folded his arms across his chest. "What would you do if there were no Gilbert McGhee to make your life hell?"

Wed Madelyn was almost out of his mouth before he could stop it. He turned away from the thought. "My mind is made up."

Ian sighed. "So I see. Very well, then. Will you go fetch her, or allow her a little more peace?"

Patrick considered. The thought of just sitting and waiting was more than he could bear. "I'll go to my house," he decided. "Stack a few rocks. Continue Madelyn's work in the garden."

He heard the patter of little feet coming down the stairs. Ah, nay, not the family. He couldn't stomach the thought of having to speak to them this morning. Jane wouldn't say anything, but she would think him a fool.

"I'd best go," he said quickly.

"Coward."

He glared at his cousin. "I'd repay you for that, but I haven't the time." He turned to go.

"Pat?"

He turn back unwillingly and waited.

"You are a MacLeod," Ian said, "and we do not run."

"Ian, I cannot kill him."

"There are ways to ruin a man without killing him."

Patrick looked at his cousin. "Does that make me any better than he?"

"It would give you your love."

Briefly, the thought of Madelyn whispered across his soul, like a gentle breeze, a breeze full of springtime.

"She is not my love," he lied. He turned and walked away before he had to face any more uncomfortable things. He grabbed his coat out of the closet and left the house. He walked quickly to his house. By the time he'd gotten there, his coat was off and he was far warmer than he'd counted on being.

He stood at the gate to his garden and looked out over the disaster. A disaster except for the large patch that Madelyn had cleared the day before. It actually looked as if something could, with enough care, grow there quite well.

He tried to ignore the relevance of that observation to his own life.

He rolled up his sleeves and set to work. And, as he should have expected, it began immediately to rain.

He worked until he was thoroughly soaked, then surrendered and went inside. He called Ian, made certain Madelyn hadn't come back, then went into his gathering room and contemplated a fire. He had a pair of hours yet before they needed to leave.

Then again, it would likely take a pair of hours to get the bloody fire going.

He threw on a log, lit it, and watched the wood smoke like a green tree. He sat down on a stool and stared gloomily—as best he could through the thick smoke—into the feeble flames.

It was likely the smoke that kept him from noticing that he wasn't alone.

He sat bolt upright and gaped at the vision that had appeared next to him.

There was a chair there where none had been a moment before. The chair was, by most modern standards, quite austere. But considering the lack of furniture in the room, Patrick found the high-backed, seventeenth-century chair to be quite luxurious. And as for the very well-dressed gentleman lounging against a large, finely embroidered pillow? He was luxuriously appointed as well.

Patrick continued to gape.

"Shut yer mouth, ye wee fool," grumbled the older man. He put his pipe back into his mouth and chewed on it.

Patrick shut his mouth with a snap and tried to breathe normally. It wasn't that he hadn't seen a ghost or two in his day. His niece—by way of the same convoluted tree Roddy perched in—had an entire garrison of specters at her command. There was also that ghostly piper who seemed to find the hill behind his house to his liking. But those shades were either at Iolanthe's house or on the hill behind his house.

They weren't in his living room.

He stared at the ghost, who seemed to have brought not only his own furniture but his valet as well. The servant set a silver tray with decanter and glass on a table near his master's elbow.

"Who *are* you?" Patrick asked. "If I'm allowed to ask."

"Archibald," the shade answered.

"The Glum," offered his valet.

"Have my reasons for that," said Archibald, rather glumly. He looked at Patrick. "First Lord of Benmore."

Patrick could hardly believe his eyes or his ears. "Well," he said. "How lovely."

Archibald fixed him with a steely glance. "Aye, it would be if ye could see yer way clear to be about yer duty of carrying on the line—now that ye have me title and all."

"Carrying on the line?" Patrick echoed.

"Why else would I be here?"

"Why indeed," Patrick managed.

"Now, be about it, man, and quickly. Where is the wench anyway?"

"The wench?"

"The Colonist. Ye are going to wed with her, aye?"

"Well," Patrick stalled. "Actually, nay. I told her I'm sending her home this eve."

"Nay!" Archibald exclaimed, looking quite horrified. "What'd ye go and do a bloody idiotic thing such as that for?"

"I'm having a few personal—"

Archibald swore. Quite inventively, truth be told. "The line, boy!" he bellowed. "Ye've a duty to the line!"

Patrick hated to dash the man's hopes, but he had to. "I'm a MacLeod," he said apologetically. "I don't have anything to do with your line."

"Why, ye wee silly fool," Archibald spluttered, "have ye never taken a peep up yer family tree? Or down it, in your case?"

Patrick opened his mouth to ask how Archibald seemed to know so much about him, but didn't have a chance.

"My sweet ma was a MacLeod, wed to an Englishman, don't ye ken. It started off a right dodgy business—thanks to a few pesky in-laws—but it turned out to be quite a love match. So ye see, my line is *yer* line. And ye'd best be about seein' it preserved."

"And ye'll do something about the dreadful state of disrepair in my home," commanded a voice that would have terrified even the staunchest of servants.

Archibald slunk down in his chair and puffed furiously on his pipe.

Patrick watched in complete astonishment as a woman in quite possibly the flounciest, most jewel- and lace-encrusted gown he'd ever clapped eyes on appeared. Her hair alone was a good three feet high. She snapped her fingers at the Glum's valet.

"Chair."

He provided one immediately. It was literally overflowing with tapestry pillows.

Patrick stood. It seemed the thing to do.

The woman sat, then waved him down imperiously.

He sank down onto his stool, feeling quite like a servant.

"My wife," Archibald mumbled. "Dorcas."

Dorcas fixed Patrick with a steely glance. "I've been waiting," and she said that in a way that implied she'd been waiting *far* too long, "for you to see to the condition of my home."

"Ah . . ."

"Use the gold buried in the garden, for pity's sake," she said in exasperation. "Under the compost heap. If you possessed the least interest in restoring the garden, you would have found it by now. And you with your affinity for plants," she added in disgust. "Inexcusable."

"But your descendants—" Patrick began hopefully.

"Fools. Not a green thumb in the lot." She looked at him narrowly. "Go fetch Miss Phillips, wed her, then be on with the business of seeing to my house." She lifted her skirts off the floor with a look of extreme distaste. "I grow weary of haunting a stable."

"Best heed her," Archibald said, shooting Patrick a look. "And ye'll do it quick, if ye're wise."

Patrick looked at Dorcas. He almost asked her if she planned to stay, then realized that would be an extraordinarily bad thing to ask—given that he was quite certain he already knew the answer—so he nodded deferentially.

"Of course," he said. "Remodeling, aye. As soon as I can manage it. I'll start with this chamber."

"The girl, Patrick," Dorcas said crisply. "Fetch the *girl*."

"Well—"

She stood. "I will expect it done immediately." She looked at Archibald. "Don't sit and smoke all day."

She gave Patrick one last pointed look, then vanished.

Archibald sighed, then rose. He looked down at Patrick.

"Best do as she says, lad. 'Tis in yer best interest."

Archibald! came the imperious ghostly shout.

Archibald sighed, then vanished.

The valet picked up the silver tray, then disappeared with all the furniture and trappings of his master.

Patrick sat and looked at his now empty chamber. He shook his head and it felt suddenly clear, as if he'd just woken from a deep sleep. The dream he'd just had, vivid though it had been, seemed to recede further with every heartbeat.

Gold in the compost pile? A ghost with remodeling on her mind? Another worried about posterity?

Absurd.

As was sitting in a cold chamber with a fire that had long since given up the ghost, as it were. He looked at his watch. He needed to leave within the hour to make the plane. He'd have to find Madelyn and get going.

He called Ian. Still no Madelyn. He felt a brief flash of annoyance run through him, but he let it go just as quickly. He hadn't done right by her. Perhaps he deserved a bit of it in return.

Or perhaps it was nothing more than a desire of hers to see the beauty of his land one last time, and see it without being rushed.

And then another thought occurred to him.

What if she'd gotten lost?

Truly lost?

He left his house, saddled the Black, and rode without hesitation to the forest. He realized as he rode that unless he found Madelyn soon, he'd just blown £4000 on a one-way, first-class ticket for no reason.

Unless he could convince himself that he really shouldn't put her on that plane.

At the moment he was beginning to have serious doubts about his doubts.

He dismounted at the edge of the forest, then looked about him. He saw the tracks after a bit. Tire tracks. Then booted feet, leading farther into the forest.

Car, then driver on the hoof, if looks didn't deceive.

He followed the footsteps. They stopped several times, then were joined—or they followed—a set of smaller boot prints.

Madelyn's.

He knew. He'd bought the boots.

He continued to follow both sets, his unease growing with every footstep. The footsteps stopped. There was some trampling.

There was Jane's mobile phone, lying there uselessly on the ground.

He closed his eyes briefly, then picked up the mobile and put it in his pocket. The smaller prints fled. They were pursued. He followed until the larger prints stopped and retreated.

The smaller prints continued.

Patrick continued to follow them.

And then they disappeared.

Patrick stopped. His heart sank and the feeling of doom descended fully. He stood there for several minutes trying to decide what to do.

There was nothing he could do. Not at present.

He turned and walked back the way he had come. He paused at the place where Madelyn's footsteps had encountered the others. The other footsteps belonged to Bentley, he supposed. But what had happened? Had Bentley come upon her unawares? Was that why she'd fled? Or had she merely caught sight of him and tried to disappear without being seen?

And disappeared more fully than she'd intended?

He stood there for several minutes, thinking, before he realized that he was not alone.

He leaned over on the pretext of fixing his boot. Whoever was watching him obviously had a low opinion of him because he sprang out immediately. Patrick had the time to determine it was indeed Bentley Douglas Taylor III, ascertain what the fool thought to do—club him with a small log—roll aside, and let his foot connect with Bentley's solar plexus before Bentley knew what had happened. Patrick stood over Madelyn's ex-fiancé.

"Interesting choice of weapons," he said.

"I left my gun at home," Bentley panted from where he lay sprawled on the ground. He heaved himself to his feet and swung the wood again.

Patrick stepped back at a leisurely pace. "Where is she?"

"Damned if I know."

"Hoping she'll return?"

"Yes. Any more questions before I kill you?"

"Certainly," Patrick said pleasantly. He didn't specifically concentrate on making Bentley look as big a fool as possible, but the temptation was overpowering. He dodged with as little effort expended as possible. "Was it you who stirred the McGhee pot?"

"Of course. Too good an opportunity to miss."

"How did you find him?"

"I'm a damned good attorney," Bentley said. "I did some investigating. For the benefit of you rustics, that means I snooped around until I dug up good dirt."

"I understood the concept, thank you. Now, call him off."

Bentley snorted, then heaved the log at Patrick. "Fat chance."

"Why not? What do you care?"

Bentley pulled out a knife. "I don't like you."

"Nor I you," Patrick said, "but that's no reason to aggravate me."

"You slept with Madelyn, you idiot. Is that reason enough for you?"

Patrick was having a hard time understanding Bentley's logic, but he supposed there were depths to the fool in front of him that he would be better off not plumbing. "You gave her the sack," Patrick said slowly. "Doesn't seem to me as if you cared whether or not you slept with her if that's the case."

Bentley threw the knife at him. Patrick shifted and the knife went sailing harmlessly past.

"I like being the first," Bentley growled. "Not something you'd understand, given all the men your sister probably had before you."

Patrick took a step closer to him. "As I keep telling you,

I don't have a sister," he said before he punched Bentley full in the face.

Bentley fell to the ground and began to scream. "Lawsuit, lawsuit, lawsuit!" he wailed.

Patrick was tempted to just walk away, but he'd had just one too many insults from this one. It was past time to encourage Bentley to perhaps get on a plane and go back home.

Of course, that didn't solve the problem of what Madelyn would do with Bentley once she was back in the States, but he would work on that later, when he wasn't concentrating on the task at hand.

Maybe he would just see that she never went back to the States.

Assuming he could find her to see to that.

He couldn't begin to think about the possibility that he might not be able to.

Chapter 24

Madelyn woke, every muscle in her body protesting, her mind a complete fog of misery. Good grief, what had she eaten? Not even her mother's hot-fudge sauce eaten in vast quantities straight from the pan could give her a hangover of these proportions. She stretched.

And found she couldn't.

She opened her eyes. And the horror became real.

She was in a cage.

A cage on a rough stone floor, a stone floor that looked like—and felt like—it belonged in the Middle Ages.

She stared through the bars in astonishment.

She was looking at a great hall. It looked like James MacLeod's great hall, only this one was not nearly so tidy, nor well built. There was a fire in the middle of the room—and she was the farthest point from it, of course. Ratty tables and equally ratty stools were huddled around the fire like hopeful hobos trying to stay warm around a metal garbage can hearth.

Even more terrifying were the occupants of those tables and chairs: unkempt, unwashed . . .

Unintelligible.

She gaped at the men who sat at those tables—and the ones that milled about the hall—and realized she couldn't understand a damn thing they were saying.

Good grief, where *was* she?

This was taking reenactment to a whole new level. A whole new *unnecessary* level.

And what was the deal with her in the cage? She looked at the bars over her head, the bars all around, the metal wickets they were fixed to the floor by. It looked like serious business. She tried to stretch out her legs.

The cage was too small.

It was then she realized her feet were bare.

Her coat was gone as well.

She took quick stock of the rest of her. Everything else seemed to be intact. Maybe that was her silver lining.

It didn't make up for the fact that she was trapped in a space that was far too small. She put her hands on the front of the cage and tried to rattle it. It was solid, despite the noise it made.

Too much noise, she realized belatedly. One of the men looked at her, shoved the man next to him, and barked out some kind of order. The man rose and walked over to her.

He didn't look like a happy person.

He tossed the contents of his bowl at her through the bars. Hot soupy slop burned her face, and she quickly dragged her sweater across her eyes. She gaped up at the man in surprise.

"What's the deal—"

Then she shut her mouth. He was lifting up his kilt.

Then he peed on her.

She screeched and backed away, but there was nowhere to go.

"Stop it, you idiot!" she shouted.

He had a dagger in his hand faster than she could blink. She didn't doubt he would have used it if the man who'd sent him hadn't barked something else at him. The man glared at her, spit on her, then resumed his place at the rickety table.

Madelyn sat on the very cold floor, smelling now of some kind of rather foul soup and something else entirely, and found herself too shocked to even cry.

Where in the hell was she?

Maybe that was the operative word.

Hell.

She could only stare, speechless, at her surroundings, at her prison, and wait as her mind tried to absorb what was happening to her. As she did so, snatches of conversation came back to her.

When was he born?

Beware of the Highland magic . . .

Do I look like I was born in the Middle Ages?
Watch out for the red dots . . .

She wished she'd paid more attention. It didn't seem at all possible that anything she'd heard could have meant anything. Too fanciful, too magical.

Too ridiculous to take seriously.

Unreal.

Unfortunately, what she was experiencing was all too real.

She wondered, all too briefly, if she was just having a really intense nightmare. Or maybe she was in a coma and this was what happened to those poor people who couldn't seem to wake themselves up. Yes, that was it. She was in a coma and the drugs they were pumping into her to keep her alive were causing ghastly dreams. That could be the only reason for the complete impossibility of her current predicament.

She closed her eyes and willed herself to wake up. She willed herself to feel a bed beneath her and needles in her arms, to hear monitors beeping and machines whirring above her.

But all she could smell was some sort of rotting meat. Oh, and that lovely biffy smell that she'd been just sure she'd never have to smell again after Girl Scout camp.

But now the latrine smell was coming from *her*.

She opened her eyes. She rubbed her eyes. No, still there. Something out of a hallucination, there right in front of her. Beside her. All around her. It was enough to make her want to scream. She was immediately past crying, or wishing she'd done something different.

Like listen to Moraig.

Like follow Jane's map.

Like take her dad's advice to stay home and find a job instead of gallivanting around Scotland.

But instead of listening, she'd leaped precipitously, sure of her own mind, as usual, and landed herself, again as usual, in a morass of her own making.

And speaking of those sorts of things, she realized quite suddenly that she needed to pee. She wondered if she could be excused for a minute to run to the bathroom.

A man walked by her, spit on her, then continued on his way.

Maybe not.

So she sat on the cold, stone floor, hunched over in a cage that was neither big enough to stretch her legs nor big enough to sit up completely straight, and let the tears run unimpeded down her cheeks. She pulled her feet up under her skirts to keep them warm.

They had, after all, stolen her boots.

She looked at her surroundings and wondered if she would have been better off if they had whacked her a little harder with whatever had plunged her into unconsciousness.

Time passed.

An eternal, miserable period of time that had passed with the excruciating slowness of a slug crossing a particularly dense bit of rain forest.

She realized that time had marched on only because dinner seemed to be winding down. Scraps of food were thrown to the dogs. A few women wandered here and there, either serving drinks, clearing wooden platters, or getting groped.

It was then that she started to panic.

She was trapped in a box not tall enough for her to kneel upright in or lie down in. And there appeared to be no way to undo the quite serviceable bars or the sturdy-looking bands that held the bars together. She started to shake the bars anyway.

No one looked.

She started to hyperventilate. "Hey!" she gasped. "Somebody . . . let . . . me . . . out. . . ."

Still no one looked at her.

"Hey!" she shouted, then gasped in precious air. "Hey!"

The leader motioned to the man who'd come to visit her before. That man rose, drew his sword—his very sharp, very medieval-looking sword—and started toward her.

She wished belatedly that she'd kept her mouth shut. She had no doubt the man either intended to kill her or take her out of the cage and rape her. The hatred in his face was something she'd never seen before. It made Bentley's worst expression look like a mild toddler frustration.

She stopped shouting immediately.

The leader called to him. He cursed, but he stopped and listened. Unfortunately, he apparently hadn't received instructions to sit back down. He continued on his way toward her.

She closed her eyes and prayed.

The slap of his sword on the metal of the cage startled her so badly that she screamed.

That seemed to be enough to satisfy him.

He spewed several things—words and spit—at her, banged several times on the cage in an orangutan-like fashion, then returned to the table to the accompaniment of noises of approval from his buddies.

So she sat, her knees drawn up to her chest, her bare feet against the cold floor, and tried to concentrate on something besides what was assaulting her nose.

Her options were nonexistent. It was a sure bet she wasn't going to get out without some help—and it didn't look as if she was going to get any help any time soon. For all she knew, she would die right where she was, lost in some unknown location, in some situation so far from any reality she could have imagined that she almost couldn't fathom it.

She closed her eyes so at least she wouldn't have to look at her surroundings. The chill floor was harder to ignore, but she tried to ignore that as well.

Heaven help her, she *was* in hell.

The sun was rising. Madelyn knew this not because she could see the sun but because hell was beginning to stir. Actually the people inside hell were beginning to stir. She wished they would stir right out of her nightmare and back into the witch's pot they had erupted out of. But on Day Three, hell and its inhabitants were still right there in the thick of things with her.

She stared at a pair of women who began to set the table. Such a perfectly normal thing to do. Never mind that she'd gotten to watch one of those women be sent sprawling the night before by the leader of the clan's hand. The woman looked perfectly content to be where she was and didn't seem to think anything of her treatment. Madelyn had begun to not think anything of it either. During each of the three suppers she'd been forced to watch over the past three days, she'd seen the same kind of thing happen to various souls in the laird's care.

Hell was a violent place, apparently.

She'd come to the conclusion that the leader had to be the laird for several reasons. One, she was in the midst of a Scottish clan. The swords and plaids gave that away. And since that middle-aged man with the scar down his face seemed to be giving the orders and no one seemed willing to cross him, she determined he must be the laird.

She took that back. There was one man who seemed inclined to cross him on occasion. She wondered if he might be the laird's brother. They looked a great deal alike, and the laird seemed to tolerate the other's interference well enough.

Madelyn didn't like the brother. He seemed particularly interested in tormenting her. He liked to poke at her with sticks, toss her indescribables from the table, and, last but not least, use her as a sort of moving toilet target.

A real prince.

One of the serving women came and poured something in the bowl at Madelyn's feet. Madelyn didn't drink it right away. Who knew if she would get more? That, of course, had to be weighed against the possibility that one of the men might toss table scraps on her.

Difficult decision.

Not one Harvard Law had prepared her for.

She lifted the bowl and sipped cautiously. It was water, not some other kind of foreign substance.

It was heavenly.

She sat back in the cleaner corner of her cage and contemplated her situation. Actually, there wasn't much to contemplate. She was in a three-foot by four-foot cage without a bathroom, bed, or kitchen. Things were not pretty.

She wondered absently how long it would be before her

muscles froze up in the position they were in. She'd had cramps the first two days. Now, she was just in such agony, she'd almost gotten to the point that she could ignore it. Never again, if she were allowed freedom, would she complain about the cramped quarters in coach. She would instead revel in the freedom to get up and go stand in line for a shot at a minuscule airplane bathroom.

Not that she would be flying any time soon.

Unless she died and joined the heavenly hosts.

She had the feeling she could be kept alive quite a long time just where she was, which didn't bode well for her getting wings and a harp any time soon.

The men were waking up. This was the part she didn't enjoy. She steeled herself for the same kind of treatment she'd received before. They would each come along near the cage, say something to her, throw something on her, then retreat to their day's duties. They all said the same thing, which she had finally managed to repeat. The first time she'd said it back to one of them, he'd laughed, then said the words back at her with a suggestive leer.

She hadn't repeated the words again.

Out loud, of course. One of the words was MacLeod. She speculated on the meaning of the word attached. She suspected it wasn't complimentary, and might have something to do with either a choice of occupations or a feminine hound. Whatever it was, it wasn't good.

Which led her to believe that she wasn't in a MacLeod stronghold.

And given the frequency with which she'd heard the word Fergusson tossed about, she began to suspect she was in the Fergusson stronghold.

She began to have unkind feelings toward Hamish Fergusson than usual. It was no wonder all the MacLeods disliked the Fergussons. Then again, perhaps it was *because* of that animosity that she found herself where she was.

The day wore on. She sat, watched the goings-on, and tried to make sense of her situation. It was the same thing she'd been trying to do for the past three days. It wasn't getting any easier, nor was it making any more sense. But one thing had changed.

She could readily believe that Patrick MacLeod could possibly have been born in 1285.

But what to do now? Begging to be released was useless. Bargaining was impossible given that she had nothing of value but herself, and she didn't think, even if she'd been willing to give it up to fifty men repeatedly, that they would be interested in what she had to offer.

Which left her where she was, lost in time, lost without friends, very much alone in the midst of a crowd.

In hell.

Chapter 25

P *atrick* adjusted the sword strapped to his back, made certain his stash of medicine was securely stashed under his shirt, then stood in the forest and willed himself to the exact place Madelyn had gone before him.

The wind in the trees didn't vary. The chill in the air didn't abate. The flora and fauna around him didn't change.

Things were not going very well so far.

Maybe he was still enjoying the events of the day before too much.

He imagined Bentley was still in bed, nursing bruises that would never come to the surface and slaps that stung but wouldn't show. He himself had never enjoyed an encounter more. He probably would have enjoyed it even more if he'd been able to really do some damage, but it was the twenty-first century, after all, and one did not torture one's rival before doing him in the most painful way possible.

Patrick almost wished he could take Bentley back with him to the Middle Ages, where he could have repaid the bastard properly for all the things he'd done to make Madelyn miserable—and for his own misery, thanks to having Gilbert McGhee stirred up.

He stood quite still.

Time passed.

Nothing changed.

He was torn between becoming agitated and becoming tired. Despite all the time he spent waiting on his charges, he wasn't one to wait willingly, especially when the saints only knew what had happened to Madelyn by now.

He looked at his watch. An hour had passed.

And then he looked at his watch. He slapped his hand to his forehead. That was probably what was causing the delay.

He took off his watch, shoved it in the pouch under his shirt so it wouldn't show, and took up his waiting again.

By nightfall he was tired, anxious, and famished. He didn't dare leave his post, but he knew staying would do him absolutely no good whatsoever. He walked out of the forest and back down the meadow to his brother's keep. If anyone would know what he was doing wrong, it would be Jamie.

Given Jamie's propensity for time traveling, that is.

After all, it was Jamie who'd discovered almost all the *X*'s on the MacLeod map. Ancient Greece, the First Crusade, the Inquisition, and, Jamie's personal favorite, seventeenth century Barbados. Ian's map had red dots on it and no labels, but it was the same thing. Patrick didn't have a map. He supposed it was just dumb luck he hadn't been thrust back in time to some unwholesome and very unpleasant destination.

Either that, or he'd been saved by his complete unwillingness to believe the gates on Jamie's land worked.

The forest's power, he believed. He'd used it himself. But the other places?

Too fanciful.

Too ridiculous.

Too much a part of the past he'd done his damndest to kill and bury when he'd met Lisa. It wasn't as if she would have believed that his birthdate was closer to 750 years earlier than the one he'd given her. At times, it wasn't as if he believed it himself.

He left the forest and saw the lights on at Jamie's hall. It always reassured him, somehow, to see Jamie's keep in its modern reincarnation. He stood for a moment and just stared at the sight before him.

He sighed. Saying that he'd forgotten his roots was a lie. He believed it every time he got in the shower and saw the battle scars he bore. He believed it every time his first tendency when faced with danger was to reach for his sword. He believed it every time he looked at his brother and remembered the moment he'd pledged his life to his new laird after their father's death.

Maybe it should have been the first thing he'd said to

Madelyn. "Hello. I'm Patrick MacLeod, medieval clansman. My sword is at my lady's service."

He wouldn't make that mistake again. He would tell her the truth.

If he could find her.

And then he would tell her quite a few other things, starting and finishing with how he just didn't think he could stand the thought of life without her.

He couldn't seem to stop himself from agonizing over her fate as he walked into his brother's courtyard. Rape, murder, beatings. The saints only knew which she'd already endured. Murder would have been the kindest of all, probably.

Elizabeth's brother Alex was waiting for him outside on the front steps. Patrick came to a rather ungainly halt in front of his brother-in-law.

"No luck," Alex said, and it wasn't a question.

"None."

"Are you doing it wrong?"

"Is there a right way?"

"Well," Alex said slowly, "that is the question, isn't it?"

Alex had had his own experiences with traveling through time courtesy of Jamie's rather magical landscape. It had won him a wife, though that hadn't come without a few trials of his own. Patrick thought, all things considered, that Alex had come out better in the time-traveling game than he had. Then again, the last nine years hadn't been a complete waste. He'd found himself in a completely foreign world and mastered it.

He'd also found a woman he thought he just might love.

He looked at Alex. "You almost lost Margaret."

"Are you reminding me of that to make yourself feel better?" Alex asked with a grave smile.

Patrick shook his head. "'Tis out of desperation."

"Now that, brother, I understand." He nodded toward the hall. "Jamie's been holding a council of war all day, waiting for you to come back."

"He thought I'd fail?" Patrick asked in astonishment.

"He thinks," Alex said with a twinkle in his eye, "that you

have some emotional issues preventing you from fully harnessing the power of the time gates."

"What a mountainous pile of rubbish."

Alex laughed. "Don't say I didn't warn you. Come on. I want to watch the fireworks."

"Go to hell," Patrick muttered at him. He received only another laugh in return. He appreciated the attempt at levity, though. It wouldn't do to panic in front of his family. Alex would understand that. Jamie would try to provoke it, so he could study it.

There were times his brother threatened to drive him to madness.

But he followed Alex inside anyway.

There were several time travelers sitting around the table in the great hall. Actually, there wasn't a soul there who hadn't used the gates on Jamie's land at one time or another, save Jane. The others, however, all had quite thorough experiences with the practice.

Take Elizabeth, Jamie's wife, who was sitting in a comfortable, finely upholstered chair. She had once found herself thrust back into medieval Scotland—onto Jamie's land no less and into the castle's pit.

Jamie was still paying for that one.

She had also subsequently gone with Jamie on several journeys through time. She didn't anymore, not with her bairns, but she knew what to expect based on her past experience.

Next to her was Margaret, Alex's wife, who had, in a former lifetime, been a medieval lady of wealth and rank who had given up the past to come forward to a time not her own. Across from Margaret sat Joshua of Sedgwick, Jamie's medieval minstrel. Next to Joshua was Patrick's own cousin, Ian, who had wished himself forward into his lady wife's bridal salon. And missing from the table were several more souls who had found Jamie's land responsive to their entreaties. In fact, it was only Jane who had never used the gates on Jamie's land.

That was probably the reason her map had red dots scattered all over it and she was religious about not stepping on any of them.

Oh, and then there was Zachary, Elizabeth's brother, who had traveled back in time with them to rescue Jamie, who had gone back in time . . . well, it was complicated. In fact, it was so complicated, all the traveling and the unreality of it all, that Patrick had made a point of trying to forget the whole business existed.

Of course, that was a little difficult with the way his brother continued to investigate the nooks and crannies of his land, popping here, tiptoeing there. When people asked him what he did for a living, he always told them he was an armchair historian.

Ha. If anyone only knew the history he viewed from a much closer perspective than an armchair!

Oddest of all, though, was the thought that he was the pioneering time traveler of this group. If only he'd just stayed home . . .

He paused.

Nay, it had been worth it.

For them, if not for him. For him, too, if he could find Madelyn.

He took a deep breath and presented himself at the table. The table itself was littered with books, plates, cups, and notes. Indeed, it did look quite like a council of some kind.

"Failed?" Jamie asked unnecessarily. "Aye, well, we've been doing some research. Sit down and listen."

Patrick sat, and he listened. The others were discussing Madelyn's last known location and trying to divine a possible trajectory and destination. He exchanged a look with Alex. There was pity coming from Alex's quarter, and Patrick took it for what it was worth.

He also accepted a plate of something hot from Jane, who squeezed his shoulder briefly before she sat down and cuddled young Sarah on her lap. Patrick ate and let the talk wash over him. He couldn't join in. He had nothing to offer. His head was too full of horrific visions: war, bloodshed, rapine. Anything could have happened to her. She didn't speak the language. She had no idea what she was getting herself into.

She was wearing modern clothes, for pity's sake. If that didn't result in her immediate dismemberment, he didn't know what would.

And that was assuming she found herself in the clutches of a reasonable MacLeod ancestor.

But an enemy?

He shuddered to think.

So he ate and forced himself not to think. He answered the questions that were put to him, questions he didn't know the answers to, such as how Madelyn would react under extreme duress, how she would fare under torture, if the journey to madness for her would be short or long.

Questions he could scarce face without flinching.

Then his input ceased to be requested. The evening waned. Ian took Jane and their children home to bed. Margaret gathered hers up and took them upstairs to put them to bed in a guest room. Elizabeth had long since disappeared with little Patricia. Jamie's lads, who had sat valiantly near Jamie, trying to look as fierce and forbidding as their father, had fallen asleep on that father. Even Zachary had succumbed to the slumber granted a man who had ingested too few vegetables. Joshua pushed Zachary out of his chair.

"You're snoring," the minstrel said.

Zachary rubbed his eyes, got to his feet, and sought his own bed upstairs.

The front door opened and closed. Ian sat down at the table and refilled his cup.

"Any decisions made whilst I was gone?" he asked.

No one spoke. Patrick looked at the men of his family and felt their concern, unspoken though it was. They offered no solutions, for there were no easy ones. They sat in silence for some time.

Alex broke the silence first. "What will you do with McGhee?" he asked. "It seems as if he bears some responsibility for precipitating this situation."

"We should kill him," Ian said firmly.

Jamie scowled him to silence, then looked at Patrick. "Aye, that is an important question."

"What has that to do with this?" Patrick asked. "Madelyn

is the one lost. She's the one we must think about."

"The other must be solved," Jamie insisted.

"Then what would you have me do?" Patrick asked.

"Kill him," Ian repeated.

"Shut up, Ian," Patrick said, turning away from that very tempting idea. It doesn't matter that I didn't kill Lisa." He looked around the table. "She was half dead when I found her."

"We know that," Ian said with a sigh. "By the saints, Pat, we know that."

"You should tell Gilbert as much," Jamie said.

"He knows."

"But he doesn't know why she put herself in that condition," Jamie said. "Tell him that. Tell him what you left out of the inquest."

"For what purpose?" Patrick asked. "Will thinking of me being cuckolded by his promiscuous daughter cause fond feelings for me to sprout in his breast? He'll think I was lacking, that I drove her to another man."

"He's no fool," Alex said. "He's just obsessed with finding a scapegoat." He looked at Jamie. "There's no point in trying to appease the man. He'll be after Pat until one of them is dead."

"Give him the name of her lover," Ian advised. "Let that lad bear the brunt of Gilbert's anger. Or," he added, "kill him. That would be easier."

Patrick rolled his eyes. "Pull yourself into the present, Ian. I cannot kill the man, much as I might like to."

Jamie pursed his lips. "As entertaining a notion as slaying Gilbert is, it isn't one we pursue with any benefit."

"Then, by all means, let us return to the true problem," Patrick said. "Finding Madelyn."

" 'Tis all part of the weave of the same cloth," Jamie said. "Gilbert's actions. Madelyn's flight. Her obvious trip through the forest. Your inability to follow her." He looked primed to begin a lecture. "There is a reason Patrick cannot bend the gate to his pleasure, and we must discover it."

Patrick snorted, but Jamie was not to be deterred by such a mild expression of disgust.

"If you find her, what will you do with her?" Jamie demanded.

"Rescue her, dolt," Patrick said shortly. "What do you think?"

"To what end?" Jamie pressed. "Do you love her? Have you searched your heart for your motives?"

"Must I have motives?" Patrick demanded. "Can it not be enough just to wish to save the poor wench a goodly bit of suffering?"

Jamie looked as if he itched to stroke his chin in the manner he usually reserved for deep thought. Fortunately Patrick was spared that by two sleeping lads who currently pinned their father's arms down.

"The gates are at times fickle," Jamie announced. "Alex can attest to that."

"True enough," Alex said. "I tried to get home from Margaret's time initially, but couldn't. Probably because I still had something to do there for her."

"Aye, such as fall in love with her," Jamie said. "Love is a powerful thing."

Patrick could hardly believe his ears. His brother, whose only love had once been a finely sharpened sword and a few tales of bloodshed and destruction put to music in a manly way, had obviously lost his mind.

"What in the bloody hell has love to do with any of this?" Patrick demanded. "I've a task to see accomplished, not a ballad to provide fodder for!"

"Your motives must be pure," Jamie insisted. "You'll never reach her otherwise."

"Are you telling me," Patrick said in exasperation, "that I'm supposed to fall in love with her before I can get the forest to work its magic for me and allow me to rescue her?"

"I daresay the falling has already happened," Ian offered with a smile.

"Shut up, Ian," Patrick growled.

Alex snorted out a half laugh. "You've hit a nerve, Ian," he said.

Patrick threw Alex a glare, then looked at his brother, daring him to add to the foolishness already being spouted. Jamie only rubbed his chin thoughtfully against his son Ian's dark hair.

Close enough to his accustomed thinking aid, apparently.

" 'Tis worth further thought," Jamie said.

" 'Tis worth nothing," Patrick said. "I care for Madelyn, true, but 'tis hardly love."

He said it forcefully.

As if he actually believed it.

But it sounded hollow, even to his own ears.

"Hmmm," Jamie said, rubbing his son's head again with his chin.

Alex stood and stretched. "Come to grips with it, Patrick. It'll go easier on you if you do."

Ian rose as well. "She's a good girl, Pat. Make a good mother for your children."

"She's a lawyer."

"Ouch." Alex laughed. "Slandering my profession. You know, Patrick, it could be worse."

Ian punched Patrick rather firmly in the arm on his way by. "Don't be an idiot," he said affectionately. "Mind the path on your way home, if you're coming to bed down with us."

Patrick scowled at the both of them, cut off anything Joshua would have said before he retreated to his bedchamber, then looked at Jamie across the table. He pursed his lips.

"And you?" he asked. "Nothing more to say? No more advice to bludgeon me with?"

Jamie was silent for several minutes, long enough that Patrick began to concede that his brother was actually giving his answer some thought, not just blurting out the first bit of fluff that frothed out of his empty head.

"I think," Jamie said slowly, "that only you can decide what lurks in the depths of your heart."

"Thank you—"

"But I also think," Jamie continued relentlessly, "that you should stop punishing yourself for Lisa's foolishness."

Patrick gritted his teeth. "Gilbert—"

"Will meet his own unpleasant end in time," Jamie said. "Mayhap he'll wander one too many times on my land and find himself in a place he'll dislike quite thoroughly. Ignore him."

"Easier said than done. You didn't bring your bride into a life with him as part of it."

"Can you change the past?"

" 'Tis damned tempting."

Jamie rose, settled his sons more closely, and gave Patrick a look that said he planned to deposit his sons into their beds and himself into his thinking chamber where he could further speculate on the sorry state of affairs in Patrick's heart.

"Think on what I've said," Jamie said meaningfully.

Patrick watched his brother walk across the hall, turn and give him one final, pointed look, then disappear upstairs.

Patrick snorted. Jamie would be far happier if he spent less time worrying about everyone else's ills and more time worrying about his own.

He banked the fire, then left the hall. He retrieved his horse and rode not to Ian's, but to a humble hut on the edge of the forest. There was a faint light spilling out through the window. He tethered his horse and walked to the door.

Moraig opened it before he could knock. She looked him up and down. "Future gear," she said succinctly. "You must rid yourself of it."

"I have medicines—"

She gave him a look of supreme disappointment. "What need you with modern medicines?" she demanded. "There are herbs aplenty for your use. Let them serve you as they were meant to. Leave your things here. They'll be kept safe until your return."

He sighed, entered her hut, and dumped everything he'd kept under his shirt onto her table.

"But the chocolate I'll keep," she said with a gap-toothed grin. "Ah, laddie, ye ken my weakness."

He smiled, then curled up on her floor just as he'd done the first night he'd found shelter at her fire.

"Thank you," he whispered.

"You'll try tomorrow," she said.

"Aye."

"And the day after that, if you need to."

And the day after that, as well. He would continue to try until he was successful. And perhaps at some point, enough hope would enter his heart that he would manage it.

He could only pray it wouldn't be too late.

Chapter 26

Bentley Douglas Taylor III walked swiftly into the forest, cursing loudly. It had to have been MacLeod to have sabotaged his car again. But this time he'd gone too far. The damned thing had made a horrible noise and subsequently begun belching smoke. Borrowing another car had taken far too much of his mental energy. MacLeod would pay for that as well.

Oh, and also for that bit of minor roughing up MacLeod had dished out. Bentley cursed again to make himself feel better. He'd had a hell of a time getting out of bed the next day—not that he'd ever admit that to anyone.

He'd given it plenty of thought over the past three weeks, of course, while he camped in the woods watching something he couldn't for the life of him understand.

MacLeod. In a skirt. Just standing in the forest. Just standing. Doing nothing else.

A strange Scottish fertility rite?

A man trying to get in touch with his inner child?

MacLeod hoping to see Madelyn reappear out of the trees?

Whatever the case, MacLeod had been waiting in vain. Bentley knew, because he'd been waiting just as long, with the same, unsatisfying results.

It was baffling, this situation. He'd been baffled three weeks ago when he'd finally caught up with Madelyn only to have her vanish without a trace. Things like that happened in the Bermuda Triangle—he knew because along with his vocabulary tapes, he had a large library of UFO materials—but not in Great Britain. And if Madelyn was still around, why was MacLeod showing up here almost constantly, just waiting around in his fairy suit, apparently waiting for something to happen?

Who knew?

It was just one of the most curious things he'd ever seen. In fact, it had unsettled him so, he'd almost been discovered. In fact, he wasn't sure MacLeod didn't know he was there. But he was sure he didn't want MacLeod to know he was there. He was still sore from their little encounter.

If he'd had a gun, he would have used it.

Or perhaps not. He definitely could have gotten one, by hook or crook. But he hadn't been all that tempted. It was far more interesting to watch MacLeod panic and wonder what he was panicking about.

He'd checked passenger lists on a couple of major carriers—it was handy to have friends with criminal backgrounds who owed him favors—but hadn't seen Madelyn's name in the past month. She was still in Scotland. She was probably not loitering in a landfill, given that MacLeod was haunting the place she'd last been with a religious commitment that bordered on obsession.

Go figure.

But what was MacLeod obsessing about?

Who knew?

Bentley reached his accustomed hiding place only to see a brief flash of plaid skirt before MacLeod was gone.

Damn.

He walked around the forest, trying to use his rudimentary tracking skills to follow any footprints that might have been left behind.

None to be found.

MacLeod was gone.

He cursed heartily, then decided that perhaps it was time to revisit the pub. Perhaps he could find that lad he'd paid to spy on Madelyn and MacLeod the last time. The boy had been full of all kinds of details Bentley hadn't been interested in.

Rumors of magic.

Tales of time travel.

Yes, a little visit to the pub was definitely in order.

He jammed his hands in his pockets and hurried on his way, leaving his lawn chair and the enormous pile of trash left over from his snacks behind him.

Chapter 27

D*eath* had to be quite peaceful, didn't it?

Madelyn scratched a mark on one of the rustier bars surrounding her. Twenty-five. Twenty-five days that she'd been sitting in her prison. Twenty-five days that she hadn't been able to straighten her legs, hadn't been able to sit fully upright, hadn't had a decent meal.

Twenty-five days was probably a short stint considering how long she could be there. They had caged nobles in medieval Scotland, hadn't they? She was certain she'd read something about one of Robert the Bruce's relatives being caged in the courtyard of some castle. She couldn't, however, remember just how long that woman had been confined.

It could have been years, for all she knew.

At least she was inside and not out in the cold. That was a bonus. Then again, if she'd been outside in the courtyard, the rain might have given her pneumonia. That was sounding pretty damn good at the moment. She could have coughed herself to death.

Not pretty, but effective.

Unfortunately, who knew how long a woman could last inside a cold medieval hall, surviving on rats and disgustingly fouled water before she expired?

Too long, probably.

Well, at least she had herself intact.

Most of herself intact.

Maybe her index finger would heal eventually. She'd made the mistake, on Day Four, of trying to get the pins out of the bars of her cage. The Fergusson's brother had caught her at it and broken her finger with the hilt of his sword.

She actually didn't remember the rest of Day Four or Day

Five. That happened, she supposed, when you were unconscious from pain.

She looked down at her finger. She'd tried to wrap it as best she could, but who knew what would be left of it when it healed properly? It was, fortunately, on her bow hand. That wasn't the best situation, of course, but it could have been worse. She hadn't suffered any compound fractures, any torture, any beatings.

Not like the man chained to the wall next to her.

This seemed to be Laird Fergusson's favorite place to hold his prisoners. He had a dungeon, but apparently there was no fun in just dumping his prisoners down there. Not that he didn't use it. He did, on your average, run-of-the-mill Scot who got in his way. She'd watched that happen a time or two—and to a couple of his own people. But it was the MacLeods he caught that were treated to the upstairs view.

Lucky her.

Unlucky the piper who was sitting next to her.

He was a good player. She knew that for two reasons. One, he'd been allowed—or forced, depending on your point of view—to play for the laird for several hours on the day of his capture. He'd played many of the songs she'd heard him play before.

Or was that after?

It was hard to know what to call it.

It was just the spookiest thing she'd ever been privy to. It was also the most miserable. She listened to him play, then watched as his fingers had been broken, one every other day, until he had no unbroken fingers left. Whether or not he'd play again was anyone's guess.

Play in this lifetime, that is.

She knew he'd play again on an instrument that wasn't of this world, and she knew this because Robert the piper was none other than the ghost who had serenaded her so often in 2003.

Looking at his hands, however, made her extraordinarily glad that the Fergusson didn't know anything about her paltry skills with the violin.

Robert had been philosophical about it all. It was what he

got for being a MacLeod, he'd told her as he'd sat chained next to her with eight out of ten fingers broken. That was during Week Two. She'd admitted to him that she really wasn't a MacLeod, she was just in love with one. And she'd been able to tell him that because he'd passed almost all of his time teaching her Gaelic. She could thank her parents for her gift for languages, because it had taken her just three weeks to pick up an excellent grasp of the grammar and an enormous amount of vocabulary. Who knew how fluent she'd be after several years of captivity?

She'd also learned the date: 1382. It seemed incredible, but so did the fact that she was a civilized woman trapped in a box.

So she'd gotten used to it. She'd gotten used to the ruin of her beautiful skirt. She'd also grown accustomed to the loss of Jane's lovely jacket and the loss of her socks. She'd also gotten used to listening to what the men called her each day as they passed by her.

MacLeod whore.

Okay, so she hadn't been called worse. At least she was just being called that, and she wasn't becoming a Fergusson one. Thank heaven for small favors.

It had been, actually, quite an education. Having nothing else to do, she'd spent all her time sucking up every nuance, every curse, every story she'd listened to. If she thought she stood a snowball's chance in hell of being rescued, she might not have bothered. But she had no hope of rescue, not with a crippled piper next to her and a hall full of men who hated who they thought she was. It was that potential Fergusson prostitute thing that kept her mouth shut about the truth of her identity. The piper, Robert, had agreed with her.

"You, they might release, but you wouldn't enjoy it," he'd said. "Me, they'll just torture, then kill."

"I thought pipers were revered."

He'd laughed. "We're on Fergusson land. The world as we know it ceases to exist at the border."

She liked him very much. She wished she'd gotten to know him better as a ghost. Then again, maybe they would have a nice long time to chat while they were hanging out in chains.

She leaned back against the bars of her cage to contemplate life. She tried to be positive. As long as she was in the cage, life could only head up from where she was. Of course, she would probably never walk again. She was fairly certain her legs were becoming fused in their bent state. At least burying her would be easy. They wouldn't have to break her legs to get her in a box, if they bothered to use a box.

It wasn't as if she'd spent her entire tenure in Laird Fergusson's cage thinking about death. That had been only the first few days.

During Day Six through Day Twelve, she had wanted to get home and completely annihilate every bad guy she could come across—this because she'd come to loathe Laird Fergusson with a passion. She'd entertained fantasies of crushing evil-doers and the male members of her former law firm under her heel with equal abandon. She'd wished for freedom and a sharp sword to slip between the Fergusson's ribs.

It was during that same period that she'd begun to get in touch with her darker side.

Fantasies of inflicting all sorts of unusual and painful tortures on her enemies had given way to a more thorough reconsideration of her priorities. It was very easy to put one's life into perspective when everything else was merely speculative.

Work? Who needed it? There were too many lawyers in the world as it was. Her piece of paper from Harvard would make a great wrapping for the pen and pencil set the firm had given her for acing the bar—highest score in firm history—when she donated the set to the local charitable organization.

Her wardrobe? She'd keep what Patrick had given her and make do with that until she had to buy things for summer, then she'd either beg Sunny for hand-me-downs or head to the local thrift store.

Sunny. Oh, it was the thought of never seeing her sister again that really got to her. Her parents would be sad, but they'd get over it and get back to their crusade to keep Latin alive and well. Sunny, though, would grieve. It would probably throw her karma way off and kill all her houseplants.

And Patrick? Well, the jury was, as usual, still out on him. Who knew what would have happened if she'd actually gotten on the plane with him that day? Would he have changed his mind at the last minute? Professed undying love right there at the terminal? Begged her to stay and make his life complete?

Dyed his hair pink and put on a tutu to match?

All that speculation had faded sometime after Day Seventeen. It was then that she'd begun to think of other things. A home. A garden. Other things that grew with tender care, like children.

Children she would never have.

But that hadn't stopped her from her fantasies. Not only had she envisioned a home, she'd furnished it as well in tasteful Shaker style. Every room in it she'd decorated from floor to ceiling. Of course, at some point she'd realized that the house she was decorating did not resemble in the least Patrick MacLeod's derelict hall.

That had bothered her.

She'd begun to wonder how Shaker style would look in a house that was supposed to resemble a castle.

She'd considered antiques at that point.

And once she'd thought about his little castle, and furnished it to her satisfaction, she'd turned her mind to his garden. That had been easier to see to than his house, probably because she'd already had her hands in that dirt. Roses, trailing vines of wisteria and honeysuckle, shrubberies and rhododendrons. The list had gone on and she'd planted each one with great care. She'd also done him up a very fine vegetable garden because during the winter, she supposed he didn't eat what he hadn't either stored or canned. No sense in buying produce of uncertain origin when you could grow it at home and know just what kind of pesticides you'd used.

Sunny used beer for her slugs.

Madelyn wondered if they had slugs in Scotland.

She was pretty sure they had all kinds of beer. She wasn't

sure if slugs were attracted to whiskey, and she was even surer that Scotland produced all kinds of whiskey. Had they initially produced it just to drink, or to keep their gardens pest-free?

Hard to say.

It had been sometime during the slug speculation that she'd begun to fear for her sanity.

So for the next day she'd done nothing but listen, try to ignore what few scraps she had to eat, and not think much at all.

But thinking about nothing had led her to thoughts of death, and that's where she was at present. Looking at the marks in the rust of her cage and praying she wouldn't make so many of them that she'd have to scratch over the first set.

Please, let death come first and let it be swift.

She had no hope of escape.

None, but that sweet release.

She shook herself sharply. Good grief, what was she doing? Giving up? Letting herself be beaten down by lousy food and crappy water? She wasn't a MacLeod, but she was a Phillips and that was good British stock, wasn't it? There was a MacKenzie sitting in her family tree as well, which might count for something. She had a stiff upper lip and she could certainly use it. She might be hunched over, but she was still alive. And where there was life, there was hope.

Hope for what she didn't know.

That an entire platoon of MacLeods would come rushing through that door to rescue their piper and she would get rescued right alongside him?

It could happen.

Laird Fergusson could also choke on a bone and his brother would take over, the brother who called her a whore with more venom than the rest of the crew.

That could happen, too.

She could also grow thin enough to slip through the bars, but that would probably take a while. It wasn't that she didn't have time on her hands. She could wait herself out. Wouldn't Bentley be surprised to see the lack of flesh on her bones.

Nah, he would still think she was too fat. There was a man

who would call the sky red and the grass purple just to be contrary.

Too bad he hadn't gotten sucked back in time with her. He could have used a few humbling years in a cage. It was very tempting to wish for that, but she knew it was futile. He would continue to thrive, continue to lie his way to success, continue in his quest to replace Dean Anderson.

It probably bugged the hell out of him that she'd gone to Harvard. Succeeded at Harvard. Gotten the kind of grades he could only dream about.

And where were they now?

She was in a cage and he was driving a Jaguar.

Somehow, it just figured.

She took a few hours to contemplate the irony of that. He was sliding around on fine Corinthian leather seats; she was sliding around on a layer of slime. He had legroom; she had none. He was driving over pedestrians; she was driving away all sensible souls with her smell alone. He had lied, cheated, and probably stolen to get to the top; she'd been honest, hardworking, and thrifty on her way to the bottom.

All right, so she hadn't been that thrifty. She was probably going to regret that corporate wardrobe to the end of her days. If she'd just been frugal, she would have had extra money to replace the clothes Bentley had stolen from her, she never would have had to rely on Patrick's charity, and she wouldn't be sitting in a cage seven hundred years in the past wondering why in the hell she was there when her former fiancé was sitting in the lap of luxury, treating everyone around him like complete crap.

The thought of that was almost more than she could bear.

And so she snoozed. She never really slept. Every time she tried during the day, some noble soul or other seemed to find it his duty to come wake her up in an unpleasant manner. At least they didn't poke at her with their swords. She was grateful for small favors.

So she closed her eyes briefly and tried to look as if she were merely thinking on her suffering, not trying to catch twenty winks.

And she marveled that she still was able to maintain such a cheerful outlook.

She should have been bawling her eyes out.

But that drew attention to her as well, and drawing attention to herself was something she had learned to avoid at all costs.

The tears leaked out and ran down her face just the same.

S_{he} realized she had slept only because she woke up—and that on her own, miracle of all miracles. She looked next to her to find Robert sitting with his back against the wall, his posture quite casual, but his eyes very alert. She'd learned to judge the mood of the hall by his eyes alone.

Something was up.

She looked for herself to judge what that something might be.

Apparently, they were having a guest for dinner. Madelyn watched with interest. They'd never had anyone over for dinner, and she wondered if the Fergussons would pull out the good china.

Well, apparently not the good china, but they did pull a couple of the tables back from the fire pit. Just enough room to give the guest and the laird's brother, who happened to be the clan's fiercest fighter—she knew this because he was the one who tended to bang on her cage the loudest with his sword to wake her up—a chance to have a little light exercise before dinner.

She looked with faint interest at the newcomer. She was far enough away that his precise details were hard to discern. His plaid was less ratty than anyone else in the hall's, his hair was a good deal shorter, and he didn't have a beard. Maybe where he came from, they actually shaved more than once every ten years.

Well, whatever his grooming habits, the man knew how to wield a sword. He held his own quite well against the laird's brother, succumbing just barely to the other man's quite impressive attack after long enough that Madelyn had grown quite bored. It was dinnertime and she could hardly wait to see what kinds of things she'd get. Rats' heads? Gristle? Gnawed-on bones? Hard to say and not worth speculating about.

The laird clapped the newcomer on the back and drew him past the high table.

"Come," he boomed. "Come and see the whore of my enemy. As a McKinnon, you will appreciate the sight."

Madelyn didn't bother to raise her eyes. The Fergusson didn't like it, so she didn't do it. She kept her eyes down and didn't lift her hand to wipe her face when he urinated on her. She would later, when he wasn't looking.

"She doesn't speak much," the Fergusson said. "Not a very intelligent whore, apparently."

"Interesting," was the comment.

Madelyn had to clutch her hands in her skirts to keep from looking up in surprise at that voice.

"And see the piper? No accompaniment to battle from that one ever again, eh?"

"Well done," came the accolade. "Your justice is swift and quite terrible. Surely all MacLeods will think many times before raising a sword against you."

"So I daresay," chuckled the laird. "So I daresay. Now, come, my friend McKinnon, and give me tidings of your clan."

She didn't dare look. The tears that fell from her eyes mingled with the other liquid on her face, so there was no danger of the Fergusson or his men noticing anything untoward.

She sat in her cage and cried.

The newcomer was Patrick.

He had come for her.

Chapter 28

Patrick sat next to Simon Fergusson at the table and did his damndest to listen with rapt, fawning attention. Fawning didn't come easily to him, but he would have kissed the bastard's sorry arse if it meant the Fergusson would think him friend and not foe. At least for as long as he needed to in order to do what he'd come to do. Which didn't, unfortunately, include carving an intricate design in the man's flesh with a dull blade prior to beheading him.

It was, he decided as he listened with a false smile of admiration on his face, something to hope for.

It kept him, that hoping, from looking over his shoulder to find out what was happening to the woman he loved.

He didn't even dare close his eyes and offer up a brief prayer of thanksgiving. It was nothing short of a miracle that he'd found Madelyn, nothing short of the same kind of miracle that he'd even managed to get the forest to work for him. After three weeks of waiting, he'd begun to suspect that it just might lock him in the future forever.

Waiting had given him far too many hours to imagine what had befallen Madelyn, far too many hours to examine the feelings of his heart, far, far too many hours to determine where he'd gone wrong in the course of his relationship with her. He'd begun to suspect that he would never have the chance to make it right.

But, against all odds, there he sat at Simon Fergusson's table, a mere ten feet away from a woman who, if he hadn't recognized a bit of the skirt pattern beneath the layer of filth, he didn't think he would have recognized as the one he loved.

He hadn't been able to meet her eyes. He'd been afraid to, lest she gasp out his name or give some other sign that she recognized him. So instead, he'd listened and admired the Fergusson's skill at catching and caging a woman.

He was powerfully tempted to put the whoreson in that cage himself before the tale was finished.

But that would come later. Now, it behooved him not to grimace as he drank disgusting wine and ate revolting meat. By the saints, he'd been too long out of the Middle Ages. Not even his father's table had boasted fare so foul.

"Meat's good," the Fergusson said, as he selected more of that fine meat. "Are things so fine in the McKinnon hall?"

Patrick shook his head—his supposed McKinnon head—regretfully. "Times are hard and my cousin's cook is inept."

The Fergusson grunted. "I'll gift him something from my larder. Not my finest, of course, but something tasty all the same. In token of our alliance."

"He'll be grateful."

"Daresay he will." He shoved more drink at Patrick. "Here. Tell me again what those bloody MacLeods did to anger your cousin."

Patrick obliged. He reminded himself a final time that right now he was a McKinnon, his enemies were the MacLeods, and he was here to secure Simon Fergusson's aid in repaying the MacLeods for stealing some of the McKinnon's finest cattle. Which in medieval terms merely meant cattle that were still on their feet and had some imagined bit of flesh still on their bones, but who was he to quibble? Those damnable MacLeods had made off with the poor beasts and the McKinnons were determined to overcome the slight mistrust between themselves and the clan Fergusson to rout out their common MacLeod enemy.

Navigating the complexities—and the enormous egos—of those relationships was something, fortunately, he hadn't forgotten. Mayhap all those years of flattering his brother hadn't been wasted. So, whilst his golden tongue gave wing to a tale worthy of song, his mind raced.

Almost four weeks. Madelyn had been in that cage almost four weeks. If her mind hadn't flown, her ability to stand certainly had. But at least he'd found her. Perhaps that was miracle enough for them both.

Why the forest had taken so long to work, he still couldn't say. Mayhap it had been Bentley reclining with crunchy snacks at his elbow and cans of soda and beer crushing on a regular basis that had stopped him initially. Doing damage to Bentley's Jaguar had been the reason for his success, of that Patrick was certain.

He'd felt the forest shift just the slightest bit, like an earthquake of immense proportions that lasted only the fraction of a second—so short a time that he had to convince himself he hadn't imagined it. He'd left the forest and walked to his ancestral keep to find it in proper medieval condition. He'd arrived only to find it an uproar over a certain Thomas McKinnon's escape and alleged kidnapping of Duncan MacLeod. Thomas was, in a manner of speaking, Patrick's niece's husband. And it was thanks to a lengthy phone conversation with Thomas whilst Thomas was sitting safely in his house in Maine that Patrick had ferreted out all the details of that particular time frame.

Not that he'd known in what time he would be arriving, of course. That was the trick of the forest. Unlike the other X's on Jamie's land, the forest seemed to have no predictable destination in mind. It sent you where you were supposed to go and you made the best of it.

Unless you were following a certain person back in time. Then the forest, if you were lucky, sent you back after them.

Patrick had gotten lucky and he knew it.

The trick was going to be getting back home, but he would think about that later.

So, not knowing his particular destination beforehand, he had prepared as best he knew, which had included the most thorough debriefing of all potential political situations possible. It was a damned good thing he'd pried as many details as possible from Thomas, because that had enabled him to keep himself out of Malcolm MacLeod's pit. He'd blamed Duncan's capture on the Fergussons. Given that Simon Fergusson had just set his men upon a group of MacLeod scouts not a month before, Malcolm MacLeod had been more than willing to believe just about anything Patrick had said.

When Patrick had introduced himself as a long-lost cousin and then promised to rescue the piper who'd been captured soon after the raid, Malcolm had been overjoyed—overjoyed that he wasn't having to do the deed himself, likely, but Patrick hadn't complained. He'd armed himself with Malcolm's knowledge of Simon Fergusson's habits, then headed off into the sunset. It had taken only a minor amount of creativity to get himself sitting safely at the Fergusson's table.

As safely as anyone sat at that table, of course.

It wouldn't be for long. The MacLeods were, even as he babbled, preparing a raid. When that was discovered, Patrick would free the piper, free Madelyn, and ride like hell for safety. Ride thanks to a MacLeod stallion that ran like the wind.

"You look like a MacLeod," the Fergusson said suddenly. "I'd recognize those bloody green eyes anywhere."

"Aye," said the man on Simon's other side. "Damned odd, those green eyes."

"Shut up, Neil," Simon said, waving his hand. "I'm having my look."

Neil, who Patrick surmised by the familial resemblance was Simon's brother, fell silent. But he wasn't happy about it.

Interesting.

Patrick bent his head, trying to look as shamed as possible. "I'm a bastard," he lied easily. "Child of rapine, as fate would have it."

"Why didn't your mother drown you after you were born?" Neil demanded.

Simon backhanded his brother across the mouth, then looked at Patrick. "Why didn't the laird kill her before she birthed you?" he asked.

Patrick narrowly avoided choking on his wine. By the saints, who was worse? Neil the fool or Simon the merciless? "His mistake," Patrick managed. "Perhaps 'twas for revenge. A child bred to hate is a powerful tool."

Neil grunted, but ducked when Simon raised his hand

again. Simon studied Patrick for a moment or two.

"I suppose so," he said slowly. "And do you hate?"

"Deeply."

Simon stroked the table with the point of his knife. "Who, in particular?"

"Malcolm MacLeod."

Simon looked at Patrick. "Your sire?"

"He was a very young one at the time."

Simon laughed. "Aye, well, he was quite the wanderer, or so I've heard." He nodded in satisfaction. "Won't he claim you?"

"Worse yet. Killed my dam."

"Unsurprising," Simon grunted. "So, you do have good reason to hate him."

"Can you fault me for it?" Patrick asked.

Simon scratched his neck with the edge of his blade. "Nay."

"Revenge as well," Patrick added. The Fergusson would understand that well enough. "With the aid of the most cunning laird in the Highlands, I'll see my dam avenged one way or another." *And see you dead for what you've done to my woman.*

Apparently the sentiment, if not whom it was silently directed at, rang true enough to silence any of the Fergusson's remaining doubts. Patrick received a hearty slap on the back, more wine in his cup, and the offer of a fine-looking—the Fergusson's taste, not his—wench to warm his plaid that night.

Patrick accepted the wine and declined the wench. And when he spewed some long, convoluted tale about his preraid policy of abstinence, the Fergusson vowed he would try the like himself.

"But not tonight," the Fergusson added with a leering grin. "Take your ease, my friend. We'll plot more on the morrow."

The keep began to settle down for the night once the laird had selected his bed partner and retreated upstairs to bed her so thoroughly it was a wonder anyone managed to hear anyone else bid them good night.

Of course, this all happened after a handful of lads had

indulged in a few minutes of heaping abuse on the prisoners. The piper cursed them and dodged their blows, but his chains didn't let him dodge far. Madelyn didn't respond, but she did flinch when they poked at her with sticks.

Patrick marked each one who took sport of her. He also marked the keeper of the keys. Those he would need later.

He laid down near the door, his sword by his side. The fury in him burned brightly.

He didn't sleep.

It was almost dawn when a watchman burst into the hall.

"Raid!" he bellowed.

Patrick leaped to his feet. "Fetch the laird!" he shouted. By the saints, this had come more quickly than he'd dared hope. In truth, he was surprised it had come at all. Malcolm's commitment to his piper hadn't seemed that deep.

"They're looting the cattle," the poor scout wheezed.

"Who?" another demanded.

"MacLeods," the scout managed. "Bloody whoresons."

"Are you sure?" Patrick asked. He made a great show of concern, especially when the Fergusson came stumbling down the stairs. Too much drink, Patrick decided. It would catch him up someday.

"Who?" Simon asked in a gravelly voice, belting on his sword.

"MacLeods," Patrick said, trying to appear as if he could barely contain his enthusiasm. "Let me lead. I've never had the pleasure—bastard child and all—"

Simon looked at him blearily, then shook his head. "You'll come along, but leading is my right." He started barking orders to his men.

"But I—" Patrick interrupted.

The Fergusson's glare, bleary though it was, was formidable. "You'll stay well to the back. Iain, Neil, come. We'll see these cowards put to the sword without delay."

Patrick made a great show of preparing himself. He'd shown a bit of what he could do the night before, but purposely not the whole truth. And now he continued the ruse,

worrying over his gear, dawdling on his way to the stables.
The Fergussons were almost frothing at the mouth, so eager
were they to get their swords into MacLeod flesh.

Patrick tried to put that possibility for himself out of his
mind.

He got on his horse, dawdled some more, then hung to the
back as the force left the keep, their bloodcurdling screams
ringing out in the predawn air.

"My knife," Patrick said in dismay to anyone who was
listening. He turned around and started gingerly back to the
keep.

No one paid any heed, save Neil, who cursed him thoroughly for being an idiot.

Perfect.

He made it back to the keep within minutes, dismounted,
and walked swiftly into the hall. Five men were there plus
the keeper of the keys. He walked up to the latter.

"Unlock the prisoners," he said.

The man looked at him with narrowed eyes. "Why?"

"Because if you don't, I'll slit your belly open and strangle
you with your entrails."

The man's mouth fell open. He looked at Patrick as if he
couldn't believe what had just come out of his mouth. Patrick
grabbed the fool by the front of his plaid and reached for the
keys.

The keeper of the keys shouted for aid. Patrick buried his
knife in the man's belly, removed the keys from his fingers
as he fell, then turned to meet the other five he was certain
would be hard upon him.

They were.

He drew his sword and took out three swiftly, and one not
so swiftly. The last, who looked to not want to be done in
at all, he shoved across the hall so he could toss the keys at
the piper.

"Free yourself and the woman!" he shouted.

He didn't wait to see what would happen. The last Fergusson standing threw himself toward Patrick, his sword
bared. Patrick glared at him.

"I've no time for this," he said, backing up a pace. "Be off with you."

"Are ye daft?" the other bellowed. "Who'n the bloody hell are ye? A MacLeod?"

"You'll never know," Patrick said. He fended off a moderately skilled attack, received a scratch or two, then ended the man's life with a sword through his belly. The Fergusson clansman fell, then lay perfectly still.

Patrick took back his sword, sheathed it, then leaped over the table to where the prisoners were being held. The piper was trying unsuccessfully to use the heavy key. Weakness from being captive, no doubt. Patrick took the key away and freed the man. He hauled him to his feet, then knelt and quickly opened Madelyn's cage. He pulled her out and swung her up into his arms. She weighed nothing.

"Thank you," she whispered.

He was halfway across the great hall before he realized she'd said it in Gaelic. He left that as a mystery to be solved later. For now, he had to get them out of harm's way.

He turned toward the door.

And then he froze.

He let Madelyn slide down. The piper took hold of her and helped her sit on the ground. Patrick pulled his sword free and looked at Neil Fergusson.

"I *knew* it," Neil said triumphantly. "I knew you couldn't be telling the truth."

"Congratulations. Now, move aside."

"Bloody whoreson," Neil Fergusson spat. "You'll never set foot outside my hall."

" 'Tis your brother's hall, you fool," Patrick said, "and this is my woman your brother caged there—"

"MacLeod whore," Neil rumbled.

"She's a MacKenzie, but I'll make her a MacLeod soon enough. And I'll make you regret everything you've done to harm her. Now, either you die or I do. Shall we get to deciding whom it will be?"

"Won't be me," Neil said.

And that was the last thing he said for quite some time. Patrick supposed the whole thing didn't take more than three or four minutes, but when every minute meant possible discovery, those were four minutes too many.

He didn't kill Neil. He cut him, broke his nose, and stomped him quite vigorously in the bollocks before he plunged him into unconsciousness with some well-placed weight on a pair of vital pressure points, but he left him alive.

Why, he didn't know.

Maybe there was no sense in leaving the Fergussons with another soul to avenge.

He put up his sword, then gathered Madelyn up into his arms and ran out the front door. The piper followed silently.

His sturdy MacLeod steed was standing where he'd been left. Patrick paused, then had his first good look at the piper.

The hair on the back of his neck stood up. The other man seemed to think nothing of seeing Patrick, at least nothing untoward. Then again, the other man wasn't looking at Patrick after having known him almost eight hundred years in the future as a ghost.

"My thanks for the rescue," the piper said with a smile. "Robert MacLeod, in your debt."

"Patrick MacLeod, and I wish I had come sooner," Patrick said. He had something else quite pithy to say, but he made the mistake of looking down at the man's hands.

Not a finger occupied its proper angle in the man's hand.

By the saints, the Fergussons were a thorough bunch.

Patrick took a deep breath. "I'm sorry about your hands."

The piper shrugged. "I've played enough for one lifetime."

"You'll play again," Patrick said. *Years from now*, he added silently. Then he hesitated. "I could reset your fingers, if you like. There are herbs that could repair the breaks properly, if I can find them."

Robert looked like a man who didn't dare hope. "Not at the moment, you won't," he said gamely. "Later perhaps." He tilted his head and smiled. "You *do* look quite a bit like a MacLeod. And you certainly don't carry yourself like a lowly bastard."

"Long tale," Patrick said. "Let's find a horse for you—"

Robert shook his head. "I'll be safer on my own two feet."

He put his hand on Madelyn's head. "Until later, my lady. I'm sure we'll meet again."

"Thank you, Robert," she said, her voice shaking. "Thank you with all my heart."

Robert turned back to Patrick. "There's a hut, north of the keep, if you've a mind for privacy."

Patrick lifted one eyebrow. "Aye, I know the place."

"Haunted, they say. Deserted, always. And you know these Fergussons. A very superstitious lot. Doubt they'll make any forays up there."

Patrick nodded. The spot where Moraig's house would stand centuries from now had been rumored to be haunted by all sorts of bogles, ghosts, and foul woodland creatures, even in his day. It was perfect for his purposes.

He put Madelyn up on the horse. By the time he had mounted as well, Robert was slipping out the gate like a shadow. Patrick didn't like leaving the man without a horse, but perhaps he would be all right. He took the reins and pulled Madelyn back against him.

"This is going to hurt," he said.

She coughed. "Just go."

And so he went. He horse leaped across the courtyard and was at a full out gallop thirty feet outside the front gates. The beast should have been a racehorse. It was tempting to take him home and see what could be bred from him.

Assuming he could get himself, Madelyn, and a horse home.

It was not something to be thinking about now.

He turned east, away from the battle, away from his own ancestral lands. He would double back when he was well out of the way of any battle. He knew very well where the clan borders were and could avoid any other unpleasant encounters.

He bent over Madelyn, to shield her some from the wind, but mostly to offer her some sense of protection. Something he should have continued to offer her in the past. The future.

Damnation, whenever it was he should have offered it, he should have offered it properly.

He rode hard, hoping his mount would forgive him for it

later, and forced himself to disallow any reflection on his situation. He had made his decisions, Madelyn had made some of her own, and the forest had seen to the both of them in its own way. They found themselves in the past and that was all that mattered. He could survive quite readily, even though it had been almost a decade since he'd had to.

He focused his attention on his surroundings, on observing the countryside, scanning the terrain for potential foes.

The morning passed. Two hours later, he was walking his mount across his own land. It sent chills down his spine to see it, empty as it was of even a hint of any kind of dwelling.

He negotiated a nonexistent path through Moraig's forest. He could only hope he didn't plunge them into a century they weren't prepared to live in by stepping on a bit of unassuming moss. The thought of being transported to those mid-1700s was enough to give him chills. He thought he had problems now with a difficult laird in charge back at the keep in the late 1300s.

He paused. There, up ahead in what was now the depths of the forest, was something that might be mistaken as a hut. Patrick sighed in relief.

"Almost there," he said to Madelyn.

She nodded. Or perhaps she shook. It was hard to say. She clutched the arm he had wrapped around her and said nothing.

He closed his eyes briefly, grateful beyond measure for having found her.

Desperately, profoundly, thoroughly grateful.

He would never let her go again.

Chapter 29

Madelyn came back to consciousness, only then realizing she'd been out of it. She'd long since ceased to worry about what she was doing while she was asleep. Who cared? It wasn't as if she was trying to impress her audience. She slowly came back to full awareness, but stayed completely still as she did so. It had become her habit, that freezing, on the off chance that stretching would alert any of the keep's inhabitants to her conscious state.

And what was the point of trying to stretch, anyway? Her feet would just encounter hard, unyielding metal. No, better that she just remain immobile and unremarkable. That wasn't actually very hard anymore, given that her muscles had long since ceased to twitch. The pain was gone as well. She supposed her nerves had given up trying to tell her that she had been curled in the fetal position for too long.

Besides, movement garnered notice and notice brought attention and she was damned sick of the attention she'd been getting. No, staying still was the best thing to do.

But as she lay there, curled up with her knees to her chin, the cobwebs began to clear from her brain and she realized that several things were quite different from what had become normal during the past twenty-five days.

The floor wasn't the same. Instead of unyielding stone beneath her, there was something soft. Dirt? She gingerly extended her index finger and scratched. Dirt, not goo. Dirt, not stone under goo.

She breathed in slowly. The smell around her had changed. It smelled of earth and rain and other things that might resemble something quite pleasant if she could get past her own offensiveness. And there was no draft. That was surprising enough that she opened her eyes to find out why.

The first thing she saw, the first thing her pitiful gaze fell upon was a man sitting with his back against the wall of what appeared to be a small hut.

Patrick MacLeod.

Looking perfectly comfortable in his medieval Highlander garb.

She closed her eyes and started to cry. She couldn't seem to stop herself. It was as if almost four weeks of misery had finally gotten to her, filled her cup right up to the top and spilled over with the relentlessness of Niagara Falls.

"Oh, Madelyn," he said.

She felt rather than heard him move across the little room. He lay down behind her. And then his arms were around her, his strong, secure arms that promised safety from all the boogeymen who were lurking out there. She felt his hand fumble for hers, then close around her fingers.

Around her broken finger.

Who knew if it was broken still. What she did know was that it hurt like hell, and she cried out in pain before she could stop herself.

Patrick leaned up and over her. "What? What is it?"

"My finger," she wept hoarsely. "I think it's broken."

"Who did it?"

"Neil."

He laid her hand gently on the floor, settled back down behind her, and gently pulled her close against him. "I'll tend it later. Now, just lay your head, love, and be at peace."

She wept until she was too tired to do it any longer. And once she was down to mere sniffles, she let the memories come back to her.

Hearing Patrick's voice while sitting in her cage. Seeing him sit at the table with the Fergusson. Watching him kill six men and make life hell for another. Then there was the ride, that horrendous ride where all she'd been able to do was clutch the horse's mane, clutch Patrick's arm, and pray with all her might that she didn't either fall off or, worse yet, stay on and shatter into a thousand pieces.

She didn't remember the end of the ride. She supposed

the end had come here, at this hut of very humble origins and no furniture.

Here, with a man who held her as if he had every intention of never letting her go.

She closed her eyes. She had to be hallucinating. Too much inedible food; too little water. Her mind had gone, and with it her common sense. She took a deep breath, then coughed. She opened her mouth to speak, but it came out as a harsh sound. She swallowed past her parched throat—or tried to, at any rate—and made another attempt.

"Thank you," she croaked.

"I tried to come sooner," he said simply. He smoothed his hand over her disgustingly filthy hair, but seemed to take no note of it. "I'm sorry, Madelyn."

She tried to shake her head, but her muscles set up an appalling protest, so she remained still. "It's all right."

She couldn't say more. What she wanted to do was weep some more, but she didn't have the strength for it. What she wanted to do was sleep, but she didn't have the courage for it. Too many dreams were lurking, just waiting to spring upon her and leave her trapped again in a cage not fit for a dog. She closed her eyes, but forced herself to remain lucid.

"What is it with Fergussons wanting me behind bars?" she managed.

"Bloody whoresons," he said quietly.

"Where are we?" she asked.

"Scotland."

She grunted. "Funny."

His hand continued its gentle motion. "In Moraig's house. Or what will be Moraig's house in the future."

"And the date?"

He was silent for a few minutes. "Do you know already?"

"I understand it's sometime in the late fourteenth century. Around 1382."

"That's correct."

"You could have told me."

"I feared you wouldn't believe me." He paused. "I regret it."

"Ha," she said, then groaned at too vigorous a movement.

"Moraig told me. I should have listened harder."

" 'Tis a bit hard to swallow."

"I'll say." She looked at his hand covering her uninjured hand. It didn't look like a medieval hand. Then again, what did she know of it? It wasn't as if she'd had the leisure to examine any of the hands she'd come in contact with over the past few weeks. She very hesitantly curled her fingers toward his. "Did you really think I wouldn't believe you?"

He laced his fingers with her good hand. "Aye."

"What did it matter to you whether or not I believed you?"

"It mattered," he said quietly.

She hardly knew what to make of that, so she decided to make nothing. Maybe he'd tried to tell other people, and they'd thought he was nuts. Maybe he'd never told anyone before, and she had a trustworthy face. The *maybes* could go on forever, and she'd probably never hit on the right one. There was no sense in trying to figure it out, especially in her current state of misery.

She wanted to say something cheerful, something along the lines of *Well, here we are in the Middle Ages, so let's go out and sightsee some things that are still under construction, shall we?* but she couldn't manage it. It was all she could do to breathe through her smell.

Not that she hadn't struggled with that before. But it was one thing to stink when the place you were stinking in smelled just as bad. It was another thing to stink in front of a man you had tried, at various and sundry times, to impress.

"I smell," she announced.

"I've smelled worse."

"I don't believe it."

"I have. I'm even sure that I myself have smelled worse."

She almost managed a smile. "Prove it. Give me examples. Start from your earliest smell and work forward."

He chuckled. That sound was like rain after a drought. She closed her eyes and let it drench her soul. If he could laugh, here in this place, with a woman in his arms who may as well have spent the past month living in a sewer, maybe there was hope after all.

And how desperately she needed hope. She wondered if

she would ever forget what had happened to her. She wondered, further, if she would ever forget watching Patrick, with an enormous sword in his hand and a look in his eye that should have made anyone with sense run the other way, take out the men inside the Fergusson hall. She'd never thought she would feel anything but abhorrence for such a thing, but then again, these were men who had laughed as they'd tortured Robert the piper. They were men who had taken great delight in making her life hell. Once she'd begun to understand what they were saying, she realized that the only reason she hadn't been raped was that she was too far beneath them for that.

For the moment.

Who knew what would have happened in the end? She suspected that if it hadn't ended up being rape, when the laird had tired of having to feed and house her, it would have been quite a horrible death.

She realized she was wheezing. Patrick was stroking her hair and making shh-ing noises. She calmed her breathing with great effort.

"I was thinking," she managed.

"Aye, I gathered that."

"You're not a bad swordsman."

He laughed suddenly and she felt as if the world had trembled because of it. "Thank you, my lady."

"I'd like not to have to watch you do that business in the Fergusson hall again."

"I'll do my best to avoid it for the both of us." He caressed the side of her thumb with his own. His hand was warm. Hers was so cold, it was almost painful to have it warmed. "You learned my tongue," he said.

"So many curses, so little time," she said lightly. "Shall I impress you with what I learned?"

"As you will."

She called him several of the names she'd learned, felt him gasp in surprise, then felt it in her to attempt a small laugh herself.

"By the saints," he managed.

"I was trying to take my mind off my location." In fact,

she'd concentrated so hard on the language, she was already dreaming in it. Her father would be proud. She wondered, absently, if she would have the chance to tell him, or if she would be spending the rest of her life in the Middle Ages.

What else was going to happen? Were they going to get home? Was Patrick going to take her back home with him? Or was he going to hang out with her in the past? Would he get her somewhere safe, then just leave her there?

She blinked back tears.

She had to stop thinking so much. Her thoughts were hard, unforgiving, like slaps across her soul.

"Madelyn," he whispered, holding her hand tightly, "Madelyn, please . . ."

She began to gasp for air.

Was there anywhere safe?

The next thing she knew, she was sobbing. It was excruciating. Her muscles protested every breath, her breath came in as if it were barbed, her body convulsed of its own accord. She pulled her hand away from Patrick's and covered her mouth, lest the entire countryside hear her weeping like a madwoman.

Patrick put his mouth against her ear as he whispered words of comfort, words she recognized for the most part, but many she didn't.

She should have learned a few nice words, apparently.

She wept until she could weep no more. Then she hiccupped, which was even worse than weeping. And then even the hiccups stopped. She lay in his arms and merely drew in ragged breaths.

"Sorry," she managed.

"Nay, 'tis I who am sorry," he said. "For many things." He pulled her more securely against him. "Take your rest, Madelyn. I'll keep you safe." He leaned up for a moment, reached over, and put his sword on the ground in front of her. "I'll keep you safe," he said quietly as he lay down again and drew her close.

Madelyn looked at the blade gleaming dully in the faint daylight. In the matter of her body, she believed him fully.

In the matter of her heart?

She couldn't bear to think about it.

S*he* woke sometime later to find herself warm for the first time in almost a month. It was such a pleasure, she didn't dare move, just in case she would break the spell. So she kept her eyes closed and savored the feeling.

Patrick stirred, then leaned up on his elbow and pulled the hair back from her face.

"How do you fare?" he asked softly.

"Wonderfully."

"Liar." He sat up. "We need water. There has been a stream near here at various points during the centuries. I need to go look for it before it grows completely dark."

"Are we really in Moraig's house?"

"Aye. Such as it was."

Thinking about Moraig reminded her of everything the old woman had said. She'd been telling the truth. Everything she'd said had been true. She looked at Patrick and found it almost impossible to take in that this was a man who had been born centuries in the past, who had grown up in a time of swords and bloodshed.

But how could she now deny it?

Why hadn't she seen it before? She'd been blind, preoccupied with other things like seeing castles and learning about their history—when all along she'd been walking next to a piece of that history and never known it.

She should have. It was her job to notice things that other people didn't, to root out the facts, to uncover details that her targets didn't want uncovered.

Yes, she should have seen it. For all his polish, there was something elementally raw underneath that polish. It was certainly more pronounced in his brother, that wildness, but it still ran true beneath Patrick's surface.

"Will you be all right? Or would you like to go outside as well?"

She took a deep breath. "I don't think I can move yet."

"I'll hurry then. Water, then I'll find something to ease your pain."

She nodded, then watched as he took his sword in his hand and left the hut. He looked at her once more with a reassuring smile before he closed the door—such as it was—and left her alone.

She found she didn't like it at all. She managed to get herself into a sitting position.

That alone about killed her.

She wanted to sit against the wall, but she couldn't. So she sat in the middle of the floor and sniveled as quietly as she could. She had serious doubts that she would ever again walk as a normal person should.

It took Patrick forever to come back. At least it felt like forever, and when he did come back, the noise of him at the door startled her so badly she squeaked in fright. He opened the door and peered in.

"Only me."

She bowed her head and whimpered. It seemed like she just couldn't do anything else. She supposed she would have to run out of tears eventually. She didn't have that much water still in her system to be wasting it on luxuries like tears.

Patrick knelt down next to her. "The stream is still there." He had made a cup out of bark. "The best I could do. I'll make as many trips as you need. Drink slowly."

She tried. A good deal of the water ended up down the front of her dress, but she supposed that couldn't be anything but a good thing.

"More?" he asked.

"Please."

He disappeared, then returned, this time with a handful of weeds. He helped her drink, then paused. "Do you need to, well . . ."

"Pee? No, thank you. Not yet."

"Let me know."

"I will."

He sat down and began to sort his weeds. She looked on with interest.

"Dinner?"

He shook his head with a smile. "Healing herbs, if you can believe it."

"You're very resourceful."

He grunted. "Aye, that's me. These are good for all sorts of aches. I'll make you a plaster of them in a minute. But first, let me see if I can ease you some." He helped her lie back, then sat down and gently pulled her feet into his lap.

Madelyn shivered. All right, he could drop her like a hot potato—after he'd rubbed her feet for a few years. She closed her eyes. He was gentle, but it was still quite painful.

"They took my boots," she said.

"I daresay they would."

"And my socks. And Jane's coat."

"Anything else?"

The way he said it, so casually, made her eyes open of their own accord.

"What do you mean?" she asked.

"Did they hurt you?"

The chill in his voice chilled her. She suspected she might feel sorry for anyone who had hurt her. Maybe those Fergussons he'd done in had gotten off lightly. She suspected a rapist would have fared much worse.

She smiled weakly. "Outside of the obvious?"

"It takes little for a MacLeod to execute a goodly bit of vengeance on a Fergusson," he said easily. "I can go back. They do leave the keep occasionally. Alone. Unprotected."

"I think you executed enough vengeance."

"That was . . . collateral damage," he said in English. Then he switched back to his mother tongue. "They deserved what they received. Now, is there aught else I should see them repaid for?"

She stared at him, wondering if she wasn't seeing for the first time the man he'd been for a good part of his life, the medieval clansman he always wore buried underneath black jeans and cashmere sweaters.

She was fascinated and quite unsettled all at the same time.

"Anything," he repeated.

"Patrick, they called me a MacLeod whore. They didn't call me a Fergusson whore. Ironic, isn't it?"

"Aye, quite," he said dryly.

She closed her eyes and tried to enjoy the feeling of his hands on her feet. It wasn't hard. "Trust me, I was too far beneath them to merit rape," she said. "They just used me as their urinal. And it's all in the past anyway. Tell me of *your* past. I'm quite interested."

He hesitated. "You could consider it fiction."

"Good grief, Patrick, I just spent a month and a half in a cage. I learned Gaelic to keep myself from going crazy. I've become all too familiar with the bowel habits of a medieval Scottish laird, his disgusting sense of humor, and his hatred for anyone bearing the name MacLeod. We're either really in the fourteenth century, or everyone around us is delusional and we're all sharing the same delusion. How likely is that? Get on with the story. Either that or hand me your sword so I can poke at you with it to inspire you."

"You couldn't lift it."

"Want to test that?"

He looked down. His hands on her feet were incredibly gentle as he began.

"I'll give you the tale," he said with a smile.

"Finally. Now, do you mind if I close my eyes? I'm still listening. You wouldn't think I'd be tired, what with all the rest I've been getting, but I'm tired just the same."

"I understand."

"And keep talking in Gaelic. I need the practice."

"As my lady wishes."

She nodded and closed her eyes. She meant to listen. She really did. But she found that before he even started to speak, the feel of his hands on her feet was too much for her feeble will to remain lucid. She felt herself sinking back into blissful oblivion, and she was powerless to resist the pull.

Maybe she should have been worried about the fact that she was hanging around in a dilapidated shack with a man who, while really tough, would probably be no match against an entire clan of furious Fergussons. But despite that, she felt safe.

And at the moment it felt as if it would last forever.

She opened her eyes a slit and looked at Patrick, just to make sure she wasn't imagining him. He was staring at her with an expression it took her quite a while to identify.

Fondness? No.

Relief? No, not that, either.

It was something far more intense, something that made her pulse quicken and her temperature rise.

He looked at her as if he just might love her.

She smiled weakly, then closed her eyes quickly, before she saw anything else she would have to interpret.

For the moment, she felt safe.

That was enough.

Chapter 30

Patrick sat against the wall of the hut that was only just a hut by the skin of its teeth, and looked at the woman curled up in front of him. He held her feet, her poor filthy, cracked feet, in his hands. It would take more than just the heat from his body to warm her abused flesh. What he needed was a fire, and that was just precisely what he didn't dare build. He could stand against many, but an entire army of Fergussons might overwhelm even him.

Then again, with the reputation that their hiding place seemed to have, perhaps he could consider a fire after all.

Mayhap on the morrow. He would take some time tonight and see if there were any hardy souls who were undaunted by the hut's reputation. If there were none braving the bogles and ghosties, he would risk making Madelyn something to warm herself by. Perhaps he would be fortunate enough to find wood dry enough that the smoke would be, for the most part, unnoticeable. And he would have to find something better for holding water than two pieces of bark nestled together.

That left still his horse to be seen to. It was, he decided wryly, a good deal more trouble to stable a horse than to just park a car in the garage. And they would have to have decent food, and the sooner the better. He'd eaten all manner of animal life in his youth, often without benefit of a fire, but he wasn't sure Madelyn could manage it. Roots, herbs, tree bark could be ingested if necessary. With any luck, she would regain her strength quickly, and they could be on their way.

Though, he supposed he really had no idea how long it would take her to recover. He'd been in a dungeon a time or two, but never for more than a pair of days. He was, quite frankly, amazed Madelyn was even able to sit up at all given what she'd gone through.

So, once she was healed, they would make the attempt. He didn't want to think about what might happen if it didn't work at all.

It was definitely a possibility. It wasn't like the forest's portal was an iron-gated affair that swung to and fro at a man's command. Jamie and Elizabeth, in the days before they'd begun their family, had found themselves quite stuck for several months waiting for particularly stubborn bits of earth to take them back home to the twentieth century.

Well, for him, that was something to worry about in the future. With any luck, things would go according to plan. Madelyn would wake, begin to heal, and they would take up their journey in a few days.

For the moment, however, he had a very long list of tasks to see to. He rubbed a hand over his face. By the saints, he'd made a great hash of things. He should have told Gilbert McGhee to go to hell. He should have pulled Madelyn into his arms, kissed her senseless, and told her he was quite certain he thought they could pass the rest of their lives quite happily together, and if she wanted to continue her career in the States, well, he wasn't sure what he would have said about that, but he should have at least been willing to discuss it.

Maybe a miracle would have happened, and she would have been content to stay in Scotland.

Now, it looked as if she might not have a choice. He wondered how medieval Scotland would suit her.

He shifted, his leg brushing his sword lying next to him on the floor. He looked down at his blade. It wasn't as if he didn't train with it regularly. He supposed he did that partially because it was a fine way to keep his form in passing good shape.

It was also, he had to admit, a link to his past he hadn't been willing to let go of.

He put his hand on the cold hilt. It was odd to be centuries away from the life he knew, centuries away from his comforts of speed and flight. It was almost as momentous as it had been when he'd left his own time and stepped into the future.

Only this time the change seemed more drastic.

It wasn't as if he hadn't done it a handful of times before—that travel through time. Once to return to his father's hall and give tidings to his brother. Once more to rescue Jamie—and that one after Lisa had died. But he hadn't done it since. Indeed, there was a part of him that had begun to wonder if his past had been nothing but a dream, a fanciful, impossible dream, the clarity of which faded with each passing year.

And by the time he'd wed with Lisa, he'd all but had a lobotomy to rid himself of his memories. To be sure, she hadn't wanted to hear any of it. Looking back now, he could scarce believe he'd wed the woman with only one tentative attempt to give her the truth. When he'd been about it, she'd cut him off, telling him she understood about the lack of sophistication a lad from the deep Highlands might feel in her Swiss-finishing-school-graduate presence, so would he please not bring it up again?

He hadn't.

Except when he'd tried the portal in the forest and seen his brother one last time. He'd told Lisa he'd gone home to see to business. She hadn't asked what kind, hadn't cared to know if his parents were alive or dead, had never asked aught about his brother. And he, fool that he was, had gone along—nay, he'd more than gone along. He'd eagerly put his past behind him and become as domesticated an animal as possible to please the woman he loved.

Love, if it is to endure, must be reciprocated.

Ian's words came back to him. Aye, there was truth enough in them. Lisa had never loved him. Lusted after him, aye, been fascinated by his coarseness—her term not his—but she had never loved him. But that hadn't stopped her from using him when it suited her.

The baby isn't yours, but you'll claim it just the same, won't you?

There had never been any doubt of it. Even if the baby had been Robert Campbell's, or any of the others she'd slept with behind both his and Robert's back, he would have claimed it, and gladly. And he would have loved it, in a way he had never loved its mother.

Had he ever loved Lisa? Desired her, aye. Wanted her approval, definitely. But loved her? He'd thought so at the time.

He knew better now.

The other thing he knew now was that he hadn't trusted her. Not truly. Not enough to give her the unvarnished truth about his past. Hers hadn't been hands sturdy enough, strong enough to hold what he'd needed to tell her.

Now, her uncle, he was a different sort entirely. Patrick had told a goodly bit of his own tale to Conal after Lisa's death, during the final time he'd ever drunken himself into a stupor. He'd poured out a good deal of his heart, divulged a goodly number of his secrets, and regretted none of it as he'd hung his head over the toilet and puked up most of the whiskey he'd drunk that night.

Because Conal had believed him.

What would Madelyn have done with the same tale? Without what she'd seen?

He suspected she might have believed him as well.

Which brought him full circle to sitting with his back against a marginally stable wall, looking at a woman sleeping on the floor in front of him and planning how best to care for her with only his sword and his wits at his disposal.

And wondering why it was he hadn't allowed himself to contemplate the possibility of truly falling in love with her.

Desperately.

Without any reservations at all.

Falling in love with her as he was now.

His heart seemed to take a deep breath, then sigh out its assent.

He watched her idly, as a man might a great treasure that he was certain would still be his if he took his eyes off it for a brief moment. Was it possible this was the same woman he'd first had a proper look at on Culloden's field? It seemed centuries ago. He wondered now what those feelings she'd stirred in him could be ascribed to.

Fate?

An incomprehensible weaving of the threads of time?

And then there was Robert the piper. He had to know, in the future, of their return to the past. Surely his ghostly memory stretched back that far. Had he been waiting centuries for them to appear on the mortal scene, just so he could serenade them? So he could stand on Patrick's wall and play for Madelyn whilst she worked in the garden? So he could play for Patrick himself whilst he argued with himself over what to do about a certain Colonist?

It was all possible, he supposed, but none of it mattered. He'd met Madelyn, come to know her, grown to love her, and almost lost her.

Through his own cowardice, no less.

Well, no more. Gilbert McGhee could be ignored. After all, most everyone whose opinion mattered to him knew the truth. The rest could go to hell and take Gilbert with them. So life would be uncomfortable now and then. Madelyn could endure that, couldn't she?

Wouldn't she want to?

The thought of having to risk the asking of her made him slightly queasy.

He shook his head. He could face a hall full of angry Highlanders, but he couldn't face the woman he loved with a simple question about her stamina where he was concerned?

She shifted suddenly, stirred, then woke slowly. She looked at him and a look of relief crossed her features.

"I was dreaming," she whispered.

"They'll fade," he promised.

"I hope so." She closed her eyes and shivered. "I hope so."

He smoothed a corner of his plaid over her feet, trying to warm them. "I need to go see to our horse. And find water and food, if possible. There are roots and berries about still, I'd imagine, if you can stomach that."

"It sounds perfect. Anything's a step up from Fergusson food."

He smiled briefly. "I daresay it is. And if it eases your mind any, Simon's fare is the worst I've ever had."

She grimaced. "I'd rather not think about it." She struggled to sit up.

He leaned over and helped her sit herself up against a sturdy bit of the wooden frame. He rearranged her skirts, then squatted down in front of her. He pulled the dirk from his boot and handed it to her. "Hide this in your skirt. If anyone comes in, wait until they're close, then bury it with all your strength into their belly. Upward into the heart is best, for they'll die more quickly that way."

"Bet you didn't learn that in judo class."

"Nay, it was the first thing my sire taught me."

"What a life."

"It had its beauties as well."

"I suppose it did." She sighed. "No interruptions. No modern annoyances."

"No running water," he said dryly. "But I'll see what I can do for you." He paused. "I don't know about a wash. The stream is very cold and the only fire I dare build would not warm you adequately."

"It's your nose, not mine," she said gamely.

"And my nose finds you as sweet as roses," he said. He took her hand and kissed it gently. "I'll return as quickly as possible, hopefully with something to eat. And herbs for your finger, if you like. Keep your dirk handy and please do not use it on me."

She nodded, looking quite sure of herself. Or she would have, if her fingers hadn't been trembling so badly. He pretended not to notice.

"I won't be far," he said. "The stream is no more than twenty paces from the hut and whatever is edible will be nearby. The herbs I need will likely be deeper in the forest, but it won't take me long to find them." He stood, then turned and opened the door. He looked at her one last time. "I'll return soon."

"I know." She smiled at him. "Thank you."

"I'm certain some day I will have the flu or something equally as debilitating. You can tend me then in repayment."

She went quite still. He did, too, truth be told. If that wasn't something of a commitment, he didn't know what was. He wanted to breathe, truly he did, but there seemed to be an appalling lack of air in the hut all of a sudden.

"I'm a lousy nurse," she said finally. "But I'll try."

"Aye," he managed.

"I could learn something useful from Moraig," she offered slowly. "Herbs and that kind of thing."

"She knows much."

"Hmmm," Madelyn agreed. "I imagine you do, too."

He nodded unwillingly. "Aye. A bit." That was an under-statement, but it was something to even admit any knowledge at all. It occurred to him that perhaps it might be time to make a change in that part of his life now, too.

So many changes.

So long overdue, whispered his heart.

He took a deep breath, then smiled at Madelyn. It had come out as something of a grimace, but he was laboring under a goodly bit of self-inflicted duress.

"I'll return quickly."

She nodded. He left, before he gave up any more ground to his heart. If he wasn't careful, he was going to be blurting out a proposal soon.

He went out and found his horse where he'd left it, stand-ing quite miserably under the shelter of a tree. Patrick rubbed his ears as he took off the bridle, then rubbed the beast's nose. He continued to rub and pat as he stripped off the horse's gear. He set everything out of the wet, led the stallion to better shelter under a tree, then left him to forage for himself.

Actually, grass was starting to look rather palatable.

He walked to the stream and looked about for something to use as a waterskin. There was nothing useful, but he could likely manage some sort of marginally watertight weaving if he took the time for it. He chose the widest-leafed weeds he could find and set them in a pile. Next he leaped over the small stream and carried on with his search for something to eat. It was late in the year, but there was enough to exist on if one knew where to look.

And he knew, thanks to the lessons he'd had from different souls during his youth. He'd learned about herbs, how to use them and what to avoid, from the village midwife, a woman of indeterminate age who had watched every child in the village make its entrance into the world. His father had raged against his poor use of time, so Patrick had taken to covering his lessons with boasts of having bedded every virgin in the village.

His father had been impressed.

He had learned volumes about healing.

He'd foraged for herbs for the woman, telling his father he was going out to slay wild beasts. He'd done that as well, but he'd also always come home with bunches of useful things hidden under his plaid.

From a traveling minstrel brave enough to venture so far north in the Highlands he'd learned how to eat what the good earth provided in whatever season he found himself. The man had possessed a robust laugh and an uncanny ability to find everything edible within a ten-meter radius. Patrick had taken to heart everything he'd said. If the minstrel had been ingesting things that were poisonous, he would have been too dead to put fingers to his lute.

All of which left Patrick where he was now, kneeling in the mud next to a healthy clutch of yarrow. He let all his fears wash briefly over him, all his self-recriminations for not having saved Lisa, all his years of denying everything he'd been in his youth and everything he'd learned there. It washed over him.

And then it was gone.

And so simply, too. He sat back on his heels, lifted his face to the sky, and let the drizzle fall unimpeded upon him.

Six years of suffering, six years of agonizing, six years of foolish recriminations.

Gone.

In an instant.

He took a deep breath. He watched that polluted wave recede and vowed then to never dip his toes in it again. The ocean was full of all sorts of waves. It was well past time he started sampling others.

He gathered the yarrow, then went to look for other healing things. And once he'd filled the little pouch he'd made

from a corner of his plaid with herbs, berries, and a decent
selection of roots, he went to look for a bit of wood he could
carve into a bowl.

He retraced his steps, collected the pile of weeds he'd left
on the near side of the riverbank, and started back toward
the hut.

Madelyn screamed.

He dropped everything and sprinted for the hut, drawing
his sword as he ran. He flung the hut door open only to find
a man sprawled over Madelyn. The man was groaning. Patrick leaped forward, hauled the man away and threw him out
of the hut. He followed immediately, his sword in his hand.
But apparently there was no need for further work upon this
soul. The man looked up at him.

"MacLeod . . . whore . . ." he managed, then he said no
more.

Patrick reached down and pulled his own dirk free of the
man's belly. He looked at him in the fading light. It was a
Fergusson clansman, one he'd seen the night before looking
at him quite suspiciously. Actually, the entire clan had been
looking at him suspiciously, so this lad was hardly any different than the rest.

But to have followed them so easily?

It did not bode well.

Patrick hefted the man over his shoulder, took him deep
into the woods, and heaved his body into the underbrush. He
could do nothing else. He walked back, took the lad's horse,
and left it conversing companionably with his own—horses
had so much more sense than men—then went back inside
the hut. Madelyn was still in the same place, trying to catch
her breath. She was holding her hand up in the air. Her finger
was bent at an odd angle. He knelt down next to her and
reached out to grasp her hand.

"Broken again?"

She nodded, her teeth chattering.

"Well, that saves me the trouble of breaking it to reset it,
doesn't it?"

She looked at him, her whole body trembling violently.
She looked like a woman who had had enough. More than

enough. So much of enough that she was well on her way to a place she didn't want to go. He put his other hand on her knee, ignoring the damp place there where the Fergusson clansman had bled on her.

"Aren't you the handy one," he said lightly, "even with a wounded paw. I believe I'll keep you to guard my back."

She was still gasping for breath. "I can't joke—"

"Of course not," he said. "So, did he say anything to you?"

"He said," she began, then she took a deep breath, "he was going to do what Simon should have done to start with."

"Rape you or kill you?"

"Both."

"Well," Patrick said easily, "best that you had at him first then, aye?"

She nodded jerkily.

He would have to talk to her about it, but later. For now, he simply sat down next to her and pulled her into his arms. She made some hyperventilating sounds, but didn't weep. He supposed she was too shocked to weep. He could certainly relate to that. He'd taken another's life to keep his own when he'd been but ten-and-three.

I've killed, in defense and in anger. Do you think I don't bear the stain of that on my hands?

Jamie's words came back to him faintly, as if from a great distance. Patrick would give them to Madelyn, when he thought she could hear them and believe them. For now, he merely held her tightly against him and let silence do its work.

Eventually she stirred. She looked up at him in the very faint bit of light left in the hut.

"This is a brutal time period," she said.

He smiled. "Aye, and you, my lady, have seen some of the worst of it."

She was silent for several minutes. "I don't think I can see anything else of it right now."

He gave her a gentle squeeze. "Give it time, love. Give it time." He pulled away and rose. "I'll go fetch what I dropped, then set your finger properly."

"All right," she said weakly.

"Then we'll see if some healing sleep doesn't do us both some good."

She made a brief sound of protest.

"I sleep lightly," he said quickly. "I'll keep us safe. And if I cannot," he said, "we'll leave it to you."

"Patrick, I can't joke about this."

"I know," he said soberly. "I know, Madelyn. But it was either you or him. It's that simple."

She sighed, but her sigh was more an unsteady quaver. "It doesn't feel that simple."

"It never does," he said quietly. He picked up his dirk, wiped it off with some dirt, then laid it down next to her. "I'll return immediately."

He left the hut, stood and listened for several minutes, but heard nothing but the faint sounds of night falling. Perhaps they would be safe.

But it looked as if Moraig's spot was not going to suffice them for much longer. Perhaps for the night, then they would have to move on. It was a pity, he realized with a faint bit of surprise. He'd been looking forward to a few days of peace and quiet with only Madelyn for company.

Well, there would be time enough when they returned home and sorted things out. Aye, time enough for a great many things.

He took a final look about, then ducked back inside the hut.

Chapter 31

Madelyn stood on what served as the bank of a small stream and looked doubtfully at the water that swirled over and around the rocks. The water looked clean. It was a sure bet it was cleaner than she was. She lifted her skirts and hitched her way down a manageable bit of bank and put her feet in the water.

And she almost passed out from the chill.

She swayed, but found herself immediately supported by a pair of strong hands.

"Enough?" Patrick asked.

She shook her head. "I want to at least wash my hands and feet. Maybe my face if I can get down that far."

"I can do that—"

"I can, too," she said. She held up her skirts, reached down, and tried to wash off her legs. She was washing off all the herbs Patrick had slathered on her the night before, but he'd said he could make more. She'd taken him at his word, wanting nothing more than to actually have a part of her feel clean.

Once she could at least see a little of her skin, she decided that perhaps too much cleanliness was a bad thing. It made her realize just how awful the rest of her was. She reached down and brought water to her face and tried to do something with the grime there. It made her cheeks ache, but she continued, at least until she could touch her face and feel clean skin there.

She straightened, accepted Patrick's help to get herself over to a flat rock, then sat and looked up at him.

"What do you think?" she asked. "Do I dare attempt a whole bath, or would it be just too disgusting to bathe and then put on these clothes again?"

He held up his hands. "I wouldn't presume to offer an opinion on that."

"If I washed my dress, how long do you think it would take for it to dry without a fire?"

"Days."

"Days of stink, days of pneumonia. What a choice."

He scratched his stubbled cheek. "Aye, but 'tis the latter that gives me pause. We cannot stay here much longer. Winter is almost upon us. We will freeze without a fire."

"Do you hear me arguing? I'm all for a good fire." She knew he was purposely not talking about the possibility of them being discovered. She didn't want to talk about it, either. It would be a long time before she managed to sleep without wondering if she would wake up to see someone coming in her room with her death on his mind. She looked down and flicked at a patch of dirt on her dress. "Do you think . . ." she began, "do you think we'll ever . . ."

"Get home? Aye," he said. "I do. We will."

"Should we try now?"

He squatted down in front of her. "Truthfully? It would be difficult unless we both were able to ride."

"And I would be a"—she looked for the word, then gave up and resorted to English—"a liability."

He smiled briefly. "Nay, not that. But you need to be able to sit a horse, and ride hard. Wield a blade, if possible."

"Oh, that's me," she said dryly. "Madelyn the shield-maiden, at your disposal."

"We have a Fergusson sword and no one to wield it," he pointed out. "You could learn."

"I couldn't lift it."

"You'd be surprised what you could do if you had to."

She nodded and tried to smile, but it came out a very queasy one, of that she was certain. She looked down at her hands. They were clean, but they didn't feel clean. She had defended herself, true, but it hadn't come without a price.

Then again, what was she to have done? Allowed that man to rape her, then kill her? She hadn't had the strength to fight back. She'd barely managed to get Patrick's knife in an upright position in time for the man to fall on it while he was trying to fall on top of her. It was just plain dumb luck he'd done himself in.

But that didn't make watching a man die not five inches from her face any easier.

She shivered. The realities of medieval life were hard, hard and unyielding. She supposed she shouldn't have been surprised that such a life yielded Patrick's ability to make difficult decisions and not look back.

Like ditching her.

Though he didn't look like he planned to ditch her again any time soon.

She looked out into the forest to take her mind off that tiresome bit of speculation. Patrick had risked his life to come get her. That had to say something for him.

She put the endless speculation out of her mind and looked down at her finger. It was slathered in herbs, splinted, and wrapped with a part of his plaid. She'd tried to protest his using his plaid.

It's an antique, she'd said.

What does that make me? he'd asked.

Impossibly beautiful, she'd wanted to say, but she hadn't. Impossibly, terribly beautiful. Every time she looked at him, every time he smiled at her as if he had warm feelings for her inside his heart, every time he touched her, it was as if the whole world held its breath in appreciation of the miracle of it.

She thought she just might be losing her mind.

Or at least her heart.

"I think," he said, "that we should go."

She pulled herself away from her speculations. "Should we?"

"Would you rather stay?"

"Depends. Is this part of the Patrick MacLeod Scottish tour package, or is this a special thing just for me?"

"The saints forbid." He shook his head. "Nay, this was hardly part of what I wanted to show you. It is a very dangerous tourist attraction."

"A theme park gone horribly wrong."

"Aye."

"I think they've already made a movie out of that. Lots of people got eaten."

"And they don't here?" He winked at her. "One never knows what resides in the Fergusson's cooking pot—"

"Patrick, that's disgusting."

"Aye, so is everything his cook produces." He stood and held his hand down for her. "I think we should try to walk a little. We'll see what of that you can bear before we turn our minds to trying to get home."

"Sure," she said. She let him pull her to her feet, waited until the involuntary gasping had stopped, then nodded firmly. "I'm fine. I'm really fine. Let's go."

He put his arm around her, his strong, comforting arm around her, and gave her shoulders a gentle squeeze. "Slowly, aye? No need to rush. We've all the time needful."

She didn't believe him. He was anxious. Under that sleek, suave exterior, he was anxious. She supposed he wondered if an entire herd of Fergussons was going to descend soon, or if he just wondered if she was going to have some kind of nervous breakdown.

It had been tempting, there, for a while. After he'd removed the body, she'd been tempted. But she'd sucked it up, rationalized all kinds of things, and concentrated on keeping herself from screaming while he set her finger.

She was better this morning. It was light outside and they were still alive. She was free of the cage. Her finger hurt a little less. And Patrick MacLeod had one arm around her shoulder and the other hand holding on to hers as if she was some delicate creature that might shatter if he held her too tightly. She looked up at him and smiled.

"I'm not going to fall apart."

He paused, then smiled, looking more relieved that he probably realized. "I never doubted it."

"Patrick, you don't lie well. It's all right. You can be worried."

"By the saints, Madelyn," he said with a half laugh. "There are times I'm simply unsure how to take you."

Take me any way you want, she thought, but she didn't

say as much. She hoped that too much of it didn't show on her face. She looked down, just in case.

And then she had no choice but to concentrate on everything but Patrick. Every muscle protested the exercise. Her feet hurt, her legs, her back, and her head hurt as well. She walked in circles until she could walk no more. Patrick took her and sat her back down on the rock near the stream. He covered her feet with leaves and other soft things, then went back over to the hut.

He saddled his horse, and the other horse, strapped the Fergusson man's sword to the Fergusson horse, then tied them both up close by. Ready to go at a moment's notice, apparently.

Then he returned with a bit of curved log in one had, his knife in the other, and stood in front of her.

"We'll rest for another hour or so," he said, "then move on. We'll try the forest, if you think you can manage it."

"I can manage it."

"Then take your ease for a bit longer." He smiled down at her. "If that suits."

"It suits."

He nodded, then sat down at her feet and set to his wood with his knife.

Madelyn watched him, and while she watched, her mind wandered. She looked up above her. The sky was still the sky, but there were no telltale jet trails. Birds flew, trees swayed, clouds ambled past. There was something amazingly peaceful about the sound of no civilization. Just the scrape of a knife against wood and the whispering of nature all around her.

It reminded her a good deal of Patrick's land, as a matter of fact.

"What are you making?" she asked lazily.

"A bowl, hopefully." He looked up at her and smiled. "I'm not much of a carver."

"It looks like a bowl to me."

"You're kind."

"I'm hoping for a good drink," she admitted. "What can I do to help?"

"Just sit," he said. "Sit and heal."

"Heal," she said softly. "That's a beautiful word."

He nodded, his knife never ceasing its work on the wood. "It is." He paused, stared off into the distance, then looked back down. "It is a good word."

She watched him for a minute, but apparently he wasn't going to say anything else. "So," she said, "how did you find me? How did you even know where to look?"

"Well, that is something of a tale, isn't it?" he asked. "And so fascinating a one that it lulled you straight to sleep last night."

"That was last night. I'm very awake right now, so get on with it."

He was silent for several moments, then he stopped, put his knife down, and looked up at her. "You never should have had to come here."

"That was hardly your fault."

"Wasn't it? It was because of me that you were even in the forest that day."

"I might have been out for a walk just the same. It was running from Bentley that got me in this predicament. How is he, by the way? Have you seen him?"

"Aye, I saw him," Patrick said. "Showed him a little of my displeasure."

"You beat the crap out of him?" she asked. She wondered what he thought of the way she mixed Gaelic with English. She wouldn't, if he didn't surprise her so often. There were just some things that her own Mother Tongue was better at expressing.

"Not as much of it as I might have liked," Patrick admitted. "No bruises. No broken bones. Just aches and pains that will last for a pair of weeks without much showing."

"Goody," she said. "I hope he's still reaching for the ibuprofen even as we speak. Now, get on with your story. What made you decide I was gone, and how did you know where to look?"

"You left Jane's mobile phone behind. And your footsteps just disappeared." He looked at her briefly, took a deep breath, then resumed his whittling. "That was my first clue."

"So what is the deal with that forest, anyway?" she asked. "One minute I was running away from Bentley, the next I was running into a group of medieval Highlanders."

"My brother could give you a week-long treatise on the ins and outs of it—indeed, he did his damndest to give it to me—and it still wouldn't be the precise answer. Generally, if you're interested in following someone back in time, all you must do is go to the proper place, concentrate all your thoughts on that soul, and *voilà*, you are there."

"And that didn't work this time?"

"Aye, it worked, but not as quickly as I had hoped. I had anticipated three hours; it required three weeks."

She sighed. "Those were three very long weeks."

"I know," he said quietly. "I tried to hurry."

She watched him work with his hands and knife, smoothing, scraping, running his fingers over what he'd done. "I wonder why I got popped back here in the first place," she said with a yawn. The motion of his hands was mesmerizing.

"Jamie would tell you that you had something to accomplish here in the past."

"Hrumph," she said, trying to keep her eyes open. "To lose a few pounds, maybe?"

He smiled up at her, then shook his head and went back to his work. "I doubt that. I suppose time will tell."

She propped her elbows on her knees and her chin on her good fist. It seemed the wisest thing to do, considering how heavy her head was becoming. It was also easier to look at him and not be overcome by the simple beauty of his smile when she had some way to hold herself up.

"So, why did it take you so long, do you think?" she asked with a yawn so uncontrollably huge she almost swallowed her fist. "All part of time's master plan?"

"I daresay it had more to do with Bentley's interference."

"He's a pest," she said. "I wish he'd find his way into the Fergusson's dungeon."

"One could only hope. He sat and watched me long enough while I was trying to wrest the forest to my desires. For all we know, he will."

She lifted her eyebrows—no mean feat, all things considered. "He watched you? When? While you were hanging out in the forest each day, waiting to do a little time traveling?"

"Aye," Patrick said, holding his remarkably bowl-shaped bowl up to study it. "He sat on a damned chair with several cans of soda at his elbow, watching me day after day. Listening to him belch was damned distracting."

She laughed. She couldn't help it. Patrick looked up at her in surprise, a smile on his face.

"That sounded like you," he said.

"I feel more like myself," she said with a smile. "Maybe I'm not going to lose my mind after all."

"You're handling this quite well."

"It's just the thought of Bentley in a recliner, watching you like he might have some Saturday afternoon college football—" She shook her head. "It's just so him. But if he was watching you all the time, how did you get him to stop?"

"Ruined his Jag."

Madelyn blinked. "You're kidding."

He looked up at her. "I would never jest about a Jaguar."

She could hardly believe her ears. "Are you telling me that you were desperate enough to actually do damage to an automobile?"

He smiled, but he didn't look up at her. "Desperate times call for desperate measures."

"What did you do?"

"I put sand in the oil reservoir."

"Wow," she said, stunned. "You must have been worried."

He nodded, but didn't look up. "*Frantic* is more the word I would choose. For you see," he continued softly, "I knew the perils of the time. And the thought of you having to face any of them . . . well, it almost drove me mad."

He looked up at her.

And the look on his face almost knocked her off her rock. A more foolish woman might have mistaken it for a quite serious emotion.

It was the same thing she'd seen in the hut the day before.

She turned away first. She didn't want to speculate on his feelings. She didn't want to let herself sink into that look and lose more of her heart than she'd lost to him so far.

Though she wasn't sure her whole heart wasn't gone already.

"Well," she said, looking up into the gray sky and marveling that it looked and felt so much like snow already, "tell me what you did when you first got back here. How did you know where I was?"

"I didn't know," he said. He started whittling again. "I went to the MacLeod keep, made friends with the current laird, acquired a horse, and came up with a tale believable enough for a Fergusson."

"You thought I might be there?"

"You weren't at the MacLeod keep. I was told there had been a small skirmish with Fergussons recently, so I suspected they might have captured you. Had you come to this time, of course. I could only hope that was the case."

She shivered. "I could have gotten very lost."

"Aye."

"No wonder Jane has red dots on her map."

He nodded. "She fears them."

"Well, at least she already speaks Gaelic. That would have to be a bonus."

He looked up at her. "Jane is a wonderful woman," he said. "I daresay, though, that only you could have survived what was put upon you." He paused. "It would have broken her."

"It almost broke me."

"Did it?" He shook his head. "You are much, much stronger than she is. But if you repeat that, I'll deny having said it."

She snorted. "Coward."

"She feeds me regularly."

"Your secret is safe with me," she said, and she felt a funny warmth begin near her heart. That was a compliment he'd paid her, wasn't it? It felt like one.

A damned difficult thing she'd had to go through to get it.

"I have to say, I've never been happier to see anyone in my life than I was to see you," she offered.

He looked up at her and smiled. "Me either."

"Really?" she asked in astonishment.

"Is that so surprising?"

"A little," she said dryly.

He put the bowl down, rested his knife on top of it, and looked at her. "We should talk."

"Later," she said, heaving herself to her feet. She almost heaved herself into the stream. The only thing stopping her was Patrick leaping to his feet and grabbing hold of her.

"By the saints, Madelyn," he said with half a laugh, "you needn't flee."

She looked down at the ground between them, and there wasn't much ground between them, and found that she had no desire whatsoever for any talk. She didn't want to know what he was feeling. She didn't want to know if along with all the details about the forest, his brother had given him advice on how to get ride of a pesky Yank. She could just hear it now: *Drop the wench back in the Middle Ages, Patrick.* It was sort of like taking out the trash, only you didn't have to worry about the landfill issues.

Patrick put his arms around her and pulled her close. "If you've no stomach for speech now, we could attempt it later."

She took a deep breath. "I don't think I can stand much more today," she said. She made herself look up at him. "I've had a bad couple of weeks."

He tucked her hair behind her ears and smiled down at her gently. "I have an idea," he said.

"A fire?"

"That, too. Nay, my idea is this: Why do we not just take the days as they come, together?"

"What other way is there?" she asked. "It isn't as if you can just leave me here and go off by yourself."

He pursed his lips. "You're damned argumentative."

"One of my best traits."

He surprised her by smiling. "Aye, it is. Take the days with me, Madelyn. Together. We'll take them as they come and see what comes of them."

She nodded with a sigh.

He kissed her forehead, then kept his arm around her and

turned her toward the horses. "Let us see if you can even ride. If you can, we'll try the forest. If not, we'll try the MacLeod keep."

"The keep?" she squeaked.

"Fire. Food. Perhaps even a comfortable scrap of floor to call our own. If I flatter the laird enough, he might offer you a bath."

A bath. The thought of it was enough to make her feel quite spry. She would have danced a jig if she'd been capable of it. It was amazing that even what she was certain would be quite primitive conditions sounded so luxurious. If she ever managed to get herself to even a one-star hotel, she wouldn't complain about lumpy, disgusting mattresses again.

Then she hesitated.

"What will they think about me? Do you want me to come up with a story?"

He looked faintly alarmed, then smiled quickly. "Leave it to me."

"It is your era, after all."

"It is that."

"We're going to have to talk about that, too, you know," she said as she stood in front of the current-day mode of rapid transit. "All those comments to the tour guides. All those complaints about the Crown Jewels. That *river* of bilge you gave me about having read so many history books that it was almost as if you'd lived it." She scowled up at him. "Deceitful. Dishonest. Bordering on unethical."

"I couldn't up and give you the truth right off, could I?"

"You could have."

"Aye, well, we'll have to talk about that, too," he said. He looked at the Fergusson horse, then at her. "What do you think?"

She thought that if it meant getting the absolutely disgusting crust of filth off her, she would jump right on that horse with a vertical leap that would have impressed any NBA star. She looked at Patrick. "Let's go."

He made her a stirrup of his hands. She put her foot in, only to have the horse shy away. The beast must have been bred to hate MacLeods.

Patrick clucked his tongue. "You're supposed to let him know you are the master."

"I tried. He's not convinced."

"You'll ride with me," he said. He put her up on his horse, swung up behind her, and took both horses in hand. "We'll go easily at first. I'll find us somewhere warm and safe, I promise."

She closed her eyes, held on to the horse's mane and Patrick's arm. Did such a place exist in the Middle Ages?

Well, if anyone could find it, she supposed it would have to be the man holding on to her as if he cared.

"Trust me," he said.

Heaven help her, she did.

Chapter 32

P *atrick* was beginning to wonder if his glib tongue had deserted him for good.

He'd promised Madelyn somewhere warm and safe. He'd actually been hoping for Ian's living room in front of that massive fireplace he had. Or maybe even a pair of chairs in front of Ian's shiny red Aga stove. Even his own hearth, well laid with a small, dry tree, would have done in a pinch.

He hadn't been planning on Malcolm MacLeod's dungeon.

He blew on his hands to keep them warm and reexamined his day to see where his plans had gone awry. Maybe he should have given the forest more time. But given that spending the majority of the day standing in the shade had accomplished nothing more than to give Madelyn a stuffy nose, he'd decided that a night or two at the keep to regroup was the thing to do.

Unfortunately, they'd arrived only to find Malcolm off repaying a few McKinnons for trying to lift a pair of his prize cattle and his bumbling son Angus in charge. Angus had put them into the pit without hesitation. Apparently someone after Jamie had decided that having a dungeon was a good thing, because they'd dug up the bloody pit that Jamie'd had filled in to please Elizabeth.

It would have been bad enough that he stood up to his ankles in that dungeon's slime, but Madelyn was with him, sitting in the slime with her teeth chattering. Had that been the extent of things, he would have counted himself fortunate. Unfortunately, the insanity didn't end there. He and Madelyn had been deposited none-too-gently into the dungeon only to find it already inhabited.

By one Bentley Douglas Taylor III.

Who was, lamentably, babbling like a madman.

Patrick had understood why they'd thrust Bentley down into the noisesome hole. Indeed, he'd understood why he and Madelyn had been put there. Angus was not, as they say, the sharpest tool in the shed. Patrick had tried to point out to Angus that they had met before, but Angus had been either too stupid to have remembered it or too terrified . . . nay, he'd just been too stupid. Patrick had allowed himself to be disarmed simply because he couldn't bring himself to shed any familial blood when he'd been quite certain that their stay in the dungeon would be very brief. But to pass those few hours in Bentley's company?

Aye, now, that was hell indeed.

"Bloody hell, Angus, ye wee fool, what have ye done with them? He bloody rescued me!"

Patrick closed his eyes and sighed in relief at the voice from above. Robert the piper, to the rescue. He reached over and pulled Madelyn to her feet. "Come on," he said, "we're saved."

"Wait," Bentley demanded, reaching out for him. "Get me out of here, too. I've been here almost two days. At least I think it's been two days. Whatever it's been, it's been long enough that whoever I find up there is going to get his sorry ass sued. In fact, let me go first. I have quite a bit to say to the ne'er-do-wells—"

Patrick pushed Bentley back away from the ladder. "Ladies first, you idiot."

Bentley struggled.

Patrick put his thumb behind Bentley's ear in a particularly tender spot, waited until he was gasping in pain, then gave him a healthy shove. Bentley began to complain loudly from where he lay sprawled in the mud. Patrick took that opportunity to get Madelyn started up the ladder. And once he'd started her up, there was no sense in not following her up and out.

And there was certainly no sense in not just shaking that ladder free of any other climbers.

"Hey!" Bentley bellowed. "Let me up! Let me out of here, you morons! I'll sue!"

Robert the piper looked at Patrick. "Who is he?" he asked in Gaelic.

" 'Tis a very long tale you would find almost unbelievable."

"I've listened to him," Robert said, looking faintly alarmed. "He spouts nonsense."

"He's a madman," Patrick said. "An Englishman who wanted to wed with my lady here. He cannot seem to accept the fact that she wants none of him."

"True," Madelyn said, leaning heavily on him. "All true."

"Do you know the man?" Angus asked, blinking furiously. "Perhaps you should return to the pit with him—"

Robert glared Angus to silence, then looked at Patrick. "My apologies, and the apologies of my laird. Come, sit at the table and take your ease." He looked at Madelyn and smiled. "How do you fare, my lady?"

"Better," she said, smiling weakly and rubbing her arms. "Better. And you, Robert?"

"Well enough," he said gamely. "Come, my friends, and let us repair to the fire. Angus will no doubt be very interested in your tale, and his sire will be pleased to know Angus made great efforts to offer you the hospitality of our hall after such a grievous error in your arrival."

Angus looked baffled at so many words strung together. Patrick had to shake his head. Jamie would have been appalled to think that such a one as this would be in charge of the clan when his time came. Maybe it was little wonder that the keep had, in the end, fallen into such a state of decay. Too many lairds such as Angus and the entire clan would bolt just to save themselves.

Patrick put his arm around Madelyn and helped her hobble out into the great hall. She hesitated, looked around her, then shivered.

"Spooky," she whispered.

"Aye," he agreed. It was like seeing before and after pictures, only this was in reverse. He gave her shoulders a gentle squeeze. "Fire first," he said, nodding toward the opposite wall, "then something to eat."

"And new clothing," Robert said. "My lady Grudach likely

has something that would suit you. I will prevail upon her to share."

The way he said it made Patrick wonder just how selfless a soul Grudach might be. Then again, he'd heard quite a bit about her from her half sister, Iolanthe, who happened to be sitting quite happily in her beautiful house in Maine with his nephew, Thomas—another member of that convoluted family tree—who had gone back in time to rescue her.

"What are you thinking?" Madelyn asked as she hitched along next to him.

"I was just pondering the impossibility of trying to map out a proper family tree with my kin," he said with a smile. "I've heard tell of both Angus and his sister Grudach from their sister. Their half sister, actually."

"Does she live near here?"

"Maine, actually."

"With her modern-day husband, of course."

"Who else?"

Madelyn shook her head. "If I'd only realized a simple thing such as a trip to Scotland would have led to all this . . ."

"Do you regret it?"

She paused and looked at him. "No," she said softly. "No, I don't."

"And what of Bentley? Do you mind if we leave him below?"

She hesitated. "It doesn't seem very nice, does it?"

"Think *three weeks in a cage*, Madelyn," he said dryly.

"Then by all means, let him season down there for a while," she said. "It'll do him some good. I'm not sure what we'll tell him afterward." She looked up at him with a smile. "Maybe we can convince him he was abducted by aliens."

"We'll think of something." He led her to the fire, then helped her sit down in front of it. He sat down next to her on the bench and held his hands to the flames. There was nothing quite like feeling some small bit of warmth after a goodly time without it.

He looked at Angus, who sank down nearby and nervously fondled a cup of ale. Angus looked as if he were about to be whipped senseless for having done something incredibly stupid. He looked at Patrick with a sick smile. Patrick smiled back.

"You know," Patrick remarked, "my lady has spent quite a bit of time in the Fergusson's keep without food or water. Perhaps she might appreciate a bit of ale. Something to eat. A bath."

"Oh, aye," Angus said, jumping up. "Aye, I'll have it seen to immediately."

"Thank you," Patrick said. "I will speak kindly of you to your sire."

That seemed to be enough for Angus. He began bellowing for sustenance and demanded that a tub be filled in the kitchen for his lady's pleasure. Patrick looked at Robert.

"So," he said, "is this the way of things?"

Robert rolled his eyes. "You've no idea."

"I can imagine. I have some acquaintance with his sister Iolanthe."

Robert sighed deeply. "That poor gel. I know young Thomas McKinnon tried to find her, but we fear they are both dead. We've had no word from either. Have you occasion to have heard from them?"

Patrick chewed on his answer for several moments, then decided it was perhaps better to let it lie. Not all questions had to be answered, especially when the answer would do none of the parties any good. He shook his head. "I've had no word from them recently." He'd talked to Iolanthe on the phone during his three-week wait, but that hadn't really been recently, had it? "One can only hope that Thomas found her, and they are living out their lives in some quiet corner somewhere."

"Aye," Robert agreed. "Iolanthe was a good gel. Nothing much like her sister," he said in a low voice. "Ah, here is food, my lady Madelyn. Eat your fill, then we'll provide other things for your comfort."

Patrick held a wooden trencher for Madelyn, filling his own belly as he could. She ate everything that was put before her, even the more disgusting things. Patrick ate just as heartily, grateful all the while that he could look forward to better fare when they returned home.

Madelyn drank deeply from her cup, then smiled. "Better," she said.

"And here comes the accompaniment to your bath," he said as Grudach swept into the hall.

Grudach was, he decided after ten minutes of listening to her rail upon her brother, every bit as offensive as Iolanthe had said she was. And when she fixed her sights on Madelyn, Patrick knew something had to be done. He stood and gave her his most dazzling smile.

"You must be my laird's beautiful treasure," he said. "I've heard tell of you."

That Grudach didn't look around her to see if he might have been talking about someone else was telling. She certainly seemed to think the problem of Iolanthe had been solved. That was interesting.

Grudach looked him over as if she sized up a prize steer. "Who are you?"

"Patrick," he said with a bow. "I was here a pair of days ago to ask your father for aid in finding my lady."

Grudach turned a very unfriendly glance Madelyn's way. "She smells as if she's been living in the cesspit."

Madelyn smiled politely. "I have been, actually."

"Don't want you befouling any of my clothes."

Robert the piper stood and looked at her without any friendliness at all. "Then fetch something of Iolanthe's. There should be aught there, given that she wasn't allowed to take anything with her."

"It was given to the poor in the village—"

"Bollocks," Robert said crisply. "I saw you wearing her finest dress not two days before I found myself out on an errand which put me straight into the Fergusson's hands. An errand, I might add, that you saw me sent on."

"You dare—" Grudach spluttered.

"I dare much. Fetch the dress."

If she could have killed him, it looked as if she would have. She spun on her heel and marched away. Patrick looked at Robert.

"You're a brave one."

Robert shrugged with a smile. "What have I to fear from her?"

"You would know better than I," Patrick said, though he had to admit that he knew far more than he wanted to.

Robert smiled, undaunted. "She'll surrender something for our lady to wear." He looked at Madelyn. "I'll see that none of Grudach's ilk aid you with your bath."

Madelyn looked so grateful for the chance to have a bath, Patrick suspected she didn't care who helped her. She flashed him a look.

"Will I have any privacy at all?" she asked.

"I could stand guard."

Her eyes grew quite wide.

Robert offered her his arm. "Survivors of the Fergusson hell must watch over each other. I will be the one to stand guard for you, my lady, and do it with my back turned. Don't mind my lack of useful fingers. I can keep all at bay with my sharp tongue alone."

Patrick offered a mild protest, but Robert gave him a look of amusement.

"I'll watch over her well, my friend," he said.

Patrick couldn't deny that Robert had certainly done that in the future. Perhaps that was reason enough to trust him in the past. He looked at Madelyn. "Are you all right?"

"If it means a bath, I'm perfect."

He rose, helped her up, then put his arms around her briefly. "You are a wonder," he whispered in English. Then he handed her over to the piper. "Take good care of her, my friend."

"I will protect her with my life," Robert said.

"Hopefully it won't come to that," Madelyn said with half a laugh.

"With Grudach, one never knows," Robert said dryly. He offered her his arm, then walked her slowly across the hall.

Patrick watched them go, then sat down to warm himself by the fire. He didn't like to think about the strangeness of sitting by the fire he'd spent the greater part of his life sitting by—except that now he was sitting by it in a century he'd never been in.

But there was something to be said for it. Perhaps they could spend a day or two in a place of relative safety, long enough to let Madelyn heal a bit. Besides, who knew when the gate would let them get home? Or what it was they had to accomplish here in the past?

He stared into the fire and gave that a great amount of thought as he nursed his rather drinkable ale—whatever else his faults, at least Malcolm spared no effort to produce a fine cup of ale. He stared into the flames and pondered the possibilities of a few days of nothing to do but sit with Madelyn and talk. In Gaelic, no less.

The woman was, as he continued to tell her, amazing.

The front door opened. Patrick looked up automatically, expecting to see someone from his family coming inside. He stared at Malcolm for a few minutes before he realized whom he was staring at. He rose immediately and assumed a deferential mien.

"My laird," he said.

Malcolm must have had a successful hunt, for his humor was fine. He motioned with an expansive gesture for Patrick to join him at the table. He called for wine and meat to be brought, then proceeded to regale Patrick with an exceedingly bloody tale. Patrick counted himself blessed to have spent his youth discussing such things over supper, for he managed to eat yet another supper without flinching during even the most gruesome of details.

Suddenly he felt the air in the room change and knew without looking that Madelyn had come into the hall. It was a feeling akin to what he'd felt the first time he'd laid eyes on her. He turned his head to look at her.

And she fair took his breath away.

She was wearing clothing not her own, but it suited her as if it had been made with her in mind. Her hair was nothing short of a rampage of curls. Her face was fresh-scrubbed, her clothing clean, and her expression one of great relief. Indeed, as she walked next to Robert, she laughed easily at something he said, as if she'd done nothing more strenuous in the past three weeks than a bit of touring. Of course, she wasn't walking all that well, and she was having a hard time straightening up completely, but that would pass in time.

And then she looked at him.

And her smile turned into something else entirely. Something private, something full of a mixture of uncertainty and hope.

"By the bloody saints, Patrick," Malcolm grunted, "the wench wants you."

Patrick managed to clear his throat without choking and making a proper fool of himself. "Apparently," he said.

"Lovely gel," Malcolm said, slapping Patrick on the back. "Taking her away from the Englishman, are you?"

"Aye," Patrick said.

"No reason you can't wed her today. Put her forever past his reach."

Patrick didn't mean to gape at him. It wasn't that he hadn't had the thought of marriage cross his mind before. Fleetingly. Briefly.

Or lingeringly, as of late.

But a marriage today?

"I'll see it done," Malcolm said, rising. "I'll rouse the priest."

"But—"

Malcolm looked at him with a glint in his eye. "Don't think you should be wandering about with a wench of her breeding and not be wed to her, do you?"

"Ah—"

" 'Tis the least I can do for a cousin," Malcolm said. "If you *are* a cousin. You look a great deal like a proper MacLeod, but these are perilous times. . . ."

"Aye," Patrick managed, "they are."

"My pit has housed more friendly souls than you."

The threat was implicit; the choice was clear.

Damnation, if he had to choose between wedding the woman and languishing in Malcolm MacLeod's pit, what was he to do?

He wondered if he could manage to look pained by it well enough to have Malcolm—and everyone else—believe he was being forced to the altar.

Was that why they'd come to the past? To be wed?

By the saints, he didn't want to believe that time thought him such a fool that only machinations of that magnitude would bring him to his senses.

"No time like the present," Patrick said heavily, "to see to one's duty."

Malcolm grunted, but there was a very visible twinkle in his eye. "Robert!" he bellowed. "Fetch the priest!"

Robert deposited Madelyn in the chair next to Patrick, then went to see to his laird's pleasure. Madelyn smiled at Patrick.

"What's up?" she asked.

He looked at her solemnly. "A marriage."

"Whose?"

"Let's put it this way," he said, "We may not have much time for any conversations of a serious nature . . . before . . ."

"Before what?" she asked.

He was suddenly afraid to answer.

Malcolm, bless his conniving heart, was not.

Chapter 33

The fire crackled exuberantly in the hearth, spreading warmth and good cheer. A candle or two added to the ambience, to the feeling of tranquility, to the overall sense of peace in the room. The floor was strewn with soft bits of straw that smelled—well, they smelled, but perhaps a girl couldn't ask for anything else in the Middle Ages. Madelyn knelt next to Patrick MacLeod and was grateful for a fire, clean clothes, and a marginally clean floor to kneel on.

The clean clothes she would have to thank Iolanthe for when next they met. The dress was a handful of inches too short, but at least it covered everything else it was supposed to. It would have to do because she'd had her clothes consigned to the fire. It had seemed the safest thing to do, given their condition and the very modern tags and fasteners attached to them. A good, hot fire had seemed the best way to take care of that problem.

The hot fire was something she could thank Malcolm for later. After a month of being chilled to the bone, its warmth was absolutely heavenly.

She was also quite thankful that she was even marginally capable of kneeling. Her body was healing in a remarkable fashion, though she supposed it would take her several more days to feel fully herself.

Briefly, she stole a look at Patrick to see how he was taking it all. The firelight flickered over his handsome features, cast his dark hair into deeper shadows, caressed the backs of his scarred hands. His shirt was a bit frayed at the cuffs and his plaid a bit worn as well, but it covered broad shoulders and strong arms. He looked not unhappy to be where he was, doing what he was doing. Indeed, he was listening to the priest with a completely serene expression on his face.

A priest who was standing—and she had to use that term loosely—in front of them and coming close to knocking her flat with his breath alone.

She paused.

At least Patrick hadn't had to likewise strengthen himself by ingesting vast quantities of alcohol.

She could be grateful for small favors, she supposed.

So she looked down at her fingers interlaced with Patrick's and marveled, gratefully, at the complete improbability of what she was going through at the moment.

Marriage.

To a man who didn't look at all disappointed by the turn of events.

Oh, he'd protested, in a token fashion, to Malcolm's strong-arming him. He'd gone to the makeshift altar—a bench placed on the cleanest bit of floor Robert the piper could find—dragging his heels.

But he'd knelt without hesitation after having helped her to do the same with the utmost gentleness, and he'd taken her hand with the same kind of care, given her a smile that said he actually didn't mind in the slightest, then paid complete attention to the man who stood in front of them, pontificating quite nicely in Latin.

Well, in somewhat slurred Latin.

Slurred, but intelligible.

Now, if she just hadn't been able to understand what he was saying, she would have been fine.

"Oh, for the days of repairing to the pub," the good friar said, closing his eyes briefly and looking quite solemn, "for a pint of the local brewer's finest—and that after a hard day perfecting my craft in the wind and driving rain. Who would have thought I would have had to leave it behind me to come dwell in a place where links describe naught but the makings of a good, strong chain?"

Madelyn hardly dared look at Patrick. His hand around hers was warm and comforting. He seemed not to be bothered by the fact that the man proceeded to describe in gory detail the last golf tournament he'd played—and lost. For herself, she could only stare at the priest in complete astonishment.

The man was twenty-first century. She would have bet her life on it.

But given his numerous references to his bookie, she wondered if she shouldn't bet her life on his being a priest.

And if he wasn't, who was marrying her?

The priest who might or might not be a priest continued with the service, seemingly dragging himself back to the usual text with a herculean effort.

Well, at least he knew the service. And his Latin was quite good, when he managed to shake himself back to coherence long enough to articulate it.

When it was her turn, she nodded and said "aye."

When it was his turn, Patrick nodded and said "aye."

The priest sighed deeply. "Never found myself anyone to love in my day"—he slid Grudach a brief look, then turned back to them—"but that shouldn't stop you two from enjoying yourselves."

Grudach? Madelyn filed that away for future reference.

"Kiss her, man," the priest said, "and hurry. Before she changes her mind."

Patrick seemed to understand that. Maybe he just figured it was the thing to do. Madelyn thought about pointing out to him that he'd been married by someone who might or might not have the authority to do what he'd just claimed to do, but she found herself distracted quite thoroughly by the feeling of Patrick MacLeod's mouth on hers.

Good grief. If this was what being married to him entailed, she wasn't sure she would survive it.

The kissing went on for quite some time. She was pathetically grateful she was kneeling so she didn't have to humiliate herself by having her knees buckle underneath her.

Then, quite suddenly, Patrick was pulled to his feet and presented with a hefty cup of wine. She would have been treated in like manner had Patrick not bellowed for her handlers to take their hands off her. He put his cup down on the bench, then very carefully helped her to her feet, found her a chair near the fire, and put her just as carefully into it.

Then he took up his wine and submitted to a quite thorough round of backslapping and congratulating.

She was allowed to remain in her seat, which she desperately needed after what she'd just listened to. She sipped her wine as she watched the good friar move among his flock, dispensing blessings and other things in Latin. He finally settled onto a bench near the fire and held court with those who eschewed drink for something of a higher nature. Angus, whose conscience was undoubtedly pricking him for having dumped her in the dungeon right off, had approached for some sort of instructive conversation. He was obviously not one to give up his drink, though, because he'd brought a jug of something in his hands. That was good enough for the good father. He held out his cup and began to hold forth, in Latin, as if he distilled something which was of great import on Angus's sorry soul.

"You see," he began, "I'm a man lost in time."

Madelyn felt her jaw slide south. She retrieved it with an effort.

"You wouldn't know it to look at me, but I was once a powerful vicar. In the late twentieth century."

Angus looked confused. Madelyn was relieved. At least she was legally wed.

"Well, perhaps *powerful* isn't exactly the case. I made money enough for my needs. But it was, as you might imagine, my illicit pleasure that was my downfall."

Angus listened with rapt attention. Madelyn did as well.

"I told my parish that I was off north to visit the poor."

Angus nodded wisely.

"But," the priest said, leaning in close, "I wasn't."

"Ah," said Angus.

Madelyn leaned forward as well.

"I came for the purpose of a bloody brilliant bit of golf."

Madelyn wondered if a few golf courses in Scotland should be drawing red dots on their maps as well. She looked at the vicar and wondered if he was happy with his lot, or if

he wanted to go home. Not that she could promise him anything, of course. But imagine, to be stuck back in time with
no knowledge of how you'd gotten there, nor any idea of
how to get home.

Should she tell him?

If she did, would she have to discuss with Patrick the
contents of their marriage contract, which had included a
lengthy reminiscence about the pleasures of modern life,
modern sporting events, and modern food. Would he consider that a less than proper ceremony?

Did she care?

Yes, she did. Very much.

And who should appear at that moment to further exacerbate her dilemma but its major component, Patrick
MacLeod himself. He held out his hand.

"Food?" he asked.

She was starting to understand his fondness for it. "Always," she said.

He very carefully helped her up, then put his arm around
her and helped her hobble over to the high table where the
wedding feast soon ensued.

It was a very interesting evening. Robert the piper could
not play, but he turned out to have a very beautiful voice.
Madelyn managed to enjoy things up to the point when she
realized that if she had to sit much longer, she was going to
cry. And at the precise moment when she knew she could
bear it no longer, Patrick took her hand and spoke to Malcolm.

"My lady tires," he said. "Is there a place—"

"Grudach's chamber," Malcolm said without hesitation.

"Father!"

He silenced her with a single look, then looked at Patrick.
"My daughter will be pleased to let you have the very luxurious chamber that she doesn't deserve."

"Not that they'll use it properly," Angus guffawed. "The
wench can hardly walk, much less . . . ah . . ."

Madelyn only caught the remnant of the look Patrick had
sent Angus. Angus shut up immediately and found the con-

tents of his bowl before him to be quite fascinating.

"Thank you, my laird," Patrick said. "We'll make good use of it."

"I daresay you will," Malcolm said with a booming laugh. "Leave something left of her, lad. I've a few questions to put to her regarding that foul bit of refuse leading the Fergusson clan."

"I'll do what I can," Patrick said dryly.

Madelyn found herself soon swept up into his arms and carried up the stairs. She had no idea what he planned, but if anyone was asking her opinion, she didn't particularly feel like having a wedding night when she wasn't sure she could even get herself to the bathroom without help.

He opened the door, went inside, then shut the door with his foot. Then he looked down at her with a smile. "Alone, at last."

She wondered if she looked as green as she felt.

She must have because he only laughed at her and carried her over to the bed. He laid her down, took off Iolanthe's shoes that were only marginally too small, then covered her with a blanket. He smiled.

"Sleep. You need it."

She stared up at him in surprise. "Really?"

"Madelyn, I'm not a barbarian."

"I wasn't worried about that. You were, after all, the one who was urged to that makeshift altar by the point of a sword."

"I was not." He leaned over her with his hands on either side of her head.

She felt a little faint.

All right, so she felt a lot faint.

"You weren't?"

"I didn't need a sword in my back," he said with a small smile.

"Didn't you?"

"Nay, Madelyn," he said quietly, "I did not. You?"

She shook her head slowly. "Me neither."

He stared at her for a moment or two in silence, then

cleared his throat. "We should talk, perhaps," he said softly. "There are things we must discuss."

Her heart sank. "Patrick—"

He leaned down and kissed her. Gently. Sweetly. Thoroughly.

Then he lifted his head. "Later," he said. "We'll talk later."

She took a deep breath. "All right."

"You should rest. There's time for talk in the future."

"And what are you going to do?"

"Rest right next to you and dream of Lilt and scones with clotted cream."

"You are a complicated man."

He laughed and straightened. He then walked around the side of the bed nearest the door. He removed his sword, pulled the knife out of his boot, then lay down next to her. He rolled toward her and carefully put his arm around her. "Can you bear the weight?"

She looked into fathomless green eyes and thought she might be able to bear a great many things if he were next to her.

"I can," she answered.

"Then take your rest, love."

"You'll keep watch?"

"Aye. I'll not fail you again."

"Patrick—"

He shook his head. "I have in the past, but I won't in the future. Now, sleep in peace and safety. I think I can guarantee you no more trips into Malcolm's pit."

Madelyn was tempted to give Bentley a passing thought, but the thought passed before she could hold on to it. He deserved what he was getting. They could probably get him out eventually anyway, later. When they went home.

Which was sounding less appealing by the heartbeat. Where would she be back in the future? Probably not on a mattress made from unidentifiable substances with Patrick MacLeod breathing softly in her ear and stroking her hand fitfully as he fell asleep.

Then again, maybe she would.

She was after all, according to an inebriated refugee from the twentieth century, his wife.

She sighed deeply, happily, and closed her eyes with a smile.

Chapter 34

B entley Douglas Taylor III stood up to his ankles in muck and wanted to cry.

He didn't cry often. He was more inclined to complain, rage, or threaten to sue.

But that was when he was in his home environment.

He didn't know where the hell he was now.

He looked up at the square of light three feet above his head and wondered how it was that Madelyn and MacLeod had escaped the tortures and he hadn't. MacLeod had been speaking the language of his captors; maybe that was it.

Maybe MacLeod was trading Madelyn for special treatment.

It was something Bentley would have done in his place.

He wished he'd had her to hand when he'd been captured. Now, that was a bad dream he doubted he would ever forget. There he'd been, innocently wandering out of the forest after having spent a night there to verify the utter stupidity of a pub rumor that such camping would produce time traveling, when what should he have innocently wandered into but a rather rustic session of the Highland games.

Only these rustics didn't speak English, and they'd carried damned large swords.

He'd threatened to call the authorities.

They'd looked at him blankly, like the brainless natives they were.

He'd given them a brief listing of the clients who owed him favors and what those clients would do to them if they didn't put away their damned large swords.

He didn't remember anything after that. Maybe someone had clunked him on the head.

Maybe he'd been abducted by aliens and anesthetized so

he wouldn't remember their painful medical experiments conducted on his admittedly superior physique.

That didn't explain why he was standing up to his ankles in mud, or why Madelyn and MacLeod had been there with him only briefly, but perhaps the mystery would be solved later when he was released.

Too bad he didn't have Madelyn to bargain with.

Well, whatever the case, Bentley knew he was in deep crap with no hope of escape. His fertile mind ran amok with possibilities of what the future could hold.

Torture.

Debriefing with sharp instruments.

More days in the mud hole with things he couldn't see and didn't dare identify crawling up inside the legs of his pants.

He began to have serious regrets about having followed Madelyn to Scotland. Scotland, of all places! He should have left her to her men in skirts and her inns with no cable. Did he really need her to get in good with her dad? For all he knew, her dad didn't like her any better than he himself did. Maybe agreeing with the man on that was the way to win points with him.

He would try that.

Just as soon as he figured out how in the hell he was going to jump three vertical feet, lift the grate keeping him down in the mud, and swing his 190 pounds of muscle out onto the floor above him without alerting his alien captors to his intentions.

He stared up at the light.

"Let me out, or I'll sue," he whispered.

No one heard him. No one came to rescue him.

He hadn't expected they would.

Chapter 35

$\mathbf{M}$adelyn walked through the village, holding Patrick's hand, and feeling quite grateful she was doing both. After three days spent either in bed or taking invalid-paced walks, she was feeling almost herself again. She still wasn't sure her back would ever be the same, but Patrick was convinced that with a few more herbs and a visit to the chiropractor when they got home, she would be fine.

When they got home. He made it sound as if they were just on vacation.

She hoped it wouldn't be a permanent one.

At least her time at Club Medieval had allowed her body to begin to restore itself to its proper working order. Either that or it was aiding her in avoiding having any more serious conversations with Patrick by propelling her out the keep's front door where there were many things around that would serve as a distraction from the more serious matters that lay between them like a heavy bolster.

Matters such as: How would they get home and how would they live once they got there? As man and wife?

She just could bear to know yet.

That imaginary bolster hadn't, however, stood in the way of several quite lovely kisses and a great deal of snuggling. Patrick had seemed quite enthusiastic about both—and more, truth be told.

After all, they *were* wed.

As far as Father John was concerned, at least.

She supposed they weren't going to get a decent opinion on the matter from a man who was continually drinking himself into stupors because of unrequited love.

The object of his affections being one Grudach MacLeod.

Grudach was having none of him, it seemed, or so Robert said with disgust. Madelyn wondered if that meant the friar would spend the rest of his life pining and drinking. She supposed it could have been worse. He could have been drinking and golfing. At least this way, no one was going to get beaned by stray golf balls.

All of which left her in the unenviable position of now knowing just how authentic her marriage was. She started to ask Patrick about his command of Latin the night before at supper, but he'd been distracted from his answer by a call to go help them settle the prisoner in the dungeon. For all she knew, he had a coliseum full of words at his command.

If it came right down to it, though, she didn't really want to ask him what he had understood—in case he didn't think their marriage was worth the parchment it was written on.

She'd also begun to wonder how long they were going to be guests in Grudach's room. She'd broached the subject with Patrick at breakfast, asking him in an offhanded way what he thought the keep was thinking about them being sequestered in their room for so long. He had lifted his sword, admired it, then looked at her and asked her if she thought they would actually dare inquire.

She'd said she didn't suppose they would.

He'd assured her he would take care of any questions. After all, they were wed, weren't they?

Madelyn hadn't wanted to discuss it further, and she'd been more than willing to escape the house that day so she didn't have to face that issue.

Cowardly? You bet.

Preserving the fragile state of her heart? Most definitely.

All of which left her holding Patrick's hand—silently and not offering any answers to questions she didn't want asked—while they walked through the village on their way to a particularly useful bit of countryside he was certain would still have a few of the herbs he was looking for. Apparently one of the things on the docket for the day was the resetting of Robert's fingers.

She wondered if the priest would give up some of his grog for the occasion.

She shivered as she walked and found herself immediately with a strong arm around her shoulders. She was growing far too accustomed to the feeling of it—and to the sight of his sword strapped to his back, the sound it made as it occasionally slapped against various parts of his anatomy, and the thought of having it used in her defense.

She'd obviously been too long in the Middle Ages.

"Cold out," he remarked.

"It is."

"We won't be long."

She nodded and continued on with him, torn between looking at a village that boasted the kind of poverty she'd never seen before and looking at Patrick, who strode through that village like some Roman deity come down to survey his domain and offer his sword in their defense.

She would have been willing to let him.

Based on the looks he was getting from the villagers, she suspected they would have as well.

He nodded to elders, he bowed to women, he ruffled the hair of children and generally left all in his wake looking as if they would have liked to have trailed after him forever.

She understood completely.

He kept her close as they left the village and started out into the meadow. It was indeed quite cold out, far colder than she would have supposed it to be, but it was, November after all. Maybe it was even colder in the past than it was in the Novembers of the future. She didn't protest when Patrick put his arm back around her.

"Are we actually going to find anything useful in this frigid wasteland of winter?" she asked, her teeth beginning to chatter.

"Winter?" he asked with a snort. "This is but late fall. Winter is much worse than this."

"I don't know how you survived it," she said honestly. "The cold. The food." She almost brought up the sanitation issues, but she'd had more than enough experience with medieval sanitation to suit herself, so she let it slide.

"I told you I grew up being cold all the time."

"Were you *never* warm?" she asked.

He winked at her. "Aye, of course. In July."

She rolled her eyes. And she declined the offer of a seat on a fallen log while he was about his searching. What he thought he was going to find in the patches of weeds he was searching in, she didn't know. Sunny probably would have been perfectly content, grubbing around and looking for things with strange names like yarrow and mullein. She preferred things like antibiotic and antiseptic, but when in Rome . . .

She was contemplating the fine view presented by Patrick's backside as he bent over to pluck up a few things to help him with Robert's fingers later on that morning when she had the unsettling and quite familiar feeling that she was being watched.

Patrick froze. If she hadn't been watching him, she wouldn't have noticed. He very carefully pulled his last weed, turned, and came over to where she was standing.

"Is your knife in your boot?" he asked quietly in English.

"You bet." Iolanthe's old boots were tight, but they sure held a knife next to her calf like nobody's business.

He smiled, handed her the herbs to put in the cloth she'd brought for that purpose, then took her hand and walked back to the village with her.

It was all she could do not to break into a run.

Patrick, however, walked at his normal pace, but she could feel every bit of him transformed into some kind of enemy antenna. The feeling followed her, and apparently Patrick as well, until she was in the middle of the village, and then it dissipated. Patrick didn't stop this time to make polite conversation. He told the people he saw to stay inside their houses unless the laird called for them to come up to the keep.

"War?" Madelyn asked.

He shook his head. "I think there was only one of them. It wouldn't surprise me to find it had been a Fergusson scout. I think our troubles with them are far from over." He looked down at her and smiled gravely. "It might behoove us to make our way home in a pair of days, lest we find ourselves in the middle of a battle we've no stomach for."

"Can we leave?"

"It isn't our war. At least not this century."

"No wonder no one likes Hamish Fergusson."

He smiled, a true smile. "Now you understand why Jane was less than forthcoming with her last name the first time she met Jamie, though we don't hold her parentage against her. We have much to hold the Fergussons accountable for."

Madelyn chewed on that one for quite a while, that thought of war.

She contemplated it during the setting of Robert's fingers, a miserable, terrible business she could hardly bear to watch. She'd watched them be broken the first time. She should have known better than to watch them be broken a second time, even if that subsequent breaking was for his good.

She thought about it during lunch, during which time Grudach sat next to her and disparaged her as bluntly as she could manage with her father in earshot. Madelyn hardly noticed. She smiled politely, thought about bodies strewn on a battlefield, and suggested to Grudach that she stop being such a pain in the butt and pay some attention to that nice priest who was in love with her.

And Grudach, for a change, shut her mouth, blushed furiously, and had nothing further to say for the rest of the afternoon.

Madelyn knew just exactly how little Grudach had to say because she spent the afternoon watching Patrick and Malcolm discuss the Fergusson threat. Afternoon turned into evening and she excused herself to go upstairs. Patrick promised he would follow, which raised a quite vocal chorus of suggestions, only half of which she understood.

Robert apparently hadn't seen her as educated as he might have, but she decided to complain later, when her face had stopped flaming from the things she had understood.

She went to bed and fell asleep.

She woke at some point during the night to the sound at of the door shutting.

"Patrick?"

"The very same."

She put the dagger back down on the floor. She heard him

set his sword down on the other side of the bed, then he lay down next to her. She went into his arms as if she'd been doing it for years.

It was frightening, how easy it had become.

"What did you decide?" she asked.

"That Simon will not stop until every MacLeod is dead, but that he hasn't the energy to come stalk us. It must be Neil, or another clansman with initiative."

"It doesn't sound good."

"It isn't. I want to leave before hell descends," he said, "Tomorrow, at first light, if we can."

She supposed she could have asked him if he thought the forest would work. She might have asked him if he thought they would get to keep the horse they'd been riding, and if they could take the Fergusson gelding as well to tie Bentley to. She could have even speculated about the possibilities of finding themselves in a nest of Fergussons once they left the keep and if Patrick thought she would be an asset or a liability. But that wasn't what she asked.

"Do you," she asked, "speak any Latin?"

He went still, then slid his hand up into her hair and kissed her. "*Amo, amas, amat,*" he began. He paused. "*Amamus.*"

We love.

She looked into his eyes. "Then you understood—"

"I did."

"And you—"

"Aye," he said, leaning down to kiss her. "Aye to it all," he breathed against her mouth. "Aye, to it all."

That was good enough for her. If she were going to give herself to anyone, it would be to him. They were married enough apparently for the both of them.

And war was about to knock on the downstairs door.

She surrendered to kisses that simply took her breath away. Touches followed, ones that she'd felt before, but never in a way that made her feel as if she might expire from the intensity of the feelings they stirred in her.

He pulled her even closer.

She was about to say something. Really, she was. And it would have been a really good something.

It was interrupted by the door bursting open.

"Fergussons," Angus squeaked. "My father calls for you!"

"Bloody hell," Patrick snarled. He looked down at her in the torchlight coming in from the hallway. "Now, they've really gone too far."

She would have laughed, but he was up and halfway to the door before she realized that it might just be the last time she would see him. She sat up, rearranged her clothes, and gaped at him.

"Patrick—"

He looked at her. "Knife in your hands at all times," he said briskly. "I'll return."

"But—"

He strode over, kissed her hard on the mouth, then turned away. "I'll be back, Madelyn. We have unfinished business, you and I."

He made it sound like a threat. So much the better, if it kept him alive.

Hours later, while she was standing in the great hall with her back to the fireplace and a dead Fergusson clansman's knife in her hand, the door opened and Patrick came inside. She stared at him in horror. He was covered in blood.

But as she watched him move, she realized that most of it couldn't be his. Either that, or he had more stamina than anyone she'd ever seen.

Not that she'd seen many bloody people.

She realized, quite suddenly, that she was babbling inside her own head. It was terrifying to think what might come out of her mouth if she opened it—and she an experienced, collected trial lawyer who had dissected so many witnesses over her six years at DD&P that she'd acquired a reputation for ruthlessness—she might not be able to stop the flow of drivel.

Patrick handed her two large pieces of plaid. She didn't ask him where he'd gotten them. She suspected they might have been liberated from a dead Fergusson clansman.

"We're leaving," he said. "We'll fetch Bentley. Tie his

hands, gag him, and bind his eyes. Rip up what we'll need."

She tried, really. Her hands were shaking so badly that she dropped her knife several times on the trip across the great hall. By the time she, her knife, and three strips of cloth made it to the dungeon, Bentley was up and Patrick was clipping him quite smartly under the jaw. Bentley slumped to the ground with a groan.

Patrick tied his hands behind him, blindfolded him and gagged him for good measure. Then he hefted Bentley over his shoulder and looked at her.

"We're off."

"How do things look?"

"A rout for the MacLeods. I've done my part. Let's go."

She didn't have to hear that twice. She kept her fingers crossed that the forest would actually work, then followed Patrick out of the keep. He put Bentley on the Fergusson horse, mounted the horse he'd rescued her on, then pulled her up behind him.

"Hold on," he said.

She held on. Though he didn't exactly gallop out of the courtyard, he didn't linger, either. How Bentley remained on top of his horse was obviously some kind of guy mystery she didn't want to solve. She held on to Patrick, said a prayer or two, and kept her eyes closed. Whatever was out there to see was surely stuff she didn't want being deposited in her subconscious.

She felt the air change when they reached the forest. Patrick swung down, then held up his arms for her. She held tightly to his hand and stood with him next to the horses and the unconscious windbag.

They were being watched.

Madelyn felt the hair on the back of her neck stand up. Patrick's sword came from its sheath with a fierce hiss. Before she could think to pull her little dagger out and hold it in front of her, Patrick was fighting off Neil Fergusson.

"You'll not escape so easily this time," Neil snarled.

"I've no stomach for slaying any more of your kin," Patrick said. "Be off with you and spare yourself."

Neil snorted. "My blade will taste MacLeod blood today,"

he vowed. "For the insults to my family, you'll pay dearly."

"Insults?" Patrick asked. "And what of the one you did to *my* woman?"

"MacLeod whore," Neil spat.

Madelyn wondered if Patrick might have heard that just one too many times. He spared no effort to show Neil how his patience had ended.

"I'll kill you," Neil promised, stumbling backward finally, his chest heaving, "and I'll take your body with me, just as you've done with my kin, so yours will have nothing to bury."

Patrick lowered his sword. "How was that?"

"Your body," Neil spat. "That your kin will have nothing to bury. You never return any of our dead. I won't return you."

Madelyn frowned. She wasn't sure what Neil was getting at, but maybe it was something that was too deep for her. Patrick didn't seem to think it was anything Neil needed to be worrying about—and this she discerned by the way he ceased using his sword and used his feet instead. Poor Neil. He was no match for whatever degree black belt Patrick held. Neil's sword went flying. Then Neil went flying.

And then Neil disappeared.

Madelyn stood still, gaping in astonishment at the place where Neil Fergusson had lain, sprawled unconscious, not a moment before. She looked at Patrick.

"What happened?"

"Either we went forward or he went somewhere entirely new."

"Spooky."

"To put it mildly." He put up his sword, then mounted, pulling her up behind him. "Let us see where our good forest has taken us."

"I shudder to think."

"Have faith, my love. It could be better than we dare hope."

She was going to take his word for it, but she sure as hell wasn't going to look for herself. She assumed the position she'd assumed as they left the medieval MacLeod keep—

that of her head plastered against his back to the right of his sword, against his back, her eyes closed, her arms as tight around his waist as she could get them and not permanently wear the indentation of his sword in her bosom.

They rode for quite some time. Longer than she would have supposed.

Longer than she was comfortable riding.

And then they stopped. She sniffed. It smelled like fire. Granted, the fireplace flues hadn't been all that advanced at Malcolm's keep, but there hadn't been this much acrid smoke in the air.

She opened her eyes and looked around Patrick's shoulder.

And she couldn't believe what she was seeing.

Chapter 36

P *atrick* slid down off his horse in a daze. He could hardly believe what he was looking at. It was his house, of course. He noted impatiently that his house was in the condition he'd left it, so it was a safe bet they'd returned to the proper time.

Aye, the place was his.

And his garage was on fire.

He ran, but before he could get anywhere near to saving what he owned, his garage blew up. He probably would have blown up with it if Jamie hadn't appeared from out of nowhere and borne him down to the ground.

"Leave it!" Jamie bellowed into his ear.

"Get off me, you fool!" Patrick shouted.

"You'll replace it!"

He fought, but found himself being dragged back behind his courtyard wall by both his brother and his cousin. He shook off their restraining hands.

"I'll leave it be," he snapped. "What kind of fool do you take me for?"

That neither Jamie or Ian offered any comment was telling enough.

Patrick stood there and watched as several hundred thousand pounds of metal went up in smoke. And while it burned, he gave thought to who might have done such a thing.

The answer was immediate and definitive.

Gilbert McGhee.

Patrick looked at Jamie. "Why?"

Jamie shrugged.

He looked at Ian. "What in the hell am I going to do now?"

"Kill the bastard," Ian said simply. " 'Tis obvious he'll stop at nothing."

"What if I'd had a . . ." He could hardly manage to get the word out. "A child," he finished. "A child playing in the garage. A family waiting to nip into town for a bit of shopping whilst I ran back in to fetch my lady's forgotten purse. What then?"

"He doesn't care," Ian said.

"Wait," Jamie said slowly. "Stop and think. You don't know it's McGhee. It could have been anyone. It could have been a stray spark."

"Look to the tyre tracks," Ian suggested. "I daresay you'll find them matched easily enough."

Patrick looked down and started to do just that. He walked about, looking at the ground, simply because he could do nothing else. He couldn't watch the ruin that had once been his speed and freedom. He couldn't look at his family. He couldn't look at his love.

By the saints, Madelyn.

He did look at her then. She had slid down off the horse and was looking at him with an expression he couldn't quite read.

Pity.

Mingled with fear.

Aye, and well she should. He turned away from her and continued his search. Fortunately for him, dawn was breaking and he had light. Jamie elbowed him aside and bent to retrieve a lighter.

"Evidence," his brother said wisely.

"Impossible to say whose it is," Patrick pointed out.

"Fingerprints," Jamie insisted. "Forensic evidence."

Patrick briefly speculated on the possibility of this event taking his brother's library in an entirely new direction, then looked at the lighter Jamie was putting into his pocket.

"It won't prove anything," he said heavily.

"We wouldn't need to prove anything if we just made him disappear," Ian insisted.

"Look at this," Jamie said, picking up a wad of pounds and unfolding the notes. "A hundred quid on the outside, one pound notes on the inside." He swore in disgust. "Pompous, treacherous whoreson."

"Aye, he is at that," Ian said, the he paused. He stooped down suddenly and retrieved a piece of paper that had been trampled underfoot. He unfolded it, read it, then went quite still. Then he looked at Patrick and handed him the slip of paper.

Your toys this time. Your woman next. Or your children, if it pleases me.

The missive was typed. Gilbert typed everything. Correction: He had his secretary type everything. The secretary that his wife had bought to keep him busy in a business his wife had bought to keep him out of the house each day.

Patrick didn't doubt, though, that this missive hadn't been typed on any typewriter Gilbert owned. If there was one thing he wasn't, it was stupid.

Patrick felt a sick feeling of finality settle into his belly. He couldn't let Madelyn stay. He'd known it. Hadn't he known it? Hadn't he known there was something in the future that would make them, as a couple, impossible?

He didn't stop to think. He certainly didn't stop to prepare a speech. He looked at Ian.

"Are her bags still packed?"

"Patrick!" Ian exclaimed softly, aghast.

"Are her bags still packed?" Patrick demanded in a low voice.

"We left them as she—"

"Fetch them. Fetch your car."

"I will not—"

"Do you expect me to use one of mine?" Patrick snarled, gesturing toward his ruined garage. "Fetch yours, damn you to hell, and get her to Inverness."

Ian looked at him silently for a moment or two, sighed, then turned and walked away. He didn't walk very quickly, and Patrick toyed briefly with the idea of telling him to make haste, then discarded it. He looked at his brother.

And he found he had nothing to say.

Jamie only stared at him just as silently.

Patrick turned and walked over to the horses. Madelyn was

holding on to the stallion's reins. She didn't speak to him and he returned the favor.

He pulled Bentley off his horse, but left him gagged, bound, and blindfolded. No sense in borrowing trouble. He laid him out facedown on the ground. He stared down at the fool, who was now wriggling around. Patrick could only imagine what he was saying. There had to be lawsuits somewhere in the offing.

What to do with Bentley? He could untie him, certainly. Better yet to untie him and have a means of transporting him back to his hotel. He couldn't ask Ian. Madelyn didn't deserve that on top of everything else. He looked at his brother. Jamie would do. Jamie could put on his medieval laird persona. That would keep Bentley in line.

"Jamie," he called, "did you drive?"

"Aye," Jamie said, looking at Bentley, then back at Patrick reluctantly. "Unfortunately."

"Take him back to his hotel, will you?"

Jamie sighed heavily. "As you will."

Patrick leaned over and ripped off Bentley's blindfold. He stared down into very wide, very terrified eyes.

"You're safe now," Patrick said. "You were . . . away for a while."

Bentley was suddenly quite perfectly still.

"You were . . ." Patrick began slowly, seriously, "abducted."

Bentley blinked.

"Aye." Patrick nodded. "By them. You know who I'm talking about."

Bentley nodded.

"Behave," Patrick said. "Do good. Give away all your gold jewelry. Do work for free. Twenty, thirty hours a week. Or they'll be back."

Bentley nodded again.

Patrick looked at Jamie. "Take him off my land."

"Happily." Jamie hauled Bentley to his feet. "So, my wee friend, you've been on a bit of a journey—"

Patrick watched his brother take a very filthy, unsettled

attorney and put him in the back of his car. Patrick was a
bit surprised Jamie didn't hose him down first, but perhaps
his brother had smelled worse.

Patrick turned his attentions back to his garage. And as he
stood there, he wondered what in the hell he was supposed
to do now. Hose the building off? What was the point? It
was halfway to the ground as it was. His cars were destroyed.

And this was apparently only the beginning.

"Why don't you fight?"

He looked next to him to find Madelyn standing there,
looking at him with fire suddenly in her eyes. It matched,
incidentally, the fire in his outbuilding.

"Fight?" he echoed. "Fight what?"

"Fight Gilbert."

"Why?"

She looked at him as if she'd never seen him before. "Patrick, he burned down practically everything of value you
had."

Not everything. The thing of most value was standing right
beside him.

It was the one thing he dare not not keep.

"There's no point," he said flatly.

"I can't believe you!" she said, sounding stunned.

"What would you have me do, Madelyn? Go at him with
my sword? This isn't medieval Scotland. I can't take justice
into my own hands."

"Then fight him in court."

"I can't prove anything."

"You won't even try!" she exclaimed.

He looked at her, tried to memorize everything about her,
every expression of disbelief, pain, and anger that crossed
her face. Those he would file away with the more tender
expressions he had already collected over the past month.

Love.

Hope.

Desire.

"There is no point," he said quietly.

He was certain that moment would be burned indelibly
into his mind for the rest of his life. The crackling and the

occasional mild explosion coming from his garage. The smell
of things that continued to burn. The chill in the air. The
flicker of fire against the stone wall, against Madelyn's hair,
on her beautiful face.

He would never forget any of that.

He would also never forget the moment when she realized
what he was going to do.

"Oh, Patrick," she whispered.

He pulled her into his arms so he didn't have look into
her eyes. He clutched her to him, buried his face in her hair,
and tried not to break down. He couldn't now. He would
later, when he was shoveling out.

Alone.

He held her while she sobbed until he heard Ian pull up.
Then he pushed her back, put his arm around her, and led
her over to the car.

"Ian will take you to Inverness. I'll have the plane waiting."

She didn't say anything.

What was there to say?

"I'll call you," he offered.

She looked up at him then and her tears were gone. In
their place was something he was actually quite sorry to be the
recipient of. Her look spoke volumes about what she thought
of his level of courage. She opened the car door, then paused.

"I liked you better in the Middle Ages."

She got into the car, pulled the car door shut, then turned
her face away from him.

He watched the car drive away. He didn't suppose he
could blame her for her sentiments. He had liked himself
better then as well.

But he couldn't fight. How could he? It had nothing to do
with Gilbert. If it had been only him and Gilbert in a field
and both of them lacking any family, he would have cut the
bastard to shreds as slowly as possible, making him suffer
for hours before he finished him.

Unfortunately, Gilbert did have family, and Helen Mc-
Ghee had asked him specifically not to hurt her husband.

And so he complied.

Unwillingly, but he complied just the same.

He watched Ian's taillights disappear into the forest, then bowed his head and blew out his breath. He stood there until he realized he'd been standing there for too long. It was cold. He looked at the horses he'd brought with him and wondered if he dared put them in his stable. Or if he dared leave his own beasts there. Jamie had room. Ian had room. Who would torture him worse with their lectures?

Ian, he decided. Besides, Jamie was going to be gone for a while. He went over to the MacLeod stallion and swung up on its back. He took the reins of both horses and started toward the keep he'd just left almost eight hundred years in the past.

He rode, trying to empty his mind of the thoughts he knew he didn't dare face. Even so, he couldn't rid his mind of Madelyn's final words.

I liked you better in the Middle Ages.

By the saints, he did, too.

Chapter 37

Madelyn walked up the jetway, feeling unaccountably apprehensive. All she needed was a lecture right off. Her parents would find her haggard face appalling, but her clothes worthy of further study. Jeans were, they would announce, a pleasant change from her courtroom attire. Her hair wouldn't fly in academia, but it would be deemed a far sight less severe than her power chignon.

To reevaluate would no doubt be the first verb she would be required to conjugate. That would be followed immediately by a command that she translate *eat a huge slice of humble pie* into a variety of other languages where the idiomatic meaning was the same: i.e., she'd seen the error of her ways and was prepared to put in her application to any number of grad schools and get back on a proper course.

She clenched her jaw, swung her violin case over her shoulder, and stomped through the gate, ready to tell her parents to go to hell.

But who should be there to greet her but Sunshine Phillips herself, in crumpled linen.

Madelyn almost cried.

Sunny hugged her. "I can't decide if you look great or like hell. *Where* have you *been?*"

"Long story."

"I have the time. No births imminent and I farmed out my yoga classes and massage clients for a couple of days."

"Sunny, you are a walking cliché."

"Yeah, see how you feel after a massage and some tea."

"It sounds like heaven."

Sunny took the violin and put her arm around Madelyn's shoulders. "Come on, Sis. Let's go home."

* * *

T_{wo} hours and a massage later, Madelyn sat at Sunny's kitchen table, staring out over her sister's garden. She sipped a cup of something good for her. The rain that fell was typical Seattle drizzle, not really enough to warrant an umbrella, except for those really fond of their hairdos, but perfectly capable of leaving anyone brash enough to go out without one completely soaked in no time.

It was good to be home.

"All right," Sunny said, sliding into the seat across from her, "give."

"I hardly know where to start."

"Start at the beginning."

"Before or after I found out that Bentley had poached my first reservation?"

"That pig." Sunny took a delicate sip of her tea. "Count yourself lucky you never married him. You would have wilted." She shook her head. "No, start before that. When you landed in Scotland. Who was the first Scotsman you saw? And who's the guy you fell in love with?"

Madelyn looked at her in shock. "What?"

"What's his name?"

Good grief, did the woman do psychic readings now as well?

"Patrick," Madelyn said weakly. "Patrick MacLeod."

"And why is it you're here and he's there?"

"It's a long story."

"So you keep telling me." Sunny sat back. "Cough up the details. I'll feed you when you start to look weak. Well, weaker than you look already. Good heavens, Maddy, you're skin and bones. I knew I should have given you some money before you left."

"It just would have gotten stolen with everything else."

"Well, I'll feed you now instead. Now, go ahead. All the details, if you please."

Madelyn took a deep breath. All the details? She wasn't so sure about that. She'd have to see how Sunny reacted to a brief testing of the waters before she gave her the unvarnished truth.

And quite suddenly she understood completely Patrick's reticence about disclosing several important facts pertaining to his past.

She took another strengthening sip of tea, set her cup down, and put her hands on the table.

"Here goes nothing," she said.

She started from the beginning.

Her tea lasted through her encounter with Patrick at Culloden field. A second cup took her through several bouts of sightseeing. She needed cookies—and why was it Sunny never had any chocolate in her house?—to get through her trips to Moraig's and the dinner at Jamie's.

The time traveling took dinner—a decent dinner where the vegetables were smothered with lots of the reconstituted cheese sauce that Sunny always kept on hand just for her.

She couldn't quite bring herself to discuss the marriage, so she left that out.

She was lingering over more tea when she finished up at the ruin of Patrick's garage.

"This Gilbert McGhee sounds like a real winner," Sunny remarked.

"Yeah, he's a prince."

Sunny reached over and took Madelyn's hand. She looked at her finger. "Your Patrick looks to have done a decent job resetting this," she remarked mildly.

"You would like him. He has a whole relationship with weeds that only you could appreciate."

"I'd like to compare notes someday." She looked up. "So, what happened once you got to the medieval MacLeod keep? The part that you're leaving out?"

Madelyn took a deep breath. "We got married."

Sunny blinked. "What?"

"We were married by a priest who apparently was in fact a priest, but had some issues with golf."

"Marriage," Sunny said, shaking her head. "I can't believe it. I can't believe he let you go. What was he thinking?"

"Who knows?"

"Don't think about it. It'll all make sense in a few days. So, tell me what happened after the marriage, or should I ask?"

Madelyn sighed, then gave her, in as few words possible, a description of their time in the Middle Ages. She'd described the trip with Ian to Inverness, which had been accomplished mostly in silence, though it hadn't been an uncomfortable kind of silence. It had been the kind of silence a man maintained while sitting next to Vesuvius.

Sunny had understood.

Poor Conal. Not even the consolation prize of a first-class ticket home had been enough to keep her silent on the flight from Inverness to Heathrow. He'd listened, he'd nodded, and he'd said Patrick would come to his senses. Madelyn hadn't cared. She'd even been too upset to enjoy those first-class amenities on her flight home.

"Oh, that is pathetic," Sunny said with a laugh.

"I thought so, too. But at least I don't have jetlag."

"It'll catch up with you."

"I could only hope. I would like to be unconscious for a few days. Maybe when I wake up, life will be different."

"Maybe," Sunny said. "So what's it like to be married?"

"By a priest who could hardly stand up?"

"Yes. That." Sunny looked at her. "Did Patrick know what he was saying?"

"I think so."

"And you both agreed to this."

"It would seem so."

"Yet he sent you home."

"Yep."

Sunny shook her head. "Weird."

"Yes," Madelyn said with a yawn. "Very."

"You should sleep on it. It'll be clearer after a good night's rest."

"Right."

"I'll cancel dessert with Mom and Dad tonight."

"Even better."

"You don't look like you feel well."

Madelyn looked at her sister with something of a scowl. "I've had a rough month."

"I'll say. Go to bed, sis."

Madelyn went.

A week later Madelyn sat at Sunny's kitchen table, sipping tea, and feeling quite a bit more like herself. If feeling like herself again was anything she was capable of recognizing, which she wasn't sure she was. Everything had changed. She'd been to a foreign country, another planet almost, and had too much time to think while there. She couldn't look at a cup of tea without having her eyes well up with tears of gratitude.

"How're you doing?"

Madelyn looked up at her sister, who had come home and was setting her keys and an enormous all-purpose purse down on the counter. "Doing?"

Sunny laughed. "You look better, but you still sound like you're sleepwalking. Come to any conclusions during all that dreaming you've been doing over the past week?"

"Only that I'm incredibly grateful for your couch."

"It's yours for as long as you want it. And I won't put you through any linguistic tortures for the privilege."

"No, you'll just make me close my eyes and sniff things. 'Whoops, wrong answer; you get the floor.' "

"Right," Sunny said dryly. She poured herself something out of the fridge, then sat down at the table. "All right, I've put off the parental units as long as I can. They're coming for dinner."

Madelyn sighed. It had to happen sometime. "What's that you're drinking?"

"Wheat grass. Want some?"

Madelyn flinched. "How about something with sugar? Caffeine? Artificial color? Other harmful additives?"

"You have tea. Drink it. You'll need your strength."

Madelyn put her head down on the kitchen table. "If I get my strength back, then I'll have to face real life. I think facing Mom and Dad is about all I can do today."

"Well, buck up, little sister. Before dinner you need to know what happened while you were out of the . . . um . . . country."

Madelyn lifted her head and rubbed her eyes. "I don't know if I can handle that yet."

"Mom and Dad will tell you anyway."

"Before or after they remind me of my loan balance, my lack of employment prospects, or all the ways I've received my just desserts the last two months?" She shivered. "Sunny, I wonder if I really have made horrible mistakes. If I'd never gone to law school—"

"If you'd practiced the violin harder in high school—"

"If I'd acquired an ear for Latin before sixth grade—"

"If you'd just done better in kindergarten," Sunny finished with a laugh. "Good grief, Maddy, where does it end? You made the choices you made and you have to live with them."

"But my life's a mess," Madelyn said.

"Everyone's life is a mess."

Madelyn shook her head. "I can't look back on it that I don't cringe."

Sunny took another healthy swig of wheat grass without so much as a pucker of distaste.

Appalling.

"This is my theory," Sunny said.

"I can hardly wait."

"Mock if you will. It's profound."

"Then lay it on me, baby. I can take it."

Sunny sat up straighter. It was probably some yoga thing. "It's like waterskiing," she began.

"Waterskiing?" Madelyn echoed. "Who, you?"

"I didn't say I did it. I'm saying life is like it. Reserve judgment, counselor, until I get to the end of my analogy."

Madelyn lifted her tea in salute. "Forge on ahead."

"Think waterskiing," Sunny continued. "You're looking ahead, in front of the boat—"

"You're behind the boat when you waterski."

Sunny threw a dishtowel at her. "Shut up and listen. This is deep."

"Hmmm," Madelyn said. "If you say so."

"You're behind the boat. You're looking ahead. The water's like glass. Pristine. Untouched."

"Unmauled."

"Exactly. It's looking good till you get there. Then you take a look at what you've left behind."

Madelyn shuddered. "I can just imagine."

"The thing is, though," Sunny continued, "it's the stuff behind you that's interesting. It makes for waves, stuff for other skiers to jump over—"

"Those are moguls and that's snow skiing and those aren't made by other skiers, they're made by rocks under the snow."

"What I'm *saying*," Sunny said, looking for something else to throw at her and finding nothing, "is that everyone has a wake behind them. It's just part of life. Expecting it to be as perfect as the water in front of you is unrealistic."

"I don't like my wake."

"You can't change it. Learn to live with it."

"I don't like your analogy."

"Then let's think of our past as a really nubby tapestry, full of flaws and interesting bits of string hanging from it—"

"I like that even less," Madelyn said.

"Then how does the fact that our great-grandmother left you her house grab you?"

Madelyn blinked. "Huh?"

"Dewey," Sunny said. "She left you the house."

Madelyn would have thought she was dreaming, but she'd caught up on her sleep and was fairly certain she was fully awake. "This isn't another analogy, is it?"

"The house is the upside. The downside is that it's probably been stripped by Uncle Fred and his kids by now. If you have a carpet left to lie on, I'd be surprised. But it's yours."

"But," Madelyn began. "But, why me?"

"Maybe she liked your wake."

"What'd she leave you?"

"Buckets of money," Sunny said with a grin. "Enough to start my own herb shop if I like. Or pay off this house and then never have to work another day in my life."

"So you'll be delivering babies for free now."

"Maybe."

Madelyn could hardly believe it. "What am I going to do with a house?"

"If it makes you feel any better, Uncle Fred has already been contacted by half a dozen people dying to get their hands on the property. You could sell it and get yourself out of debt. Probably take another vacation to Scotland if you wanted."

Madelyn flinched and Sunny reached out her hand. "Sorry, Maddy. I didn't mean it that way. He'll come to his senses."

"He already did."

"No, he didn't. If he had, he would be here."

"His life's a mess. He probably doesn't want my mess adding to it. You know, Bentley and all."

"Oh, didn't I tell you?" Sunny asked mildly. "Heard via the grapevine that Bentley's back in town."

Madelyn's ears perked up. "How did you hear this?"

"Stella DiLoretto comes in for a massage once a week. Twice if her husband's getting on her nerves. Apparently, Bentley's been back at work, but not doing very well."

"Poor Bentley."

"He locks himself in his office. Doesn't come out much. The rumor is, he's writing a few pieces for *The Confessor*."

Madelyn laughed. "*The Confessor*? That tabloid? You're kidding."

"I'm not. Stella says he's working on some sort of alien-capture exposé."

"I can't wait to read it."

"Well, he'd better make a ton of money on it because he's going to lose his job if he doesn't get back to work."

"Cry me a river."

Sunny smiled. "It's bad karma to wish him ill."

"I'm not wishing him ill. I'm wishing him what he deserves."

"Well," Sunny said with a smile, "that's a different story entirely. How does vegetarian chili sound for dinner?"

"Perfect. Got any of those cheesy rolls to go with it?"

"For you, sister dear, always."

"Real butter?"

Sunny only smiled and started pulling things out of her fridge.

Madelyn sat back. A house, the house of her childhood vacations and long summers, unexpectedly hers. Interesting news regarding Bentley and his state of mind. Cheesy rolls slathered with real butter.

Life was looking up.

The doorbell rang.

"Mom and Dad," Sunny announced. "They're early. They must be anxious to see you."

All right, so life wasn't looking up that much.

She resolutely shoved thoughts of Patrick aside. She'd need all her stamina just to endure the grilling. The only mystery that remained was how many languages she'd be bombarded with.

Hopefully not any more Latin. She'd had enough of that to last a lifetime.

Chapter 38

Patrick drove along behind an incredibly slow caravan in his new Vanquish and didn't have the strength to pass it. He merely drove with the window rolled down, his arm hanging limply out the side, and medical clinic waiting room music on his stereo.

All in all, a very forgettable morning.

It should have been a good morning. He had a new car, courtesy of his insurance, which would no doubt reach ridiculously new heights of premium. The weather was unusually fine, with the sun actually making an appearance. The roads bare and dry. Yet all he could do was languish behind a thirty-year-old caravan and breathe things that should have been outlawed thirty years ago.

Frightening.

When he had finally reached the turnoff to his house, he was half-dead from exhaust fumes. It took him all the way home to breathe enough fresh air to feel halfway back to himself. Not that being back to himself was a place he looked forward to being.

His life was, you might have said, in the toilet.

Which in his house wasn't functioning, either. He wondered what else life was planning to throw at him in the near future. That was probably something he didn't really want to know.

He drove into his courtyard, looked dispassionately at the shell of his garage. At least most of the debris had been removed. He knew, because he'd removed what of it he could lift himself. And he'd helped with the rest.

It had taken his mind off other things.

He got out of his car, shut the door, and set the alarm. He shuffled across the courtyard—and when was the last time he'd shuffled, he wondered—and paused in front of his door. There were three pieces of paper attached, two with tape, one with a dirk. He pulled the knife free first and read the barely legible note.

> *Pat,*
>
> *Put that Yank barrister on the plane meself two days prior. Told him ye'd be pokin' him with this if he didna just go peaceful like.*
>
> > *Bobby*
>
> *P.S. Conal made me come. Yer haime is a wreck. Get a bloody stick o' furniture, would ye?*

Patrick would have smiled if he'd had it in him. He stuck the dirk back into the door and removed the second note. It was a dinner invitation from Ian, when he felt like eating something besides tinned beef.

The third note was from Jamie. It also concerned dinner, but it was not a request.

Well, so his laird called, it seemed. Patrick crumpled up that note along with the rest, sighed deeply, and went inside his house, unfurnished wreck that it was. He shut his front door, opened the shutters over his windows, then dropped his coat on one of the stools.

He trudged wearily into the kitchen and surveyed the contents of his fridge. There was nothing edible there—even by his very low standards. He shut the door and went back to sit in his hall. His great hall, if it could be called that.

He built himself a fire, lit a candle, then sat in the one proper chair he owned. He prepared to indulge himself in a well-deserved afternoon's brood.

And, as if on cue, it was then that the piper started up.

"Oh, by all the bloody saints!" Patrick shouted, jumping to his feet. He threw open his front door, stuck his head outside, and shouted. "Robert, shut the bloody hell up!"

Robert, who hadn't deigned to show himself of late, merely played on.

Patrick slammed the door shut, turned, and stomped back over to the fire—just in time to be forced to jump aside as a chair much finer than his materialized directly in front of him.

He suppressed the urge to roll his eyes. Would he never know another moment's peace?

Apparently not.

First came that hale and hearty curmudgeon, Archibald the Glum, first lord of Benmore. He was joined by none other than his ever obedient and relentlessly agreeable valet, Nelson. Patrick waited until Archibald had seated himself before he took his own seat. He watched Nelson see to his master's comfort and wondered if perhaps he might be happier with a valet.

He didn't have long to contemplate that possibility before the peace of the afternoon was relentlessly shattered.

Dorcas burst into view, bedecked with jewels, lace, and enough flounces to clothe a dozen women. Nelson hastily provided her with a comfortable chair. This one was from a different century. In fact, Patrick wasn't sure Nelson hadn't pinched the idea for the thing from a local furniture store. The pattern looked quite modern.

"Patrick, sit yourself down," Dorcas said briskly, "and let us put this foolishness behind you."

"Dorcas," Archibald grumbled, "this is man's busi—"

"It most certainly is not." She pointed a rather bony, ring-bedecked finger at Patrick. "Sit. Listen. Prepare to mend your ways. And afterward I will instruct you on how to make this horrifyingly spartan hovel a place your bride will want to come to."

Patrick sat. He looked at the Glum, who was puffing quite enthusiastically on his pipe and apparently was physically incapable of staring at anything but the fire. He sighed and looked at Dorcas.

"I'm listening, my lady."

"I should hope so."

* * *

Two very trying hours later, he was released to go to dinner
at his brother's. He wasn't looking forward to that being any
less torturous than what he'd just endured, but he went just
the same. Too many years of obeying his laird, mostly, without question left him driving down and showing up at the
table without complaint.

Dinner was nothing out of the ordinary. Elizabeth was up
and about quite nicely. The baby was beautiful. Holding her
fair broke his heart.

Dessert was finished far too quickly.

Jamie rose and walked toward the stairs.

Patrick sighed, rose, and followed. He felt again a lad of
thirteen summers, on his way to receive a fine reprimand. He
was hard-pressed to remember he had five-and-thirty years
behind him.

He walked into his brother's study and sat down in the
chair next to the desk. Unbidden came the vision of the same
chamber as it had been some seven hundred years in the past.
Grudach's bedchamber. Sitting in a chair by that bed, watching Madelyn sleep. Waiting for her to heal.

Lying with her in that bed and coming damn close to making her his wife in truth.

"Any tidings?" Jamie asked.

Patrick pulled himself away from the vision with difficulty
and focused on his brother. "Tidings?" he asked. "From Gilbert or Madelyn?"

"Either."

Patrick shook his head. "Nothing from him. Not that I
expected to hear anything."

"And from Madelyn?"

He looked at his brother. "Did you think she would call
me?"

"Not after the way you sent her off."

"What was I to do?" Patrick demanded.

"Not what you did, I'd say," Jamie said, unperturbed.

"Did you summon me here to berate me for that or did

you have some other bit of wisdom to bestow on my poor self this evening?"

"I thought that after a fortnight, you might have managed to remove your head from where you've been keeping it. Have you? Have you found sense yet?"

Patrick cursed. "I made the best choice I could."

"You didn't make a choice," Jamie said stubbornly. "You allowed Gilbert McGhee to make that choice for you."

"And should I have made the choice to put Madelyn in harm's way? My children? Would you do the same thing?"

"You cannot ignore him and hope he will tire of the chase. The man is obsessed."

Patrick stared at him in irritation. "And just what is it you would have me do?"

"Sue the whoreson for slander. We've all heard what he calls you." He gestured to a book lying open on his desk. "I've been reading about the law. I can help—"

Patrick stood quickly. It was either that or take that bloody book and club his brother over the head with it. "Many thanks, I'm sure. I'll seek your advice straightway, should it be required." *And that would be when hell froze over.*

"Or sooner—"

Patrick started toward the door. "I'll give it thought."

"Patrick."

Patrick stopped, bowed his head, and sighed. He knew what that tone of voice meant. Jamie had been thinking again. It was never a good thing. He turned around reluctantly. "Aye?"

"Do you love her?"

If that wasn't the question that he asked himself constantly . . . He shrugged. "I don't know."

By the saints, he was a liar. He did love her.

Desperately.

Hopelessly.

So much that even thinking about her was like a dagger in his breast.

Jamie leaned back in his chair and looked at Patrick with undisguised pity.

"You poor fool," Jamie said. "Forgive yourself for a bad

choice the first time with Lisa. Everyone deserves love. Forgive yourself, let your heart heal, and let it hope."

Patrick stared at his brother. He could scarce believe so many sentimental things had come out of the man's mouth at one sitting. He pursed his lips. "And Gilbert? What am I to do with him?"

"He'll come to his own bad end. No one can fault you for protecting yourself on your own land. No one," he repeated.

Patrick closed his eyes briefly. It was tempting. It was tempting to do his enemy in once and for all.

"Go home and think about it," Jamie said.

Patrick nodded, turned, and left. The hall was empty, so he didn't have to face any more of his family. He left the keep and drove slowly home, Jamie's last words echoing through his soul.

Forgiveness.

Healing.

Hope.

It was the last, he realized with a start, that he'd felt listening to Madelyn's music.

Hope.

Something she had. Something he didn't.

He sat in front of his house for a very long time, letting the word seep down into the very bones of his soul.

Hope.

His heart echoed the word with a gentle whisper.

He got out of his car and walked into his house. Archibald was still warming his toes against the embers of Patrick's fire. Patrick stood near the hearth and looked down into the ruins of his latest effort.

"Goin' to fetch the gel?" Archibald asked.

Patrick sighed. "I may never have any peace if I don't."

"And I'm here to tell you, you won't if you do—"

Archibald!

The Glum ducked his head, but looked at Patrick meaningfully.

Patrick laughed uneasily and walked back to his bedchamber. Lady Dorcas hadn't given him any suggestions for improving the decor here, so he assumed he was safe taking off his clothes and going to bed.

Just to be safe, he turned off the light before he stripped.

As he lay there in the dark, he let himself think about what he had been pushing aside for a fortnight.

What could she possibly be thinking? Was she waiting for him to call, or was that misplaced arrogance on his part?

I liked you better in the Middle Ages.

He sighed deeply.

He could lie down and let Gilbert make his choices for him, or he could choose for himself and take the consequences like a man. It wasn't as if he could take a sword to Gilbert—or couldn't he? Self-defense was self-defense.

It was so much more clear-cut in medieval Scotland.

But what was clear to him in present-day Scotland was how much he did love Madelyn. He found himself looking for her as he went through his miserable days. He found himself listening for her laugh, waiting for her smile, turning to talk to her about the things that were close to his heart.

He found himself thinking about bloody castle stairs and imagining how she would enjoy them.

He sat up, reached over, and fumbled in his jacket pocket for his mobile phone. He knew her sister's phone number. It had seemed an intelligent thing to do—the getting of that phone number. Just in case he needed to reach Madelyn and give her important tidings.

He dialed, then paused.

It was too early in the morning there. He might try again later, when he figured out what in the hell he was going to say. When he'd decided if he could bear to hear her tell him to go to hell.

He put the phone down on the floor, lay down, and closed his eyes.

Sleep did not come easily.

Chapter 39

M adelyn dragged her sleeve across her forehead. How was it possible to sweat when it had to be forty degrees outside? All right, so it wasn't really that cold. But Dewey's house was a block from Puget Sound, a Victorian amongst other Victorians in a little port town, huddled together as if they thought company would keep them warm, and even a block away from the sea meant a chill during winter.

It was a great house. Madelyn knelt in the upstairs room, a large room that ran almost the length of the house, and looked around. Dewey's was a house of many gables, a house with nooks and crannies, the house where she'd spent the summers her parents had passed in countries not child-friendly enough to suit them.

She had loved those summers, truth be told.

She shut the trunk in front of her and gave its lid a little dusting with a very, very dusty dust cloth. She looked around her at the treasure trove of furniture Uncle Fred and her cousins hadn't been able to get at. Maybe they'd assumed there was nothing on the second floor. Maybe they'd been too dazzled by the goodies on the main floor. Maybe they'd had some sort of spell cast over them that prevented them from seeing the staircase that led upstairs to where the really good stuff was.

Maybe they hadn't had a key to the industrial-sized padlock that had kept this long room locked.

Whatever the case, even though the first floor had been plundered, the upstairs still contained enough things to keep her busy for weeks.

Two weeks, so far.

Making it four weeks since she'd last seen Patrick.

She tried not to think about that very much.

She rose and crossed over to a chair under a window, pulled the dust sheet off it, and sat down with a sigh. She stared out over the fog-shrouded landscape in front of her and let her thoughts wander as she hadn't dared let them in weeks.

What was Patrick doing? Had Gilbert killed him yet, or had Patrick killed Gilbert and was now languishing in Hamish Fergusson's jail cell? Had he rebuilt his garage? Was Robert the piper still serenading him, or had he given up in disgust and ditched him? She certainly hadn't heard the familiar sound of bagpipes lately, so she supposed Robert was still on Patrick's hill.

She had started to wonder, occasionally, if she'd dreamed the entire thing.

Maybe there was something to Roddy's claim of Highland magic. It was as if the minute she'd set foot on MacLeod soil, she'd been transported into a world where everything felt like a waking dream. Ghosts, pipers, medieval clansmen—all walking around in broad daylight as if they belonged there.

Unreal.

She might have suspected she'd merely dreamed the whole thing if it hadn't been for her finger that ached when it rained and the little piece of Patrick's plaid he'd wrapped that finger in, a plaid that she had tucked in the top drawer of the dresser she was using in her great-grandmother's room.

She stared out over the garden and rubbed her finger absently. A waking dream.

A pity she'd woken up.

She sighed and got out of the chair. Lots to do and not much time to do it in. She was going to have to get serious about a job search very soon. The modest monetary inheritance Dewey had left her was keeping the student loan folks at bay and a few things in her fridge, but that would only last a couple more months. By then, she'd better have a good employment under her belt or she really would be doing the unthinkable and accepting one of the offers to sell.

The will had stipulated that she, Madelyn, receive not only

the house but a small chunk of change for the service she
would render in going through the contents of the house.
Though Uncle Fred had done a pretty thorough job of re-
ducing the downstairs inventory—against his grandmother's
express wishes—Madelyn suspected that Dewey had left her
in charge of sorting through her private things simply because she'd known Madelyn would send things where they
needed to go. She had piles all over the parlor.

Even a pile or two for Uncle Fred.

She put her hands on her lower back and stretched. She
still wasn't fully recovered from her ordeal at the Fergusson
keep, but she was getting better. There was a good chiropractor in town. A single, handsome chiropractor.

She'd been singularly uninterested.

He didn't carry a sword, after all.

She clapped her hand to her head, sending up a substantial
cloud of dust, and coughed her way down the stairs to the
kitchen. The floorboards creaked in a very comforting way.
She stood at the sink and looked out over the garden. Her
viewing angle was a bit different than it had been during her
youth, but she felt as if she'd stepped back in time a dozen
years. She could hear her great-grandmother talking about
the properties of this plant or that, the growing season of this
flower or that, the endless tasks of gardening that kept her
moving easily from year to year, allowing her life to follow
the cycles of the earth.

Madelyn paused and held her breath.

Good grief, if she wasn't careful, she was going to start
sounding like Sunny soon.

She'd obviously had one too many cups of tea at *that*
kitchen table.

She reached for a slicker and walked out into the back
garden. It was enormous, for the area, and full of plants that
Dewey had spent years tending. Had the green thumb ended
with Dewey?

Madelyn looked down at her own as-yet-untried green
thumbs.

They were dirty, but it wasn't from a ballpoint pen. Somehow, when the choice was between slaving for the Barracuda

and tending a Victorian garden, there was no choice.

She had the luxury, at least for the next few days, of pretending she could do something different. She stood in the rain, looked around her, and wished she could do something different forever. She didn't want to sell this house, but she didn't see how she could afford not to. Even if she found a job down the street at the local law firm, it wouldn't be enough to pay off her loans and keep herself eating. The work hours alone would make it so the garden would never have anyone tending it.

And she couldn't bear the thought of the garden going to weed.

She closed her eyes and prayed for a miracle.

She wanted to grow things.

She wanted, heaven help her, to plant children and see them grow.

She wanted, she decided as the rain fell softly on her face, a man she would never have.

She'd almost come to terms with what he'd done. He'd been trying to keep her safe. In his own hard, unyielding, take-no-prisoners medieval kind of way, he'd been trying to keep her safe. That didn't make it any easier to accept, but at least she understood it.

She took a deep breath, and opened her eyes, letting the tears slip down her cheeks. It didn't matter. It was raining out. A little more moisture wouldn't make any difference.

Then she froze.

There, under the little arched trellis that supported climbing roses that had woven their way around the wood for two decades, stood a man.

Dressed in black.

As usual.

She was so surprised to see him, she could only stare at him in complete astonishment.

"Wha—" She swallowed and tried again. "What are you doing here?"

He didn't move. If she hadn't known better, she would have thought he looked the slightest bit unsure of himself.

"You promised me a tour of Seattle," he said.

More tears joined the ones that were already running down her cheeks. She managed to nod. "So I did."

He seemed to be considering his words. Madelyn wasn't about to put any in his mouth for him. She was still recovering from the initial volley.

"And I think," he said, putting his hand to his forehead, "that I might be getting a cold. It may require tending. You promised me that, as well."

She smiled. It felt as if the sun had just come out. She hugged herself and tried not to do anything too exuberant, like half a dozen backflips.

"You need yuckenacea," she said solemnly.

"That's echinacea."

"Have you tasted that junk?" she asked. "It's disgusting."

He smiled and took a step out of the arbor. "I can handle it." He took another step toward her. "I take it this is yours?"

"Can you believe it? I can't afford to keep it, but I'm pretending right now. Want the tour?"

He shook his head.

She shook her head as well. "You don't want the tour?"

He crossed the distance between them with even, measured steps. He stopped a foot away from her.

She looked up at him. The look on his face made her mouth go dry. "What do you want?" she asked.

"You," he said simply. "If you'll have me."

Well, there was nothing quite like a man who cut to the chase. She swallowed with difficulty. "Maybe we should go inside."

He swooped her up into his arms. She threw her arms around his neck and held on as he carried her inside.

"Patrick," she began breathlessly.

He set her down inside and stood as close to her as he could without touching her. "We have things to decide."

"Do we," she managed.

"You wed me, if you remember."

"You sent me home, if you remember."

He looked at her without smiling. "I was a fool."

"Well—"

"I cannot promise you a safe life," he continued. "Gilbert

hunts me. The saints only know what he'll try next. If you agree to be mine, you agree to that danger."

That was sobering. She looked up at him and found it in her to nod slowly.

"But I vow that my sword will always be raised in your defense. In the defense of our children. I will," he said, each word clear and crisp, "keep you safe."

"Will you leave again?"

"Never."

She looked down. The zipper on his jacket became quite fascinating to her all of a sudden. "Where will we live?"

"Together."

She looked up quickly and found that he was smiling faintly. "That's not an answer."

"It's the best one I can give." He took her hands in his. "I love Scotland."

She nodded. "I can understand that."

"But," he said and he reached in his pocket for something, "I love you more."

She caught her breath as he slipped something on her finger. Her ring finger. She looked down. "That's quite a rock—I mean admission," she managed. She blinked at the sight of the diamond on her finger, then looked back up at Patrick. "You can't leave your land, Patrick."

"We'll work it out. You'll need time with your family as well. We'll find a balance. If you're willing."

She considered. She looked at the ring on her finger. She thought about what it would mean to have Gilbert McGhee in her life.

She thought about life without Patrick.

Then she thought about sunshine suddenly bursting forth all around her on a cloudy day.

She looked up at Patrick. "If I say no?"

"I'll prod you to bed with my sword."

She laughed. He smiled before he bent his head and kissed her thoroughly.

"Say me aye," he whispered against her mouth. "Say me aye."

How could she say anything else?

So she said him aye.

And she was, she had to admit a good deal later, extraordinarily glad Dewey's brass bed had been too much for Uncle Fred's bad back.

It was very late in the day that she sat at her greatgrandmother's kitchen table and watched Patrick make something with eggs and a few of Sunny's vegetables she hadn't gotten around to eating.

"So," she said casually, "how long are you really here for?"

He looked at her in amusement. "I have an open ticket."

"Oh."

"And if you still have to ask me that question, I have obviously left my work undone."

"Is that possible?" she mused.

He turned and looked at her, spatula in hand. "Is it our marriage that troubles you? If you're uncomfortable with our medieval ceremony, we can be wed again. I didn't propose very well the first time."

"You didn't propose at *all* the first time."

He laughed and turned back to the stove. "I've tried to remedy that this afternoon."

He certainly had. He'd asked her to marry him several times. In between doing, well, other things.

"Your sire might like to give you away," he offered.

"There is that," she agreed. "He might have a few things to say about our good vicar's interpretation of the marriage rites."

He brought over two plates, set them down, then sat down across from her. She smiled weakly.

"This is very domestic."

"We have to keep up our strength."

She found herself smiling. In fact, she had a hard time not smiling continually. And when she wasn't smiling, she was staring at the beautiful man across from her and marveling that not only did she know him, she *knew* him.

He had accepted that serious commitment from her with the appropriate amount of solemnity.

"Your sister is a goodly wench," he said, admiring his breakfast. "Nice veg, what she grows."

She choked. "You didn't call her a wench, did you?"

"Aye."

Madelyn gaped at him. "Did you call her that to her *face*?"

"I called her several things far worse than that, especially after what she fed me. She invited me for supper when I arrived and fed me some sort of chocolate cake laced with lobelia."

"Sunny? Chocolate?"

"Perhaps it was to cover the vast quantities of lobelia."

"Is that nasty?"

" 'Tis an emetic." He smiled wryly. "I spent the rest of the evening with my head in the loo."

"Gross."

"Especially since it was her loo I was occupying for the rest of that night. She merely stood there and watched me retch. Nary a word of comfort did she offer."

Madelyn pointed a forkful of egg at him. "The chocolate should have tipped you off. She doesn't usually have it in her house."

"She took special thought for me, then."

"She's just avenging my honor. I bawled on her couch for two weeks."

He reached for her hand. "Did you?"

"Didn't you?"

"I don't cry."

"Hmmm," she said with pursed lips. "Then what did you do?"

"I stomped about a great deal."

"Same thing."

He smiled gravely. "It is."

She picked at her dinner for a while, then looked at him. "You're really staying," she said.

He sighed, put his fork down, then took hers out of her hand. He stood, pulled her up, and into his arms.

"I can see I have more convincing to do."

"Patrick, you can't just haul me around like a sack of potatoes every time you want to get your way."

"Can't I?" he asked.

"You can't."

"Why not?"

"Because I'll never get a full meal. I'm starving."

He let her slide to her feet, then took her face in his hands and kissed her until she began to think that food maybe wasn't all that interesting after all. When he released her mouth, she looked up at him.

"This is going to be complicated, isn't it?"

He looked at her solemnly. "Aye. But worth it?"

She went into his arms, rested her head against his chest, and sighed. "Definitely."

He kissed her forehead, held out her chair for her, then sat down across from her. Madelyn tried to eat, but she found that she couldn't do much more than attempt to shovel in a few bites in between bouts of intense smiling.

There she was, not in the land of waking dreams, yet still dreaming all the same.

But if it was a dream, she never wanted to wake up.

Chapter 40

Patrick stood at Sunshine Phillips's front door and waved good-bye to his in-laws, unwholesomely grateful that he was seeing the back of them. It wasn't that he didn't like Madelyn's parents. He did. Her father was tall, distinguished-looking, and quite obviously brilliant. Her mother was handsome as well, with a scholarly mien and a sharp eye for any misstep.

But they both had the very disconcerting habit of changing tongues in the middle of conversations, a habit that had left his mind reeling—and he was not unfamiliar with many of their favorites.

And that had just been casual dinner conversation.

He'd wondered, during dinner, why everyone was so matter-of-fact about the glorious fare. Then he'd realized it was because they were all gearing up for his grilling.

Madelyn's mother had come first. Her testing of him in Latin had been uncomfortably thorough and he'd had no choice but to reveal exactly what he knew. Fortunately, he and Madelyn had had the time to discuss their time in the Middle Ages from the comfortable perspective of truly married souls and his lady wife had no more illusions about his skill with that mostly deceased tongue. So, he'd been tried to his utmost and come away mostly unscathed.

Madelyn's father had taken over, first in French, then in a handful of other languages Patrick couldn't speak very well, then finally in Gaelic. It was when he had found himself comfortably in his own tongue that he'd begun to relax.

His mistake, of course.

After dessert they moved to the living room, where he juggled more questions from his new in-laws in their inexhaustible supply of languages.

And the questions were ones he hadn't answered very well.

Who married you?

Where were you married?

Why weren't we invited and if the service was done in Latin, why weren't we consulted about its accuracy?

He'd stalled, he'd hedged, and he had outright lied to soothe and placate. And he'd felt the assessing gaze of Sunshine Phillips on him the entire time.

It was when Madelyn's parents had asked him where he planned to live, how he intended to support Madelyn, and how happy Madelyn would be in the wilds of Scotland, that an unaccustomed sense of nervousness overcame him.

He feared he didn't have any good answers for any of those questions either.

Somehow, though, Madelyn's parents had apparently come to some sort of conclusion about him. They had found him worthy of his degree, congratulated Madelyn on choosing an appropriately intelligent mate, then departed for their ivory tower with smiles, waves, and plans to attend another wedding in Scotland quite soon.

They hadn't seemed unhappy with Madelyn's choice.

Sunny was a different tale entirely.

"I brought pictures to sort," Madelyn said as they stepped back from the door. "Sunny, are you up to it?"

Patrick looked at his sister-in-law and imagined she was up to quite a bit more than just sorting pictures, but he was in her house, so he couldn't throw her out of it before she got to it.

"Pictures?" Sunny echoed. "Sure." But she was staring at Patrick purposefully, and he received the message quite clearly.

The Inquisition was nothing, laddie, compared to what you've yet to experience.

Or a sentiment to that effect.

Patrick smiled weakly, took Madelyn's hand, and made himself comfortable where she put him on Sunny's couch. He watched his lady wife sit on the floor before him, then looked around himself in an attempt at distraction. Not that he hadn't been here before, but that had been under less than ideal circumstances. Tonight, at least, he had survived dessert at Miss Lobelia's table.

Sunny's home reminded him a great deal of Moraig's—because of the herbs, not because of the crooked walls. She dried herbs in bunches from the ceiling, she had pots aplenty on shelves that were the slightest bit uneven, and the whole house smelled of things that were good and wholesome.

Now, if he'd just been as comfortable here as he was at Moraig's, life would have been fine.

He looked at Sunny as she sat on the floor across from her sister. He supposed she sat there so she could shoot him meaningful looks from time to time. She was quite beautiful, he conceded without hesitation, looking a great deal like her sister, with dark hair and fair skin. But he suspected Sunny had never worn her hair back in a chignon, nor put on a business suit. Stockings? He doubted she owned any.

But the fire in her soul was a great deal like his wife's, and he suspected the man who learned to be near her and not find himself scorched would be a happy man indeed.

Much like he himself was, warming his hands against that raging inferno that was Mistress Madelyn MacLeod.

He looked at the reason for that ridiculous bit of happiness and found that he couldn't stop himself from reaching out to touch her. He ran his hand down her mane of riotous hair, received a quick smile over her shoulder in return, then shivered as that echo of Culloden magic whispered through him. He'd almost grown used to the fact that it seemed to have taken up permanent residence inside him, always there under the surface when he was around Madelyn. He didn't know why it was there, but he suspected that something had been trying to tell him she was meant to be his.

He wished it hadn't taken a trip back in time to convince him of what he should have seen from the start.

But he couldn't, in all honesty, say he regretted it. He was married to the woman he loved. Could he, really, ask for more?

Well, perhaps a vote of confidence from her sister, but that likely wouldn't come without a price.

Madelyn reached up and covered his hands that rested on her shoulders. She twisted around to smile up at him.

"They liked you."

He took a deep breath. "A man could hope."

"My father is flying to Scotland without the excuse of a paper to deliver," she said. "He likes you."

"And your mother?" he asked.

"She's coming, too, without a professional reason. No higher praise."

"You know, they could be coming to see you get married," he said dryly.

"They wouldn't bother if they didn't like you."

He could scarce believe that, but he wasn't the one to say. Madelyn's parents were an unknown quantity; if she said they were pleased, then he would believe it.

He squeezed Madelyn's hand. "What do you suppose your sister thinks of me?" He looked at Sunny then, giving her his most charming smile.

Sunny regarded him coolly. "Her sister is still unconvinced."

"Sunny," Madelyn chided, "stop."

"He hurt you," Sunny said.

"He made up for it."

"Pretty is as pretty does," Sunny said stubbornly. "I'll watch him a while longer before I decide."

"I cleaned up the loo after myself," Patrick offered.

She was having none of that. "You might have picked up the bathroom, Patrick," she said crisply, "but you didn't have to pick up the pieces you left of my sister."

He nodded. "You're right."

"If you hurt her again, I'll be the one coming after you. And don't think I can't use a sword, because I can."

"You can't," Madelyn said placidly.

"I can learn."

"Sunny, I love her, too," he said.

"So you say, but how are you showing it? What are your plans for the future? What are you asking her to give up? What are you giving up for her?"

"Sunny," Madelyn warned, "you're pushing it."

"I'm asking the questions our father is too feeble to ask. He looks at Patrick as an opportunity to brush up his Gaelic. I'm looking at him as your potential husband."

"Potential?" Madelyn asked dryly. "That's sort of a case of the cow already being out of the barn, isn't it?"

Sunny glared at her sister, then turned that glare on him. "Well? Any good answers on what you're doing to prove you're worthy of her?"

"Sunny!" Madelyn exclaimed.

"Think of it as repayment for Conal's torture of you," Patrick offered, giving Madelyn's shoulder a gentle squeeze. He looked at Sunny. "I'm not afeared to answer what you want to ask. And I hope I'm not asking your sister to give up all she holds dear. Her great-grandmother's house is hers—"

"For the moment," Madelyn said with a sigh.

"For as long as you want it," he said. "I paid off your loans, so you needn't sell it."

Madelyn dropped the handful of photos she was holding and turned fully around to gape at him. "You didn't."

"I did."

"Patrick," she said, looking quite stunned, "that was over a hundred grand!"

He shrugged.

"You can't—"

"I already did."

"But that's my debt—"

"And Gilbert's mine," he said. "It weighed on you and I could ease that. So I did."

Madelyn started to cry. Patrick slid down to sit on the floor, then put his arms around her and pulled her back against him.

"Patrick," she whispered against his neck, "you really didn't have to—"

He stroked her hair. "I didn't have to," he agreed, "but I wanted to." He waited until she'd pulled back to look at him before he spoke again. "'Tis but money, Madelyn. Now you're free, to work if you will or turn your hand to other things—without any burdens weighing on you."

"I don't know how to thank you."

"You said me aye," he said with a smile. "That was enough."

She kissed him. "I suppose that now you've razed your bank account, we'll be camping in your house?"

He laughed. "I think I might have enough left for a chair or two. We'll see to it when we go home."

"And that's another thing," Sunny said briskly. "Where will she call home? Are you dragging her off to the Highlands? And what are you going to do for money, now that you've spent all yours on her loans?"

"I have enough to see to her quite comfortably, even after that," Patrick assured her. "As far as where we'll live, we're still thinking on that. And as far as work goes, I can't say as of yet. I am without employment at present."

"I can relate," Madelyn muttered.

Sunny scowled at her. "Not funny. This is important to me." She looked at Patrick. "Are you giving up that bodyguarding business? That's not the kind of work a man with a family takes lightly."

"I'm not going back," Patrick said.

"Are you sure?" Madelyn asked.

He nodded. "Conal knows I've grown weary of it. I'll find something else to do."

"Your brother will be happy," Madelyn said with a smile.

"He'll be overjoyed," Patrick said dryly. "It will give me ample time to restore that wreck of ours."

"Hmmm," Sunny said, studying him. "And when that's done, what are you going to do?"

Madelyn sighed and reached for more pictures. "I really hope you guys work this out soon. I don't think I can handle a lifetime with you not getting along."

"It isn't that we don't get along," Sunny said. "We're just getting the rules of the game straight."

"Your sister is right to see what I'm made of," Patrick agreed. "I've no quarrel with her over that."

Madelyn looked at the two of them, then shook her head. "You are two peas in a pod. Maybe that's it."

Sunny nodded thoughtfully. "We *are* irritated the most by flaws of our own we see in others."

"Not another waterskiing analogy," Madelyn pleaded. She looked at Patrick. "Agree with her quickly so we don't have to listen to it—"

Sunny threw a pillow at her sister. Madelyn only laughed and looked at Patrick. "I think she sees a lot of herself in you and it drives her nuts."

He smiled. "Aye, I understood that—"

Then he stopped smiling. It was as if his entire existence had ground to a painful, full stop. He closed his eyes at the sense of déjà vu that washed over him in a wave so fierce, he could scarce catch his breath.

A memory of Lisa's mother saying the same to him came to him, saying it during a conversation in which he'd wondered aloud what he could do to please her husband.

"He dislikes you because you are too much like him," she had said. *"He refuses to speak of his youth or of life in the Highlands. You, Patrick my lad, are very much like Gilbert when I first met him. Full of that Highland fierceness."*

He sat there and stared at nothing. Highland fierceness? What had she meant by that? He'd been three weeks in the present when he'd left Moraig's and walked to Inverness. He'd had a job tending Helen McGhee's garden a week after that.

Highland fierceness.

Was it possible Gilbert was more than he seemed?

"Patrick?"

He blinked, looked at Madelyn, and smiled faintly. "Aye, love?"

"You were very far away."

He shook his head. "Foolish thoughts." He paused, then shook his head again. "Nay, quite foolish." He looked at Sunny. "Do you have more questions for me? Ask me whatever you like, sister, and I'll answer as I can. And I hope my answers will satisfy you in regards to my intentions to care for Madelyn. I do not fear work, so she will never lack for food on her table. I am not afraid to fight, so she will never have to live in fear for her life. And I am not too proud to admit when I am wrong."

"You've apologized enough," Madelyn said firmly. "Sunny, let it go."

Sunny pursed her lips. "All right. I'm not thrilled about your occupation—since you don't seem to have one at the moment—but I'll get over that."

"Why don't you start a business together?" Madelyn asked. "You know, herbs and things."

Patrick felt a small chill go down his spine. "Herbs?"

Sunny also looked a little unsettled. "A business? Together?"

"You should," Madelyn said, seemingly oblivious to the undercurrents. "Patrick, as you might imagine, is really good at all that survival stuff. Finding herbs in the wilderness." She smiled up at them. "Books. Classes. Wilderness training." She looked at Sunny. "You'd have to come to Scotland. A lot. Maybe move there."

"Scotland," Sunny said, sounding bemused. "I've never been to Scotland."

Patrick looked at Madelyn with a smile. "And so it begins."

"We'll tattoo a map on the back of her hand."

"That might be wise." He smiled at Sunny. " 'Tis an interesting idea."

"I've always wanted to write a book," she admitted. "Pass on some of the things I've learned."

"Begin your treatise with an entry extolling the virtues of lobelia," he advised.

Sunny actually smiled at him then, and he felt as if he'd passed some kind of test. It was important to him. Madelyn loved her. If Sunny didn't care for him, things would no doubt go quite ill for him at family gatherings.

And the thought of a business was intriguing. His cousins had put their knowledge of various things to good use. Perhaps he could start up some kind of school with Ian and teach not just swordplay, but survival. Who was to say that in difficult times, a knowledge of how to heal the body with herbs from the field wouldn't be useful?

He put the thought aside for examination later, when he had the leisure for it, and turned his attentions back to the conversation at hand which was, fortunately, in a language he could understand. The future would take care of itself, as it generally did. When Madelyn had her great-gran's house sorted out properly, they would go back to Scotland.

"More dessert, Patrick?" Sunny asked pleasantly.

He looked at her assessingly. "Aye, if you taste my portion first."

She was an herbalist after all, and he'd tasted her wares before.

"Maybe Madelyn would play her violin for us while we eat," Sunny offered.

"As long as I'm not listening to it from the loo, I'll be delighted," he said.

So he sat quite happily with dessert that hadn't been tampered with, and listened to his lady wife play her violin for them for a goodly part of the evening. He closed his eyes at one point, simply because if he'd left them open, the tears would have been running down his cheeks.

By the saints, there was something about her music that stirred his soul.

It gave him hope.

And it made him very glad he had the remainder of his life to listen to it.

Thoughts of Gilbert teased at the back of his mind, but he pushed them aside. There would be time enough to think about them later. For now, he would listen to Madelyn's music and let it soothe him.

A fortnight later he couldn't bear his gnawing thoughts anymore. He left Madelyn happily sitting before the fire reading and walked down the block to the local library. He sat down at the computer and started looking.

Fortunately, genealogy sites were numerous. Clan sites had become so as well. It took him no time at all to find himself standing boldly in the Fergussons' great hall, as it were, and looking up their family tree. It gave him the chills, somehow, just looking back over the generations of lairds. That, at least, was complete. The other names he supposed they would find in time, if at all. But the laird and his immediate family? Aye, those names were there for anyone to read.

The Fergussons' genealogists had been thorough and apparently quite determined.

Patrick felt another chill creep down his spine.

He went straight to the place where he thought he might find what he sought. 1362. A son, William, was born. That son grew up to become the laird. He had sons as well. They were listed, apparently, from youngest to eldest.

1348, a son was born and named Neil.

1344, a son had been born and named Simon.

And a third entry. An entry he hadn't anticipated, but honestly wasn't surprised when he saw.

1342. A son had been born to William Fergusson and Mary McGhee.

A son named Gilbert.

Patrick closed his eyes and took many deep breaths. Indeed, he took so many, he thought he might begin to hyperventilate soon. He put his face in his hands and shook.

"Sir? Sir, are you unwell?"

He looked up at the librarian, who was watching him with concern tinged with suspicion. He smiled weakly. "Genealogy."

She nodded knowingly. "We call it the 'royalty or rustler' syndrome. I had a lady faint last week because of it."

"Was she related to a king?"

"The other kind," the woman said in hushed tones. "It happens all the time. I'll get you water if you need it."

"I'm fine," he said, trying to look fine. "Am I allowed to print this?"

"Certainly."

Ten minutes later he was stumbling from the building clutching something that might or might not change the course of his life.

Gilbert McGhee?

Son of William Fergusson and Mary McGhee?

It could happen, he supposed. Indeed, he was living proof that it could.

He walked up the street to Dewey's house, stepped inside the gate, and stood for a moment in the garden. It was raining, but that didn't trouble him. The garden was a haven, a place of complicated beauty, something that had been created with loving care over the course of decades.

He wondered if his children might come to look at his garden the same way.

Well, they wouldn't if he didn't do something about weeding out the weed that would continually crop up until it was eradicated once and for all.

The back door opened. Madelyn stood there, smiling.

"Hey," she said, "you weren't gone long."

"I missed you," he said simply.

Her smile deepened and she stepped backward. "Then come in, my lord, and tell me all about it."

He would, but later.

For now, there were other things on his mind.

Chapter 41

M adelyn set aside an empty box and bent down to rip off the tape on another. She opened the box, put her hands in the small of her back, and stretched. The feeling was altogether too familiar. It seemed as if all she'd been doing for the past three months had been packing and unpacking. First packing Dewey's house up, then her own stuff, and now unpacking things from both places into Patrick's house.

Sunny shouldn't have worried about them not having any furniture to sit on, or about having funds enough for a few renovations. Madelyn had seen Patrick's bank accounts, been rendered speechless by the numbers they contained, and subsequently stopped telling him he shouldn't have stretched himself to pay off debts that were hers.

Well, not that she still couldn't believe he'd done it, but now she knew that doing so hadn't put so much as a dent in his monthly pocket change.

None of which really changed her fiscal outlook, though. She still made him hunt around for the best deals on furniture, fixtures, and contractors. She cared; he didn't. He just wanted things done quickly.

And he still bought her clothes, despite her protests.

She shuddered to think what he would do when he found out she was going to need maternity clothes soon.

But that was a story for another day. Maybe she could talk him into a weekend away from all the souls who seemed to have taken up residence in their house with them. The sooner the better, though, or he was going to know without her telling him that she was pregnant and getting more so with each week that passed.

She grabbed a handful of things out of the box and decided, as she did so, that perhaps she was done for the day. Morning sickness was starting to kick in in a big way and she would rather face it lying down, thank you very much.

She crossed over to the armoire, opened it, and shoved her shoes inside, avoiding the spot where Patrick kept his sword.

She paused, straightened, and contemplated.

Shoes. Swords.

Her life was indeed very strange.

But wonderfully so. She shut up her shoes, left room for Patrick's gear, and went in search of something to ease her queasiness. Patrick's sword wasn't in the armoire because he was off engaging in his morning habit of trying to kill his cousin. She'd gotten used to that, too. Sometimes Patrick went to Ian's to train, sometimes Ian came to their house to train.

And sometimes they all went to Jamie's, and she went along just to gape at the three of them and remind herself quite unnecessarily that she had married into a family of medieval clansmen who were quite firmly in touch with their past.

She wondered if her parents should be seeing that when they came over for the wedding. Maybe she would do well to keep them in the house while Patrick and his menfolk were at their work, lest they stumble onto something that might set their heads to spinning. Or, as was more likely the case, something that would set her father to thinking he might improve his Gaelic if he had a sword to wave around.

She could only imagine how that might go over at his faculty teas.

She walked back to the kitchen and stopped at the entrance to it. It looked better than it had when she'd arrived two months ago. There were dishes now in the cupboards. They'd found a large farmhouse table with comfortable chairs. She'd hung curtains on the window. The walls had been covered with a fresh coat of paint and the floors covered in hardwood that was relatively warm under her feet.

Life was pretty good.

She also had a phone installed in that kitchen, which either she or Patrick used once a week or so to call Bentley and check in. He answered only because he didn't dare not. Patrick had promised him that if he didn't, he would find himself in dire straits indeed. Worse ones than just being ignored by *The Confessor,* that discriminating rag that found Bentley's stories too weird even for their pages. So they called, Bentley answered, and they checked up on his progress with his UFO reporting and his pro bono work.

Life was very good.

Her sister was sitting at the kitchen table, which made life even better. Sunny had farmed out yet more of her clients and her yoga classes and come to stay for a while. She and Patrick happily discussed herbs, healing, and things that grew beneath the eaves of the wood. That suited Madelyn perfectly.

Given that she was growing something quite lovely beneath her heart.

She put her hand over her belly. Two months and counting. It was hard to believe how much her life had changed. She couldn't help but be grateful to Bentley for that. If she'd never come to Scotland, she would never have met Patrick, and, well, the rest was wonderful history.

She'd worried, of course, about Gilbert and what he would do next. They'd talked to Conal often, and bummed rides off him several times in his Lear. They'd discussed with Conal what Patrick had discovered about Gilbert's potential background.

Conal had been speechless. Gilbert a medieval clansman? It had almost been too much for him to swallow. It was one thing to believe it of Patrick; it was another thing for Conal to believe it of his brother-in-law.

He'd also said that Gilbert had been unusually quiet as of late, as if he was going through some sort of soul-searching.

Patrick had been skeptical.

Madelyn hadn't dared speculate.

And then Sunny had come over and Madelyn had given up speculation for the pleasure of family. Gilbert would keep. There was no point in worrying about him. What were they to do, live their lives in fear?

So she'd taken the map Jamie had made her, which looked

quite a bit like Jane's, then taken her sister to roam for hours over Patrick's land. She'd introduced Sunny to Moraig and watched them fall into each other's arms like long-lost relatives.

"Need tea?"

Madelyn realized she was staring at her sister without looking at her. She shook her head to clear away the cobwebs, then shook her head again. "Thanks, but no. I'm fine."

"You should rest."

"I rest too much. Much more rest and you'll be worrying about me beaching myself on that couch."

"Gain what you need to. Your body will tell you when it's enough."

"My sister, the midwife."

"You'll be grateful for it when you're in transition screaming at your husband that this child will be an only child and if he disagrees with you, you'll make sure of it."

"Do laboring women have enough breath for sentences of that length?"

Sunny threw a dishtowel at her. She always seemed to have them to hand. Maybe that was all part of her mystique as well. Madelyn smiled and crossed over to the fridge to peer inside and see if there was anything useful in there. Well, at least what was there wasn't covered with mold. Even so, not a thing appealed.

"Got anything for morning sickness?" Madelyn asked, shutting the fridge door.

"Always. Why don't you go find somewhere comfortable to sit and I'll bring you some of it?"

Madelyn considered. The living room was still a work in progress. The bedroom contained the bed, and if she went back in there, she would make use of it. There were other bedrooms, of course, but again, the bed thing would happen there, too, and if she had to sleep any more, she would scream.

That left either the study or the sitting room.

She hesitated. She knew what both would contain.

The study was a place that Archibald, first lord of Benmore, had laid claim to the moment the dark brown leather club chair had been installed. He could be found there most

afternoons, puffing on his pipe, contemplating this book or
that—books he seemed to have brought with him, apparently,
because she and Patrick certainly didn't own any of that vintage. He always seemed very pleased when she came to sit
with him, but she suspected he liked her because she gave
him some hope of posterity.

He was, she had found, very big on genealogy.

She liked Lord Archibald very much. He was gruff, he
was a bit on the gloomy side, but he was always very solicitous. And he had begun to put out his pipe whenever he
saw her, when he had determined that she was in an . . .
um . . . delicate condition.

Why the ghosts and sundry knew and Patrick didn't was
something she would think about later.

But she was too restless to sit, and she wasn't really in the
mood to make polite conversation while trying to ignore the
queasiness that raged throughout every cell of her body.

That meant the sitting room was out, too. Lady Dorcas,
now that the rest of her home seemed to be approaching her
standards of civilization, continually tried to decide on what
decor she thought appropriate for her sanctuary.

Sunny didn't like that.

Madelyn refrained from criticizing. She was perfectly willing to let Lady Dorcas do what she wanted. It had been, after
all, her house first.

But the thought of having to accustom herself to another
decorating scheme, or turn pages of home improvement mag-
azines for Lady Dorcas while she tried to decide what style
she liked best, was just more than she thought she could
handle.

A walk in the garden was what she needed. Patrick was
due home any minute, and she wanted him to find her rosy-
cheeked, not looking as if she was about to puke her guts
out. She could look like that tomorrow, after she'd given him
the good news.

She paused for a minute in the living room and looked at
the painting Patrick had hung over the mantel. It was a painting of their little castle that he had had commissioned from
some struggling artist he'd met on the street in Inverness. It

was quite good, actually, and the artist had imbued the view with a great deal of that Highland magic Roddy MacLeod was so convinced of. Madelyn looked at the picture, just sure that at any moment, things would show up in it that hadn't been there at painting time.

Time travelers.

Sprites and elves from Moraig's neck of the woods.

Ghostly pipers tramping about happily atop Patrick's hill.

Ghosts appearing at other times and places in their house.

Nothing she had anticipated that first day in Inverness when she'd exited the train station and taken her first deep breath of Highland air.

She smiled, grabbed her coat, then headed toward the kitchen. Sunny had made a list of things she was perpetually in need of, and Madelyn never went out into the garden that she didn't look hopefully for something on that list to be popping up from its winter slumber.

She picked up one of the baskets that seemed to have taken up residence all over her kitchen and headed out the back door into the garden. It was actually quite cold outside, but she could handle it. What was a little residual snow in the garden when a woman had morning sickness to escape?

She walked along, keeping a close watch on the terrain under her feet so she didn't slip. She followed paths she and Patrick were beginning to painstakingly lay out and smiled at the sight. It might never look like Dewey's garden, but it had its own charm. And it was theirs. You couldn't argue with that.

Though she did have to admit she missed Dewey's garden, which was so beautiful even in winter. Well, it was in good hands for the present. She and Patrick had loaned it out for the year to one of her cousins, a gardener by trade, who was trying to get back on her feet with her two kids. Madelyn had wondered, often, if that wouldn't be the best use for Dewey's house. A place to heal. The garden alone would be enough to soothe a troubled soul. And at least there, you could just walk where you wanted and not worry about hot spots on the ground. Here, you just never knew.

Even in her own garden, she was never sure. All she

needed was to accidently find one of Jamie's gates while on an innocent walk outside to pick a few flowers. It was almost enough to convince her to be more careful where she was putting her feet, so she didn't run into anything scary.

And then she found herself running into something scary just the same.

For a moment, she thought she'd run into the house.

She looked up and realized she'd just run into Gilbert McGhee.

She didn't have time to even blurt out a pleasant "how do you do" before he had grabbed her by the hair and was jerking her along after him. She wondered if he was going to kill her right there between rosebushes or if he would drag her into a car and take her somewhere less thorny to do the deed.

She screamed, just on principle.

"Shut up," he snarled in Gaelic, giving her hair another jerk.

She clutched her head to save herself pain.

Then she found herself hauled in front of him with his arm across her throat. She tried to grind her heel into the top of his foot, but he was wearing boots and her slick move didn't pan out. She tried for his groin, but he grabbed her arm and wrenched it up behind her back. He shoved her forward, toward the garden gate.

Too bad Patrick hadn't gotten around to teaching her some of his more lethal moves. She also wished that she'd taken to wearing a dirk in her waistband as he'd tried to convince her to do.

Her mistake.

Gilbert stopped suddenly. Madelyn found it in her to look up from where she was walking.

Patrick stood just inside the wall, a vision of fury in black. His sword was bare in his hand. His expression was chiseled straight from granite.

She almost wet her pants and she was his wife.

Gilbert, unfortunately, was less impressed. "Too late," he spat. "Too late to save her, MacLeod."

"Coward," Patrick sneered. "Do you have the bollocks to come at me truly, or will you hide behind a helpless woman?"

Madelyn wished, absently, that he hadn't said that. She was just certain Gilbert was going to slit her throat, but he bellowed suddenly and grasped his head with both hands. Madelyn found herself pulled out of the way by Ian, who boosted her over the rock wall, then quickly followed.

"My contribution to the cause," he called to Patrick. He looked at Madelyn. "Had a rock to hand and couldn't stop myself from using it."

She looked at him in shock. "Well, why didn't you completely disable him?"

"And have Pat furious with me for the rest of his life?" Ian asked, wide-eyed.

"Ian!"

"Patrick can see to himself."

"Easy for you to say."

"If he truly begins to look as if he'll fail, I'll offer him a bit of aid."

It wasn't a good answer, but it was an answer. Madelyn stood there and watched her husband and his former father-in-law go after each other as if they had every, *every*, intention of killing each other.

"What in the world are they doing?"

Madelyn looked at her sister, who had come to stand next to her. "Fighting."

Sunny's mouth was working but nothing was coming out. Madelyn understood completely.

"He's trampling your rosebushes," Sunny managed finally. "They both are. And all those lovely herbs. Of course, not that the herbs are up yet, but there are seeds in those weeds and those seeds will eventually—"

"Sunny, you're babbling."

Sunny shut her mouth, took Madelyn by the arm, and clung.

Madelyn understood that as well.

She also understood, quite suddenly and forcefully, how awful it must have been to have been married during the Middle Ages and have to watch your husband go off to war.

Or have had war come to him.

Only she wasn't in the Middle Ages, she was in the middle of her husband's garden. War wasn't coming to him; his former father-in-law had come, with no good intent.

And there wasn't a damned thing she could do about it.

"So he finally showed himself," Jamie said.

She looked around Ian to find that Jamie and his wife's brother Alex had somehow found their way to the scene of the disaster as well. They were leaning on the wall casually, as if they watched nothing more interesting than a mildly entertaining sporting event.

"We knew he would," Alex said.

"Should have killed him sooner," Ian intoned. "I was for that from the beginning, you know."

"I'd imagine Patrick will see to that today," Jamie said.

Madelyn felt Sunny's fingers dig into her arms. "Kill him?" she whispered. "Patrick's going to kill him?"

Madelyn didn't have a good answer for that. All she could do was stare at the horrific sight in front of her and pray.

Patrick had shrugged out of his leather jacket and thrown it toward them. He was now standing there in a black turtleneck, black jeans, and black boots.

If he didn't scare the hell out of Gilbert McGhee just by that alone, Madelyn wasn't sure what would.

Then again, Gilbert looked every bit as comfortable with his very medieval-looking sword as Patrick did, so maybe he'd seen worse.

And if she hadn't been so dry-mouth scared, she might have found the scene before her to be quite interesting. It wasn't every day a woman watched her modern-day husband wielding a sword with as much ease as he might have a Weedwacker. And if there was anyone who made it look like a dance, it was Patrick. He was, she had to admit in a detached way that frightened her but seemed like a good way to cling to her sanity, a very lethal man. He held his sword easily, he parried without effort, he seemed perfectly comfortable with the fact that the man facing him had every intention of trying to do him in.

Only she'd seen what Patrick was capable of, that morning in the Fergussons' hall, with Simon Fergusson's men.

Gilbert's brother's men.

Did Gilbert have any idea whom he faced?

Or was he sure enough of his skill that he didn't care?

She wasn't sure she wanted to know, but she knew she would be finding out the answer soon enough—whether she wanted it or not.

She could only pray it would be the one she wanted.

Chapter 42

Patrick fended off Gilbert McGhee Fergusson's attack and tried to clear his mind of distractions. His life depended on that. Well, he supposed if he truly began to look feeble, Jamie and Ian might come rescue him, but he would have to look damned feeble before they would offer aid.

And it wasn't as if he had any desire for aid. This was his problem, his trouble, his responsibility. It wasn't for his brother or his cousin to see to. Though he was tempted to tell them if they didn't shut up, they would be next in line after he finished with the whoreson in front of him.

"I think Pat's suspicions were spot on, don't you?" Ian said idly.

"Of Gilbert being Simon Fergusson's older brother?" Jamie asked. "Aye. He looks just like every other bloody Fergusson I've ever seen."

"Careful," Ian growled.

"I'm convinced that there is little Fergusson blood running through your lady's veins," Jamie said easily. "She actually has the look of a Campbell about her. Surely there's one in her family tree somewhere."

As if Jamie would recognize a Campbell if one clubbed him over the head with a picture of himself, Patrick thought with a snort.

"Have you looked into her roots?" Jamie continued.

"We've been a bit busy," Ian said dryly. "You know, watching after a pair of bairns, seeing to her weaving, running my school, keeping me fed."

"Well," Alex said with a laugh, "the last is a full-time job, no doubt."

Patrick cursed. "Will you all shut up?" he demanded. "I'm busy here."

"He's touchy," Jamie said, in only slightly softer tones. "That doesn't bode well for his concentration—"

Patrick threw his brother a look. He would have thrown something else as well, but he didn't dare. Gilbert seemed to have no trouble ignoring the inane conversations going on not twenty feet away from him. Patrick turned his attentions back to where they should have been. Gilbert not only owned a broadsword, he knew how to use it. Patrick would have tried to determine where and when the man trained, but he found that the swordplay demanded the whole of his attention.

Well, except for that small part of his mind that was accustomed, after so many years, to listening to Jamie continue to blather on.

"Patrick should train harder," Jamie said blandly. "I keep telling him, but he never listens. The folly of youth."

Patrick promised himself several months of grinding his brother into the dust as reward for doing in the ruthless bastard in front of him.

That was assuming he managed that.

He looked at his former father-in-law and wondered how he could have missed the obvious. There was something about the man, something wild, something quite uncivilized.

Something so appallingly similar to Simon Fergusson.

"Met your brother a couple of months back," Patrick said casually.

Gilbert's sword dipped, but he recovered quickly. "Don't have a brother."

"Don't you? I think you actually have two. Simon and Neil, if memory serves."

Gilbert's sword definitely faltered in its arc. He looked at Patrick narrowly for a moment, then put his sword point-down into the dirt at his feet. He breathed heavily.

"So," he said flatly, "you know."

"I know," Patrick said. "What I don't know is why you hide it."

Gilbert rolled his eyes. "You bloody fool, why would I show it?"

"Is that why you took your mother's name?"

Gilbert tightened his lips. "I took her name to honor her. And to escape my sire."

Patrick had no trouble understanding the last of that. "Then what is your quarrel with me?"

"You fool, you killed my daughter!"

"You know I didn't—"

"And you're a MacLeod," Gilbert continued, wrenching his sword free of the ground and taking up a fighting stance. "Isn't that reason enough?"

"Eight centuries ago, maybe. Today? I wonder."

" 'Tis reason enough for me," Gilbert said. "Now, are you going to talk me to death, or lift your sword and show me something more impressive than the womanly swings you've mustered up so far?"

Womanly swings? Patrick almost responded to that, but didn't have the chance before he was interrupted by something else. Robert MacLeod appeared suddenly on the wall, filling his pipes with air and beginning the strains of a battle dirge that would have inspired the most faint-hearted of men.

Then the walls were suddenly covered with Highlanders—probably the same ones who had guarded Madelyn that one afternoon. They were all facing in, staring at him with fierce expressions that bespoke their determination to see him preserved at all costs.

Wonderful.

Sunny groaned loudly enough that Patrick heard her. He chanced a look in time to see her slip down behind the wall, likely in a dead faint.

Gilbert fared no better. He almost dropped his sword. He turned around in a circle, gaping at what he saw.

He stopped, looked at Patrick, and swallowed very hard.

"What evil is this?" he rasped.

"No evil," Patrick said pleasantly. "Just ghosts."

Gilbert crossed himself against Patrick, then lifted his sword. "I knew you couldn't fight me by yourself. No MacLeod has honor enough to rely on his own skill. Always looking for some kind of aid—"

"Ach," Jamie said in disgust, "fight, you fools, and let us be done with this. I've a mind for a decent lunch."

Patrick turned and looked at his brother. "Is it possible *you* might find it in yourself to be silent? If you offer your opinion one more time—"

"Patrick!" Madelyn screamed.

Patrick leaped aside in time for Gilbert's sword to make a great rip in his shirt. He looked down. No blood spurting, at least. He flashed his wife a look, then turned back to Lisa's sire.

"We could end this peaceably," Patrick said, fending off a parry or two. "I did not kill Lisa. She killed herself."

"Liar!" Gilbert spat. "You're a MacLeod. You're a liar by blood."

"I did not kill your daughter," Patrick said. "And I don't have to kill you. Not if you vow to walk away from this. Leave my land, leave my woman, go in peace."

Gilbert flung himself at him with a *never* spewing out of his mouth along with a goodly bit of spittle. Patrick jumped aside, then found that words were no longer going to be a part of the afternoon's activities. Gilbert came at him with a ferocity that left him calling upon reserves of skill and courage he hadn't tapped in a very long time.

If ever.

But while Gilbert fought for hate's sake, Patrick fought for his wife, his future children, his own family's honor.

He was, after all, a MacLeod.

And a MacLeod did not cower.

A MacLeod also didn't trot out his black belt during a duel with medieval weapons, but he was damn tempted. He could have disarmed Gilbert and plunged him into unconsciousness with but a handful of well-placed blows. But that would have left the man alive, likely quite free of any long-term jail cell, and shamed enough to attack again with redoubled destructiveness.

Nay, 'twas better he finish this with a blade.

The morning wore on. He was vaguely aware of the addition of one Dorcas, first lady of Benmore, who had come to complain about them turning her garden into a muddy field. Robert continued to play songs that Patrick had heard in his own day on the field of battle, songs that stirred his blood as they were meant to.

His brother was, mercifully, silent.

He grew weary. Maybe Gilbert trained more often than he let on; maybe he was determined to spill MacLeod blood that morn or perish in the attempt. Whatever the case, Gilbert seemed to draw on an inexhaustible supply of fury.

Patrick pushed Gilbert back, his chest heaving.

Gilbert regrouped and went on the offensive.

Patrick stumbled. He fell. He rolled just before he lost his head. And in the process of rolling, he caught Gilbert's feet with his own and felled him with a modern move that he should have used an hour earlier.

He was tired. He just couldn't help himself.

Gilbert fell backward into the compost pile.

And he disappeared.

Patrick sat up and gaped. Even Robert the piper faltered in his music. Patrick struggled to his feet, stared a bit more at the mound of dirt piled up against the back wall, then looked over to his right to see if anyone else was as surprised as he was.

Madelyn was leaning against the wall, her eyes wide. The rest of his family merely stared at the heap with expressions of disbelief. All but Jamie, who peered with great interest at the spot.

"Well," Jamie said enthusiastically, "another place for travel. Though," he continued, sounding as if he regretted the idea quite thoroughly, "perhaps you should plant something feisty there. Nettles. That no one travels through that gate lightly. This is your garden, after all."

"Good idea," Patrick said. He walked across the ruined garden and heaved himself over the wall. He set his sword atop the wall, then pulled Madelyn into his arms. "Are you all right?"

"Perfect. You?"

"Never better."

"Where did he go?"

"I have no idea," Patrick said, "and I've no mind to go investigating." He looked at Lady Dorcas, who was tapping her fan on top of the wall thoughtfully. "You said there was something in that heap, but it escapes me what."

"Gold," she said archly. "And a goodly amount thereof."

"Well," Patrick said, dragging his sleeve across his brow, "I've no mind to investigate that either."

"I will," Jamie said, jumping spryly over the wall. He took Patrick's sword and poked about in the heap. He found nothing but dirt for some time, then came the sound of sword against something solid.

"Rake," Jamie commanded.

A rake was fetched. Then a shovel. The dirt was dug and a trunk uncovered.

"Hold on to something of me," Jamie commanded.

Patrick swung himself back over the wall with a sigh and deigned to hold on to the back of Jamie's shirt while his brother bent and heaved out a medium-sized trunk. He set it on the ground and opened it up.

"Doubloons!" Jamie exclaimed happily. "I'd recognize them anywhere."

"Then you'd best not go back to where they were minted," Patrick said dryly, "lest you encounter our good Gilbert Fergusson and find him quite annoyed by his journey."

Jamie ran his fingers through the gold. "There is quite a bit here, Patrick. Enough to put your wee ones through college, I'd say."

"And yours, too," Patrick said with a snort. "Maybe Ian's as well." He looked at Madelyn. "I'll plant nettles."

"Good plan."

"They're medicinal as well," Sunny offered weakly, apparently having recovered enough to lean on the wall.

They were, but he wasn't sure he was going to be harvesting anything from that patch any time soon. He took his sword back from his brother, then went to stand across the wall from his wife. It was then that he noticed that she was quite pale.

"Are you unwell?" he asked, jamming his sword into the dirt and grasping her by the shoulders.

She looked quite green all of a sudden.

And just as suddenly, she pulled away from him, stumbled away, and retched.

Patrick looked at the men of his family. They were looking quite green themselves.

"Patrick!" Lady Dorcas snapped.

He snapped to attention in spite of himself. "Aye?"

"Put your lady to bed. A woman in her delicate condition does not need to watch the excitement you've put her through this morning. I daresay she will require quite a bit of your solicitous care, if you can manage it. If not, Mistress Sunshine and I will see to it."

Now Sunny was the one who was starting to look a bit green. He suspected she wasn't quite adjusted to the otherworldly occupants of his and Madelyn's home.

And then it hit him.

"Delicate condition?" he repeated.

Madelyn straightened, turned, and smiled weakly at him. She looked pale.

He felt a little pale himself.

But he was, after all, a MacLeod, and a MacLeod did not run.

And he was quite sure a MacLeod did not receive the news of his impending fatherhood flat upon his arse.

He hopped over the wall, then crossed the distance between them in two strides and pulled her into his arms.

"A babe?" he whispered.

"Yes," she said, leaning heavily against him. "And one who'll grow up safe, thanks to you."

He rested his cheek on top of her head and closed his eyes. He sighed deeply, unsure if he was more relieved that his enemy was out of reach, or more overwhelmed that he was going to be a father.

It was, perhaps, a bit of both.

He pulled back and looked at Madelyn. "Let me see you inside."

She nodded.

He put his arm around her shoulder, then turned them around so he could look at his piper. "Thank you, Robert. Very inspiring."

Robert nodded. "A pleasure, my friend. 'Twas the least I could do after all you've done for me."

Patrick looked at the other Highlanders lining the walls. He wasn't sure who they were—

"My posterity," the Glum said proudly. "Fine, strapping lads, those. I imagine they'll be around when ye need them, as well they should be to protect their laird."

Patrick shut his mouth around the question of whether or not Lord Archibald was now going to be divining his thoughts with regularity. Better not to know that one, he suspected. But he nodded his thanks to that posterity of the Glum's just the same, then turned to his own family.

"Well," he said, looking at Ian and Alex, "that's done."

"Finally," Ian said. He stretched his hands over his head, yawned, then scratched his belly. "Entertaining morn, Pat, but I've things to do. Have a new class coming in this afternoon and I'd best be ready for them. Alex, have you time to look over a bit of new paperwork for me? I've no mind to see myself in jail for scratches I might leave on these lads, and I suspect one of them is of the ilk to cry foul when bruised."

"Sure," Alex said easily. He clapped a hand on Patrick's shoulder. "Good work, brother. He was a tough one."

Patrick nodded in agreement. Gilbert had been very skilled and quite ruthless, making his brothers in the past look quite incompetent by comparison. Patrick didn't want to admit that he had been forced to stretch himself to best him, but there it was.

He was remarkably relieved that was over.

He watched Alex and Ian walk off toward Ian's house, laughing companionably. He shivered, once, in spite of himself. Odd how life and death could play out so seriously one minute, then life could go on so easily the next.

He turned and looked at his brother, who was still fondling doubloons. "Well?" he asked.

Jamie looked up with a frown. "I'll have to consult my coin man for a proper value for these. You'll want to bring them inside, of course, out of the chill and out of sight. You

never know who might wander over your land, see them, and
think to help themselves."

"How about you worry about that?" Patrick said. "I think
I'm going to be busy for the next little while. My wife is, as
you may or may not have noticed, in a delicate condition."
And he hadn't asked for his brother's opinion on a chestful
of gold; he'd asked, foolishly, for his opinion on the morning's events.

Jamie stood, tried to heave the trunk up and failed, then
looked at Patrick. "I'll need your aid," he admitted.

"That must have cost much," Patrick said with a snort.

Jamie looked at him thoughtfully for a moment or two.
Then he put his hand to his chin and stroked.

Patrick made preparations to flee.

Jamie closed the lid of the trunk, then came over to the
wall. He hopped over it, took the three paces required to
reach Patrick, then put his hand on his shoulder.

"You fought well," he said simply.

Patrick wanted to tell himself he didn't care. He was, after
all, a man with five-and-thirty summers behind him, not a
green lad of twelve. But he couldn't deny that praise from
his elder brother didn't leave him completely unaffected.

He nodded. "Thank you."

"Perhaps we can examine later why it is you feel the need
for this validation—"

Patrick rolled his eyes and turned away before he said
something to ruin the moment. He looked at Sunny.

"Welcome to Scotland," he said.

She smiled weakly. "Great place. I'll go make some tea."

"I'll help," Lady Dorcas said with an imperious wave of her
hand. "Archibald, go stoke the fire for the sweet gel. Come,
Mistress Sunshine, and we'll chat whilst we steep. You've a
particular style about you that soothes me greatly. Perhaps you
might come offer me your opinion on the decor of my parlor."

Patrick watched as Sunny trailed off after a still-speaking
Lady Dorcas—who was trailed by a hangdog Lord Glum—
toward the house. Jamie gave him one final look, promised
to return with aid for the moving of the gold, then left as
well.

Stroking his chin.

Patrick knew that boded ill for his peace of mind.

But at least he finally found himself alone with his lady. No ghosts. No family. No former in-laws with mayhem on their minds. He looked down at Madelyn.

"Forgive me," he said quickly, "I should have gotten you to bed—"

"I'm fine now," she said. "A little queasy, but the air seems to help."

"Well," he said quietly, "that's that."

"That's that," she agreed. She looked up at him. "What will you tell Conal? Or Lisa's mother?"

"Probably everything now. Helen deserves the truth about Lisa. I daresay she won't be sorry about Gilbert. He was abusive to her, I think. Conal won't be surprised to learn of his end. He'll likely be relieved he doesn't have to go about behind his brother-in-law, cleaning up his messes."

"Will there be an inquest?"

He sighed deeply. "There may be."

"What do we tell them?"

He looked at her seriously. "The truth, unfortunately, is unbelievable. I suppose we'll just have to say we saw him last in our garden and that he went missing after that."

She shivered. "I hope he doesn't come back."

" 'Tis unlikely."

"Life is complicated." She paused. "I can see why you didn't go after him after he set your place on fire."

"No proof," he said quietly. "No point." He took her hand and kissed it. "It will all disappear in time. We'll have our peace. Helen will find hers. Conal will have his."

"And we'll plant those nettles."

"It would be best."

She nestled herself closer in his arms. "Thank you, Patrick."

"I'm simply trying to make good on my promise of peace and safety."

"You did. As difficult as it was to watch . . . you did."

"Did you think I would lose?" he asked, pulling back to look down at her in surprise.

"Get real," she said with a smile. "I just figured you hadn't had enough of a workout this morning and didn't want to end it too soon. Really, Patrick, you should train more and get out all that excess energy Moraig claims you have."

He scowled at her and ignored the laugh he received in return.

"Then again, you'll probably be expending lots of energy chasing after your child in a year or so, so maybe you should rest up."

"Excellent idea," he said, though he doubted he could rest at the moment. He was far too full of life and death and feelings that threatened to overwhelm him. He would put his lady wife to bed, then search for a clutch of nettles to transplant onto his compost heap. It would keep anyone from their day from falling into the past, and it might keep Gilbert at bay, should he somehow manage to come back the same way he'd gone. A few howls from an errant time traveler coming through their garden's time gate might be enough to at least alert them that something had gone amiss.

Then he would call Conal and Helen. He needed to be finished with that chapter of his life.

And once he'd seen to that, he would allow himself to sit and think.

About the miracle of life.

About the pleasures of family.

And about the blessing of the woman walking with her arm around him who had come into his life and given him a reason to live again.

To love again.

"I think you stroked your chin."

He blinked and awoke from his thoughts. "I didn't," he said, aghast.

She only laughed and tightened her arm around his waist.

Patrick called her a saucy wench under his breath, received another laugh in return, then kissed the top of her riotous head of curls and walked with her back to the house.

Epilogue

Patrick supposed there were advantages to having a sister-in-law as a midwife. It saved him the worry of transporting his wife to hospital, though Jamie had rented a helicopter just in case. It was sitting behind Patrick's house, waiting patiently. And Sunny was waiting just as patiently, ignoring his pacing, ignoring Madelyn's swearing.

"What in the *hell* was I thinking?" Madelyn gasped as she clutched the side of a birthing tub Sunny had demanded be imported. She looked around desperately. "This is too much."

"It's transition," Sunny said serenely. "Just hang on."

"Hang on!" Madelyn shouted. "You go through this and then tell me to hang on, you—"

Patrick listened, openmouthed, to a very long list of names his wife called her beloved sister. He gaped at Sunny as she turned and smiled at him.

"Would you believe," she said, unruffled, "that Madelyn worried that women in labor didn't have enough breath for long, involved sentences?"

"That wasn't a long sentence," Patrick ventured. "It was a long list of very foul names." He looked at his wife. "Really, Madelyn, perhaps—"

"And *you*," she said, gasping, with tears streaming down her face, "*you*—"

The list was even longer. It was in Gaelic. He decided that he would perhaps have to have a word with Robert MacLeod. Too many foul words had been taught to his wife for his comfort. If she would just throw in a few nice ones, he would feel a great deal better. He'd heard stories about the joy of childbirth, the overwhelming nature of the experience, the bonding that occurred between husband and wife.

In reality, it looked like a lot of work to him.

And he suspected that his wife wanted to kill him.

Nay, he didn't suspect it. He *knew* it.

But two hours later the work was done, his daughter had made her entrance into the world, and his wife was looking up at him with love in her eyes and tears streaming down her face.

Sunny handed him the baby.

Patrick accepted her, that small, helpless creature that had lived nestled under his wife's heart for a se'nnight shy of ten months, stared down into her fathomless gray eyes, and found himself rendered quite speechless.

His life shuddered from the joy of it.

He met Madelyn's eyes. "She's beautiful," he whispered reverently. "Thank you."

She smiled through her tears. "She is."

He held the baby as Sunny tended to Madelyn, gave her up to her aunt's loving arms to help Madelyn out of the tub, then knelt down by the bed as Madelyn held her ten-minute-old daughter and put her to her breast. Madelyn looked at him.

"What should we call her?"

He'd thought about it for months. Almost ten months. A name for the first flower to bloom in their garden.

He hoped Madelyn would agree with him.

"I have a name in mind," he began.

"What is it?"

He paused, looked at the wee babe, then back at his love. "I think," he said slowly, "that we should call her Hope."

"Oh, Patrick," she whispered.

"It's what you brought me. Twice now. First when you came into my life, and now again with the gift of my daughter."

His heart settled within him and whispered contentedly of peace.

And beautiful things blooming in his garden.

And of hope.

It was enough. .

Look for Lynn Kurland's new romantic fantasy novella
in a collection that also features
Patricia McKillip, Sharon Shinn, and Claire Delacroix.

Coming from Berkley Trade in July 2004!

ROMANTIC ROOTS

MACLEOD

Robert ●————————————————● Douglas

Ian
m: Jane Fergusson

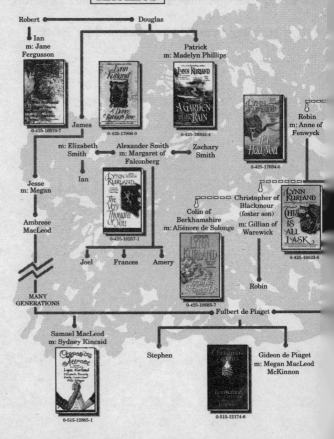

Patrick
m: Madelyn Phillips

0-425-16970-7

0-425-17906-0

0-425-19202-4

Robin
m: Anne of Fenwyck

0-425-17694-0

James

m: Elizabeth Smith

Alexander Smith
m: Margaret of Falconberg

Zachary Smith

Ian

Jesse
m: Megan

0-425-18297-1

Colin of Berkhamshire
m: Aliénore de Solonge

Christopher of Blackmour (foster son)
m: Gillian of Warewick

0-425-18033-6

Ambrose MacLeod

Joel   Frances   Amery

Robin

0-425-18685-7

MANY GENERATIONS

Fulbert de Piaget ●

Samuel MacLeod
m: Sydney Kincaid

Stephen

Gideon de Piaget
m: Megan MacLeod McKinnon

0-515-12865-1

0-515-12174-6

family lineage in the books of
LYNN KURLAND

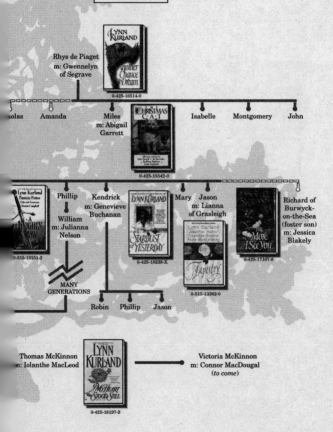

DE PIAGET

Rhys de Piaget
m: Gwennelyn
of Segrave

Another Chance to Dream
0-425-16514-0

...olas   Amanda   Miles
m: Abigail
Garrett   Isabelle   Montgomery   John

The Christmas Cat
0-425-15542-0

This Is All I Ask (?)
0-515-13151-2

Phillip
↓
William
m: Julianna
Nelson

Kendrick
m: Genevieve
Buchanan

Stardust of Yesterday
0-425-18238-X

Mary   Jason
m: Lianna
of Grasleigh

Tapestry
0-515-13362-0

Richard of
Burwyck-
on-the-Sea
(foster son)
m: Jessica
Blakely

The More I See You
0-425-17107-8

MANY
GENERATIONS

Robin   Phillip   Jason

Thomas McKinnon
m: Iolanthe MacLeod

My Heart Stood Still
0-425-18197-9

Victoria McKinnon
m: Connor MacDougal
(to come)

continued . . .

If I Had You

"Kurland brings history to life . . . in this tender medieval romance."
—*Booklist*

"A passionate story filled with danger, intrigue, and sparkling dialogue . . . "
—*Rendezvous*

"A heartwarming book."
—*Old Book Barn Gazette*

The More I See You

"Entertaining . . . The story line is fast-paced and brings to life the intrigue of the era . . . wonderful."
—*Midwest Book Review*

"The superlative Ms. Kurland once again wows her readers with her formidable talent as she weaves a tale of enchantment that blends history with spellbinding passion and impressive characterization, not to mention a magnificent plot."
—*Rendezvous*

Another Chance to Dream

"Kurland creates a special romance between a memorable knight and his lady."
—*Publishers Weekly*

"[A] wonderful love story full of passion, intrigue, and adventure . . . Lynn Kurland's fans will be delighted."
—*Affaire de Coeur*

The Very Thought of You

"[A] masterpiece . . . this fabulous tale will enchant anyone who reads it."
—*Painted Rock Reviews*

This Is All I Ask

"An exceptional read." —*The Atlanta Journal-Constitution*

"Both powerful and sensitive . . . this is a wonderfully rich and rewarding book." —Susan Wiggs

"A medieval of stunning intensity. Sprinkled with adventure, fantasy, and heart, *This Is All I Ask* reaches outside the boundaries of romance to embrace every thoughtful reader, every person of feeling." —Christina Dodd

"In this character-driven medieval romance that transcends category, Kurland spins a sometimes magical, sometimes uproariously funny, sometimes harsh and brutal tale of two people deeply wounded in body and soul who learn to love and trust each other . . . Savor every word; this one's a keeper." —*Publishers Weekly* (starred review)

"Sizzling passion, a few surprises, and breathtaking romance . . . a spectacular experience that you will want to savor time and time again." —*Rendezvous*

A Dance Through Time

"An irresistibly fast and funny romp across time." —Stella Cameron

"One of the best . . . a must-read." —*Rendezvous*

"Lynn Kurland's vastly entertaining time travel treats us to a delightful hero and heroine . . . a humorous novel of feisty fun and adventure." —*A Little Romance*

"Her heroes are delightful . . . A wonderful read!" —*Heartland Critiques*

Titles by Lynn Kurland

STARDUST OF YESTERDAY
A DANCE THROUGH TIME
THIS IS ALL I ASK
THE VERY THOUGHT OF YOU
ANOTHER CHANCE TO DREAM
THE MORE I SEE YOU
IF I HAD YOU
MY HEART STOOD STILL
FROM THIS MOMENT ON
A GARDEN IN THE RAIN

Anthologies

A KNIGHT'S VOW
(with Patricia Potter, Deborah Simmons, and Glynnis Campbell)

LOVE CAME JUST IN TIME

THE CHRISTMAS CAT
(with Julie Beard, Barbara Bretton, and Jo Beverley)

CHRISTMAS SPIRITS
(with Casey Claybourne, Elizabeth Bevarly, and Jenny Lykins)

VEILS OF TIME
(with Maggie Shayne, Angie Ray, and Ingrid Weaver)

OPPOSITES ATTRACT
(with Elizabeth Bevarly, Emily Carmichael, and Elda Minger)

TAPESTRY
(with Madeline Hunter, Sherrilyn Kenyon, and Karen Marie Moning)